DEVIL'S NIGHT

Penny Wright Series Book 1

A.N. WILLIS

This is a work of fiction. All characters and events in this work are fictitious. Any resemblance to real persons, living or dead, is coincidental.

Copyright © 2021 by A.N. Willis

All rights reserved. No part of this book may be reproduced or transmitted in any form or by any means, electronic, mechanical, photocopying, recording, or otherwise, without prior written permission of Observatory Books. If you would like to use material from the book (other than for review purposes), please write to observatorypublishing@gmail.com.

Paperback ISBN 978-1-7343597-8-7

Produced by Observatory Books

Denver, Colorado

DEVIL'S NIGHT

FIVE MILES WEST OF ASHTON, COLORADO, NESTLED INTO a dead-end canyon at the end of a dirt road, lies the abandoned town of Eden. Once, Eden was a bustling mining enclave, full of men hoping to strike it rich and women dreaming of a better life.

Then, on July 17, 1894, came the Devil's Night Massacre.

Today, Eden is one of the best-preserved ghost towns in the United States. It's also the most haunted.

In July 2000, I spent Devil's Night in Eden to investigate. I wasn't alone. Working alongside me were the other members of the Ashton Paranormal Society. And we had the services of a talented, if unusual, medium: my five-year-old daughter, Penny.

-from A DEVIL IN EDEN by Lawrence Wright
(*Ashton Press, 2001*)

CHAPTER ONE

2019

The Paradise Hotel was just as Penny Wright remembered it: crumbling red brick, warped wood floors. Thick paper peeled in sheets from the walls, revealing moldering lath and plaster beneath. A few windows still held wavy panes of glass.

Linden Hao snapped a photo, her phone aimed at a bullet hole in the wood.

"It's even creepier than I imagined," Linden said.

"But what do you think?" Penny asked.

"Are you kidding? You were right—it's perfect."

Penny nodded, more to reassure herself than to agree. She'd been working on this project for months, but planning from her desk in Los Angeles was nothing like being here in person. This was the first moment that it all felt real.

They stood in the hotel's lobby. All the furniture and opulent fixtures were long gone—maybe pilfered over the decades by visitors who came here to bask in the haunted ambiance.

Penny had been one of them, years ago. But that had been a different life.

Most of the buildings on Eden's Main Street were gutted, rotting, or had fully succumbed to the harsh Colorado winters.

But the Paradise had kept a regal sort of beauty, despite its dark history. It was just the place to kick off the festival—assuming they could get all the details finalized in time. But she'd find a way.

"You did good." Linden bumped Penny's shoulder with her fist.

Penny brushed aside her nervousness and smiled. "Hell yeah, I did."

Linden took a hesitant step up the staircase, then came back down. "That doesn't seem stable, does it?"

Linden was five-nine and slender, no more than a hundred twenty pounds, most of that her new Patagonia hiking clothes and heavy Columbia boots. They'd landed in Denver yesterday and stopped for the night, making a pilgrimage to the massive REI to pick up gear before dinner in trendy RiNo. In the morning they'd taken a puddle jumper to Montrose and made the hour-and-a-half drive to Ashton, where they swapped out their rental sedan for the waiting Jeep. Then the final bumpy miles to Eden. Yet despite all that, Linden still looked dewy-cheeked, her black hair long and smooth.

Penny hadn't fared so well. Her plaid cotton button-down no longer smelled fresh. Sweat plastered her bangs to her forehead. Her stomach wouldn't settle, though she'd had no appetite for breakfast. But there was also something exhilarating about being here, back in this place she hadn't set foot in over six years.

"Excuse me, Ms. Hao?" someone said, poking his head through the hotel's entrance.

"Be right there. Hey, Penny? I need to sign some more papers for the contractor."

In just over a week, Eden would be the venue for Sterling PR's biggest event of the year—the launch of a caffeine-laced drink, Dark Energy, for a huge new client. Penny had pitched a three-night music festival culminating on July 17, the 125th anniversary of the notorious Devil's Night Massacre. It was macabre, and it was more than a little crass. But Penny—and more importantly, the client—knew that it would be social media gold.

Would Eden's ghosts make an appearance? Penny had been counting on it. Yet her shoulders were tensed, waiting for the first sign. Ghosts rarely made her nervous. Not anymore. But Eden wasn't just any place.

She walked over to the bar, which was off to the right of the lobby. Here the ceiling lowered, and ancient bottles of cloudy glass still stood on a top shelf. Penny put her hands on the bar, the wood oiled smooth by countless hands and spilled glasses of whiskey. She brushed dust from her fingers against her jeans.

Beyond a carved wooden archway, a single table stood on spindly legs. The dining room. Penny crept closer. A shiver ran up and down her spine as she looked up at the tin ceiling. A gaping, cracked hole showed where the chandelier had been.

She'd never been to this room before. Her last visit to Eden had been at night, and neither she nor her friends had been brave enough to venture this far. Plus, she'd been...preoccupied that night. She'd still managed to get scared out of her wits and do some other stupid things besides.

But she knew the story of what had occurred here. Ernest Fitzhammer, the owner of the Paradise Hotel, had been found hanging from the chandelier. Penny felt a shift in the air. A hum of electricity increasing in frequency. She flinched, imagining the swing of a man's body, listing on a frayed rope.

She was a long way from that eighteen-year-old kid, terrified by what she'd seen in Eden. And she was even further from the five-year-old who'd come to Eden with her dad on Devil's Night. *Ghost girl*, the other kids had called her.

Something moved in the corner of her vision—the doorway across the room.

It had been a swish of fabric, like a full skirt twirling around legs. A wave of cold moved through her. A chill that began inside of her instead of out.

She crossed the dining room before she realized she'd moved.

She looked into the kitchen. Against the wall sat an iron stove, the plaster blackened from soot. A thin chimney ran from the stove into the roof. Someone had replaced the back door with an incongruous modern version, the deadbolt locked.

To the left, a hallway. It led into darkness.

That sense of deep cold remained, that same ever-present hum in the air. Penny backed away as her heart thumped an unsteady beat. The dead had always been clearer to her in Colorado than anywhere else, especially this close to home.

She focused on closing herself off from these sensations, something she'd learned well in the years she'd been away.

Ghosts were not conscious. They had no intent, ill or otherwise. They were trapped in a single moment of their greatest regret or fear, and for someone sensitive like Penny, those impressions could become overwhelming. As soon as the construction crew moved in, the thrum of living people would drown out most of these remnants of the dead.

Of course, Eden would still look like the set of a horror movie. Hopefully, *some* signs of the haunting would remain. Just enough to give festival-goers the scare they'd be craving.

"Everything okay?" Linden asked.

Penny spun around. Linden stood in the middle of the dining room wearing a hard hat. It was orange and slipped a bit to one side. She started fiddling to adjust it.

"We're both supposed to be wearing these, apparently," Linden said. "Insurance."

"Right." Penny forced a smile. "I'm just soaking in the ambiance."

"The outside shots have been great, but I can't believe we almost missed these details." Linden had made a trip to Eden two months ago for site recon, but Penny hadn't been able to come. Their planning budget was too tight.

Linden pulled out her phone again to take a few more snaps. "What should the caption be?"

Penny swallowed and wrapped her arms around her middle,

wishing she could banish the chill. She'd never enjoyed being frightened. To her, ghosts were too real to be funny or exciting. But she wasn't the target audience. *Haunted is exactly what we want*, she'd said in her pitch. That was the whole point of hosting their event here—Eden's reputation. She needed to capture that creeping sensation, bottle it up and make it into something that would sell.

"This is where it began," Penny said. "Where they found the first bodies."

She pointed at the wall opposite the window. The wallpaper had long since been torn down here, any traces of red gone.

"The word 'Marian' was scrawled there in blood."

Bloody Marian. The butcher of Eden.

Linden pretended to shiver, then smiled mischievously. "I'm in awe of you right now."

Penny swatted her arm. "Shush."

For much of her life, Penny had lived in the shadow of this place. It was past time that she changed the narrative. Reclaimed Eden for herself.

If she did things right, this year's Devil's Night would be one that nobody would ever forget.

CHAPTER TWO

They went back through the lobby toward the hotel's entrance. "Turns out the general contractor is busy in Ashton today," Linden said. "Which kinda pissed me off, since he didn't say a word on the phone yesterday. But that was until I met his foreman. Guy's a mountain-man hottie."

"I didn't know you had a Paul Bunyan fetish," Penny said.

"Quiet." Linden giggled. "You're going to diminish my aura of unattainability."

They walked down Main Street. The day was already growing hot, sweat trailing down Penny's back. July in the mountains wasn't nearly as hot as central LA, but they were at nine thousand feet and the sun could be scorching in the thin air. The town was set into a box canyon between towering sandstone cliffs. Mountain peaks rose in the distance. The view still took Penny's breath away.

Once, the town of Eden spread throughout this canyon. But now there was little apart from Main Street. Some buildings had collapsed, barely leaving a hint of what they'd once been. A few of the wooden structures still stood: saloons; a mercantile, where townspeople had bought their flour and mining tools and roughspun cloth. In the window to the blacksmith's workshop, you could still see hunks of rusted metal and a black cast-iron furnace where tools were once melted and shaped.

Then there was the Paradise Hotel, still standing an impressive three stories of brick and stone cornices. The Eden Bank was a twin to the hotel on Main Street's far end. But a fire decades ago—set by squatters—had gutted it on the inside.

Teenagers came to Eden to get drunk, and vandals had caused damage or graffitied walls. But somehow, there'd been enough fascination with Eden to keep it standing.

"There's the foreman," Linden whispered, poking Penny in the side. Then Linden straightened, calling out to him. "Matthew, this is Penny Wright. She's the one who's really in charge here if anybody asks. And she still needs a hard hat."

Penny looked over.

His sharp features were more filled out than she remembered, yet instantly recognizable. His dirty-blond hair hung over his forehead, his eyes skeptical as he watched her. He was standing with the construction crew, arms crossed, a jean-clad hip cocked out, tan work boots on his feet.

Matthew Larsen.

Oh my God, she thought, *what is Matthew doing here?*

He grabbed a hard hat from a flatbed and started towards them. Her heart was writhing in her chest, wanting to reach for her former best friend—the first boy she'd ever loved—just as much as it wanted to get the hell out of there.

"Hello." Matthew didn't seem surprised to see her. He held the hat out to her. Penny fit it onto her head. The thing felt heavy, but also reassuring. If only it could cover the rest of her face. She was sure she was blushing underneath her freckles.

Linden started to introduce him. "Penny, this is—"

"Matthew Larsen. I know. We've met."

Your move, she thought.

"We met a long time ago," he corrected.

"Oh." Linden was glancing between them, trying to read what was being left unsaid. "Good, then." She lifted her eyebrows at Penny, which clearly meant, *You'd better tell me everything.*

Matthew's gaze was flinty. Like he was annoyed at *her.* Like he wasn't the one who'd vanished from her life, ignoring her emails and calls. But that had been "a long time ago," just like he'd said. They were both grownups, and Matthew had always been responsible. She just needed him to do his job.

He produced a clipboard. "I hear you've got more to add to the project?"

"Actually, we were hoping our GC would be here," Penny said. "Is he on his way?"

"Sully's back in Ashton, working out some issues that came up with the permitting and inspections."

Linden held up a manicured hand. "Wait, what issues? Anvi didn't mention anything like that."

Anvi Narayan—another member of their event team. She'd been in Ashton for several days already, handling legwork and logistics.

Matthew shrugged. "The electrical's way behind schedule, as you must've heard. We just got the new electrician up here a few days ago. Sully will know more. As for the permit, I'm not sure. Right now Sully's meeting with Harry Wright. Um..." He nodded at Penny.

"My Uncle Harry," Penny said. "Remember?"

"Our inside man." Linden sighed, taking off the hard hat. "I need to make some calls and talk to Anvi. Penny, can you handle the walk-through with Matthew? I'll let you know what I find out. And call your uncle when you have a chance."

Linden strode toward the trailer, phone in her hand.

Penny crossed her arms, scuffing her hiking boot in the dust. Matthew tapped on his clipboard, waiting for her to say something.

It wasn't that she'd forgotten about him. Quite the opposite. She'd spent plenty of sleepless hours thinking of Matthew since dreaming up Devil's Fest.

The last night she'd seen him had been right here—in Eden. One of the best and worst nights of her life.

But eight thousand people lived in Ashton. She'd assumed Matthew would continue avoiding her and that she would do the same.

So why was he here?

CHAPTER THREE

Matthew had known for weeks that Penny would be coming. He'd been nervous about seeing her again. But she wasn't the same girl he'd grown up with—not in essentials. She'd lived in Los Angeles for years now and had rarely deigned to come see her family. Her only reason for coming home was this ridiculous festival.

Devil's Fest. What was she thinking?

If he'd been the boss, Matthew would never have gotten involved in this. Though the corporate sponsor was paying everyone well. So that helped.

"We should get started," he said.

Penny chewed her lip, shaking her head. She looked so much like when they were kids—long strawberry-blonde hair that glowed in the sun, the freckles that dotted her cheeks and nose. And her mouth curved into that same defiant frown.

"I'm not going to say it's good to see you," she said. "Because you clearly don't seem to feel that way. But we can at least be civil."

Penny had never hesitated to speak her mind. At least that much hadn't changed.

"I wasn't being civil?" he asked.

"I'm sorry about your mom. And I'm sorry I haven't had the chance to say that in person till now."

"Thank you." Matthew looked away into the distance. Penny hadn't come to the funeral. She'd sent a letter, though, and a bouquet of hydrangeas, his mom's favorite.

"How are you doing?" Penny asked, twisting her hands together.

Matthew sighed. Did she really think this would change anything? This superficial attempt at small talk? "I'm good, Penn. How've you been? How's LA?"

"It's...sunny."

Yeah. Exactly.

What had happened between them years ago—almost happened—had been a mistake. It had been a moment of weakness, wanting a girl who'd always been off-limits.

"You're right," she said. "We should start. Believe me, I *know* how much work has gone into getting this place ready. But we've made a slight change to the plan."

Penny pointed at the hotel. Sun reflected in its windows.

"I want to host the VIP welcome party inside the hotel. It needs to be impressive. As for bathrooms, we're renting trailers. So that's already taken care of."

For a moment, he couldn't speak. "Wait, you want the hotel ready in a week? The upper floors are in bad shape. If I had a couple months, maybe, but one week? Why didn't you decide this earlier?"

"Because I didn't *think* of it earlier," she snapped. "Not the *whole* hotel. Just the lobby, bar and dining room."

He tried not to roll his eyes. Classic Penny. She could never make up her mind.

Matthew crossed his arms over his clipboard, gazing up at the brick building. For decades, Ashton's Historical Club had been doing basic maintenance on Eden's structures. Keeping the roofs from caving, replacing door hinges. So it wasn't as bad as it could be. Penny wouldn't need plumbing or heat or the typical features that made a place livable. But one week? Really?

"It would be a lot easier and less expensive to host your party in a tent like you planned," Matthew said. "You sure the hotel is what you want?"

"*Yes,* we're sure. The hotel is going to be the centerpiece of opening night. I realize you think this is silly, but I know what I'm doing."

"I meant no offense," Matthew said softly.

"It's fine."

It was not fine.

"Anyway." Penny tucked her hair behind her ear. "We want to keep all that character. The peeling wallpaper, the off angles. The creep factor. It's all about the details. That's what'll play on social media."

"Got it." Matthew's pen scratched against his notepad. "Creep factor. Off angles. I'll talk to our structural engineer and make it happen." Somehow. He couldn't believe he'd said yes to this. But then again, he never could say no to Penny Wright.

"Thank you."

They walked towards the far western end of town, which faced the dead end of the canyon.

As Penny spoke, he snuck glances at her. Her hazel eyes were green sometimes; at the moment they were dark blue. As always, she'd rimmed them with dark eyeliner.

Good Lord, this girl. His chest felt tight looking at her.

"Do you still see them?" he asked suddenly. He hadn't even thought about it beforehand. The words just came out.

Penny stopped talking and looked at him.

"See what?"

She knew exactly what he was talking about. Everybody who grew up in Ashton in the last twenty years would know what he was talking about.

The ghosts, Penny, he thought. *Whatever you saw the last time that we were here in Eden. The last time we were together.*

"Never mind."

Let her go, Larsen, he told himself. *Like you thought you did a long time ago.*

"I'll let you know if there are questions."

That wasn't the way he usually spoke to clients. But he needed to get out of there. Matthew turned and walked away from her.

CHAPTER FOUR

A loose shutter creaked on the hotel's facade. Penny tried to ignore it. She went over to Linden, waiting at a respectful distance until her friend—and superior at Sterling PR—finished the call.

"Matthew's cute," Linden said, pocketing her phone.

"He's obnoxious."

"Okay, I need info. *Now*. Who is that guy?"

Penny considered how to put it. She didn't want to spend the next several hours talking about Matthew, which would be necessary to convey just how much his presence had affected her life. How he'd been her friend and confidante and then, after she went to college, had caused her nothing but heartache.

"You remember the guy I mentioned before, the one who stomped on my heart?"

"That's *him*?"

Linden put her hand on her chest, turning to stare at the construction crew. Penny let herself look. Matthew was going over the plans with his team, nodding his head while they spoke. He'd always been good at listening. Saying what he really felt? Not so much.

"You know, he's not *that* cute." Linden's head tilted, clearly checking out the way Matthew's butt filled out his jeans.

Penny put a hand between her friend's shoulder blades. "Thanks for trying. But you're not the best liar."

"Not true—I'm an excellent liar. But not about sexy men. Can't hide that truth. Sorry, sweetie."

Linden turned back to face her, crossing her arms and putting on her *let's-talk-business* expression. "I got our contractor Sully on the phone, and he swears that any bumps on the permitting are minimal. I'm working with the client on our updated budget. That leaves..." She put a finger to her chin. "About a thousand more tiny details, most of which are waiting in your inbox."

"Perfect." Penny smiled.

Thank goodness for the satellite internet hookup. Several carriers provided decent cell coverage in the area, but data was notoriously unreliable.

Dust rose on the road into Eden.

"That must be Anvi." Penny tried to keep the attitude out of her voice. Linden didn't like conflict between members of their team.

A white pickup roared into the canyon, hauling a massive, beige-and-black travel trailer. Their living quarters. Linden had wanted to be here, on site, at all times during the final prep phase. The drive into Ashton was five miles over unpaved road. Twenty minutes max. Penny didn't think it was that big of a time loss, but she understood Linden's point. Sterling PR expected twenty-four-seven commitments from its employees.

Besides, staying up here meant less time that Penny would deal with her family. Uncle Harry was one thing. But her father? Please, no.

Anvi got out of the pickup truck. She sported a pixie cut, ample curves. But no smile. Even on Instagram, she rarely cracked a grin. Her face was angular and serious, as if planning important things.

Anvi strode over to Penny.

"It's good you're finally here," Anvi said. "Why did you change our content schedule? The new tweets?"

"I spoke to June about it yesterday," Penny said, "and she liked it."

"But you should've asked *me*. We made those decisions weeks ago."

Technically, Penny was the senior associate. Anvi was new, just hired after graduating a year early with her public relations degree. But Anvi had a habit of asserting dominance. She and Penny had clashed in the office—Anvi was anal about doing things a certain way, while Penny preferred to go with her instincts. Linden wanted them to figure it out. *I'm not a micromanager*, she'd said. *You and Anvi will have to find a way to work together.*

"We can talk about it," Penny told Anvi. "Later." Just add it to the list.

A black Jeep pulled into the wide, flat area they'd designated for parking.

"Game faces, people," Linden murmured. "The client awaits."

A thin, petite woman jumped out of the Jeep. June Litvak, their liaison from SunBev. She wore jeans, ankle boots, and a hesitant smile.

"It's so good to see you again." Penny opened her arms for a hug. June's honey-blond hair bounced in thick curls, tickling Penny's cheek. She smelled like fruity gum and floral perfume.

"How was the trip in?" Penny asked.

They found some shade while they chatted. June had arrived in Ashton last night from Phoenix, where SunBev had its headquarters.

"Linden," Anvi said, "could I get your input?" Linden jogged off again.

Penny looped her arm through June's. She'd spoken to June at the pitch meeting, of course, and countless times on the phone afterward. But they hadn't had the chance yet to really get to know one another. Whenever Penny had tried to steer their conversations toward personal, non-work-related matters, June got tight-lipped.

So Penny had given in to the siren's call of Google. She found out that June was a competitive figure skater in high school. Now, she worked in SunBev's marketing department. Beyond those bits of trivia, June was an enigma.

"I'll be honest—I'm so nervous." June fidgeted with Penny's sleeve. "I feel like I'm wearing all the wrong things. I should've brought hiking boots, shouldn't I? You told me to, and I completely forgot."

"I'm sure we can find you a pair. Linden and I can take care of whatever you need. Just let us know."

"I'm not usually forgetful, I swear. I've had a lot on my mind lately."

"Oh? I'm free for rants, too," Penny said. "I love a good rant."

June smiled shyly. "It's...nothing about the festival."

Penny couldn't tell if June wanted to say more. After several seconds, she still hadn't elaborated. Instead, she gazed up at Eden's buildings.

"This town really is incredible," June said. "It's just so perfect for Dark Energy—the vibe, the history."

June was obviously changing the subject. But Penny couldn't help thinking of the day she'd had the idea. The Sterling PR team had been sitting around the conference table, their orders from Linden's coffee-shop-of-the-moment already distributed. Tripp Sterling had leaned back in his chair, eying them as he recited facts about SunBelt Beverages. SunBev had started out as a mom-and-pop artisan root beer maker and had grown into a regional force in naturally sweetened beverages. But the company wanted to go nationwide.

"They've already got the name: Dark Energy," Tripp said. "But they need a signature launch. Something unique. We need this account."

Nobody mentioned the disaster of late last year. A makeup company they represented had gotten sued for dangerous heavy metals in their formulations. Sterling had been in charge of marketing tainted foundation and lip gloss to teens. They hadn't known, of course. But the scandal made Sterling PR look just as toxic.

Penny needed a win, too. Tripp had been eying her skeptically in the hallway, like a piece of furniture that could stand to be replaced. Student loans were eating her alive, and she'd already downsized her beautiful Wilshire apartment to a Culver City house share she'd found on Craigslist. If she failed, she'd have to move out of LA—no more walks on the beach on the weekends, no more people-watching on Melrose Avenue or staying up late brainstorming with Linden. She'd have to go back home to Ashton for good, to the town where everybody knew her history. Where she could see the dead end coming a mile away, just like that canyon beyond Eden's Main Street.

Sitting at the conference table, the idea just came to her. Penny blurted it out without a moment's hesitation.

"Devil's Fest."

When Tripp's eyes lit up, she knew she'd done it.

She just wished she'd had a brilliant idea that involved somebody else's home turf. But this—Eden, its history—was what she knew. She'd have to work with it, ghost sightings and all. If she didn't...

No. There was no "if" about it. Devil's Fest was her big gamble, and she was all in.

Penny continued June's tour of Main Street, describing how everything would look in just a few days. When they'd finished, Penny said, "This afternoon we'll have a little thank you dinner for our crew. Anvi ordered barbecue. In the meantime, feel free to make use of the trailer if you don't want to go back to Ashton."

June turned to her. "Oh, crap. One more thing, super quick. Our hotel has all this construction going on. Like, jackhammer in the lobby. It was okay last night, but super loud when I left this morning. I'm not that picky, but the execs will be annoyed. Anything we can do?"

Penny stared, mouth open. *Breathe,* she thought. *Things like this happen all the time.* "Of course—I had no idea. If it's okay with you, we've got an extra bed in the trailer and we'd love for you to join us tonight. I'll find you a new hotel."

June headed for the trailer. Penny cursed to herself. *Find June and the rest of the SunBev VIPs some fancy new digs on a day's notice. No problem.* She'd thought that Anvi had double-checked all the accommodations. But she wasn't about to ask Anvi for help now. Penny would have to fix this one herself.

She'd have to ask her family for a favor.

PENNY'S UNCLE HARRY arrived at the same time as their dinner. He strode over to her while the caterers unloaded.

"Penny-girl," he announced, and gave her a kiss on the cheek. "Don't you look grown up!"

Harry wore a brown polyester suit and a tie designed to look like the Colorado flag. He had questionable taste in clothes, but her uncle was someone you could count on to make things happen in Ashton. He had his hand in any number of business ventures, some of them borderline shady. Like the campground timeshare program that hadn't gone so well.

"I heard we hit a snag with the permits?" Penny asked.

Uncle Harry gave his dazzling smile. "A hiccup. No concern."

"But what was it?"

"Just some local who's upset about you holding an event up here. Superstitions about Devil's Night. Complained to the mayor, but it's no big deal."

She had expected some pushback in Ashton, given Eden's history. "But I thought you'd already 'smoothed the way,'" she said, using her uncle's words. "Wait, was it *Dad* who complained?"

Nobody was more obsessed with Devil's Night—and its ghosts—than her father. She should have told her dad about the festival already, but she'd kept putting it off. He could be so dramatic. And now he'd heard about it on his own.

Uncle Harry laughed. "Oh no, not Lawrence. He's not exactly happy about Devil's Fest, mind you." He held up his hands. "But hey, that's just an FYI. Your business is your own."

Great. "Thanks for the warning."

Harry was her dad's younger brother, and the two didn't get along very well. So far, Harry had been essential in putting together Devil's Fest—from signing the lease with the landowner to getting on the good side of local officials. She couldn't have done this without him. Which would probably annoy her dad all the more.

She'd already called her mother to ask for that favor—a dozen rooms at the Ashton Valley Inn, which her family ran. Her mom had promised to figure something out, but only if Penny came to see them. *Tonight*.

Before, Penny had been noncommittal about when she'd have time to swing by the inn. Her mother had known a few details about the festival and this trip, though Mom had readily agreed they should wait to share the information with Dad. That was how things ran in the Wright household: Mom tried to manage everything, including Dad's blood pressure. These efforts were not always successful.

"Don't you worry," Harry said. "I'll make sure all those permits and inspections and bureaucratic nonsense don't cause you any headaches." He looked over at the catering table.

"But dang, that brisket smells good!" Harry announced, voice booming. "I guess we'd better eat while it's hot?"

No one disagreed. They grabbed plates of food, plastic cups of foamy beer, and seats around the temporary picnic tables. Penny sat down between Anvi and June. Harry went over to join their general contractor, who'd finally arrived, and the construction crew. Harry clapped a hand on Matthew's back. They both looked toward Penny—were they talking about her?—and she glanced away.

Linden clinked a fork against a wineglass she'd procured from somewhere. Because *of course* Linden had a real wineglass, even out here in the boonies.

"Thank you all for being part of the Devil's Fest team. This whole shindig was Penny's idea, as everybody knows."

Linden reached down to pull on Penny's arm. "Come on," she said quietly, "this is your show as much as mine. You're the local girl, charm them."

Penny stood. Twenty sets of eyes looked back at her.

And Matthew Larsen was sitting just a few feet away, his gaze seeming to lock onto hers every few seconds.

CHAPTER FIVE

Linden watched her friend face the gathering. Penny waved at them, shifting her weight from foot to foot. Usually, Penny didn't need any encouragement to get up and speak.

It's Matthew, Linden thought. *He's a distraction.*

"Hey, everyone," Penny finally said. "Thank you for being here. Like Linden said. Um…"

This was going nowhere, all thanks to the broad set of shoulders in the first row. Linden opened her mouth, about to take over. But then Penny forged ahead.

"This town isn't just brick and glass and broken boards. It's not even the stories we've all heard. The murders. The ghosts." Penny paused, her eyes darting to the side in thought. "Eden is also the people who called this place home, their wishes and dreams that didn't quite come true. The light that can't really be seen without the juxtaposition of darkness and death."

Keep it moving, Linden thought. *Don't go English major on them.*

Penny was so earnest sometimes. So free with her emotions. She didn't have an instinct for self preservation, which was a skill that Linden had finely honed growing up in an overachieving family. But at least with Penny, you always knew where you stood.

The sun had dipped behind the mountains, and Main Street was descending into shadow. Glowing lanterns had appeared on the picnic tables, provided with perfect timing by Anvi.

"Even though we're here to tell the story of Dark Energy, we're also giving Eden some much-needed TLC," Penny said. "We're preserving history and benefiting the community of this entire region. Let's leave this place better than we found it."

Coming from anyone else, those bold statements would've sounded disingenuous. But Linden was sure that Penny believed every word. The crowd clapped—some more enthusiastically than others—and Linden wrapped an arm around her friend's shoulders.

"You see?" Linden said quietly. "That's why I need you. You're the heart of this event."

Penny hugged her back. "Thank you for believing in me."

LINDEN AND PENNY had first met in a psychology class at UCLA. Linden had been a year ahead, nearly finished with her communication degree. Confident in her skills. But Penny's ideas for their group project had intrigued her. Penny had refused to follow their prof's specific guidelines, and predictably, they'd gotten a B+ despite all their hard work. Yet Linden had agreed—those guidelines were stupid and arbitrary. Linden was still proud of that project, though her parents had of course scoffed when she didn't get an A in the course.

Linden's father was a world-renowned neurosurgeon, her mother an entertainment lawyer who negotiated deals for Hollywood's biggest studios. One of Linden's brothers had received a MacArthur Genius Grant. None of them could believe it when she'd chosen UCLA over the Ivy League. But Linden knew their not-so-hidden secret: *her parents were freaking miserable*. She wanted more out of life—success *and* happiness.

But was she going to work every one of the Hao family's contacts in LA to achieve that?

Rhetorical question.

When Tripp Sterling hired her for his public relations firm, she knew she was trading on her family's cachet. That didn't bother her. Tripp was handsome, exciting, ambitious. Unbelievable in bed. He was also demanding and judgmental, which somehow only heightened his sex appeal. It made him good at his job. Penny didn't even know that Linden had been sleeping with their boss. Linden preferred keeping her secrets close.

Linden was already in love with him before she realized it— she'd fallen for a man whose personality was exactly like her father's.

The pressures of the last year had been getting to all of them. But Penny's Devil's Fest idea was the perfect antidote. After their firm pulled this off, Penny's place at Sterling would be secure, and Tripp would stop stressing so much. And maybe, just maybe, he'd be willing to consider an actual commitment. Linden wanted that diamond ring—and her parents' joyous approval—more than she liked to admit.

They had already visualized every aspect of the event. Dark Energy was the sponsor, but not the overt star of the festival. These picnic tables would be out of sight, and the decorators would transform Main Street into a nighttime playground. The promotions would be subtle: cans held in the hands of the social media influencers they'd invited, artsy banners hanging above the stage at the end of Main Street. Only about five hundred festival-goers had gotten tickets each night, distributed via online lotteries in the last month. Most of the bang of Devil's Fest would take place on Instagram, Twitter, and TikTok. A Facebook Live stream would chronicle the music acts. Stories would run in niche-specific publications during and after, all leading up to Dark Energy's official launch date in stores.

After dinner, Linden asked Penny about the walk-through

with Matthew. "Does he think his team can get the hotel ready in time?"

Penny nodded. "We can count on him."

"Good. I'll double check the numbers, but this should work within the current budget. Just in case, let's keep the big tent on standby. If the hotel party doesn't come together, we'll go outdoors."

Linden was happy to let Penny run with her ideas—even if Penny had a tendency to come up with newer, better ones after the planning should've been finished. From the start, Penny hadn't been a perfect fit at Sterling PR. She had a tendency to get distracted by a big-picture concept and let small details slip through the cracks. But time pressure seemed to bring out the best in Penny. Linden wasn't about to stifle that creativity.

Penny's gaze had landed, once again, on their sexy construction foreman. Penny's ex-flame. A complication that Linden had not anticipated.

"Is he going to be a problem?" Linden asked. "I can ask the GC to replace him if you need."

"No, it's fine, I—"

June screamed.

Conversation ceased, all heads turning in her direction.

"I'm sorry, it's just—there's somebody up there." June pointed at the hotel. "In the window."

The others were looking around, confused. But not Penny. She was staring at the upper floors of the hotel. Linden saw nothing different from before.

"What is it?" She touched Penny's arm.

Someone from Matthew's construction crew stood up. "Right there. Looking out at us."

Before anyone could stop her, June ran toward the building. Then Penny took off after her.

CHAPTER SIX

Penny held June by the shoulders at the hotel's entrance.

"Somebody's up there," June said.

"I know. But you can't just charge in."

Penny had seen a face looking out from the hotel's second floor. There'd been something insubstantial about the figure. And now that she was closer, Penny could feel the pull of loneliness.

Help me, she heard in her head.

"What's going on?" Matthew had caught up to them. The others were hanging back not far behind, murmuring to each other. "Is there somebody upstairs?"

Penny shook her head. "I don't think so."

"But I saw," June protested.

Matthew pushed the heavy door open. The hinges squealed.

"We can't have people messing around in here," he said. "If they're hurt, we'll be responsible."

"Matthew, listen to me. It was just..."

But he'd already gone inside.

"Stay here," Penny said to June. She followed Matthew through the low-ceilinged entryway.

The lobby was much darker than it had been that afternoon. Cavernous. Beyond the check-in desk, the staircase led up to a second-floor balcony overlooking the lobby. From there, the balcony curved around to the other side of the floor. The same pattern repeated with the third floor above it.

One door on the second level was open.

A shadow began to move, almost out of sight in the dark. For an instant, a shape resolved. A swirl of long hair moved across the landing.

A draft of cold air hit Penny head-on, like it had swept down the staircase. The chill passed straight through her body.

Don't let him hurt me, a voice said.

Penny gasped.

"Penn?" Matthew's hand grazed her elbow.

She put her mental defenses back into place, and the strange thoughts vanished.

"Did you feel that? The cold?" she whispered.

"Yeah," he murmured. "I did."

"The voice?"

But he shook his head.

That didn't surprise her. Matthew had never shared her ability when they were growing up. Few people did. Though some of the others had seen that figure in the window, too.

The lobby floor creaked as Uncle Harry came in behind them. "Is there really somebody upstairs?"

"Nobody alive."

When Penny turned, she found Linden watching from the doorway.

"I guess when you said Eden was haunted," Linden said, "you really weren't kidding."

IN THE TRAILER, June kept shifting around, arms and legs akimbo. "That person I saw, that was a ghost? Really?"

"Apparently so," Linden said. "It was our welcome dinner, after all. The ghosts decided to say hi." She unzipped her suitcase, digging through her neatly folded clothes.

"Your first time?" Penny asked June.

She'd told them the rumors about the haunting. But experiencing such phenomena was different than just hearing stories.

"Definitely." June shook her head. "It was so real. And I ran *toward* it. I have no idea why I did that."

"You never know how you'll react until it happens."

"Why did only some of us see it?" June asked.

"It's easier to see spirits around dawn and twilight. Those are in-between times. Usually in Eden it's just sounds, voices, the occasional cold spot. I guess we were lucky tonight."

Penny was acting nonchalant, but she was unsettled. Matthew's construction crew hadn't mentioned a single strange incident in the weeks they'd been here. And then two sightings today, right after she'd shown up. A little haunting was local color; a lot could be disruptive.

"How do you know so much about this stuff?" June asked.

Anvi snorted a laugh. She was sitting at the little banquette in the trailer's kitchen area. Her legs were folded, long pink nails scrolling on her phone.

"What?" Penny asked.

"It's time you told us, don't you think?"

So Anvi knew. Maybe Linden had shared the information. Linden knew about Penny's ability—or curse, whichever it was. Penny didn't try to hide it. She didn't bring it up, either. But now, it was time to have *that conversation* with June.

ONE OF THE first was at the inn Penny's family owned—an elderly lady with pink hair who'd died in a second-floor room. She'd smelled of pineapple candies, which she'd dispensed from her sweater pocket. She had pinched Penny's cheeks the day before and called her "Little Missy." Penny watched her walk across the lobby, her bathrobe hanging open, at the same moment that a medic wheeled her out under a sheet.

Very quickly, Penny realized that other people didn't see such things. It was an isolating experience, realizing just how little you knew about the world. She didn't tell every random person she met day to day. *I can see ghosts.* But she wasn't ashamed of her ability, either.

Penny gave June the condensed version of her past. The starter package—just enough detail to sketch out her ability without getting too personal or too weird.

"Folks around Ashton have their share of ghost stories," she explained, "and not just about Eden. Usually it's strange noises in old houses. Lights in the woods that they can't explain. Why some sense an apparition at a particular moment and others don't, I really have no idea. I just happen to see ghosts a little more frequently. It's something I've learned to live with."

"A little?" Anvi's tone was light, but clearly this was a loaded question.

Penny shrugged. "Maybe more than a little."

"I read that book in the Ashton Visitor's Center gift shop. *A Devil in Eden?* Written by someone named Lawrence Wright—any relation?"

Anvi had indeed been productive during her week in Ashton.

Penny hadn't realized that anybody sold copies of that book anymore. So far as she knew, you couldn't even buy it online. She herself had read it only once, in seventh grade. Of course, she had lived it. The people of Ashton would never forget, but Penny had convinced herself that the rest of the world either didn't know or didn't care.

"Yes, my dad wrote a book about Eden. Featuring me. Published by a small local press almost twenty years ago, and out of print for a while now. Though I guess a few copies are still floating around."

They were getting into the unabridged version of Penny's life.

She didn't mind sharing this information. But throughout her childhood, that book had defined her.

When Penny's father discovered her ability, he encouraged her. *You have an incredible talent*, he'd said. *It's not wrong to want to use it.* But Penny felt like her father had used *her*. The book was about Eden and Bloody Marian, but it was also about Penny herself. *My five-year-old daughter, the medium.* Now that she'd grown, she refused to accept the role her father had assigned her.

"I don't blame you for keeping all that to yourself," June said. "I probably would, too."

Anvi went back to scrolling her phone. "It's a fitting backstory to Devil's Fest though, isn't it? If I were Penny, I'd be using it in the media kit. And a ghost showed up, right on cue. It's too good to pass up."

Linden held up her hands. "Okay, I think we're all tired. Let's worry about work tomorrow, shall we?"

The tension remained in the room, but both Penny and Anvi knew better than to speak now that Linden had quashed the conversation.

Penny started packing an overnight bag. She still had to go into Ashton to see her family. June slipped into the bathroom, and Linden put in her earbuds. Anvi stayed at the table, still absorbed in her phone.

Penny had known for months that Anvi didn't like her. They had completely different work styles, and they'd clashed over projects before. But Anvi's statements tonight had felt unnecessarily personal.

Penny set down her toiletry kit and went over to Anvi, lowering her voice. "Were you accusing me of something earlier?" she asked. "Planting someone to play a ghost?"

"I didn't say that." Anvi seemed to think, then set her phone facedown. "Here's how I see it. Your dad went on and on in the book about how Eden's ghosts are dangerous. Which I'm sure made it sell better, back in the day. So shouldn't we *hope* they're not real? I'm just saying—you're kind of being inconsistent, but it's still a good story. We should use it in the campaign."

Which was the last thing that Penny wanted.

"Not everything my father wrote is true—you're right. But this event is about Devil's Fest and Dark Energy. Not about my father or me."

But Eden *was* a part of her family history. Even if Devil's Fest was the huge, smashing success that Tripp Sterling expected it to be, Penny was afraid she'd be out of ideas. She had no other urban legends or scandalous ghost stories waiting in the wings to turn into the next big promotion. She didn't want Linden to know just how much she was putting on the line here.

Penny glanced over at her friend. Linden was turned away from them, typing an email on her laptop.

"That's not the only connection that you have to Eden, though," Anvi murmured. "You're related to her, aren't you? To Bloody Marian."

Wow, thought Penny, *she really did read that book*.

"Marian was probably my ancestor. If you believe the stories. My great, great-grandmother. But I don't see how that's…"

Anvi leaned her elbows against the table. "So actually, 'this whole thing' is *all* about you. What's the point in pretending otherwise?"

To that, Penny had nothing to say.

AT THE TIME OF THE DEVIL'S NIGHT MASSACRE, MARIAN Smith was around twenty years old. Her true last name isn't known. According to some stories, she was the daughter of an East Coast railroad tycoon and ran away from home. Others claim she was a former prostitute. Or perhaps a miner's wife who'd abandoned her husband and child.

In the summer of 1894, Marian and some number of her acolytes set out toward Eden. Whether Marian's party also had killing on their minds or if the robbery simply went terribly wrong, no one knows.

-from A DEVIL IN EDEN by Lawrence Wright

DEVIL'S NIGHT - 1894

Dust rose in the distance. Excitement flared in Marian's chest.

They're coming.

She'd worried when the coach didn't come through on time. She thought she'd lost this chance—her only chance. But here it was, and all was well.

She crawled along the ground to Douglas Perl. Dirt snuck into her mouth and scratched her skin. She liked the immediacy of these sensations. The fluttering in her stomach that came from being in control.

"When they stop, do not rush. Let the scene unfold as I described."

Douglas was reclining with his back against a rock, his hat over his forehead to keep the sun from his eyes. But his hands betrayed his anxiety—Douglas kept rubbing his palms against the threadbare knees of his britches.

"I still think it a poor contrivance," he said. "They mayn't believe it."

Marian's mouth curved at one side, the closest she ever got to a smile. "Just mind Tim doesn't get excited."

She preferred to take them unawares, before any blood had

been spilt. Blood would come later. Her heart beat faster, thinking of it. Her fist squeezed, then relaxed. She bit her lip, trying to come back to the moment.

She and Douglas were on a ridge looking over the road below, where the landscape shifted from open valley into foothills. Fitzhammer's coach would have to climb through these highlands before it could descend into the canyon, where the town of Eden lay.

As long as Douglas followed her plan, they'd be all right. She had a begrudging respect for him, and she believed that Douglas felt the same about her. As much as any man could respect a woman's intelligence, anyway.

Douglas knew the ugliness of life just as well as Marian did. Marian understood his motives—to feed his family, to right certain injustices without doing more harm than good. He might not approve of Marian's true mission today. But Douglas knew all that she desired him to know.

"We've got fifteen minutes till they reach the choke point," she said.

Douglas nodded, his hat still over his eyes.

Marian backed up, snaking along the ground, until she reached the cover of the trees. She got up, shaking the layer of beige dust from her clothes.

She'd hidden her change of costume behind a rock formation. Today, as on most days, she wore a man's vest, wool coat, and duck canvas trousers. She stripped off these beloved items until she wore only her drawers. On went the corset, cinching her waist. It was tighter than she remembered. The dress was calico, just a touch of ruffling at the neck and sleeves. Lead shot was sewn into the fraying hem to keep it down. Buttons trailed from her throat down to the seam at the top of her hips. She hated the thing, what it represented. It wasn't really *her*. Not anymore.

She thought of the dress that her mother used to wear—pale

blue satin that bore indelible stains, white lace gloves that had turned a dingy yellow. There was always something dark red on the gloves' fingers, though Marian couldn't tell if it was lip rouge or dried blood. Probably both. White had dusted her mother's front from the flour she used as face powder. Marian had scrubbed those clothes on Sundays, wishing that her mother would show a small measure of pride. *What's the point?* her mother had asked once. *The dress will be just as filthy by the end of Monday. You think the men care?*

Marian tucked her dark brown locks into a bonnet. Last, she reached for her weapons. She slid her tiny derringer into the top of her boot.

But when she reached for the knife she'd set down just moments ago, it was gone. Someone had been here—snuck up on her while she'd been *dressing*.

Marian drew the derringer from her boot. "Douglas, did you take my knife?"

But when she leaned out from behind the rock, it wasn't Douglas she saw.

Tim stood there with her knife balanced on his palm. He stared sheepishly at the ground. "I'm sorry, Miss Marian. I didn't saw noth—" The words dissolved into a fit of coughing.

"'I didn't *see*,'" she corrected. The derringer went back inside her boot.

She didn't like that Tim had gotten so close without her knowing. In the past, he'd made his amorous feelings clear. She'd tried to dissuade him, gently but firmly. But she doubted he'd actually been spying; he didn't have the wits to lie.

Consumption gave Tim a weak constitution, though he was also a crack shot with an iron. His devotion made him loyal to her. But Marian didn't trust any man entirely.

Marian held out her hand. "Give me my knife."

"But—" He coughed again, clearing his throat. "It needn't be you, Miss Marian. I don't wish to see you hurt."

Douglas was watching from his lookout spot, frowning.

She came closer to Tim. "And should I be subject to your whims?"

"I don't reckon so."

Which wasn't quite an answer. Tim handed her the knife. Without hesitating, she sliced the sharp tip across her palm.

Bart Adams spurred the horses onward. They were supposed to have arrived in Eden an hour ago.

They'd been wrapping up certain of Fitzhammer's assets in other mining towns. Quite a few investments had gone belly-up in recent months. It was time to gather up what was left and plan for the future. But, as usual, Bart's employer had been distracted by something fragile and beautiful. Fitzhammer had insisted on meeting a railroad heiress for breakfast before they left Ouray. Fitz thought he could convince the girl to invest in Eden, though the town had been a hopeless cause since the price of silver crashed. But Bart's employer was a proud man, and stubborn besides. He hated to admit a wrong.

The truth was this: Eden was nearly bust already. Nobody counted people in mining towns. They counted saloons and dance halls, and Eden had just a handful of the former, none remaining of the latter. Bart had his own loose ends to tie up in that town—urgent problems that demanded his attention—but he was eager to put Eden behind him as soon as Fitz agreed.

Bart glanced at the angle of the sun to judge the time, though he could've checked his watch. He *hated* being late. He liked to think himself clever and well-prepared. Ready for any problem that might arise.

So it came as quite a shock when he glanced back at the road, and a woman suddenly appeared.

She stumbled out a hundred yards ahead, holding the scraps of a torn shawl around her shoulders. Bright red blood was smeared across her face, which made Bart cringe in disgust.

Bart didn't recognize her as one of the few females still living in Eden. But folks passed through often enough. One never knew.

He eyed the hillsides, keeping on his guard. His Spencer repeating rifle was tucked near his feet within easy reach.

She trotted unsteadily toward them, holding out a hand. "Help me! Please!" Her bonnet was askew, dark ribbons of thick hair tumbling out. She was younger than he'd thought at first. Maybe nineteen, twenty.

"What is it?" Fitzhammer called from the coach, lifting the leather flap to look.

"Not sure. A girl, seems to be."

The girl kept coming closer. Her waist was tiny beneath her dress. Her lips were full, swollen from being struck. His skin crawled as he looked at the blood. Bart didn't well abide the sight of blood.

Then her shawl shifted, and he saw her dress—ripped open at the side. The beige of her undergarments was visible beneath. His disgust lessened a bit, replaced by interest.

"Seems she may've been attacked," Bart added.

"Stop, then," Fitzhammer said. "Let me speak to her."

Old Fitz did like to play the hero.

He slowed the horses. "You a'right, miss?" Bart asked cautiously. "Something happen?"

She pointed behind her in the direction of Eden. "There's been a brawl in the street, sir! You got to help, please."

"A brawl?" Fitzhammer said. The door to the coach swung open, and the man himself stepped out, just donning his traveling hat. He was past sixty, though Fitz didn't like to own up to his exact age.

Bart was nearing forty. In the past, some said he favored Fitzhammer, almost as a son favored a father. They had a similar height and clean-shaven chins. Though Bart considered himself the more attractive, especially these days. True, he wasn't as dashing as he'd been growing up in New Orleans. Back then he fancied himself a card player and thought there were riches to be made hustling poker. Nearly getting shot at the table taught him pretty quick. Working for an important man like Fitzhammer was a better long-term plan, and less likely to cut short his life.

Fitzhammer held out his hand to the girl. "Now, tell me exactly what the trouble is."

Fitz took her hand, drawing her closer to the coach. There was something familiar about her. Perhaps she just fit the type that usually caught Fitzhammer's eye—the dark hair, the pouting mouth and pale skin.

"They was fightin' and one grabbed me," the injured girl was saying. "I nearly didn't escape. Frightened me somethin' terrible. We have to go and fetch help." She clutched at Fitzhammer's elbow.

"Nonsense," Fitzhammer said, glancing at the smears of dust her fingers left on his coat. "My man here is well armed. He'll take care of the ruffians."

Easy for you to say, old man, Bart thought. "How many of them was there?"

"Two. One of 'em the man I come to town with, but I don't like him much. He's the one what hit me."

There was something about her mannerisms that didn't sit right with Bart. He couldn't quite say. She was doing an awful lot of talking for a young girl with a split lip. And she kept that bonnet pulled so low across her eyes.

Again, he craned his neck, gazing at the hillsides. Was there a spot of movement? A shape that didn't belong?

"Now, now," Fitzhammer said. "We'll get this sorted, don't you fear. Why don't you come along with us?"

Bart started walking toward the coach door, where his employer was already helping the girl inside. As she sat down, she looked at Bart from beneath her bonnet. That single flash of her dark, devilish eyes was enough.

Holy Hades. It was *her*. The last time Bart saw her, she'd sworn she would kill him and Fitzhammer both.

Bart went for his revolver. "Boss, it's that bitch. It's Marian!"

Fitzhammer's eyes went round at the name. Bart had his Colt .44 Peacemaker cocked and aimed in less than a moment, but Marian was now pointing a silver derringer at Fitz's forehead. She grinned, and her teeth were painted red with blood.

"Hello, Bart. It's been quite a long time."

CHAPTER SEVEN
2019

Penny made sure that June was settled for the night. Then Anvi called her a ride to Ashton. They'd hired a local company called Alpenglow Guides to handle transportation; Alpenglow had already been ferrying Anvi and June around. Once the festival started, Alpenglow's drivers would pilot the shuttles bringing ticket holders along the difficult road to Eden.

Penny put on the small leather backpack that she used as a purse. It held her clothes for the overnight trip. She stepped out of the trailer. Linden joined her.

The night was cool, the moon a crescent hanging over the peaks. Something hooted, and brush rustled. Penny had remembered how cold it could get up here at night, even in July. She'd warned them all to bring layers and heavy blankets. Still, she shivered in her sweatshirt, wishing she'd brought along her down coat. At least she could breathe out here. The trailer had felt extremely close with the four of them in it, though the website said it supposedly slept ten.

It would be good to get some space from the others tonight, even if that meant descending into her parents' oppressive domain.

"I'm worried about June," Linden said.

"June? Why?"

"Because she jumped at the Devil's Fest idea, yet she freaked out at the first sign of something weird."

Penny glanced at the trailer. "June said earlier today that she's been preoccupied, though she said it's not about the festival. She seems like a private person."

"So she might just be stressed." Linden chewed her lip. "I'll see if she wants to talk tomorrow. Last thing we need is an upset client."

June hadn't seemed upset, really. But if she was already feeling tense, then the dark atmosphere of Eden—and its equally dramatic history—probably wouldn't help.

"Maybe we shouldn't let her wander around Eden alone," Penny suggested. "Especially at sunrise and sunset. Do you think?" Even that was probably more caution than necessary. But it wouldn't hurt.

"Works for me." Linden crossed her arms over her sweater and balanced on one foot, the other leg notched in a tree pose. "Why didn't you tell me that stuff about your dad and his book?"

Penny turned her face to the night sky. "I didn't want you and Tripp to think this is all about my story."

"But you didn't tell *me*."

Did Linden mean "me," your best friend? Or "me," your boss?

Penny grimaced, though Linden couldn't see her expression in the dark. "There's something so ridiculous about all this. My outlaw ancestor, my dad's melodramatic book. He called me a 'spiritual medium.' Like I should have a hotline advertised on late night TV."

Like many compelling tales, her dad's book was one part truth and ten parts exaggeration. In other words, marketing.

"See, your mistake is thinking that other families are so different." Linden wrapped an arm around Penny's shoulders, sharing the warmth between them. "Everybody I know is embarrassed by their parents. No matter their circumstances. Though your case is...unusual."

"But you know what I mean."

Linden had gone to all the right schools. She'd mentioned a prestigious elementary school that required letters of reference to get in. The Hao family lived in Bel Air, a fifteen-minute drive from UCLA, though of course Linden had lived in her own apartment in Westwood during college instead of their mansion.

"You're unique and adorable, and I love that about you," Linden said.

Just what Penny had expected. Linden did not understand.

"But Tripp expects me to know everything that's going on," Linden continued. "He doesn't want there to be any surprises, you know? Tripp's got a ton of money riding on this. SunBev has even more at stake. We have to get it right."

Penny's cheeks were burning. Actually, her entire body was overheating. She'd forgotten about the cold.

"You can count on me. Everything's going to be perfect."

"Of course it will. I'll see you in the morning." Linden gave her another squeeze.

Penny walked toward the parking lot, hoping her ride would appear soon. She had to get her head straight so she could focus on her job—not ghosts, not her parents, not her past.

Then she heard footsteps behind her. She spun.

Matthew stopped short, holding his keys in one hand and a messenger bag in the other.

They both spoke at once. "What are you—"

Jinx, Penny thought, which she would've said if it were years ago and they were still kids.

"Waiting for my ride," she said. "My mother has summoned me."

"Ah." He jangled his keys on his palm. "I was working on my plans for your hotel party. Trying to catch up since we're already behind."

She crossed her arms, turning away. Not another lecture already.

"Come on," he said, heading toward a truck. "I'll drive you."

"That's really not—"

"I'm sure we can be 'civil' for fifteen minutes."

Penny looked toward the road, willing her driver from Alpenglow to roar in and save her. But there was no sign.

Matthew's engine revved to life.

She reached for the passenger door handle on Matthew's truck. He was facing the windshield, not even looking at her. His hair was pale, bluish in the low light and the glow from the dashboard.

She climbed up and slid into the seat, copying Matthew's expression—eyes forward, face impassive. The cab smelled just the way she remembered, like pine needles, laundry detergent, and the spicy-scented deodorant that Matthew had always worn.

They pulled away. Penny sent off a quick text, cancelling the ride she'd requested from Alpenglow Guides.

She glanced at him. His profile she knew by heart. The angle of his nose, the curve at his lower lip, both highlighted against the darkness. There were so many things she could say right now. Things she probably shouldn't say for the sake of Devil's Fest. But then the words started coming.

"Did you know before today that I was involved with this project?" she asked. "That we'd be working together?"

"Does that bother you?"

"I have no opinion. I was just curious."

His eyes cut over to her, shining in the dimness. He had such expressive eyes. Penny had always been able to read exactly what he was thinking in them. Right now they said, *I'm calling bullshit.*

"Okay, fine. I was more than curious." *But that's all I'm saying*, she thought, *and you just have to deal with it.*

"Your hair's natural again," he said. "I always liked it best that way."

She'd colored it every few months in high school. Black, platinum, dark brown. Even pink with purple ends, which her mother had *loved*.

"Been like this for years. I stopped dying it in college."

He was quiet for a moment.

"Already a ghost sighting today," he said.

"That's why we're holding the festival in Eden—people love ghost stories."

He shook his head. It was barely a movement. More a flinch, really. But it was enough.

"You don't approve of what I'm doing here," she said. "Devil's Fest. This energy drink thing."

"We all gotta make a buck."

She leaned her elbow on the passenger door and looked out the window. The dark landscape flew past, silhouettes of trees.

"I was surprised, though," he said. "Considering your history with Eden. Of all the people who'd be planning an event like this, making money off a bunch of murders, I never thought it would be you."

She sighed and turned back to him. There was something fragile about his features. Heavy eyelids, like he was always sleepy or thinking deeply. When they were young, the other kids had made fun of him for it. Most of the time he laughed it off. But on those few rare occasions, the hurt had shown so plainly on his face.

"Look, let's just agree to keep this professional, keep our past out of it, and it'll all go smoothly."

His mouth quirked. "Our past? What are you referring to, exactly?"

She settled back in the seat. The truck bumped up and down. "Go to hell, Matthew," she murmured, wishing that the wind would carry her words away. That he wouldn't hear in her voice how much she still felt for him.

"Your Devil's Fest is in less than a week," he deadpanned. "I'd say we're all going to hell."

CHAPTER EIGHT

They parked in front of the Ashton Valley Inn. Penny grabbed her pack, got out and slammed the door.

"Thanks for the ride," she said over her shoulder.

"My pleasure," Matthew called back.

He was a funny guy now, apparently. Jokes and sarcasm. He'd definitely changed in the last six years.

She jogged up the steps. The door opened onto a familiar scene: green carpets, burgundy drapes, striped wallpaper. The inn had once been the stately home of Judge Beau MacKenzie, one of Ashton's founders. He was also the man who discovered the bodies after the Devil's Night Massacre in Eden.

Nobody was manning the desk, so Penny rang the bell. Her mom swept out of the office, a romance paperback still poised in front of her face. "One sec," she said, "this is a really good part." Her dangly earrings—bright blue frogs today—danced from the movement.

She glanced up and immediately dropped the paperback onto the floor. "Penny. Penny! Baby girl, get over here." Her mom skirted the desk and pulled Penny into a hug. "Lawrence, get out here. Krista, you too! Penny's here!"

Penny cringed and gritted her teeth, hoping her eardrums

could survive the onslaught. The last time she'd visited was Christmas three years ago, though her parents had trekked to LA a few times. She and her mom spoke on the phone every few weeks about trivial things. Her mom had been bugging her constantly to make the trip home, but she hadn't had the vacation time. Or the energy.

She'd never had a falling out with her parents—nothing so dramatic. Penny just didn't like how she felt here, in Ashton, around her family. Like she was still the same little girl and couldn't possibly have changed.

Ten minutes later, they'd gathered around a table at the back of the on-site bar along with Penny's sister.

Her dad sat with both hands wrapped around his Coors bottle. He looked pensive, lost in thought. He'd pulled his graying hair back into a ponytail, and his green flannel button-down had tiny acorns printed on it.

Penny's mom, Debbie, set two glasses on the table. Amaretto sour, her signature drink.

"Lime wedge instead of a cherry," Debbie said with a wink, as if Penny had never encountered this concoction before. "Not too tart, not too sweet."

Same way I like my ladies, her dad usually followed up. But tonight he stayed quiet, still staring at the beer label.

Penny clinked her glass against her sister's pint of local IPA. They'd already exchanged small talk about Penny's trip and Krista's current lineup of online college classes. As usual, Krista had her dark hair in a French braid. She wore a pair of the neon running shorts she favored, her feet clad in Tiva sandals.

Nobody had mentioned Devil's Fest yet. Though Penny was sure that her dad had plenty to say.

Then Krista nudged her elbow. "So can you get me tickets?"

"No." Lawrence's fist came down on the table, making them all jump. "Krista is not going. This Devil's Fest thing is a disaster waiting to happen. Bryce agrees with me."

Their older brother. In the last year, Bryce had opened a

restaurant on Ashton's hopping tourist strip, right between an art gallery and a shop selling crystals and tarot. Bryce was also Matthew's best friend. Thankfully, Penny's brother had better things to do than hang out here at the inn.

"It's just a festival," Debbie said, stroking her husband's hand. "Penny's a grown woman now. She deserves to make her own choices. Even when we don't agree."

"Thank you," Penny said. "I need this, Dad. This job is important to me."

"Selling what happened in Eden like it's one big commercial?"

Penny's drink had left a wet ring on the table. "You're the one who wrote a book about it."

"A book about the terrible things that happened there. My book was a warning. Not a bunch of perverts dancing naked on PornTube."

Krista giggled. "Do you mean PornHub? What've you been watching on your phone, Dad?"

An older couple occupied a nearby table. They were looking over. Penny leaned in and lowered her voice.

"Nobody's going to—"

"She just needs to be different, Lawrence," Debbie said. "Let Penny be Penny. Isn't that what we've always said?"

Penny stared at the slick surface of the table. She knew her mom was trying to be helpful, to defuse this fight before it got going. But the words stung. *She just needs to be different.* Like this was one more frivolous venture, like when Penny was a dog walker for all of three days. Or her brief stint as an interior decorator. The pre-med major that didn't last past organic chemistry. Or the master's program in Modern American Literature that she quit before it even began. She'd been at Sterling PR for almost two years, but her parents still saw her as a flake.

Her mom had it wrong: Penny didn't want or even need to be different. She simply had always been different. She came into the world that way, named for the rust color of her hair when she was born, hair that only a couple of random cousins on her dad's side shared. The rest of them all tan-skinned, raven-haired.

Bryce and Krista both took after their mom—whip-smart, quick with an opinion, then a joke to soften the blow. Like their dad, they worshipped the mountains like it was their religion. They'd never thought for a moment about leaving Ashton. This corner of Colorado was the closest to paradise that they could imagine.

Penny was the one who'd left paradise to move to smog-filled, crowded Los Angeles. They'd never understood why she enjoyed living there—the character of each small neighborhood, the bustle and excitement and anonymity.

She loved her family. But she hated how people called her "ghost girl" growing up. How they always asked about her dad's book and about Bloody Marian. *Did you really see her? Did she really speak to you?*

And yet Penny had come back. Maybe Devil's Fest really was her one and only idea. Then she'd have to start all over the way her family expected. The way she always did.

THE FAMILY HAD a wing of the inn to themselves, but Penny asked for a separate room. "I'm not sharing a bed with Krista," she said. "She never stays on her side." So her mom handed her a key for the second floor and promised to work her magic for the SunBev executives that would arrive soon.

Throughout this exchange, Penny's dad hovered by the front desk. Then he walked with her up the stairs.

"You don't have to show me," she said. "I know the way."

"Of course you do," he retorted. "But I don't get to see you much, do I? Not anymore."

Black-and-white historic photos decorated the walls: Ashton's Main Street filled with horse-drawn carriages; Ashton's V-E Day celebration in 1945. There were various images of the inn, both when it was Beau MacKenzie's house and then a century later, when the Wrights remodeled.

The night after the massacre in Eden, Marian Smith had traveled under cover of darkness to abandon her child in Ashton. Beau MacKenzie had found the crying little girl on Ashton First Methodist's front steps. Lawrence had written about all of this in *A Devil in Eden*. It was a strange family inheritance, rife with ambiguities. Penny remembered being confused as a child. Was Bloody Marian evil? What did that mean for her descendants—Penny among them?

Penny's father became obsessed with understanding the paranormal. But she just found the debate tiring. It would be easier for everyone if the dead stayed in their place.

She and her father reached the second floor and turned down the hallway. More photos adorned the walls: Lawrence and his siblings as children, growing up at the inn. Then photos of Penny and her brother and sister. Like this was their private living room and not a public hotel hallway.

"I understand you're still mad at me about the book," Lawrence said. "You felt you needed to rebel. Moving to LA was one thing, but this?"

She groaned, closing her eyes. "I'm not mad. I'm sick of hearing about it. There's a difference."

"What you're doing is *dangerous*. Don't you remember what happened to us up in Eden, when I took you there?"

Penny recalled only pieces of that day. The drive up to Eden with her parents and their friends. Her first glimpses of the ghost town—the stately brick hotel and the imposing canyon walls. Her dad had formed some sort of "Paranormal Society," devoted to researching the unknown. He loved that his daughter could see ghosts. And Penny had loved the attention.

They'd wanted to test Penny's abilities. Her mom went along reluctantly, urged on by Penny's enthusiasm. Right away, things got out of hand. They heard noises coming from the buildings. Saw a door move by itself. She had sensed angry spirits there.

Penny got scared—really scared—and her mom insisted on taking her home.

Penny's dad had refused to go, determined to stay in Eden through Devil's Night.

"It was one of the worst mistakes of my life," her father said. "I swore to your mother I'd never let you set foot in that place again."

Penny turned to face her dad. "You're not responsible for Devil's Fest. I am. You're not 'letting' me do anything."

"The ghosts in Eden could hurt you. Or someone else. They nearly killed me that Devil's Night. You're going to pretend that didn't happen?"

She resumed walking toward her room. "You slipped and fell. You weren't even hurt."

Her dad stayed where he was, his voice following her down the hall. "Something *pushed* me."

"So you thought. Power of suggestion."

"You told me that Marian could sense us. *She knew we were there.*"

Penny spun around to face him.

"But I lied!"

A door opened, and a hotel guest peeked out hesitantly. Lawrence apologized, then hurried after Penny. She'd made it to the end of the hall and unlocked the door to her room. He stopped her from going in.

"What do you mean, you lied?"

Penny closed her eyes. She hadn't wanted to get into this. And she certainly had not intended to have a shouting match with her father in the inn's second-floor hallway. But it was past time for the truth.

"I was just a little girl who wanted to make her father happy. I told you what you wanted to hear."

She'd come across countless ghosts in her life. They'd been lost and sad. Often confused. And yes, sometimes angry. But none had ever communicated with her directly. So she *must* have been embellishing when she was five and claimed that Bloody Marian had actually spoken to her. There was no way that Marian had been aware of Penny's presence. Ghosts didn't work that way.

Kids made up stories all the time. Normal parents didn't publish those stories in books and call them true.

"I'm sorry, Dad."

He shook his head. "I know what happened back then. The ghosts there are...persuasive."

What was that supposed to mean? "Believe whatever you want. I'm tired. I'm going to bed."

"At least promise you won't go anywhere in Eden alone. Please, Penny. I'm begging you."

"Goodnight, Dad. I love you." She went into her room and shut the door.

CHAPTER NINE

THE TRAILER'S SCREEN DOOR SQUEAKED AS IT OPENED. ANVI cringed at the noise, looking behind her. She didn't want to wake the others. But Linden didn't stir. June was still snoring away in the trailer's rear alcove.

The cold pinched her skin as she stepped outside. The sky was brilliant with stars; Eden's Main Street lay in darkness. She closed her eyes and inhaled, holding the breath until her lungs ached.

She missed her cheap hotel room in Ashton. She might've grown up in West LA, Beverly Hills adjacent—in a quaint little Spanish-style house, certainly no mansion—yet Anvi had simple needs. A warm bed, Netflix, a nice bottle of aged rum, and decent bandwidth. She liked taking her morning run through city streets, dodging trash trucks and delivery vans. Her favorite coffee shop at home was open late, and sometimes she continued to toil on her laptop while office workers sipped mojitos and listened to live acoustic.

But now, Linden insisted they sleep up here by the ghost town, crammed into that trailer. Except for Penny, of course. Somehow, none of the usual rules applied where Penny Wright was involved.

Anvi had never been the girl with the most friends. When she was a kid, the rest of her Brownie troop barely spoke to her. They said she was mean; she didn't smile enough. But when Girl Scout cookie season arrived, she made a plan that helped them sell more boxes than any other troop in the county. She ended up quitting a year later—all those boring badges—and some of the girls had actually begged her to come back. She'd never forgotten that lesson: you couldn't force people to like you, but you could make sure they realized your value.

Anvi took out her phone. The screen seemed bright as the sun in all that darkness. It wasn't the iPhone that Sterling PR paid for, with her work email and social accounts and client photos. Linden was way too nosy with that phone. This was Anvi's personal Android, a phone that Linden didn't even know about. Anvi preferred to keep it that way.

Walking farther from the trailer, she thumbed to her list of favorite contacts and hit send.

He answered on the second ring. "Hey. I was hoping you'd call."

Her pulse jumped at hearing his voice. They'd been texting often since she arrived—on her private phone, of course, which stressed her a bit with constantly juggling two devices. But she also didn't want to give him the impression that she was indifferent. He wasn't the kind of guy who waited around.

"We had some excitement this afternoon," she said. Anvi described how Penny, June and a few others claimed to have seen a ghost. It was a ridiculous charade, only sensible if they made it part of the Dark Energy campaign.

She'd hated Devil's Fest from the minute those words left Penny's lips. Anvi had been ready with her own campaign for Dark Energy: a huge party on the grounds of the Griffith Observatory, complete with contortionists, avant-garde acrobats and street magicians in futuristic costumes. Anvi's grandfather had inspired the concept with his love of astronomy and all things sci-fi. He'd shown her every Star Wars movie, bought her Philip K. Dick novels every birthday.

She'd really thought everybody at Sterling would love the idea. They were *supposed* to love it.

And then Penny shot down the entire concept. *A sci-fi theme? Isn't that taking 'Dark Energy' a bit literally?* Linden, of course, had agreed. Because Penny could do no wrong.

All that work, the outpouring of Anvi's heart, instantly down the toilet.

Now, Anvi was killing herself to pull off Devil's Fest. Soon, Tripp Sterling would understand what she had to offer. When it came time to expand Sterling PR, Anvi would be in the perfect position to jump into a partnership spot. Right over Penny's head.

She heard a high-pitched noise and whirled around. It had sounded like the hinges on the trailer's screen door.

"Hello?" she said into the dark. "Linden?"

Nobody answered.

"What's going on?" His voice was breaking up.

"Nothing," she replied into the phone. "Thought I heard someone. Never mind."

Just imagining things, she thought. *Letting Penny's stories get to me.*

Anvi didn't understand Penny's stress about that book. Why not tell the world about *A Devil in Eden?* They were already plugging Eden as the most haunted ghost town in America; why not leak reports that an actual medium dreamed up the festival after she encountered Eden's ghosts as a child? The blog posts would write themselves. People would eat it up.

And not only that—a "ghost" had just been spotted, right before Devil's Fest.

Was it really a stunt pulled by Penny to impress their SunBev rep? If so, Anvi was impressed. She hadn't thought Penny so capable. But Anvi didn't really care either way, so long as they could make Devil's Fest a success. And if she could get the credit. So if some influencers just happened to get an email with certain insider information...

The temperature had dipped below freezing. Anvi pulled her hands inside her sweater sleeves. The fingers holding her phone were growing numb. She spent a bit longer on the call, lingering over their conversation. Parsing every word that he said for meaning.

"I'll see you soon," he said. He ended the call. Not the warmest goodbye, but he was rarely effusive. His tone was flirty, though. Just the right amount of suggestive. She smiled to herself, her blood heating. Things were looking up.

She was about to head off to bed—if she could somehow tune out June's snoring and Linden's flowery-scented moisturizer. But then rocks scattered nearby. As if someone had knocked them over.

Anvi froze. She'd heard about coyotes, mountain lions. But it wasn't an animal.

There was a person standing there in the shadows.

"Who's there?" Anvi said.

No answer. The figure didn't move. Suddenly the cold was more than Anvi could take. She felt it seeping through her sweater and deep into her skin.

"What do you want?" Shivering, Anvi unlocked her phone and turned on the flashlight. She aimed the light at the figure.

June held up a hand to shield her face, blinking in the bright beam.

Anvi lowered the phone to her side. "What are you doing out here?"

June looked around herself, as if just realizing where she was. "I just...needed some air. Who were you talking to?"

"Nobody," Anvi said, then realized how that sounded. "My grandfather. We talk every day." That was usually true, though Anvi hadn't remembered to call him in the last two.

But June didn't even seem to be listening. "Did you say my name before? I thought I heard...something."

Anvi steered June back toward the trailer. "Probably just a dream. You were crashing pretty hard earlier."

Penny's stupid stories. Anvi laughed at herself for being so paranoid. All the same, she checked the lock on the trailer door —twice—before finally drifting off to sleep.

CHAPTER TEN

PENNY HIT THE BREAKFAST SPREAD IN THE MORNING. SHE'D slept well overnight, no dreams. She'd hardly thought of Matthew at all.

The buffet was arranged on her mom's floral-patterned china, doilies underneath the serving dishes. She grabbed a strawberry yogurt and a banana and ducked into a corner booth.

It wasn't so bad being home, however much she'd hoped to avoid it. Penny had actually loved growing up at the inn. There'd always been somebody to talk to. The bustle of the inn's dining room. The constant stream of people to watch.

Like that disheveled woman who'd just wandered in, her wide eyes roving across the room in search of someone. She was around Penny's mom's age. Probably had a story to tell. A late night, perhaps? A straying spouse?

"Morning." Krista, Penny's little sister, slipped into the seat across from her. Krista held out a muffin wrapped in a napkin. "Dora sends her love."

Penny smelled vanilla, butter and dark chocolate. Dora, the inn's head chef, was famous for her chocolate chip muffins. Penny took a bite of the still-warm streusel topping and made a mental note to visit Dora later. Another part of her old life in

Ashton that Penny had missed. It hadn't all been angst and ghost sightings, though she might sometimes remember it that way.

"So I was serious about the tickets to Devil's Fest," Krista said, folding her arms on the table. "I need four."

"I don't want Dad any angrier than he already is."

"Like Dad's ever mad for more than five minutes. He's probably forgotten what he said by now."

Penny lifted a skeptical eyebrow, tucking more muffin into her mouth. Chocolate melted on her tongue.

"I gotta get back to the kitchen. I'm on buffet duty. Don't forget the tickets, 'kay?" Krista got up. "Oh yeah, and Matthew's waiting for you by the front desk."

A chunk of muffin went down the wrong way. Penny coughed. "He's what? Why?"

"He said he's your ride up to Eden." Krista's eyes narrowed as she smiled. "He lives here at the inn. You knew that, right?"

Penny groaned. She'd had enough of Matthew last night.

Krista walked away from her table. At the same moment, the disheveled woman started marching over—the same woman Penny had noticed earlier. She stopped in front of Penny's table. Buttons were missing from her cardigan.

The woman leaned in too close. "You're her, aren't you? Penny Wright?"

"Um..."

"How could you, of all people, risk holding a big festival up in Eden? On Devil's Night, no less? Someone's going to end up dead."

Penny couldn't help laughing. "I'm sorry, who are you?"

The woman grabbed a glass of ice water from the next table. "You need to wake up." She splashed the water into Penny's face.

Penny gasped at the sudden cold. Her shirt was soaked through. The rest of the dining room had gone silent, everyone staring.

Krista came back over. "Excuse me? What is going on?"

"Someone will end up dead!" the woman shouted.

"Ma'am, you need to leave. Before I call the police."

She left, still glaring at Penny on her way out. Krista got a pile of napkins and helped Penny sop up water from her clothes.

"I'm so sorry about that," Krista said. "Sometimes people wander in for the breakfast, and we don't worry too much about it. But I can't believe..."

"Do you know who she is?" There'd been something vaguely familiar about the woman.

"No clue."

"Uncle Harry said somebody complained to the mayor. Maybe it was her." One naysayer in their entire town wasn't so bad. Two if she counted her father. Well, three including Matthew. Maybe better not to keep a tally.

The rest of the diners had gone back to their breakfasts, though they kept stealing surreptitious glances in her direction. Penny stood up, helping to gather the wet napkins and tablecloth.

"I need to get going."

"Okay. Hey, Matthew's probably still waiting. You'll have a story to tell on your way to Eden."

"Tell him I already left."

Krista tilted her head disapprovingly. "I don't know what happened between the two of you, but—"

Penny darted toward the back door. She'd managed all right the past six years without Matthew in her life. She didn't need his help, and she certainly didn't need his approval.

CHAPTER ELEVEN

Penny called Alpenglow Guides—the local company they'd contracted with—to give her a ride. A twenty-something guy named Scott Mackey showed up, wearing a bright orange cap featuring a snowboarder and the words *"Ride or Die."*

"Good to finally meet you." He took off his orange cap and ran a hand through his sweaty mop of hair. "I heard of you before, but like, Krista's talked about you, too. You work with Anvi, right?"

He was talkative on the drive, his mouth running while he kept eying the wet splotch on her chest. Apparently, Scott and Penny's little sister were good friends, which might've shown dubious judgment on Krista's part. But the guy seemed harmless.

When they arrived at Eden, Penny jumped out of the Jeep, barely pausing to say goodbye. She just wanted to get to work.

The sounds of hammering and air-powered nail guns echoed across the canyon. Matthew's crew was laboring outside the Paradise Hotel, moving around gigantic pieces of lumber and plywood. Penny waited until no one was watching, then snuck into the hotel's entrance, snagging a hard hat from a table.

The lobby was already cleaner than yesterday. The crew had

left tools in various places along with more wood. But nobody was there at the moment, which made things easier. Matthew would probably tell her she shouldn't be inside, hard hat or no. But she wasn't going far. She was barely going to touch anything. She just needed to take some new photos.

Penny hurried into the dining room. She'd borrowed Linden's fancy SLR camera from the trailer. Technically, she already had plenty of content for their campaign. Not to mention pages of copy written by the team. For weeks, they'd been posting teasers about Devil's Fest, securing placements on blogs, influencer social feeds, and in the media. But Anvi had been all over Instagram the past few days, and Penny had to keep up. She wanted something fresh. Plus, it felt good to stay busy. If she filled every moment with work, then she wouldn't have to think about annoying things. Like that crazy woman at the inn who'd ruined breakfast. Or Matthew.

She took a few shots of curled wallpaper; a close-up of weathered floorboards. The building across the street shot through wavy glass.

Something creaked over her head. Penny glanced up. Tiny bits of plaster were drifting down from the ceiling. The building was shifting, that was all. Matthew's crew was working.

Next, she snapped another pic of the notorious crack in the ceiling where Ernest Fitzhammer, the hotel's owner, had been hung from the chandelier.

Past the dining room, Penny came to the kitchen and the corridor she'd seen yesterday. Light barely filtered through the dirty windows. She took a few photos of the iron stove, which had little rosettes stamped into the metal. It seemed like everything from the nineteenth century had some kind of decorative flourish. Little feet that curved into claws, or crystal knobs for handles. She snapped a photo of the stove's feet, too, and then turned around.

Her breath stopped in her chest.

There was someone standing in the hallway. The woman in the long dress.

Penny blinked at the darkness. She could only see the woman's lower half—billowing fabric that didn't quite brush the floor, and the pointed toes of sturdy shoes. She was so real. More solid than Penny had grown used to seeing in Los Angeles—faded impressions of people like old photos. She tried taking a picture, but the camera's display screen showed just black.

The woman walked away. The figure reached the end of the hall and turned right, where the corridor continued out of sight.

Penny thought of the ghost last night who'd crossed the second floor.

Was it Marian?

In the legends, Bloody Marian was the villain of the Devil's Night Massacre. The ominous figure that witnesses had seen walking down Main Street, covered in blood. But nobody knew all the details of what happened on the original Devil's Night—why Marian had killed those people, including some of her own men.

What if Penny could use that in the Devil's Fest marketing, somehow? Play up that mystery? She could bring her father's book into the narrative without putting the focus on herself.

Penny let her mental walls slip—just a bit—and listened.

Don't let him hurt me, a faint voice said. As if it had whispered from behind a crack in a wall.

The sound of crying came from somewhere deeper in the building.

Penny walked down the hallway. The camera bumped against her stomach on its strap. She had to use the light on her phone to see. *Go, leave me alone,* she heard. But inside her, the pull to follow only grew stronger. There was a musty smell, more intense here than the rest of the hotel—rotting wood, mold, ancient dust. Her fist clenched around her phone, the screen growing slick from her sweat.

Penny rounded the corner. She spotted the ghostly woman again. The specter walked through a closed door.

"Wait!" Penny said.

She hurried toward the door. The knob made a shrill sound, metal grinding against metal, as it turned. It opened on a small room with a bookcase on one wall. The shelves had collapsed, all the books long gone.

The ghost stood by the remains of the bookcase. Then she walked through the wall and vanished.

Here, the voice said. *I'm here. Please.*

Penny reached out to where the ghost had disappeared. There was an odd flaw in the wood paneling. Penny traced the small opening, and her finger slipped inside.

She pulled. A section of the wall moved on creaking hinges. Opening. Then another room appeared.

A collapsed brass bedstead slumped against the opposite wall, the mattress rotted into dust. A rod still hung over the window, though the curtains were just shreds. A pile of ancient trash lay in the corner—cans nearly rusted away, empty glass bottles.

Penny stepped inside.

The crying started again, now louder. She didn't know why she'd come here. She didn't want to be in this place. This room. Her head was swimming. The room began to rotate. She squeezed her eyes shut.

I'm scared he'll come back. What if he doesn't come back? It was the ghostly woman—her thoughts and feelings flooded Penny's mind. But the thoughts were contradictory. Penny couldn't make sense of it.

"I'm Penny Wright," Penny said aloud. "I'm leaving now." Trying to convince herself.

Ghosts were just shadows left behind after a living person had gone. They were like a replay of a video; mere remnants of the past, not the present. Ghosts couldn't hurt you. Only fear could.

She tried to close off her mind, but the foreign thoughts kept pushing in.

Be quiet. He'll hear.

The secret panel in the wall slammed shut.

She tried to find the latch again, but this side was smooth. Splinters dug into her fingertips as she searched for the edges of the door.

"Hey!" she said, banging with her fist against the wood. "I'm stuck in here!" Matthew's crew wasn't far. They'd hear her. They had to.

Then she felt hands on her back.

Each finger was distinct, pressing into her shoulder blades. They *pushed*.

The hands threw her up against the door. Her face hit the wood, the roughness scratching her cheek. The hard hat clattered to the floor. She screamed, but the sound was muffled. Fingers wrapped around her neck. Pressed.

Help me, please. She coughed, trying to breathe.

Penny squirmed away and spun around. But no one was there —neither living nor spectral. She had to get out of there before they came back. *He*. Before *he* came back.

She ran for the window across the room. Ripped aside the tattered curtain. The frame no longer held any glass, leaving a narrow gap about two feet high.

She pushed herself up on the ledge, maneuvering sideways through the opening. Her foot touched down, but she didn't land evenly. Her elbows landed hard on the ground a moment later. The blue sky was bright in her eyes.

Penny was gasping, unable to catch her breath. She sat up and brushed dry grass from her hair. She seemed to be in a space in between buildings. A postage stamp of dirt and weeds, enclosed by walls on all sides but open to the sky above. It smelled like mildew, the air stagnant. Three of the walls were brick, as if the hotel had been constructed to partially enclose this space. The last wall was wood, only about two stories high. It didn't budge when she tried pushing on the boards.

She looked up at the brick walls. The second and third floors had duplicates of the narrow rectangular window. The second floor one was boarded up from the inside.

No way out from here. She'd have to go back the way she came.

But that room...Someone had been in there with her. A ghost had actually touched her. *Pushed* her. She'd never experienced anything like it. Hadn't even thought it possible. Her dad had claimed something similar in his book, but she hadn't believed him.

Tears sprang into her eyes. She was just now grasping the awfulness of what she'd experienced.

Someone had tried to hurt her. Why?

"Can anyone hear me?" Her voice sounded weak. Strangled. Now that she was outside, she could hear the banging of the construction nearby, which was comforting in a way. *Stay calm*, she told herself. *You're okay*. Linden's camera was a bit scratched but otherwise intact. Penny felt for her phone, but it wasn't in her pockets.

She cursed. She'd dropped her phone in that room.

Penny went back to the window and looked in. Her phone lay on the floor.

A new feeling surged through her—he was coming. The voice spoke again.

Don't make a sound. Please, just leave me alone.

The world tilted. She stumbled and fell to the dirt, cradling her head in her hands. Nausea rose in her stomach, and she gagged.

"This isn't happening," she told herself. "It's not real."

But she kept hearing that plaintive voice in her mind: *Don't hurt me again. Please.*

She sat there in the dirt, head between her knees, until the feeling began to pass. The sky had stopped spinning, and her stomach was calming. She put her hand down, bracing herself. But her finger caught on something. She pulled to free herself, and skin tore from her fingertip. Blood welled from the cut.

She looked down. It took another surreal moment to understand what she was seeing.

There was a human skull half-buried in the dirt beside her.

EDEN SPRUNG UP ABOUT THREE YEARS BEFORE THE DEVIL'S Night Massacre. Ernest Fitzhammer, a wealthy businessman and owner of many mining claims in that region, spent extravagant amounts to build the Paradise Hotel and bank. Fitzhammer envisioned a microcosm of a city block in New York or San Francisco, though he never was able to replace Eden's other buildings with more permanent stone or brick.

But since it was built, the Paradise was plagued with rumors of a haunting. Guests would report odd noises. They heard crying at night, though the porters could never discover the source. Even before Eden's luck turned, the Paradise grew unpopular among the town's visitors. So perhaps the place was always cursed to be the site of terrible events, as some newspapers later claimed.

-from A DEVIL IN EDEN by Lawrence Wright

DEVIL'S NIGHT - 1894

Fitzhammer stared at her in dismay. "Marian? Is that really you?"

Slowly, she got out of the coach, positioning Fitzhammer in front of her. Bart's eyes flashed with fury. His finger tightened on the trigger.

Marian pulled back her bonnet, exposing her face. Her hand was sweating. The derringer slipped against her palm as she held it. But Fitzhammer's shock was like fresh water to her, calming and cool.

"What do you want?" the man asked. "Money?"

Douglas appeared from his hiding place, advancing slowly toward them.

She held the derringer to Fitzhammer's temple. "Drop your weapon, Bart. You're outnumbered."

Douglas pressed the barrel of his gun between Bart's shoulders. "You heard the lady."

Marian saw the hesitation and hatred in Bart's eyes. But he did as he was told. His gun thudded onto the dirt.

"Bart, you're going to drive," Marian said. "Ernest, you'll get back in the coach. We have a trip to make."

"Now be reasonable," Fitzhammer said. "Why not just take what's in my purse and be done with this?"

"Don't you see?" Bart asked. "She's going to kill us. This is her revenge."

"No one's going to die," Douglas said in his baritone voice. "Not if you do what we ask. Get back up onto the driver's bench."

Bart turned around, reaching for the bench. But then he suddenly dropped to fours, scrambled beneath the horses, and ran. Douglas fired, but his bullet went high. Bart sprinted uphill for the nearest copse of trees.

Another shot rang out. Smoke rose in the air.

Tim emerged from his cover of bushes, his gun tight in his fist. He jogged down to where Bart had fallen. Bart was screaming, clutching his thigh.

"Lord in Heaven." Fitzhammer grabbed the bowler hat from his head and pushed it to his chest. "You've killed him. You've killed Bart."

"Get him bandaged up." Marian tossed Douglas her shawl. He trotted over to Tim. Together, they rolled Bart—who was still hollering and crying—onto his back.

Fitzhammer turned to her. Sweat was glistening on his upper lip above his pale mustache. His hair had gone grayer than she'd remembered, but his whiskers remained a golden yellow.

"Marian, I was always good to you, wasn't I? I took you in."

"If you want to live, I suggest you shut your mouth."

"Nobody else would've cared for you but me. Consider who your mother was, where you came from—"

She squeezed the grip of Bart's gun. "*Stop talking.*"

She'd read the story by Robert Louis Stevenson. Dr. Jekyll denied his true nature at first, too. Yet by the end, he had to face his Mr. Hyde. Fitzhammer would too, before his end.

MARIAN HAD KNOWN her mother's habits well. The woman had been drunk nearly every waking moment, trying to drown her utter bafflement at the life she'd been reduced to living. Just once, she'd spoken of loving a man who jilted her. But the next time Marian asked, her mother insisted it never happened. *Your father was like any of them. Nobody special.*

They lived in a small crib on a side street in Telluride. As a girl, Marian remembered hiding behind the woodpile out of doors when men came to call. She grew skilled at twisting her arms out of joint to slip from a meaty-fingered grasp.

She befriended some of the dance-hall girls. Their lives did not seem so bleak as her mother's. Some of them were whores, but not all. They giggled and made up her hair and dressed her in their clothes. Made her their pet. But as Marian got to know them, their predicament became clear: either marry while still young and pretty, become a soiled dove in a parlor house, or end up in a filthy crib. Eventually, all roads led to a man's bed or to poverty—sometimes both. And Marian had no intention of being like her mother.

At fifteen, Marian met Ernest Fitzhammer. The other girls said he was kind and fatherly. Not to mention rich. There were whispers, of course. That he especially admired the younger girls. That he'd never married and lived a transient life, moving from town to town. But the girls agreed he was always generous with tips.

As far as men went, Fitzhammer was far from the worst.

He told Marian he worried for her. She was so lovely and innocent and would be preyed upon, he warned. He insisted upon saving her from a degenerate life. She understood his meaning, and she hesitated. But what he said next broke down any remaining barriers in her heart.

He promised to hire a tutor for her. She'd have a proper education.

The schooling began right away. In Fitzhammer's parlor, surrounded by ornate furniture and expensive imports, the tutor began the instruction. At first they improved her reading, then moved onto literature, classical history, and beginning mathematics.

She kept waiting for the moment that Fitzhammer would visit her at night.

A few months later, that night came. She smelled his cologne; felt his hand on her back. A few of the dance-hall girls claimed to find pleasure in the act. To Marian, it was only a reality to be endured.

She applied herself doubly hard to her schoolwork, reminding herself every day: *this determines what I am worth.* In her spare time, she was drawn to the darker stories: writers like Poe and Mary Shelley and Wilkie Collins. They perfectly captured the secret ugliness of life.

Her first pregnancy came at sixteen. In the third month, blood soaked her drawers and petticoats. She screamed and raved for hours. Fitzhammer left the house, driven by his servant Bart Adams, and they didn't return for weeks. When she came back to herself, something had ossified inside of her. As if the childish, soft parts of her had turned as dead and cold as minerals.

The next time she fell pregnant, she had a plan at the ready.

So naïve, even then.

She came to Fitzhammer in his office. He was a man of business. He spoke the language of deal-making and negotiation.

"I'm here to discuss terms," she said, keeping her eyes on the rug. Her hand curved protectively over her still-flat belly. Their prior arrangement was no longer sufficient. Surely, he would see that.

He looked up, setting his pen aside. "Terms? What are you saying?"

"I'm to have your child. I have my demands."

His mouth opened, but no coherent words emerged.

"You'll marry me. My lessons will continue, but you'll refrain from coming to my bed until after the child arrives." She was afraid that her womb was delicate and might try to reject the baby again.

The door to the office was open. He stood up and went to shut it. He leaned against the door. "I'm beginning to understand. I didn't think you capable of this, Marian."

Her eyes remained downcast. Her voice steady. But her heart had quickened—not quite as dead as she'd believed.

"The men with whom you conduct business," she said, "I will tell their wives of my situation. They may take an interest."

"You threaten me? None will believe the daughter of a common whore."

"They may." She had no idea if this was true, but she put conviction behind the words. And she knew Fitzhammer believed. She saw the fear grow behind his eyes.

Unfortunately, she hadn't predicted how that fear would make Fitzhammer react.

She refused to think of what happened at the asylum. She was the *Woman In White* from the Collins novel, wrongly committed and ill used. But at least her child was safe from him.

After a time, she escaped and decided to create a new life. She locked her memories away, like a book she swore to never again read. But she had nightmares that followed her into the day. Her heart would shake her entire body, refusing to calm. Her mind spun in circles, holding her prisoner some days so that she couldn't even leave her bed.

That book refused to stay closed.

The coach pulled up in front of the Paradise Hotel, and Douglas pulled the reins to stop the horses. "Go tell the porter we need assistance with Mr. Fitzhammer's luggage," he said to Tim.

But the porter beat them to it. He must've seen the coach

pull up. The man hurried outside, dressed in a light blue uniform.

"Mr. Fitzhammer! Welcome home, sir—Oh!"

He'd exclaimed when he saw Marian step out of the carriage. She'd cleaned herself up, and she did look lovely when she chose. Though Douglas felt a twinge of guilt at noticing. Neither his wife, Sara, nor Marian herself would've looked favorably on his opinion.

He was still ambivalent about their alliance. She was a woman of contradictions: masculine in her usual demeanor and dress, coldly intelligent, yet sometimes quick to lash out. He'd met no one, man or woman, so determined to survive. In truth, she frightened him. But if he wanted to right the wrongs done to him—and by extension, to his family—then he had no choice but to work with her.

"Fine morning, is it not?" Marian said to the speechless porter.

Fitzhammer followed her out of the coach, straightening his vest and coat and settling his bowler hat on his head. He jumped slightly when Marian hooked her arm around his. This was the most difficult moment; if Fitzhammer alerted the porter, then they might have to shoot their way out of there. Douglas looked up and down the street—hardly anyone was about.

Then Douglas looked back to Marian, and he noticed her shoes.

She was wearing square-toed, hobnail boots. Like a miner. Not the pointed shoes of a lady. Douglas felt himself go very still, watching the scene unfold.

Fitzhammer was sweating so profusely that a bead dripped off his sideburn.

The porter was studying the man, as if noticing that something was off. "How was your journey, sir?" the porter asked.

"Well enough," Fitzhammer said gruffly. Marian nudged him toward the entrance.

Fitzhammer opened his mouth, ready to say more, but then seemed to think better of it. They walked inside the hotel.

Douglas exhaled.

The porter watched them go. Or rather, watched Marian. Then he noticed Tim and Douglas, and the porter's eyes narrowed. His pointy nose sniffed, rodent-like.

"Where's Bart?"

Douglas kept his face blank. They'd dragged Bart to the top of a hill and left him tied to a juniper tree. His wound was bound tight enough that he wouldn't bleed to death. Most likely. Douglas bore the man no specific ill will. But he'd been forced to compromise quite a few ideals in the past months. Desperation had a way of turning morals into a luxury. His mother had insisted on church every Sunday, but she was gone now, wasn't she?

On the driver's bench, Douglas nudged Tim.

"Bart's not here," Tim said. "We're new. Should we bring in Mr. Fitzhammer's luggage?"

"Fine," the porter said. "You, what's your name?"

"Tim."

"Tim," said the porter, "take the coach to the stable. It's the next street to the east."

Douglas jumped down and fetched the travel case. "Take it around back?" he asked.

The porter nodded. Carrying the heavy case, he rounded the side of the building.

If Marian's plan went as she'd said, then the rest of Eden would never know anything had been amiss. Marian would secure the money that Fitzhammer rightfully owed them and persuade the rich man to stay quiet. *He's proud to a fault*, Marian had promised. *He won't want anyone to know we got the best of him.*

How she'd gleaned so many details about Fitzhammer, Douglas didn't rightly know. In an hour or two, they'd be riding out of Eden on two of Fitzhammer's horses, which Tim was going to lead back from the stable. They'd pick up their waiting supplies and exchange the horses in the hills, where they'd left them that morning. By nightfall, the three of them would be a long way east of here. And Douglas could wash his hands of this sinful matter.

He prayed that his mother wasn't looking down on him right now.

THERE WAS something unseemly about the Paradise, just beneath the surface. Marian noticed it from the moment she walked into the lobby downstairs. Angles that weren't quite true. Water stains along the edges of the wallpaper. She'd even heard a sound like distant crying, though she couldn't be sure if she'd imagined it.

When they reached his room on the third floor, Marian said, "The safe. Where is it?"

Fitzhammer blanched. "I haven't got one here."

"There's no use lying. Not to me."

After she fled from the asylum, Marian had stayed with a kindly old couple. They gave her food and helped refashion her drab wool garment so she wouldn't be recognized as an escaped prisoner. They must have known she'd come from the nearby asylum, but they didn't ask her about it. She ended up fleeing from them, too, leaving in the night because she couldn't bear their kindness. She took only a hook from the old man's meager tools to use as a weapon.

From there, she walked all the way to Fitzhammer's home near Telluride.

The place was deserted. She found a loose board and wiggled inside. Covers lay over the furniture pieces, protecting them from dust. She imagined she was a ghost haunting the place, wandering from room to room.

All she found was the safe in Fitzhammer's bedroom, its door hanging open. Insides bare.

She scraped together a set of fresh clothes—men's clothes—from abandoned linens and stole a few crystal goblets that had been left behind. Things she could sell. Next, Marian went into town. She learned from one of her old dance-hall friends that Fitzhammer had moved on to another place—Crystal, up in Gunnison County. So that's where Marian headed. She'd met Tim, with his meager intelligence yet romantic sensibility. And Douglas, whose mind she might've esteemed if she'd had time to know him better. His strong jaw, smooth bronzed skin, and lips always kept in a careful line. Perhaps a face she could've admired if she were a different woman and had lived another life.

Sometimes, she wished she'd never asked for more than Fitzhammer had deigned to give her. But even more, she hated him—hated the entire world—for the ease with which he cast her to the gutter.

Bart's gun was digging into her calf. Like the derringer, she'd shoved it barrel-first into her boot. Now she retrieved it and pointed the weapon at Fitzhammer's bloated face.

"Where is the safe?" she asked again.

Fitzhammer's finger tugged at the high, starched collar of his shirt. "At least let me have a drink first. You can afford me that much after this humiliation."

"You think you deserve better?"

He went toward the liquor cart, which was beside his desk. He reached for an amber-colored crystal decanter. Marian knocked it from his hand. The stopper flew across the rug, and brown liquid sloshed out.

Her heart was pumping like a steam engine. She advanced on him. Fitzhammer bumped into the liquor cart, knocking aside another decanter.

"I had the child, you know," Marian said.

He spat on the ground.

"Why can you not admit the injustice of what you've done?" She raised the gun, her hand trembling. This was not the plan she'd rehearsed so carefully with Tim and Douglas. She should be focused on the safe. Once she had the money, she could worry about the rest. But Fitzhammer's denials made her so ill she could think of naught else.

Then she noticed his hand had snuck behind him. He was grabbing for something inside the liquor cart.

"Get away from there," she said, reaching for him.

Fitzhammer sprang forward. He knocked Bart's gun from her grip. Then he raised his arm, a triumphant sneer on his face.

He held a pistol in his hand.

AT TWO, PENNY STARTED TELLING US ABOUT PEOPLE SHE met. There was a confused lady walking up and down the hallway, Penny said, a lady who was invisible to everyone else. There was a worried young man sitting at a table in the inn's dining room, even though the place was empty and closed. We thought she had a very active imagination.

But in the back of my mind, I wondered.

"Their eyes are sad," she told me once when she was four. "I try to talk to them, but they never look at me."

Sometimes there were small signs of corroboration when Penny had one of her "sightings." Slight temperature drops, unusual movements of shadows, knocking noises with no logical source.

I wanted to protect my daughter. But I also couldn't help wondering how far her talent might extend.

-from A DEVIL IN EDEN by Lawrence Wright

CHAPTER TWELVE
2019

Penny sat at a picnic table, picking at the Band-Aid on the tip of her finger. Just a few feet away, sheriff's deputies had cordoned off all of Eden's Main Street with yellow tape.

Deputy Ray Castillo stood at the barrier, fiddling with the radio on his belt. He glanced over at her like he'd felt her watching. A small smile lit up his face.

"You don't have to stay, Ms. Wright." He'd told her the same thing ten minutes ago. But she wasn't going anywhere until she knew what was going on.

"Any updates?" she asked softly, ignoring the discomfort in her throat.

"They're still working," the deputy said apologetically. "Need another granola bar?" He pulled a bar from one of the many pockets on his tan uniform. The wrapper crinkled.

The last one had tasted like glue mixed with sand. "No, thanks."

The sun was setting, the entire day nearly wasted. The construction crew had gone back to Ashton, for how long, nobody could say. Linden and Anvi were at the trailer, doing damage control to get ahead of the media. And it was all her fault.

After she found the skeleton, she'd crawled back inside the hidden room. Her fingers had been too unsteady to send a text. A member of Matthew's crew had heard her screaming.

They're probably just old bones, Linden had said. Linden hadn't wanted her to call the sheriff. But a crime could've been committed—one more recent than the 1890s. Penny had felt she had no choice.

Gingerly, she touched the sore places on her neck beneath her collar. But she couldn't think about how she got those. Not right now. Otherwise she might start crying in front of this sheriff's deputy, who couldn't be far out of high school.

"Your statement was plenty," Deputy Castillo said. "I can call you when anything changes. What's your number?"

She gave it to him and also added his to her contacts. "Do you think the skeleton is old? Or could it be recent?"

He opened his mouth, sneaking another look over his shoulder. In front of the Paradise Hotel, more deputies and people in plastic coveralls had gathered. Some kind of medical examiner, Penny assumed. They'd arrived in a big SUV with the acronym "CBI" written on the side.

"The forensic anthropologist has to make the determination. We'll know a lot after the investigation's done. How old the bones are, characteristics of the victim, cause of death."

Chills raced through her. Penny crossed her arms. "How long does it usually take? The investigation, I mean."

Deputy Castillo leaned his lanky form against the picnic table. "It depends. Well, usually we can wrap up the scene in a day or so. With CBI involved—that's Colorado Bureau of Investigation—their examination of the remains happens at their facility, and it takes longer. Should be only a few days, give or take."

Which could still screw their schedule.

She should've ignored the ghost when she saw it. So foolish, letting down her defenses. *But I wanted to prove Dad wrong*, she realized. Now she didn't know what to think.

The deputy leaned toward her. "My dad's Carlos Castillo, by the way."

Penny's confusion must have registered on her face, because he added, "My dad was up here in Eden back then? When you and your father were here? You know, the book."

"Oh. *Oh.* The book." The name Carlos did sound a little familiar, like many people and things around Ashton. Carlos must've been a member of the Ashton Paranormal Society, the group that Penny's father had founded. Some of the members joined the trip up to Eden when Penny was five. Mostly Penny remembered the woman, Helen. How kind she'd been.

"I lived with my mom growing up," Deputy Castillo said, "so I didn't move to Ashton till a few years ago. But my dad talks about it sometimes—kind of his claim to fame. This place scares him."

"Deputy—"

"Call me Ray." His ears were turning red.

"Ray. I don't remember your dad specifically." She wrapped her arms around her middle and shrugged. *Please don't cry*, she told herself. "My father thinks this festival is a mistake. Maybe your dad does, too."

Ray wrinkled his brow. "Our parents spent years saying how bad this place is, just so high schoolers wouldn't come up here and have fun. I'm all for public safety obviously, but people need to blow off steam, you know? The more you tell kids that a place is forbidden, the more they want to come."

"You don't believe the ghost stories?" Again, her fingers reached unconsciously for her collar.

"Nah. I've seen some stuff go down, and not once was the bad guy a ghost."

She'd never heard of anything like it, either. Not even in her father's book. The physicality of those moments. The sheer terror of being so out of control, pushed and choked by someone unseen...That wasn't supposed to happen in real life. She'd never encountered a ghost before who had such power.

Her dad's book was all exaggeration—she'd been so sure. But whatever had happened in that room inside the Paradise Hotel, it wasn't just the power of suggestion.

"Hey, I think it'll work out," Ray said. "Devil's Fest is the most interesting thing to happen around here in a while. A lot of us are excited to go—me included."

Penny tried to return his smile. From his worried look, she guessed she wasn't too convincing.

IT STARTED TO GET DARK, and another, less friendly, officer replaced Deputy Castillo. But Penny still hesitated to leave her post. Not until she had some good news to report back to Linden.

The door to the trailer slammed. Linden came out, heading over to the picnic area. Penny got up to meet her.

"Hey, the deputy said they could wrap up tomorrow," Penny said. "I'm hoping that—"

But Linden cut her off. "You've been here all day. This isn't where we need you." That vein was twitching in Linden's temple, the one that meant she was stressed. "I need you in Ashton with your uncle, pulling whatever strings you can. Not sitting here moping."

"I'm not moping. I'm trying to learn what I can about their investigation." She'd been working on her phone, too, wrestling with her lousy cell connection. "I know this delay is my fault, and I'm doing what I can to move us past it."

Linden stepped in closer, taking her voice to a harsh whisper. "This isn't just a delay. It's a freaking *dead body*. Tripp is moving up his arrival, and you *know* he's not happy about changing his plans. June's flipping out, too. She's been on the phone with SunBev since this morning, and they're wondering if they should just pull the plug."

There had to be a solution; Penny just couldn't see it yet.

"I'll...I'll go talk to June. Calm her down." She started toward the trailer, but Linden touched her shoulder.

"No. You're going back to Ashton, like I said. Matthew's waiting to drive you."

"*Matthew*? Why?"

"It was his idea. Go home. Talk to your uncle. And whatever your issues are with Matthew, figure them out. When I see you next, I want you focused completely on work."

Linden turned on her heel and went back to the trailer.

In the parking lot, Matthew was waiting behind the wheel of his truck. She hadn't noticed last night—it was the same 4x4 he'd had since high school. Memories tried to surface, but she wouldn't let them come.

He leaned his head out of the window. "I'm starting to feel like your chauffeur."

"I'll call someone else."

"Only kidding. I wanted to apologize for what I said yesterday—because I was out of line. I'm sorry. Linden told me you needed to go back to Ashton, so I'm here to help."

The gesture should've been touching, but it felt like a punch to the chest. She was already so raw after what happened inside the hotel.

"Are you all right, Penn?"

"Sure. Just great." She got in and slammed the passenger door.

The truck pulled onto the road. "How big of a problem is this?"

"I don't know. We might get shut down."

She'd only arrived yesterday. Now, her discovery had thrown the entire festival into chaos. If Penny didn't do something, Tripp was going to fire her.

But what if the festival *did* go forward? What else could those ghosts be capable of?

Matthew chewed his lower lip. He had one hand on the steering wheel, the other resting on his jean-clad thigh.

She glanced at him. *Whatever your issues are with him, figure them out*, Linden had said.

How the heck was she supposed to do that?

"When they said you were trapped in the hotel, I couldn't believe it," Matthew said. "I'm sorry I wasn't there."

"Not your job to look after me."

The truck shuddered as he drove over uneven road. "You want to talk about what happened?"

She told him what she'd said to the sheriff's people—that she'd followed a ghost into that room and gotten stuck. A couple of uniformed officers had interviewed her, and they'd smirked as she told them about the apparition. One even laughed. Ghost stories were commonplace around Ashton, yet not everyone took them seriously.

Matthew listened without judgment. He'd known for years that she saw ghosts, so it was nothing new to him. She had no idea if he believed it, deep down. But at least he didn't scoff.

Penny crossed her arms over her stomach, her body trembling again with chills.

"Hey. Tell me what you need. Dinner? A double martini?" Matthew reached out his hand, palm up.

"Why are you doing this?" Her voice was low and thick. Barely audible.

"Doing what? Giving you a ride?"

"Being so effing nice all of a sudden. Do you have any idea how much this hurts?"

He sighed, withdrawing his offered hand. "Penny..."

"No. Pull over, right now."

"Why?"

Linden wants me to sort this out? Fine. Penny couldn't do anything about that skeleton or the investigation, but she could clear the air with Matthew. So she could finally get over him and move on.

"We're talking about this. Us."

"You really think it's the best time?" But he didn't wait for her answer. He pulled the truck to the side of the road. They bumped and tilted on the angled shoulder. He swung wide so they'd be clear of any traffic and turned off the engine. He frowned at the steering wheel.

"I want to know what I did wrong," she said. "Why you cut me out of your life."

I want to know why you broke my heart.

CHAPTER THIRTEEN

She remembered the first time she saw Matthew. He was one of the boys that her older brother, Bryce, invited to play baseball in the meadow behind the inn. Matthew Larsen was the new kid, smaller and quieter than the others. Penny had been eleven, three years younger than Bryce, still tagging after him but old enough to know she wasn't really wanted. But the rejection made her defiant. She insisted on watching them play and shouting her opinions, laughing at their mistakes. All that summer, she wore the same old pair of pink pants with tears at the knees. Her favorite Pokemon t-shirt, growing tighter as her body developed.

Matthew's shaggy, dark-blond hair hung into his eyes. He kept his gaze down when he spoke, talking so quietly that the other boys had to lean in. He was the shortest of the group of fourteen-year-olds, the same height as eleven-year-old Penny. But he had an easygoing confidence about him, some impervious quality that almost always made the teasing slide off without hitting a mark.

Penny remembered his skinny legs beneath his jean shorts, his knobby knees. He stepped up to home plate holding the bat.

Swing and a miss. He struck out every time at bat that first game. Penny pulled the band from her hair and held it out, shouting that he needed to keep his bangs out of his eyes. Some of the other kids laughed; Bryce told her to shut up. But Matthew had smiled, tossing his head so his hair moved to the side, and she'd felt a flutter in her stomach. She didn't understand the feeling, that thrill, but she liked it.

She liked Matthew. He never called her "ghost girl" or pretended to see spirits to mock her. Bryce had been a decent older brother—he never let his friends tease her within his hearing. But with Bryce, there was one right way to do things, and it drove him nuts if you did anything else. Sometimes he let her play ball, but he always yelled that she was holding the bat wrong, even though she got base hits as often as any of them.

Matthew never yelled at anybody. Even if he was on the other team, he'd give her a fist bump as she rounded the bases.

When Penny was fourteen and Bryce was seventeen, she'd decided that her brother should teach her how to drive their dad's old truck. She had all her arguments ready to convince Bryce, the consummate rule follower, that she didn't need to wait for her learner's permit. "What if you're off at college, and Mom and Dad are both sick, and I have to drive Krista to the hospital?" He'd made a lot of faces, but Bryce loved bestowing his sage advice even more than he loved shutting her down, so he'd agreed.

Matthew rode along. He and Bryce were best friends by then, and Matthew had grown taller and broader. Cute enough that girls covered their mouths and whispered when he walked past. He sat in the middle of the back seat, quiet as Bryce lectured about ten-and-two-o'clock on the steering wheel. But every time she looked into the rearview mirror, Matthew was watching her, a reassuringly calm smile on his face. She felt comfortable around him. Like the bubble of confidence that surrounded him could extend out to encompass you, too, if you'd let it.

When they got to a deserted stretch of country road, she and Bryce switched seats. "Just take it nice and easy," Bryce said. "Don't kill us."

"You're making her nervous," Matthew had said.

"I'm not," Penny insisted, though she was starting to sweat.

The whole thing was a disaster, as Penny should've expected. She pushed the pedals too hard, making the car lurch forward and back. She jerked the wheel and ran the car off into the grass when she tried to turn. And all the while, Bryce kept thundering at her, "No, you're doing it wrong!"

Then a man dashed into the road.

She'd screamed and punched the brakes, which promptly locked up. They'd skidded to a stop, the smell of scorched rubber rising from the truck's tires. She started crying as she tried to explain; the man stumbling across the asphalt, blood running down the side of his face. She realized as she spoke that it hadn't been a living man, only the ghost of one. She'd nearly crashed because she was scared.

Usually, ghosts didn't appear as they did in the moment of death. They were projections, made of pure consciousness, of a particular moment in the ghost's life. She'd gathered that much. But this one, with the blood and the shock on his face, had caught her off guard.

Neither her brother nor Matthew had seen the ghost. Usually, Bryce was unfazed by her sightings. But at that moment, her story just infuriated her brother even more.

Bryce got out of the car. "I knew this was a terrible idea. There's no way you can drive."

She went back to shotgun, and they yelled at one another on the ride home. When they got back to the inn, Bryce slammed the driver's side door and stomped inside.

Penny didn't move to get out. Instead, she smacked her fist against the dashboard.

There came a creak from the seat behind her. She'd entirely forgotten Matthew was back there.

"Sorry I suck at driving," she said.

"Everybody does at first." He got out, then appeared at the front passenger door. "We can go around the block if you want to try again." He gestured for her to scoot over into the driver's seat.

"Are you serious? What if I see another ghost? I'll probably drive into the side of the inn."

"I don't think so. But if you see something, go easier on the brake."

He was so calm about it. So Penny shrugged and shimmied herself over to the driver's side. Matthew took her place at shotgun. He talked her through each step, nice and slow, in that deep, breathy voice of his.

"Have you tried using just your toes to press the accelerator?"

"I was going to do that next," she said. "Bryce didn't give me a chance."

They made it out of the parking lot, then down the road at a snail's pace. An SUV honked at her, then zoomed around. She kept glancing over at Matthew. He smelled like the autumn floral arrangement that her mom had placed in the dining room, pine cones and evergreen branches and sticks of cinnamon. He just sat in his seat, humming whatever was on the radio, even when she made the brakes squeal. Occasionally, he gave her suggestions.

By the end of the drive, she was half in love with him. Afterward, he just gave her the usual fist bump and went to find Bryce.

Over the next few years, she fell in and out of love with Matthew countless times. But everything with Penny was like that—a new hobby would take over her entire world, only to burn out after a few weeks. Her mother and Bryce would scold her for being fickle and unfocused, but she was just trying to find that perfect pursuit that would never let her down, never get old. She was trying to figure out who she was supposed to be.

The decision to go to UCLA for college was like falling in

love, in a way—just a possibility at first, and then suddenly overtaking her entire being. Los Angeles was one among several campus visits. She'd never been to California, and she figured she'd get a beach trip out of it. And then she walked UCLA's straight, wide paths with those thousands of anonymous students. She lay in the green grass beneath a perfect blue sky, her lungs so full of the rich sea-level air—she could almost smell the ocean even there, miles inland—and she just knew it in her heart. This was where she belonged.

That day, she didn't see a single ghost.

Matthew was one of the first people she told. He'd rounded the bend into his twenties by then, a surrogate big brother who listened, who asked just the right questions. Probably her closest friend. He never seemed to notice her recurring infatuations with him.

She texted him a selfie on Ocean Drive in Santa Monica, a bougainvillea plant in full pink bloom behind her, and wrote, *Who knew I was really a California girl?* He texted back a picture of a surfer. Part of her had been wondering if he'd be sad. But she'd given up hoping that someday Matthew would long for her the way she longed for him.

At the end of the summer after her high school graduation, she got ready to leave. Her high school friends wanted to take her out for one last wild night.

After a day or two of debate—*do I dare?*—she picked Eden.

She hadn't been back there since childhood. Since the infamous Devil's Night that formed the basis of her father's book. Her parents had actively forbidden her, and for many years, she'd listened. But the Old West town represented everything she was leaving behind—her family history, the small town environment where everybody knew her quirks.

It was August, and that year's Devil's Night had already passed. Which was fine. She wasn't ready for *that* level of rebellion. Penny just wanted to watch the sun sink behind the canyon walls and maybe hear Eden's ghosts whispering and know she was almost free. Her friends would be right alongside her, and she wouldn't stay the night. Matthew would be there, safe and steady as always.

When she saw Matthew that night, she knew something about him had changed.

Her brother Bryce was taking summer classes at the University of Colorado at Boulder. He was about to start his senior year as a business major. But Matthew hadn't gone away to school. Instead, he was taking night courses at a local community college and working construction during the day. All that summer—after her high school graduation—there'd been a weird tension between him and Penny that she couldn't put her finger on. There was more weight to his silences. More meaning to his looks. But she dismissed it. If he really felt something for her, then she was sure she'd know.

But she remembered how he looked at her that night. That last night. They were in the parking lot of the inn, her friends sneaking sips of cheap whiskey from a flask. She had invited Matthew to her going-away celebration, though he didn't really know her other friends well. But Matthew never seemed awkward with new people. At least, not until that night.

Matthew had shown up right at eleven. He stood apart from the group, his hands in his pockets and his lips pressed together.

Penny sidled over to him. "What is it?" she asked. "Something on your mind, Larsen?" She tapped his forehead. He caught her hand.

"You sure this is a good idea, Penn? You going to Eden? Your brother would flay me if he knew I came along."

"Then make sure Bryce doesn't hear about what happens tonight. It's our secret." She was flirting with him a little. She felt wild, like a bird ready to open its wings and fly. Two shots of whiskey, and her nerves were singing.

"Just promise me it's what you want," he said, voice lowered. "I need to know they didn't pressure you into this."

She leaned in closer, her mouth an inch from his, and whispered, "I want this." She just wanted to see his reaction. And react, he did. His nostrils flared. Matthew's eyes flashed in the dark, like two sparks alighting from a campfire.

"Let's load up," somebody said. They were all supposed to ride up to Eden together, cramming into her friend Jimmy's Dodge Quad Cab. Penny grabbed Matthew's arm and they walked to the truck, where the others were already climbing in. There were eight of them and only six seats, so a few would have to double up.

Matthew leaned in to say, "Sit with me?"

"Okay," she said, her throat constricting.

Matthew got in first and went to the back. She tried squeezing in beside him, but he pulled her onto his knees. The engine started. The cab was dark, and Luke Bryan played on the radio. The others were talking and giggling, pushing at each other, not paying attention to her or Matthew.

She sat against him, sliding fully into his lap. His chest rose and fell against her back. His hands held her by the hips, gripping tighter when the truck bumped or turned.

She couldn't breathe. She thought maybe her heart had stopped.

"Is this okay?" Matthew murmured.

She turned her body to the side, so she could see him. His eyes were bright, his mouth slightly open. "Yes," she whispered back. They went over a bump, making her rock against him.

He put his mouth against her ear. "Tell me again what you want?" he asked, so low that she felt the words more than hearing them.

She smiled and touched her finger to his chest. His Adam's apple moved down and up as he swallowed.

When they reached Eden, her friends piled out, running and laughing. They made a ring of rocks in the middle of Main Street, gathered kindling, and lit a fire. Penny's girlfriends danced with her and took slugs of whiskey and sang. Matthew stayed close, his hand touching hers in passing, his fingers grazing her body in the dark.

She looked for him constantly, and his fire-lit eyes kept saying the same things. The night felt dreamlike. A balloon that had broken away from the earth and was drifting and spinning away. It was all wonder and beauty, no ghosts anywhere. As if ghosts belonged to a different world, the world of her past, and she'd left it all behind.

Jimmy had brought his guitar, and someone pulled out a pipe and a tiny baggie of weed. It was hot and bright by the fire, but even a few steps away you could vanish into the dark. She reached out to where she knew Matthew was standing. He felt her hand and pulled her close. Crickets were chirping. The air had gone cold, her breath clouding in front of her face. But he was warm as the fire.

"Come with me," she whispered.

Hand in hand, they walked away from Penny's friends and the fire.

She knew there was something cruel about this—what they were doing to one another. She was leaving in the morning for college. Why did they have to wait until now? But she had wanted him so much and for so long that she didn't care. She needed to know how he felt. How he tasted.

She didn't know quite where they were on Main Street. The abandoned buildings were there, towering in the darkness. An animal howled somewhere, the sound echoing across the canyon.

They wandered for a bit, fingers entwined. Then she recognized the Paradise Hotel. Penny pulled Matthew towards its entrance.

"We shouldn't get too close," Matthew said. "The buildings aren't safe."

"But I thought getting close was the whole idea," she teased.

Penny thought the door would probably be padlocked, like the other doors she'd seen on Main Street. But the lock must've been broken, because the door creaked open when she pushed.

She stepped into the darkened entry. "Penny..." Matthew began. But he followed.

The space was freezing. The ceiling stretched far over their heads. But then Matthew pulled her against him, and she stopped seeing the room at all.

Heat radiated from him. He ran his hands along her sides. She squeezed his shoulders and his biceps, the lean muscles that she'd always wanted to touch. But they still didn't kiss. That would really change everything. She hesitated, though she wanted to feel his mouth on hers. He didn't make the move, either. Maybe he was waiting for her to cross that final distance. So he wouldn't be to blame.

She pressed her body fully against his, and he made a low sound in his throat. She kissed him, somehow knowing just where his lips would be in the dark. Matthew reacted instantly, his arms taut around her waist, lifting her off her toes. His tongue slid against hers. She sucked his lower lip, and he tasted like salt and campfire.

After a few incredible moments, she stopped to take a breath.

"Penny," he said, "I..."

Then an icy shock of fear ran through her. There was someone else here in the dark.

A figure with long, tangled hair stood a few feet behind Matthew.

Penny shouldn't have been able to see her. But the woman was glowing faintly silver. Black hair hung into her face. But her eyes stared out, at once lifeless and terrified.

He's coming, a voice whispered.

Penny screamed.

The night ended abruptly then—Penny running out of the hotel, her friends trying to calm her and packing up to go. Matthew had gone back to the fringes. The spell between them had broken.

She took shotgun on the drive back home. Cold air blew through the open window against her face.

"Promise you're okay?" Matthew whispered from the seat behind.

"I'm good. But you were right. Eden was a bad idea."

At the inn, Matthew gave her a hug goodbye. But his touch was perfectly chaste. That spark of heat had vanished from his eyes. As if it were yet another phantom.

CHAPTER FOURTEEN

"I don't know how to answer that question," Matthew said.

She'd asked him, *Why did you cut me out of your life?* Seemed clear enough to her.

They were sitting in his truck by the side of the road. The darkness reminded her of that drive they'd taken to Eden, back when she was eighteen and he was twenty-one and she was foolish enough to risk everything for a kiss.

"Was it the ghost stuff? Is that what scared you away?"

After Matthew, she told any guy she was serious about. *This might seem strange, but.* Some of them got out quick, but a few stuck around. It took her years to learn how to keep the ghosts at a distance. To make them disappear when she wished.

"You know that never bothered me," he said.

"Then did you just lose interest in my friendship when I was at school? Out of sight, out of mind?"

He ran a hand through his hair. "Come on, Penny."

She'd emailed him that first semester. He wrote one sentence replies. It hadn't mattered so much; she'd been busy with her classes, her friends, a new life in a new city. She wasn't naïve enough to think that Matthew was hers just because they'd kissed. But it would've been nice to hear from him.

"When I came to Ashton for Christmas," she said, "you avoided me."

His eyes flashed. "You were with that...*guy*. You brought him home with you."

"You mean my friend, who happened to be a guy? I brought him here because he was getting over a nasty breakup. With his *boyfriend*. And his family wasn't supportive."

Matthew blinked at her. "Oh."

She huffed. "Are you telling me you didn't talk to me for almost six years because I brought home a male friend?"

"It wasn't really that. There were a lot of reasons, and you know as well as I do."

But she *didn't* know. She didn't get it at all. "Were you embarrassed that I kissed you? You thought—what, that I'd expect you to marry me because our tongues touched?"

The muscle in his jaw tensed. "I *did* want more. But we were in completely different places. And not just our locations. It wouldn't have worked."

"So you admit that you felt something for me."

"Jesus, Penn. Of course. I was in love with you."

She squeezed her eyes shut. Those words ripped her open down the middle. He was holding her bloodied heart in his hands.

"You don't get to say that. Not now." She brusquely wiped the tears away.

"It's true."

She tried to breathe through the pain. "Back then, I loved you, too." There. It felt good to say it. Freeing. "Long before you even noticed me," she added.

His mouth cracked into a smile. "It's not a competition. And anyway, I doubt it."

Outside, tree branches rustled in the wind.

"I agree that it wouldn't have worked out between us," she

said. Penny's college friends with long-distance boyfriends ended up with horror stories to tell. She and Matthew probably wouldn't have lasted if they'd tried a relationship.

"But you threw out our friendship, too," she said.

"I didn't think of it that way," he murmured. "I admit that I made mistakes, and if I hurt you—"

"You did."

"Then I'm sorry."

"You don't have to keep apologizing." Although she'd been wanting an apology. And now, she had it. Right now, she needed to steer them to a different subject. One that didn't feel like a double bypass surgery.

"Why are you living at the inn? What about your parents' house?" She'd have heard if he sold it.

"That's complicated."

She shook her head, wanting an explanation, but he continued. "It's nothing about you. It's just hard to talk about. I don't even talk to Bryce about it. Maybe...another time."

"Okay. So we're friends again?" She wanted that, even though being near him again hurt more than she'd ever imagined. Okay, if she was being honest, she still wanted *him*, though she wasn't dumb enough to do anything about it.

"I'm willing to try," she added. "If you are."

"Yeah. I'm willing."

Their eyes locked. They both quickly looked away. Nope, not ready for that yet.

"Let's head to the inn." He twisted the key in the ignition and put the car in gear. "Linden asked me to text when I got you safely there, and I don't want her to send out a search party."

CHAPTER FIFTEEN

WHEN THEY GOT BACK, ALL WAS QUIET. MATTHEW SAID HELLO to the night receptionist, and he and Penny went straight to the kitchen. It was like high school, staying up late, raiding the inn's refrigerator with her. Only Bryce was missing. Back then, Matthew would've given anything to get rid of Bryce for a few minutes to be alone with Penny. Now, he had her to himself, yet his chance to do something about it had passed long ago. In a week or two, she'd be heading back to Los Angeles.

Penny found some buttermilk biscuits from that morning's breakfast. Matthew warmed up a pot of sausage gravy.

"Do you think your uncle can get Eden opened up again?" he asked. The microwave hummed, the gravy spinning around.

"I've been texting him." Penny checked her phone, then tucked it back into her pocket. "We'll see. Can we not talk about Devil's Fest right now?"

She still seemed upset. Matthew didn't know if it was because of him, or because of what happened earlier in the day—finding the bones. But he chose not to press her.

They ate standing at a butcher block counter. Most of the lights were off, highlighting the curves of Penny's features. Her lips were fuller than when she'd been a teenager. Her eyes were more knowing. More beautiful.

So it was out in the open now. The truth he'd been hiding for all those years: he had loved her. He'd adored Penny since they were kids. She was funny and outspoken and completely unpredictable. But by the time she was fourteen and he was seventeen, his feelings took on a new level of intensity. He thought about her constantly—his best friend's little sister. When they had video game tournaments in his living room. When they played friendly games of touch football and he "accidentally" tackled her to the ground. Staying over with Bryce when Penny was asleep in the next room. He vacillated between swearing he'd never cross the line, and dreaming of the day she'd be old enough that he could make a move.

And then, suddenly, she'd been eighteen and about to leave Ashton. That night in Eden, he'd given in. He turned off his brain and did what felt good. And when Penny responded, when she kept escalating, he wasn't about to say no. He wanted whatever she would give him. He was about to confess to her how he felt.

But then she screamed, and she was that little girl again, afraid of the ghosts in the dark. He'd only been twenty-one, but he'd felt like a dirty old man.

And yes, he'd been jealous when she brought some other guy home at Christmas. But Matthew's mom was having another round of chemo then, and she needed constant care. Work and online classes overwhelmed him. Penny lived in Los Angeles; she had moved on and showed no signs of ever wanting a life in Ashton.

He couldn't be her friend anymore because it hurt too goddam much.

He was glad they'd finally had an honest conversation on the drive down. But Matthew had kept something else from her: he was pretty sure he felt the way he did back then.

He just didn't know if Penny was still that girl.

In the inn's kitchen, Penny took a bite of gravy-soaked biscuit, closed her eyes and moaned. "This is crazy good. I don't know how Dora does it. If she and Samantha ever break up, I'm going to propose and take her back to LA with me."

Dora was nearly eighty years old, and she'd been with Samantha for decades.

"Don't you already have good food in a big, fancy city like Los Angeles?"

She smirked. "It's still not Dora's food."

Then why don't you move back to Ashton? Matthew thought. He didn't ask it out loud.

But then, he just couldn't help himself. He asked, "Are you seeing anyone in LA?"

Why did that matter? He was just torturing himself.

She broke off a piece of biscuit and popped it in her mouth. "Not at the moment. I'm focused on work."

She didn't ask the natural follow up. *Are you seeing anyone?* Matthew was not. He'd had girlfriends over the years, of course, but nobody momentous. Nobody who'd been able to erase Penny from his mind.

"There's something I didn't tell the officers today." She was breaking up the remains of her biscuit. "Something pushed me against the wall in that room. While I was trapped."

"What?" He dropped his fork. "Someone was there?"

"Not some*one*."

"You're saying a *ghost* pushed you against a wall?"

Penny nodded. "Do you believe me?"

"Of course I do."

Even when they were kids, he'd never doubted her. But after his mom died, he'd had an odd experience himself. He still didn't know what that was, that presence he'd felt in his childhood home. It had been so upsetting, so personal, that he'd never told another soul. Maybe he would've told Penny. If anyone could help him make sense of the experience, it would be her. But she hadn't been around.

"But I thought ghosts couldn't touch you," he continued. "They barely even know that we're there." That was what she'd told him. Penny's father believed something different, but Matthew figured that Penny would know what she was talking about.

"That's what I thought." Her voice cracked. Her hand covered her mouth, and she turned away. "It felt like someone was actually trying to hurt me. It—he, maybe he, I don't know—choked me."

He did what? Matthew wanted to demand. He tried to stay calm.

"Hey." He touched her shoulder, and Penny spun around. She pressed her face to his chest. She was crying. He hugged her against him. Her hands were still in between them, crossed protectively over her middle, but it felt good to hold her. Too good.

He looked down at her. Penny was wearing a button-down shirt with a collar. Using a finger, he gently bent the fabric away from her neck.

"Penn, there are bruises here."

"Really?"

Purple splotches, like fingers had been squeezing. Adrenaline rushed through him as his anger rose. "What the hell." It probably wasn't possible to kick a ghost's ass, but he was ready to try.

Penny wiped her face and stepped away from him. She went over to the shiny, stainless-steel hood above the griddle. The bruises showed in the reflection.

"It hurts, but I didn't know it was visible. That's...surprising."

That wasn't the word he'd have chosen. Horrifying, maybe?

He watched her pick up her plate and start washing it off in the sink. "You don't need to wash up," he said. "I'll do it."

"I need to do something normal right now." Her voice shook. She moved slowly and methodically. He was standing behind her, holding his plate. She took it from him. His hand brushed her arm.

He wanted to do something—anything—to make this better. But he knew Penny well enough to understand that she didn't work like that. She'd always wanted to fix things for herself.

"I'm not even sure how many ghosts there were," she said. "I definitely saw a woman. I'm pretty sure she's who I saw that night six years ago, when you and I...When we were up at Eden."

"I remember." Did he ever remember.

"My father would probably say she was Bloody Marian. But I think it was someone else entirely who pushed me and...hurt me. A man. But how many malevolent ghosts does that town have?" She shut off the faucet, dried her hands on a towel, and turned around.

"Are you having second thoughts about Devil's Fest?" he asked.

She shot a glare at him.

"I'm not trying to talk you out of it." Yet. "I'm just trying to understand. I've never actually read your dad's book all the way through," he admitted.

"I never thought I could forget a word. But it's been—I don't know, over ten years since I read it?" She grimaced. "I don't even think I have a copy anymore. Everything I told the Sterling and SunBev people was based on memory."

"I've got a copy." It wasn't really *his* copy of the book—someone had left it in the room, probably a previous guest. Matthew had been living here at the inn since after his mom passed. Debbie—Penny's mom—had been incredibly understanding. She refused to take his money, but he did all the handyman work for the inn, so he considered it a somewhat fair trade.

He nodded his head toward the door. "It's in my room." His pulse ticked up. "Do you want me to go get it? Or..."

She shrugged, her face betraying nothing. "Either way."

Matthew looked around the deserted kitchen, unsure. Should they stay here, on relatively neutral ground?

Had he really just asked Penny Wright up to his hotel room?

"We can both go," she said. "It doesn't have to be weird."

"Exactly," he replied on an exhale. Okay. Yes. He'd definitely invited her up. This girl was going to get him into so much trouble.

CHAPTER SIXTEEN

In the elevator, Penny waited for him to punch the floor button. She had no idea which room was his. Matthew pushed the button for the third floor, the top, and they rode in silence.

She couldn't believe Matthew had asked her up to his room. But he was acting like it meant nothing. Like he'd believed her when she said it wasn't weird.

But if he could be an adult about this, then so could she.

The hallway was quiet, the lights dimmed for the nighttime hours. Matthew took out his key and unlocked the door to 318 at the end of the hall. They walked inside. The room was decorated in the same style as the rest of the inn—floral-printed wallpaper, dark wood furniture, a thick rug. A mirror with a carved frame sat above the chest of drawers. Matthew had placed his things neatly on the desk. His clothes hung in the closet with the door slightly open.

She wondered again why he was living here, in this cramped, transitory kind of life, instead of in a proper home. In the house he had inherited from his mother. But he'd said he wasn't ready to discuss it yet. She was going to be respectful, like he was just another platonic friend. Clearly, that was what he wanted.

"Have a seat," he said, pointing at the couch. His bed was across the room, and he went over to pick up a few items of clothing he must've left there that morning.

She sat, slipped off her shoes, and then tucked her legs beneath her. Matthew went to the nightstand, where books were stacked on the lower shelves. He sorted through them, then pulled one out.

"Here it is." He crossed the room and handed it to her. "*A Devil in Eden.*"

It was a paperback, bearing a cover with a nighttime photo of Eden's Main Street lit up with a ghostly light. She'd never known who took that photo, whether it was her father himself or a friend. She knew that he used to spend a good amount of time up there, trying to study the ghosts. That was back in the 1980s and 90s when physic research was trendy, probably in the wake of Stephen King bestsellers like *Carrie* and *Firestarter*. She'd read about some experiments popular back then, things like trying to affect a random number generator with one's mind, viewing hidden images on cards from across a room. Her dad Lawrence was into all of that stuff, plus ghost hunting. He'd wanted to become a parapsychologist and formed the Ashton Paranormal Society so they could do his little experiments.

Two of Lawrence's best friends from college, Helen and Jason Boyd, had traveled to Ashton just to take part in the trip to Eden. It had all been so exciting to Penny. But by the end, Helen and Jason had gone away, and Lawrence vowed never to return.

But he was more than happy to write his book, ensuring that none of them could ever forget.

Matthew was leaning against the dresser, legs crossed at the ankles. He watched her patiently. She felt a flare of anger at that nonchalance—if he hadn't been so damned patient when they were growing up, waiting around for their relationship to magically begin, maybe things would be different now.

Maybe I'd never have left here at all, she thought.

But that would mean losing the life she'd worked so hard to

create—on her own, with nobody's help. She wouldn't be her own person.

"You going to read it?" Matthew asked. "Or just stare at it."

"I'm starting." She flipped through the pages, passing by black-and-white images of Eden in its heyday and Marian's Wanted posters. *Also known as 'The Schoolmarm,'* they said. *Armed and dangerous.* She was drawn as a striking woman, if not conventionally beautiful. Dark hair pulled back, dress buttoned up to her neck with a bit of ruffle at the collar. Only her crooked smile hinted at the wicked intelligence inside.

Penny skipped past the parts about the Devil's Night Massacre. She saw her own name on the page, and she began to read.

According to Penny, ghosts can't see or hear us because we're alive. "They don't know they're dead," Penny said that day. "Sometimes they're thinking about the people they love, or things they forgot to do. Sometimes it's a silly thing, like trying to find their glasses. Sometimes they're confused and lost. Other ghosts are upset. Even crying." She looked down at her little notebook, her lips shaking. I almost stood up, but her big brother Bryce rubbed her back, and she went on.

"Or angry," she added hesitantly. Beside me, Debbie squeezed my hand.

Am I doing the right thing? I thought. I'd ask myself that time and again over the next days. But no matter what I did or didn't do, I knew my little girl would continue to see these things. If I could have, I'd have taken away that burden from her, regardless of my desire for answers. I swear that's true. But it's never been my choice.

Penny looked up at us. "But I'm not scared. Because ghosts don't mean us any harm. If there's some way that I could help them, then I want to know how to do it. I don't want ghosts to be sad. Please, I want to know what I can do. I want to go to Eden."

Penny had read this aloud. Now, she set the book down, marveling at how innocent she'd once been. And, despite herself, she felt some sympathy for her father's predicament. If his claims could be believed, anyway.

"Do you think that's possible?" Matthew asked. "You could help ghosts..." He waved his hand, searching for the words. "Move on?"

Once, she had wished that were true. But it had been so long since she even imagined using her ability that way.

"My dad wanted me to understand my ability, but I never have. For years, I've just tried to co-exist."

"But you could do something *good* with it. Help people."

"As opposed to what I'm doing now?"

"I didn't say that."

But you were thinking it. She tossed the book onto the couch. "Maybe I should go."

"Don't do that," he said softly. "Don't run away."

Neither of them moved. It took a few moments for the bands around her chest to ease.

"Tell me what it's like," he said. "You never really described it before."

She crossed her legs. "I hear them speaking, but in my head it sounds like my voice. Like I'm the one thinking it. But it's foreign, too. Not me. I'd figure I was schizophrenic if I hadn't learned things that would otherwise be impossible to know." She'd found objects that a dead person worried about losing. Learned about events that she later confirmed in news articles from decades ago.

He said nothing. She tried again.

"It's like..." She shifted on the couch. "Imagine that your brain can tune into a certain radio station that nobody else can receive. In some ways, it might be an advantage. Maybe that radio station is broadcasting something that you need to hear. Tornado warnings. Or something you want, like baseball scores that nobody else knows. But other times, it's not saying anything interesting at all. Maybe it's even creepy and disturbing. And you can't stop hearing it."

"I'd want to make the radio quiet."

"Exactly. That's what I spent years doing. I got pretty good at it."

His brows knit as he nodded. "So, what happened today? In the hotel?"

"I turned up the radio. I listened. But I shouldn't have." Penny gingerly touched the sore places on her neck. *The ghosts in Eden can be persuasive*, her dad had said.

"Then, theoretically, you could turn the volume back down again."

"But what if the ghosts in Eden really could hurt other people? Not just me?" What if that explained the body she'd found?

Matthew came over and sat on the couch, careful to leave a couple of feet between them. "What scares me the most is that *you're* going to get hurt again." He touched her hair, just briefly, tucking it behind her ear. She breathed out slowly. Then his hand withdrew.

"Penn, if the festival might not be safe, don't you think you should cancel?"

She'd been thinking the same thing without wanting to admit it.

"Devil's Fest is barely hanging on as it is, and if I don't make it happen, I'm screwed." She'd lose everything that she'd spent her adult life working toward—a life of her own. She stood up, pacing across the tiny room.

"In the past, whenever things didn't work out, you found something new."

She stopped and glared down at him. "You mean I'm good at

quitting, then starting from scratch? You think I like living that way? I can't do it again. If I mess this up..."

There wouldn't be a next time at Sterling. Tripp would toss her out like yesterday's Instagram story. Anvi would take over her place. Or they'd hire somebody newer and better. And that meant Penny couldn't afford her rent anymore, she couldn't make the payments on her loans. She'd be a failure once again, just like everybody here at home expected all along.

But if somebody got hurt, she'd never forgive herself. In the end, this was just a PR spectacle, put on for social media. It didn't matter when compared to someone's safety. Or their life. Was that really a possibility? Or was she completely overreacting?

She sank onto the couch again, holding her head in her hands. "I have no idea what to do."

Matthew scooted toward her. He put his arm around her shoulders, drawing her closer. She put her head against his chest and let him hold her.

Once upon a time, this had been all she wanted—Matthew's arms around her and an implicit promise that he wouldn't let go, even if just for one night.

If only that were still enough.

EVERY SUMMER WHILE I WAS GROWING UP IN THE 1970S, my family visited Eden for the anniversary of Devil's Night. The ghost town had an eerie grandeur to it, and it was even better preserved then than it is today....

My mother's stories alone didn't frighten me, but my older siblings were sure to turn up the drama as high as it would go. Anything to get a rise out of us younger ones. They said that Bloody Marian had been possessed by the Devil and murdered a dozen men. If you found a mirror in one of the old abandoned buildings and said her name three times, one of her victims would appear behind you and frighten you to death. Standard stuff to scare little kids. On the other hand, my mother said that the ghosts who haunted Eden were just lost, sad souls.

I would've been in elementary school the first time that I heard something strange, unexplainable, in Eden myself. That's probably when my obsession began.

-from A DEVIL IN EDEN by Lawrence Wright

DEVIL'S NIGHT - 1894

Douglas carried Fitzhammer's baggage around the back of the hotel. At the delivery door, he stopped. Another porter—this one short, with a thin blond mustache—was smoking a hand-rolled cigarette, lounging against the railing of the wooden stairs.

"I got some luggage here for Mr. Fitzhammer, sir," Douglas said.

"I never seen you before." He'd parted his pale hair down the middle and pomaded it on each side.

"I'm new. We done just arrived, sir. Mr. Fitzhammer will be wanting his belongings."

"You heard the rumors about this place?" the porter asked.

"Rumors? No."

The blond man grinned. "Try not to soil yourself if you hear the ghosts."

Ghosts? What was the man talking about? Douglas walked past, carrying the heavy case.

In the kitchen, a sole cook listlessly stirred a single pot. She barely glanced at him, much less tried to stop him. Fitzhammer's suite was on the third floor—according to Marian's information—so he searched around until he found the servants' stairs. He left Fitzhammer's trunk in an empty room. He checked the contents quickly—just clothing, books, toilet items—before heading up.

His boots thumped against the wood as he went up one level, then up again. As he climbed, he heard no voices or commotion. The whole place had an air of loneliness, much like the boardinghouse he'd been living in when the mine closed.

The mine that Fitzhammer had owned.

On the third floor, Douglas came out onto a landing. Dusty shoe prints criss-crossed the rug. Nobody had bothered to beat them clean for days. Once again he listened, trying to make sure he wouldn't meet Fitzhammer or Marian on their way up the main staircase. But all was quiet. They must have already gone up.

Faint voices murmured from the lobby below. Douglas kept his head down. A year ago, he'd never have expected to get mixed up in a business like this.

But a year ago, he'd had a job. And his mother had still been alive.

DOUGLAS HAD a small farm back home on the eastern plains of Colorado. The land was tough, and his mother had been equally ornery. Her only vice had been a pipe every night after dinner. She'd close her eyes and puff. *Simple pleasures, Deedee*, she used to say to him. She'd always called him that, even after he was grown and asked her to stop. Sara called him Deedee sometimes, too, though he was sure that Sara only did it so he'd kiss her to hush her up.

Simple pleasures, indeed. They'd lost Douglas's brother—small pox—and Sara hadn't gotten the child she wanted yet. Yet they'd had a happy life.

But after a couple of poor harvests, there was nothing to sell and not much to eat. So, like his parents did before him, Douglas set out westward, leaving his wife and mother to wait for his return. He found a job at a mine in Crystal as a mucker. It paid poorly and was back-breaking work. His best hope was to move up to better jobs once he'd proven himself.

He met Tim there in the mine. Tim had suffered from consumption since childhood, which had stunted his growth and made him look even younger than his seventeen years. At the mine, Tim ran messages. Douglas stopped him from falling once, and after that Tim latched onto him like a puppy dog. It was all right. They pooled their earnings and shared a room at the boardinghouse. That meant Douglas could send home even more to his family. Tim had a rare talent with an iron, and on days off, Tim gave Douglas sharpshooting lessons.

Douglas spent his evenings studying the letters that Sara sent. She knew how to write, and she had very patiently taught him his alphabet and simple words. But he still struggled to decipher longer ones. Tim also wished to read and write, and he started attending a kind of "school" with a teacher he called "Miss Marian."

You should meet her, Tim said. *She's not like anybody you've met.*

Douglas had seen her around town, her odd mannerisms and intense eyes. He had no interest in getting mixed up with a crazy woman.

But then came the silver crash.

The mine they were working suddenly closed down. The owner took off with a month of the miners' pay. Then Tim came in, saying that his "Miss Marian" wanted to offer them a meal. Douglas was low enough that a free dinner couldn't be denied.

Her shack was barely bigger than the table where they sat. She'd tacked canvas to the inside walls for warmth. Her proper voice didn't seem to fit her strangely dressed body, at least at first. Her eyes were so wide and moved so often, Douglas figured she was not right in the head. Yet her words made a certain amount of sense.

"Consider the man who owns the mine where you were lately

employed, Mr. Perl. An individual by the name of Ernest Fitzhammer, if you do not know. He refused to pay your final wages, claiming bankruptcy. But has he suffered much? I guarantee not. A man like Fitzhammer thinks he can buy our very souls for a few coins, use us as he will, then toss us aside."

"She's right, that isn't justice." Tim dabbed his mouth with a dirty handkerchief as he coughed.

Douglas gently set his spoon on the table. "But what are we to do about it? Ain't nothing that the likes of us can do to change the workings of the world."

Tim leaned toward him. "Don't say 'ain't,'" he whispered.

Marian did not speak to his lapse in grammar, which Douglas later learned was atypical of her.

Tim rapped his fist against the table. "Miss Marian has a book about a man in the olden days of England named Robin Hood, and he had all sorts of adventures with his gang of Merry Men."

"Robin Hood." Douglas was not much of a reader, but he'd heard of that particular folk hero, as most children had. Nothing but fairy tales. "You're talkin' about becoming thieves and outlaws. Stealing from the rich. Tim, we best say our thanks and go. Because this woman is liable to get us strung up."

Tim grabbed his wrist. "Please, Douglas. Just listen. Doesn't hurt to listen."

Like hell it don't, Douglas thought. But he stayed. Marian said she knew where this Fitzhammer had gone now—to a town called Eden.

To Douglas, the plan seemed too good to be true. He thanked Marian for their meager dinner and dragged a disappointed Tim out of there.

Two more weeks went by with no pay, no prospects. Finally, the next letter from Sara arrived with the news of his mother. She'd succumbed because her failure of a son couldn't provide. Would Sara be next?

He went to Marian's shack in the woods that very same day. "Tell me what I'd have to do."

FITZHAMMER AIMED the gun at Marian. "Get out of my hotel."

"My men are still out there." She saw Bart's revolver in the corner of her vision. It had slid to the far side of the room. Hopelessly out of reach. "If I perish, they'll come for you."

She took a single step toward him, slowly. His eyes narrowed.

In the mirror behind Fitzhammer, there was a flicker of movement by the door. The knob was turning. Fitzhammer hadn't noticed. She didn't dare to shift the focus of her gaze.

In the mirror, the door moved inward almost imperceptibly. An eye peered through. Then a thin, gray circle of metal.

The shot was deafening.

Blood sprayed the mirror and the wall. Fitzhammer's gun went flying from his mangled hand. And Douglas stepped fully into the room, holding his still-smoking weapon.

Any moment and someone would be here to investigate the gunshot. Marian ran over and kneeled on Fitzhammer's chest. She jammed her hand over his mouth, cutting off his screams. She had to stop herself from covering his nose, too, blocking off his air until he turned purple.

We need him alive, she reminded herself. *For now.*

"We'd best hurry," Marian said breathlessly. "Keep him quiet."

She found a sock drawer and stuffed one of the soft bundles into Fitzhammer's mouth.

Douglas's usual stoic expression had given way to panic. "I had to shoot him. I thought he'd kill you."

Her plan had just gone dreadfully awry. Yet she was exhilarated. "Help me tie him up," she said.

Marian held him as Douglas bound his feet with a suspender. They turned him on his side and cinched his wrists behind his back with a necktie.

A wool scarf lay across the back of a chair. She grabbed it and wrapped the fabric around Fitzhammer's bleeding hand. He grunted into the socks.

"Search the room," she said. "Find the safe."

Douglas's eyes were glazed, and for a few seconds he didn't seem to register her words. Then he swallowed and nodded. "Yes. The safe." He went into the bedroom.

Knocking came a moment later. "Mr. Fitzhammer, sir?"

Douglas stood frozen in the bedroom doorway.

"Tell him all's well," Marian instructed her captive in a whisper. She pressed the edge of her knife to Fitzhammer's neck. Then she pulled the sock entirely free from his mouth.

Fitzhammer took a breath, then shouted, "Help, they'll kill me! Call a posse!"

Marian cursed. She backhanded Fitzhammer across the face. Douglas was still standing in place, paralyzed.

The porter outside the door yelped. They heard his footsteps retreating. She had to do something. Marian ran across the room and grabbed Bart's revolver from the floor. She crossed the suite in two bounds, threw open the door. The porter was almost to the stairs. He was blond, youthful.

"Send help!" he cried to someone downstairs.

Her shot went wide. The blond porter ducked, covering his head. His foot slipped on the stairs, and he went down, tumbling end over end. She ran down the corridor, looking over the balcony railing.

He'd stopped rolling. One foot stuck out between the balusters. He moaned.

Another porter—this one dark-haired and ferret-faced, the one who'd met them outside—was staring up at her from the lobby, his face twisted in shock. There was no way she could catch him if he ran, and no way she could get an accurate shot from this angle and distance.

But it didn't matter. Tim emerged from the shadows of the

hotel's entrance. The barrel of his gun touched the porter on the neck.

"Hands up," Tim said hoarsely. He closed his mouth on a new barrage of coughs.

The porter's arms rose. But then he crouched and darted suddenly to the side. He was running for the front desk. They'd probably have weapons stored there. Marian took aim, even though she knew she'd never hit him.

Before she even pulled the trigger, a tremendous shot rang out against the high ceiling. Then another. The porter lay sprawled on the floor in a mess of red. The top of his head was gone.

Tim's body was shaking from the recoil, but his gun remained solid in his hand.

THEY ROUNDED everyone up into the dining room: the cook, a maid, the remaining blond-haired porter—his leg broken so badly he could barely speak for the pain—and Ernest Fitzhammer. According to the cook and the maid, the rest of the hotel was empty. They hadn't seen a proper guest in weeks. That was just as well. Douglas didn't want to bring any more innocent people into this situation.

I'm a lousy criminal, Douglas thought. *But damned if I'm going to die in this town.* He'd do what he had to do. Still, he wanted to cry, thinking of that hideous mess in the lobby. Tim had pulled the man's lifeless body behind the front desk and rolled up the soiled carpet.

They had drawn the curtains across the front windows and locked the front and back entrances. But Douglas had heard people outside. There weren't many left in this town, and they had no sheriff. But some brave soul would come to investigate before long, and locked doors wouldn't be enough to keep them back.

"I'll pay you," Fitzhammer said again. He'd been prattling on. "It's all her fault. She's a madwoman out for revenge. She—"

Marian came into the room. She'd changed out of her dress. Douglas didn't recognize the clothes; he figured she'd swiped them from Fitzhammer's trunk.

"Revenge?" Douglas asked her. "What's he talking about?"

"Never mind." Marian strode over to Fitzhammer, cocked back her arm, and struck his face with the butt of her gun. The maid screamed.

"Douglas, you and I need to speak privately."

Marian went into the lobby. Douglas glanced back at the scene in the dining room. The cook and maid were crying. The injured porter moaned. Douglas looked away from them, sicker in his heart than he'd ever been. *I must see this through*, he thought.

They went to the other side of the lobby. "This isn't what we planned," Douglas said weakly.

She made no response to this. Her gaze was never quite warm, but right now, her eyes were cold and lifeless as lumps of ore. Her face had turned a yellowish pale.

She said, "There's no safe in Fitzhammer's rooms."

"*What?* You said it would be there!"

"That just means it's somewhere else. We have to find it."

"This town's going to get restless fast. Nobody's battered down the door yet, but at some point they will."

Marian turned away. She swayed, her hand going up to her forehead.

Douglas caught her by the shoulder, trying to steady her. "Are you well?" he asked.

"I am fine as I'll ever be."

Marian went up to the third floor to search, while Douglas began on the second floor. He made quick work of the guest rooms.

In the lobby, he tried to ignore the terrible stench of bodily fluids. There was a small room off to one side of the vestibule, an office of some sort for the porters. He went in. They'd stored their street clothes and sacks of lunch here. Douglas stuck a piece of bread in his mouth, but he had no appetite for the rest. He stuck the food in his pocket instead. He'd give it to the captives later.

There was no sign of a safe.

Douglas made his way into a long corridor. He went door by door—small rooms for storage and supplies, no guest rooms on this floor. Douglas had no idea how rich people lived, how they kept their valuables.

Then he heard something—a muffled cry.

Goose pimples rose on his skin. He remembered what the blond porter had said. *Have you heard the rumors about this place?*

In the dining room, Tim was leaning against a wall, scratching the bottom of his chin with his gun barrel. The man was so thick-skulled sometimes. "Careful where you aim that," Douglas reminded him.

The gun returned to its resting position, aimed at the hostages on the floor. Fitzhammer eyed Douglas with hatred, while the injured porter appeared to have passed out.

Douglas kneeled by the maid. He pulled the hunk of bread from his pocket and held it out. He gave another to the cook. "Who else is in the hotel, 'sides you four here? I heard crying."

The maid's eyes widened. She only shook her head.

The cook, a stout woman of about sixty, spoke up. "Them's the..." She bit her lip, sneaking a look at Fitzhammer. "Ghosts," she finished.

"*Ghosts?*" Tim asked.

"Haunted," the maid said in a thick Germanic accent.

Douglas looked between the maid and the cook. He couldn't understand much of what the maid said, so the cook would have to do.

"Come with me."

Fitzhammer started struggling with his bonds again. "Take

me, too. There's a reward in it for you. Be a man—don't let that Devil-woman damn you."

Douglas ushered the cook through the kitchen and into the hallway.

"Let me loose," she said. "Please. I don't know anything."

"I'll bet you do. Mr. Fitzhammer doesn't deserve your loyalty. He lies and he steals. Don't he?"

She stared back, her wide-eyes leaking tears. But he sensed agreement in her silence.

"We didn't want to hurt anybody," Douglas continued, "and I promise if you help me you'll go free."

She stilled, though the tears continued to fall. "The safe?" she whispered. "That's what you want?"

He nodded. "That's right. You know where it is?"

"It's in a room around the corner. This way."

Douglas followed her down the hall. This was the place he'd heard the crying earlier. The quiet had returned.

They came to a room that Douglas had already searched. "The safe is not in there," he said. Was this a trick? A trap?

"But it is. It's hidden. I'll show you."

Douglas followed her in, keeping one hand on his weapon. The room was tiny, the shelves filled with ledger books. Like that big book on the check-in counter, Douglas thought. Lists of names, money. Accounting, he recalled. Was that the word?

The cook went to a bookcase and removed several large volumes. Behind, set into the wall, was a dial.

The safe.

Douglas touched the dial. It glided back and forth. "You know how to open it?"

"Oh, no. He wouldn't trust me with that. No, sir."

"How did you know it was here?"

"The maid—she's afraid of this room. She says the ghosts are louder here. So I clean it for her. Mr. Fitzhammer..." She shook her head. "Some people in town say this building's cursed because of him."

Her forehead shone with sweat. "You'll let me go now, yes?"

"I'm sorry." He was a man of his word. But he couldn't let her go yet. The risk was too great. "I will, but later."

"You swore!"

She screamed and struggled as he took her back to the dining room.

CHAPTER SEVENTEEN
2019

PENNY WOKE ON MATTHEW'S COUCH. THERE WAS A PILLOW under her head, a blanket stretched over her. She heard snoring—he was asleep on the bed.

She sat up, rubbing her face. The sun was up, and that meant that she might meet somebody like Krista or their mother in the hall. And what would they think, seeing her leave Matthew's room at this time of the morning?

Not a thing had happened, of course. Neither of them were so stupid anymore. Penny folded up the blanket, grabbed her shoes. She snuck a peek at her phone. There was a message from Linden.

Get up to Eden ASAP. And bring extra coffee. We're back in action!

TRIPP ARRIVED IN THE AFTERNOON. The Sterling team gathered at the picnic tables near Main Street; Penny and Linden sitting on one side, Anvi on the other, Tripp standing at the head. June and the SunBev folks were in Ashton, probably anxiously awaiting more updates. Matthew's construction crew was back to work—for now. But that might not last after Penny said what she needed to say. Beneath the table, she tapped her heels into the dirt.

Tripp took a long look around Main Street, then at each member of his team. Building up the anticipation. The police and medical examiners had removed the bones and released the site, but there were still so many questions. And by now, Tripp must've heard about *A Devil in Eden*.

"Penny," Tripp said, turning to her. "I got some interesting news yesterday. Involving you?"

Here it comes, she thought.

Tripp wasn't an awful boss. He never screamed at them or cursed. Instead, he conveyed his displeasure through small jabs that one could dismiss as unintentional. Like the way he'd forgotten Penny's name one afternoon, though their office had just ten people. Or leaving her off the cc list for an important email. But when he was pleased, Tripp did have a certain charisma. His movie star smile felt like a special gift you'd earned. There were front row tickets to Hollywood Bowl concerts, invites to the art gallery that Tripp's sister owned. His Brazilian mother was a sculptor who worked in wood and clay, his Canadian father an art history professor. He'd filled Sterling PR's airy office with abstract pieces in muted colors by Mrs. Sterling and her equally impressive friends.

Penny loved being surrounded by so much beauty and creativity. But if Sterling PR was the picture-perfect image of a workplace, then she was the droopy pothos plant in the corner that somebody forgot to water.

So perhaps this was inevitable. She hadn't thought it would end this way, just giving in. But she had to be honest with them. *Completely* honest.

"Tell us about this book that your father wrote," Tripp said. He leaned against the edge of the table, sleeves rolled up over his toned forearms.

"I should've mentioned it at the SunBev pitch. Before, really. But I thought that—"

"You're right," Tripp cut her off. "That way, we could've worked this into our narrative earlier. But at least we have a chance to polish your delivery, because it needs polishing. The interviewer will want something exciting."

"Wait—interview? What interview?"

A breeze pushed Tripp's dark hair over his forehead. He slicked it back. "Well, this is just the first one. Right Anvi? She's been lining them up all morning."

They all looked at Anvi, who was clearly fighting back a smug grin.

"Why didn't we discuss this first?" Linden said. "Penny doesn't want to do interviews."

"You know what incredible publicity this will be," Tripp countered. "We couldn't have planned it better. A ghost leading Penny to its remains? I mean, however you want to spin it, fine," he added, turning toward Penny. "As long as we agree and then clear it with SunBev first, to make sure they're on board. But I spoke to their marketing VP Richardson first thing today, and he loves it. Anvi—see if we can include June in some sit-downs as well. I think SunBev would appreciate that."

Penny was still struggling to form a response. They wanted her to do interviews? With the media?

If Tripp was happy, then this couldn't be all bad. But Tripp wasn't her only concern.

"Wait, there's more I need to say. Right before I found the bones, something happened to me. I—" This was so hard to say. "I think a ghost grabbed me. Threw me against a wall. I realize how that sounds, believe me. But if I was wrong before, if guests at Devil's Fest could actually get hurt—"

Tripp made a face. "We'll have to tone that down. Don't want the insurance company getting antsy. We've got our safety and emergency protocols squared away, but hey, I'm thinking a roller-coaster style warning. 'Not recommended for sensitive individuals and pregnant women, ride at your own risk.' That's brilliant. Draws people in more than it keeps them away. Besides, I'm pretty sure that's what the fine print on the Dark Energy can says." He chuckled.

"I'm being serious. I have bruises." She pulled down her collar. "What if people are injured?"

"By *ghosts*? Let's not take this too far Penny, okay?" He'd barely even glanced at her neck. Tripp took out his phone, jotting something down. "Anvi, send around the list of blogs, podcasts and media outlets who want an interview. Linden, I want you to check in with SunBev and keep them informed as this develops. And Penny—draft up a script for you and June that we can circulate internally for comments."

He turned and headed for the trailer.

Penny couldn't hold back her anger. "Anvi, what the hell? You've been talking to Tripp behind my back? And *the media*?"

"I did what you should've done in the first place. News about those bones was going to leak any second, and they'd dig up *A Devil in Eden* on their own. If we're the ones telling this story, then it works for us. We're already getting requests to open up more festival tickets."

"But it's my story, Anvi. Mine." And that wasn't even true—it was her father's story. She was going to be "ghost girl" all over again.

"Listen," Linden cut in, "let's all do what Tripp asked us to do. Get to work." She pulled Penny away. When they'd gotten some distance from the picnic area, Linden said, "You really have bruises?"

Penny pulled down her collar again.

Linden sucked her teeth. "I'm so sorry."

"I'll be okay. But thank you."

They hugged, Linden resting her chin on Penny's bowed head. "I believe you about what happened, 'kay? One hundred percent. But most people don't experience ghosts the way you do."

"I know." That was exactly how Penny viewed things when this began. "But if there's any chance…"

"Do you have proof that someone, *anyone*, aside from you has ever been seriously hurt by a ghost?"

"Well...no." Penny had no idea how those bones had ended up outside the Paradise Hotel. Her father's book was only conjecture and exaggeration. A few ghosts making noise, opening doors. A little push. Scaring people—that was all.

"Think about it." Linden held her by the shoulders. "Tripp is right. This could be huge. Devil's Fest is a fun party on its own, but now? With bones and warnings about 'violent' ghosts? We could be talking national, mainstream news articles with a huge reach. Millions more eyes on our event—and on Dark Energy."

Penny's chest was unwinding with relief. She wasn't excited about these interviews. But compared to losing her job, she'd gotten off easy.

She could spin the interview conversation to Dark Energy instead of herself. And as for the ghosts, she'd do what Matthew suggested—turn down the radio in her head. She'd even take her father's advice and avoid being in Eden alone.

"But I want my family kept out of this," Penny added. "No interviews with my dad. Make sure Anvi respects their privacy."

"I'll talk to her." Linden squeezed her hand. "Penny, I know this is stressful. But Devil's Fest is going to be better than we ever imagined. And it's all because of you."

Looking over at Main Street, Penny hoped that Linden was right. Now, she had more on the line than just her job. It was her family. Her reputation. Everything depended upon Devil's Fest being a success.

CHAPTER EIGHTEEN

THE PARADISE HOTEL WAS MUCH THE SAME AS WHEN PENNY stepped inside a week ago. The wallpaper was still peeling, and shadows still played among the rafters. But now the lobby was full of people—nearly fifty of the VIPs that they'd invited from SunBev and Ashton.

"Penny!" Tripp Sterling walked over to her, his arms outstretched. Like they hadn't seen each other just that morning. He kissed her on either cheek, his beard prickling her skin.

Linden was next to him, dressed in the outfit she'd ordered for opening night: leather pants and a flowing top, black studded cowboy boots, and a belt slung low over her hips. But instead of a gun, her belt held a radio for communicating with their security team and personnel. Penny carried one too, the volume turned to a murmur.

"Loved the NPR interview." Tripp grabbed a champagne flute from a passing tray and clinked it against Penny's glass. In a corner, a musician played jazz on an upright piano. Not quite a match in terms of historical time period, but nice.

"Thanks," Penny said. She probably should've said something more ingratiating, but she simply didn't have the energy. There had been dozens of phone and video interviews in the last three days. She'd lost count. But Tripp's strategy had worked. Penny could hardly believe the response they'd had—instead of dooming Devil's Fest, the discovery of the skeleton had turned it into a viral sensation.

There had been no official word yet on the identity of the skeletal remains, nor even their age. But the Associated Press had picked up the story. Thousands of additional people had tried to get tickets to the event, and entry passes were reselling for five hundred dollars on Stub Hub.

Thankfully, mentions of *A Devil in Eden* were usually relegated to the bottom half of the written stories. There was plenty of buzz and speculation about Penny online—according to Anvi, who kept Penny more informed than she ever wished—but so far it was manageable, aside from some randomly creepy text messages and emails. She hoped the interest in her would fade now that the festival had begun.

It was really Matthew that Tripp should thank, not her. Matthew had worked long overtime hours with his crew to get the hotel's lobby, bar and dining area finished. They'd put new glass into the missing lobby windows, added hidden supports to the upper floors to steady them, and countless other little fixes that Penny had noticed.

She'd worried that Matthew would be disappointed with her for going ahead with the festival. But he hadn't said a word. She only wished Matthew were here. When she invited him to tonight's opening event, he'd politely declined. His job was over. She wasn't even sure when she'd see him again.

So much for their brief attempt at friendship.

Penny's Uncle Harry was here somewhere, schmoozing with the best of them. The guests milled about between the first-floor rooms, sampling hors d'oeuvres from platters passed by waitstaff and sipping whiskey cocktails at the newly operational bar. Elsewhere at the festival, SunBev's sodas would be the only beverages on offer.

Music thumped outside, clashing with the piano. The main

gates to the festival wouldn't open until nine, but the DJ was already playing music for the hundreds of people waiting to get in.

Several people from SunBev's sales team came over, shaking hands with Tripp and congratulating him. Tripp took the SunBev contingent over to the bar, while Linden stayed behind with Penny.

"You should be celebrating right now, but you look like you're at a funeral," Linden said. "A really stylish funeral, but still."

Penny tugged at the high collar of her long-sleeved, black lace dress. "I'm just worn out."

Although she'd been avoiding the darker corners of the Paradise Hotel—always keeping Linden or even Anvi with her—she still had those bruises on her neck, and they ached worse at night. She'd kept up her defenses, and she hadn't seen any more ghosts. But at this point, Penny just wanted the whole festival to be done with.

Maybe she could sneak away to the trailer after dinner was over. They'd parked it outside the festival's chain-link perimeter fence, not too far from the generator trucks. Linden wouldn't be there; she'd booked a room next to Tripp's at the Ashton Valley Inn for the nights of the festival.

"After tonight, we'll be a third of the way done." Linden stole Penny's wineglass and took a hefty swig of white burgundy. "I was looking online at a spa near Santa Fe. Tripp's sister recommended it. I'm going to book a solid week for when this is finished. You should join me."

Like Penny had the funds for a resort week. "I'll settle for a quiet room at my parents' place." And Dora's cooking. And Matthew...She didn't know what to do about Matthew. Maybe a room at the inn wasn't such a good idea after all.

"June's still staying at the inn, isn't she?" Linden asked.

"Last I checked," Penny said.

June and the other SunBev folks were spread among several

Ashton hotels; it wasn't ideal, but Penny's mom couldn't fit them all at the inn.

"I haven't seen her tonight," Linden said. "This is supposed to be her big moment, just as much as ours. Where is she?"

"That's a good question."

As Penny looked around the hotel lobby, she didn't see the petite blond anywhere.

CHAPTER NINETEEN

June Litvak adjusted her hair in the mirror. A loud bass line pounded, shaking the walls of the small room. She was in a climate-controlled bathroom trailer, which Penny's team had provided for the VIPs to use.

Over in the Paradise Hotel, the opening-night party was already underway.

She took out her concealer and dabbed another layer beneath her eyes. Her fingers shook. *Keep it together*, she thought. If only she'd slept last night. But she hadn't slept well in months.

She'd never expected to end up in an office job. Until she turned sixteen, her entire life had been devoted to figure skating. The sport had been her passion; her reason for getting out of bed at four every morning to train. Even now, she could replay her routines in her head, still hear the sound of her blades cutting across the ice. She'd dreamed of making it to senior nationals, and maybe even the Olympics. But that had just been a fantasy. She'd kept on lying to herself long after she should've realized that she just wasn't good enough.

Ever since, she'd struggled to trust her own judgment.

At SunBev, June was by far the youngest employee. The company was family owned, self-described as out of touch with youthful trends and new methods of publicity. They'd hired June to perfect their image before they went public. June was also the roommate of Kelsey Richardson, the daughter of SunBev's vice president of marketing, Jeff Richardson. She knew the connection had helped her get the job.

June was careful to keep her true self hidden around her SunBev co-workers. She wasn't just Kelsey's roommate. They'd been together since sophomore year at Northwestern. On one of their early dates, they went ice skating. June had done a few simple spins in the center, and afterward, Kelsey kept staring at her, smiling. They'd had their first kiss on the walk back to June's dorm room.

Kelsey hadn't even wanted June to apply for the SunBev job, but to June the opportunity was too good. Get to know her girlfriend's father, make him see how hardworking she could be? She was laying the groundwork for the day when Kelsey—finally—was ready to come out to her family.

Kelsey's father seemed nice. At first. When June felt the hand on her butt one afternoon, she didn't understand it. Then the hand squeezed and he leaned his crotch against her, and his meaning became clear enough. She'd left the office and called in sick the next day. Even thought about quitting. But then she'd have to tell Kelsey what happened.

The pitch from Sterling PR felt like a godsend. An excuse to keep her busy with phone meetings and planning sessions. She was happy to take a backseat and let Sterling's team make the decisions.

June had nearly fainted when she heard the festival might not go forward at all. But then, Linden and Penny had worked their magic yet again. June had seen the crowds at the camping grounds, the lines of buses and vans and cars vying to get in. They kept coming, even though tickets were sold out, just to bask in the aura of Devil's Fest. It was amazing, even better than June could've imagined.

So why didn't she feel happy?

Maybe she just missed her girlfriend. She'd hoped that Kelsey could make the trip, but Kelsey was afraid to call attention to their relationship. Not that those concerns were anything new. June was out to her family, but Kelsey didn't know when she'd be ready.

June snapped shut her compact of concealer. She took another deep breath, tugging up her black leather bustier. She'd worn a tasteful black linen shawl over it, just to keep the creepy oldies like Richardson from staring. Tonight, after the bosses took the shuttle back to town, she would chug a can of Dark Energy and dance the night away. Then she'd do it again tomorrow night. And the next. Kelsey would be sorry she missed it.

Someone knocked on the bathroom door.

June stepped out, nodding politely at a well-dressed woman in deep purple. She swore when she checked the time on her phone. She was really late for the party—her bosses might be looking for her.

June took a black feathered hat out of her bag and perched it on her head, joining the stream of people on Main Street. The gates had just opened. Most had dressed in elaborate black get-ups, adorned with silver and lace. There were prizes if you wore a costume. Staff handed out swag near the entrance—devil's horns, witch's hats, masquerade masks, all emblazoned with the Dark Energy logo.

June reached the Paradise Hotel, fighting her way across the stream of people. A security guard stopped her, and she flashed a special VIP badge hanging from a lanyard around her neck.

She went to the hotel's entrance, where an attendant opened the door for her. Something made her hesitate before stepping fully into the lobby. The party had obviously been going for a while. A large group, including Penny and Linden, hovered around the bar. Others sat in clusters on the sofas. She saw Jeff Richardson, who was sipping on a glass of red wine, his lips stained purple.

The room swam, and she braced herself against a wall. Not again. When she didn't sleep well, she got light-headed. Which happened constantly these days. Drinking would make it even worse. She just needed to sit somewhere quiet for a little while until the spell passed.

There was a door straight ahead of her across the hotel's entryway. The upper levels of the hotel were off-limits, but surely the first floor was safe. She quickly crossed to the door, glancing into the lobby as she passed. Nobody had noticed her.

The door had shiny new brass hinges. But it wasn't locked. She pushed inside, then swung the door behind her so it once again looked closed.

She'd been having the worst dreams since she arrived here—dreams of blood, hands wrapped around her throat. Dreams of standing on the edge of a tall, dark building, with an endless drop beneath her.

And then the sensation of falling just before she awoke, drenched in sweat.

The dreams had nothing to do with skating; she'd fallen so many times on the ice it was impossible to count. Yet her mind kept going to a particular regional competition, when she'd fallen out of a Lutz during her free skate. She finished the program, but afterward, the ankle had swollen double inside her boot. She'd been icing it, her makeup destroyed by tears, when some twenty-something guy—she still had no idea who he was—knelt beside her. He'd smiled, like he wanted to make her feel better.

Then he said, *Not everyone's tough enough for this.*

More than ten years later, those words still caused her chest to seize.

She was in a small room. June turned on the light on her phone. There wasn't much inside; just a leftover tape measurer and a box of nails. The walls and floor were unvarnished wood, bare and utilitarian. Perhaps this had been an office at one time.

The party was just on the other side of the wall. She could practically hear what they were saying. There was no place to sit, but at least she could close her eyes here and not worry anyone would notice.

She put one hand against the wall. Her lightheadedness was passing. She breathed deeply several times. The room smelled of metal and mildew, an odd mixture. She could still hear the festival music from outside through the thin outer wall.

"Okay," she said to herself, "you're fine now. Get out there."

Not everyone's tough enough for this. She thought of slamming down on the ice, failing.

Richardson's smirk when she spun around to confront him.

Nausea swept through her. She stumbled and bent over, catching her hands against her knees. *Am I sick?* she wondered. Breakfast hadn't sounded good, and she'd skipped lunch too. Her head was aching. Throbbing. She just wanted to go home—not to the inn, but all the way home to Phoenix. To Kelsey. She'd done what she was supposed to do, helped launch Dark Energy. Why wouldn't they let her go?

Why were they keeping her here?

She shook her head. Her thoughts weren't making sense. Definitely getting sick. Not what Richardson would want to hear, but that was too damned bad. She hadn't threatened to go to HR, and she probably never would. But he didn't know that.

Help me, she heard. *I need help. Please.*

"What?" June asked.

She opened her eyes. Nothing had changed in the room. But she heard the voice again. A woman's voice.

He's coming.

June shivered. She hugged her arms over her stomach.

He'll hurt me again. Please.

Using the light from her phone, she crept forward. She'd been wrong; there was something else here. A door in the opposite wall, though it was smaller than the first one. That was where the voice was coming from.

There's no way out.

Someone was crying.

"I'm coming," June whispered.

She thought of the skeleton that Penny had found around here somewhere. Though all the interviewers had asked about the discovery, Penny had remained steadfastly vague about how she found the bones. She'd only said that she saw a ghost, and then stumbled upon the grave by chance.

June, too, had seen the ghost the first day she arrived. The face in the window. Nothing could've prepared her for the experience. June had realized something about herself that day: living in the everyday real world was hard enough without bringing the supernatural into it.

But right now, June wasn't hearing a ghost. That voice belonged to someone alive. She was sure.

Incredibly, she wasn't scared. She wanted to help. *Needed* to. The door wobbled on its hinges; these hadn't been replaced. The door stuck before opening fully. She peered into a dark corridor, lifting her phone. She was in a back part of the hotel. Like the office, it wasn't decorated at all. Just rough, warped wood. In some places, bricks shown through where planks had fallen. She walked forward.

I'm so tired, the voice said.

"Hold on," June said. She had to get there. She had to help. He was going to hurt her again.

"Where are you?"

There was no answer in words. Just whimpering.

June reached the end of the corridor and found a narrow set of stairs. The kind made for servants, not grand like the staircase in the lobby. The construction crew had nailed a piece of wood across the stairway, blocking it off. But the noise came from up above. She crawled beneath the barrier, then put a foot on the first step. It settled under her weight, but held. The next step was solid too. She kept going, up and up. On the second floor, another doorway blocked her path. But this door was crooked, falling off its hinges.

She squeezed past and came out onto a thin carpet. Her feet

squished into it, like she was walking over forest moss. She was looking out over the lobby. A railing separated the landing from the open space, and the partygoers milled around below.

The sounds of the party were much louder. The piano, laughter, glass tinkling. But she could still hear a woman's voice.

I can't hold on.

CHAPTER TWENTY

THE CROWD SURGED FORWARD, AND KRISTA WRIGHT WENT along with it. The gates had finally opened for the first night of Devil's Fest. Krista had been looking forward to this ever since her older sister Penny announced the project on Instagram, which was months ago now. She'd been hurt that Penny hadn't called her first, but that was Penny—always doing her own thing in a splashy way.

Scott Mackey's shoulder bumped against hers. He was wearing that stupid orange hat that he loved so much. Krista hadn't worn a costume either, but she'd switched out her running shorts for jeans and unbraided her hair so it fell around her face in waves.

"Couldn't Penny have gotten us VIP tix?" Scott asked.

"Couldn't *Anvi* have gotten you VIP tix instead of general admission?" Krista had to shout over the music. The DJ was playing a dubstep remix of *Mad World*. She adjusted the headband someone had handed her at the gate, which sported a red pair of devil's horns.

Despite Krista's nagging, Penny hadn't come through with tickets at all. Penny just kept making excuses, probably because of their dad. Thankfully, Scott snagged some passes to the opener. He worked for Alpenglow Guides, and he'd been driving Penny's team back and forth to Eden. He'd even driven Penny up to Eden on the day that she found that skeleton. Scott had been telling everybody in town who would listen.

Scott had also been lusting after Anvi since the moment she arrived in Ashton. Not that Krista cared. She'd made out with Scott at a party freshman year of high school, and she'd felt like he was trying to give her a spit facial.

"Anvi said she didn't have any extras for me, but I'm meeting up with her tonight." His eyebrows wiggled.

"So you're ditching me?" They'd come with two other friends, but they'd already gotten separated in the crowd. Krista's head turned back and forth, trying to find them.

"Not till later. I'm all yours till then." Scott slung an arm around her shoulder. "I got a spot set up earlier for Anvi—candles, some chairs. A blanket in case things get, you know…"

"Just in case filthy, semi-public places turn her on? Next time, a bus station bathroom?" Krista looked where he was pointing. The old bank. "Penny said that nobody's supposed to go inside any of the buildings. Our tickets will get revoked."

"Anvi and I don't count. I'm practically on the staff."

Finally, they passed through the bottleneck, and people spread out over Main Street. Barriers kept the crowds from going too close to the buildings, but people were taking pictures and craning their necks like this place was the haunted mansion at Disneyland.

Krista had been to Eden several times before, just on jaunts with friends, and she had to admit that the transformation was impressive. Penny and her team had made Eden into a giant, open-air rave. Lights shaped like tiny skulls were strung along both sides of Main Street. The ghost town's windows were all lit up with orangey light, like the buildings were aflame. But as you passed each one, you could see the wrecked insides. The stage was at the end of the street, where multicolored lights strobed over the canyon walls. The whole place felt wicked and alive.

Krista felt pretty good herself. She and Scott had smoked before they came. But the security line had taken way too long, and her buzz was threatening to wear off. At least she was away from the inn. Her parents had been making her answer the phone to screen requests for interviews, which her father forbade any Wright living under his roof from accepting. Downtown Ashton was a snarl from all the traffic, and this week every restaurant had a two-hour wait to get in.

She didn't love the "Dark Energy" banners everywhere. She'd tasted the energy drink two days ago when Penny brought samples to the inn. It was too fizzy and tasted like overripe watermelon. The worst part was the color—a deep purple. Krista's mom had warned that nobody better drink the stuff near her favorite white couch.

Since she was little, Krista had grown up in Penny's shadow. Everybody knew who Penny was; the town asked about her still. *How's Penny doing in Los Angeles?* Nobody asked what was new with Krista. Secretly, Krista was glad that her sister lived so far away. It lowered the bar on getting approval from their parents. Unlike her older sister, Krista didn't have a need to constantly prove herself. She was happy to work at the inn and have ample time off for her friends, for trail running in the summer, and back-country skiing in winter. She took her recreation very seriously.

Krista occasionally wondered if she should be jealous of Penny's life. It seemed exciting, living near Hollywood with all those celebrities, the famous music venues and clubs and the crazy things that supposedly happened on Sunset Boulevard. Not that Penny enjoyed any of that. It was all *work-work-work, LA is so expensive, I was in traffic for three hours yesterday*. Her job at Sterling PR seemed like a nonstop grind, nowhere near as glamorous as you'd think a "public relations boutique"—as it said on the website—would be. Yet Penny did seem lighter there, as if she'd shed some invisible weight that she always wore back home in Colorado.

Finally, Krista spotted the two other people she'd come with: one of her best girlfriends from high school, and Ray Castillo, who worked for the sheriff's office. Deputy Ray looked cuter in his civilian clothes: jeans and a Red Rocks Amphitheater t-shirt. He was relatively new in town, still an unknown quantity. Krista had never noticed his tattoo before, a hummingbird on his inner bicep. She found it surprisingly sexy. He was single, too, and Krista's friend had sworn to have no interest. Krista wasn't looking for a boyfriend. But she was always chasing that heady mix of adrenaline and endorphins; didn't matter if she found it on a ski slope or in a hot guy's bedroom.

"What should we do?" Ray asked. "Eat?"

"I brought gorp," Scott said, scooping a handful into his mouth.

Krista's stomach was twisting with hunger, and not for Scott's sweaty trail mix. But Penny had tucked the concessions behind Main Street where they'd be out of sight. It looked better in pictures, sure, but it wasn't super practical. And who knew where the port-a-potty ghetto would be.

Krista decided to figure that stuff out later. "Let's see how close we can get to the stage." Right now, all she wanted to do was press herself against Deputy Ray and dance.

About an hour later, the screaming started. People started running toward the exits. But Scott had already disappeared.

CHAPTER TWENTY-ONE

Nobody seemed to know where June had gone. Penny checked with the security guards via radio, but they didn't know. Neither did Anvi. Penny and Linden discretely asked around as they mingled at the party, not wanting any of their guests to worry—especially not the SunBev execs. But apparently, no one had seen June since earlier that day in Ashton.

"Did she seem happy with us the last time you spoke to her?" Linden whispered to Penny. They were standing by the velvet rope that blocked off the lobby stairs.

"I think so." June had been nervous and distracted ever since that first day she arrived. But though Linden and Penny had both tried, she hadn't wanted to talk about it. And then they'd gotten so busy with their interviews.

"I hate this kind of crap," Linden said. "Some clients will act perfectly content to your face and then badmouth you to Tripp after the campaign is over. *'She wasn't listening to my needs.'* I like June, but if she pulls something like that..."

"I doubt that's it." Penny put a hand on her friend's arm. "Go have fun. I'll try to get in touch with June." If she couldn't get cell reception, she could always hike back to the trailer and get on the satellite.

"And just in case," Penny added, "you could turn up the charm with the SunBev execs. Make sure they have a good time?"

"You *are* learning." Linden smiled and gave her a wink, then headed for the dining room.

Penny slid her phone out of a hidden pocket in her thigh-high boot. She sent off a text to June and waited to see if it would go through.

Then she glanced up. Matthew stood in the hotel entryway. He was wearing a black shirt, black jeans, and his dusty work boots. Not exactly a costume, but she wouldn't change a thing. Her stomach swooped, like she was on one of those swinging carnival rides. *Just a friend*, she reminded herself. *Right.*

She went over to meet him. "Looking good, Larsen. You made it."

His hands were in his pockets, and there was hesitation in his posture. "I realized I shouldn't miss it."

Part of her wished the obnoxious Matthew would come back. This would be a lot easier. She was supposed to be working. In fact, she was supposed to be finding June.

"Why don't you grab a drink and enjoy the event?"

"Penn, wait. Please. I..." He glanced to the side. "There's something I need to say. And I'm afraid of waiting again until it's too late."

"Too late for what?"

June, she reminded herself. *Think about June.*

He took a breath, then blew it out. Put his hands on his hips, like he was preparing a speech or something. His eyes came back to her, and the earnestness there struck her right in the heart.

"I care about you," he said. "I want you to know, if you ever decide to move back to Ashton, I'd like to see where this goes. You and me."

"You and me," she repeated.

A warm flush spread across her skin. She was overheating. The lace collar of her dress was too tight.

"You're asking me to move back to Ashton? *Now*?"

"I said *if* you decide."

She was tempted—that was the worst of it. Even right now, when she should be celebrating and looking to her future at Sterling. But if he thought she'd just drop everything and move to Colorado—for any guy, even him—then he didn't understand her at all.

She put a hand over her eyes. "I have a life, Matthew. You have no idea how hard I've worked for it. And now you're asking me to give that up just to 'see where this goes'?"

Matthew frowned, a crease appearing between his eyebrows. "I don't want you to give anything up. As long as you're happy. Tell me you love Los Angeles. Say that PR is really your passion, and I'll step aside. But I don't think it is. I think you're meant for something more."

"What do you even know about—"

She looked up. Movement had drawn her eye to the second-floor landing—the balcony overlooking the lobby.

June was standing up there, her hands on the railing.

"Oh my God," Penny said. "June!"

Matthew spun and looked at the balcony, taking a few steps back. "What is she doing? Nobody's supposed to be up there."

The other people in the lobby started pointing and murmuring. They weren't sure yet if something was wrong. Penny didn't want to alarm anyone without reason.

"Hey, June." She kept her voice calmer this time. "Are you all right?"

June's expression didn't change. Her eyes were glazed, staring out over the room without seeing. She leaned against the railing.

"Hey, please back up," Penny said. "June?"

There was a terrible crack as the brittle wood gave way. June toppled forward. Several things happened at once. There were screams in the lobby. Penny gasped, covering her mouth in horror.

Matthew lunged, his arms outstretched.

Then June slammed into Matthew, and they both crashed into a heap on the floor.

CHAPTER TWENTY-TWO

THE DOOR TO THE PORT-A-POTTY SLAMMED OPEN. SCOTT Mackey rushed out into the clean night air. He shouldn't have gone overboard at the street taco stand. That habanero salsa had burned a path through his insides. Hopefully, the reek wasn't on his clothes now. He didn't want Anvi to smell it.

He lifted his shirt from his shoulder and gave it a sniff. Nah, all good.

About twenty minutes ago, he'd slipped away from his friends Krista and Ray. They were still dancing while some semi-famous DJ did his thing. But after carting the employees of Sterling PR and SunBev around for almost two weeks now, Scott knew all about the behind-the-scenes workings of the festival. Maybe his ticket didn't say "VIP," but he was planning on an exclusive experience tonight. Just him and Anvi.

Scott walked along the rear of Main Street, checking his phone for reception.

On my way, he texted to Anvi. *Meet you there?*

She hadn't seemed super eager to meet tonight, just smiling and tilting her head in that coy way of hers when he proposed it. But she hadn't said no, either. She was hot and sarcastic, and she smelled really good. Lemons and some flower he didn't know the name of. Anvi was a little mean at times, too. Really smart, but snarky. Like the time he was driving her to Eden, and Anvi couldn't stop laughing because he'd mispronounced "Kilimanjaro." Anybody could've gotten that wrong. But he wasn't averse to learning things. Expanding his horizons. Maybe she'd fall for him and invite him to visit her in LA. Probably wouldn't happen. But it could.

Scott checked his phone again. No texts from Anvi yet.

He turned up his volume all the way, then stuck the phone in his pocket.

He reached the back of the bank building. It was a rectangular hulk of brick, crumbling at the corners. He'd been hoping that he could just slip past the security guards. They didn't have nearly enough of them patrolling, and he'd even asked Anvi about it. But she said their budget was getting stretched thin with all the lighting and the sound system and the extra photographers they'd hired. Apparently, the VIP party alone was costing north of thirty-grand.

But there was a security guard resting his girth against the fence right behind the bank. Possibly a problem. But not insurmountable.

Scott came closer, recognizing one of the guys who worked as a ski instructor during the winter season. Scott nodded to him. "Kurt, hey! How's it going?"

"Hey, man. Not bad. This party's kinda weird." Kurt was a glass-half-empty kind of guy. Always grumbling about something, like not enough free granola bars in the ski lodge, which instructors weren't supposed to take anyway.

"Nice looking ladies, though. You seen the costumes?" Scott whistled.

"Naw, I can't see jack over here. They've got me stuck in no-man's-land. It's not fair."

Scott leaned a hand against the fence. He glanced over at the bank. There were no doors except the front, but there were a couple boarded-up windows at the rear. Last night, Scott had loosened the plywood of one from its frame, so it still appeared secure but wasn't attached to anything at the bottom.

"Twenty bucks, and I can keep an eye on things if you want to go check it out," Scott said.

Kurt shrugged. "I'll get canned," he said sulkily.

"I doubt it. But suit yourself. I already saw at least half a dozen girls flash their tits at the DJ. I was thinking of sneaking behind the stage, getting an eyeful..." Scott started meandering away.

"No, wait. Twenty bucks? You swear you won't leave this spot for the next hour?"

"For two twenties, I won't." Scott knew he was laying it on a little thick, but he wanted Kurt to believe him.

"Forty an hour? Jeez." But Kurt still took out his wallet and slipped a couple of bills into Scott's hand.

Scott waved at Kurt's back as the guard disappeared around the corner.

Then he jumped over the barrier, dragged over a couple wooden pallets, and climbed through the window.

His feet hit the ground, and he stumbled on the bag he'd dropped through the window yesterday. He picked up the bag and threaded his arm through the strap. The interior of the building was pitch black, save for the light coming from the higher windows. He almost tripped over a plastic-covered conduit of electrical wires. These connected all the way to the generator trailers, which were parked outside the fence to cut back on noise.

In his bag, Scott found his flashlight and switched it on. The space was gutted. A fire had gone through the room at some point. It smelled like fresh sawdust.

He made his way across the room. He walked over a thick layer of rubber matting, which had been laid down over plywood as a makeshift floor. It thumped hollowly beneath his feet.

The lighting guys had been in here. One edge of the stage was attached to the front of the building, with metal scaffolding for mounting the huge lights. From outside it looked cool, all those multi-colored lights shining on the stage. But inside the bank, things were kinda sloppy. Scott was no electrician, but he doubted this mess was according to code. A mass of heavy duty electrical cords ran up from the floor and along the inside wall. All the windows were boarded up, and the cords ran through holes in the plywood, feeding power to the stage lights and systems. It reminded him a little of the setup in his basement when he was growing up, though on a larger scale. His brother's sound board had been hooked up to different speakers and computer monitors, all the wires twisted together beneath the table.

He used to listen to his brother playing classic rock. Scott would sneak out of bed and go downstairs, and his brother would smile and make a shhh sign with his finger over his mouth. The amp wasn't too loud because Scott's mom would've gotten angry. His brother didn't play whole songs, only the guitar solos —*Stairway to Heaven, Hotel California, Free Bird* if he was in a great mood. He recorded different versions, playing them back with a serious face. Sometimes Scott would fall asleep right there on the ratty plaid couch. Any song could be a lullaby if you felt safe and warm hearing it.

Now his brother lived in an RV in Oregon somewhere. The recording equipment got sold. Whatever. Scott's stepdad used the basement for a home office; he was an elementary school counselor. Always with the questions.

He checked his phone. No texts from Anvi yet.

Earlier that day, Scott had cleared off some space beside a free-standing wall, where they'd be out of sight of the bank's front doors. Not that he expected to be interrupted.

If Anvi would just effing get here.

He went over their last conversation in his mind. She'd been flirting with him, right? She'd pretty much said she'd meet him at ten. Or at least, she hadn't turned him down. It was only ten-oh-five. She wasn't quite late yet. Maybe she couldn't get away from her bosses.

He opened his bag. A thick picnic blanket made a nice rug for the floor. A metal flask held Tito's vodka, and he took a couple swigs as he set up. Candle—check. Vape pen, loaded up yesterday—check. At the dispensary, he'd chosen the strawberry-lemonade cartridge, betting that Anvi would like it.

Then he heard a noise. The same sound his shoe had made against the floor a few minutes ago—echoing inside the cavernous space of the bank.

"Anvi?" he asked quietly. "That you?"

He got up and shone his flashlight over the dark space. There was another footstep, but this one came from the opposite direction. He spun, pointing the flashlight beam. But nothing moved. The electrical cords on the front wall looked like snakes, slithering upward.

Maybe he'd just imagined it. Outside, the DJ was still spinning and the crowd was carrying on. Scott settled back onto the blanket. Ten-ten, now. She was only ten minutes late. She'd gotten held up somehow.

He took a few more swigs from the flask. The vape pen was just sitting there, so he took a puff. Fake berry and citrus flooded his sinuses. After a few minutes, he was feeling much calmer.

But there it was again—that sliding, shuffling sound.

"Hello?"

A cold sweat broke out over Scott's chest and arms. He was sure something was moving in the dark, just out of reach of his flashlight. Every time the light moved, the thing moved too.

Was it a raccoon? A coyote? Jeez, something with rabies? But animals with rabies came straight at you, didn't they? Not skulking around in the shadows. Or so he hoped.

Scott checked his phone again, sure that Anvi had finally written him back. But he had no new messages. It was ten-twenty-three.

"I'll wait five more minutes," he announced into the room,

though he wasn't sure why. Maybe just to hear his own voice. Besides, he was totally going to wait at least ten more. Because what other hope did he have of getting laid tonight? His chances with Anvi were pretty minuscule at this point—he knew that—but a small hope was better than none.

But that creeping feeling wouldn't go away. It wasn't just the cannabis oil in his vaporizer. Beads of icy sweat were forming on his upper lip and brow. He waved his flashlight back and forth across the room.

Scott shouted. A dark shape had darted across the flashlight beam.

He was breathing hard. He tried to catch the thing again in the light, but he couldn't find it. Where was it? *What* was it?

He started backing away. The front of the building was behind him, the sounds of the party outside growing louder.

He felt something hard behind his back and nearly screamed. But it was just the electrical wiring. He was right up against the front wall. Were the wires humming? Or was that just the rushing of blood in his head?

Suddenly, a shape rushed at him out of the dark.

Scott screamed and dropped the flashlight. "Go away! Get out of here!" He kicked his leg, but made no contact. His back pressed against the wiring. He felt each thick, rubbery cord where it touched his shirt.

There was still a little light in the room from the flashlight beam and from the lights of the festival seeping around the boarded windows. He couldn't make anything out in the shadows. But there was something watching him, he knew it. He heard a whimpering sound and realized he was making it.

"Leave me alone," he said. *You need to get out of here, man,* he told himself. *Just bail. Forget Anvi.* But his legs wouldn't move. His knees were shaking.

Slowly, so slowly, a long finger moved against his neck. Tingles shot across his skin. It took half a second for him to match reality to the sensation, and another half second to realize what it was.

One of the thick electrical cords.

He tried to jerk himself away, and instantly the cord whipped around his neck and squeezed. Scott bucked his body, trying to get free, but the cord just held tighter. He tried to cry out, but could only manage a wheeze. His lungs didn't have enough air. He couldn't breathe.

Faintly, he heard sounds like screaming coming from outside.

"Please," he tried to whisper. But his voice wouldn't come. His lips could barely move. "Help." The cord kept cinching tighter around his neck, pulling him upward until his toes left the ground. His vision filled with static. The pressure in his face was unbearable.

Then the pain was in his chest, like something had viciously punched into him there. Shot. Someone had shot him. But from where? How was this happening? He was falling into darkness, tumbling end over end.

A voice whispered into his ear.

I won't let you hurt anyone else. Ever again.

THE ACCIDENTS WORRIED ME. ON MORE THAN ONE OCCASION, I saw someone fall and twist an ankle, damage a wrist. Nothing very frightening, especially given that many visitors on Devil's Night were drunk or under various influences. But people kept reporting strange sounds, even words, right before they were injured. The intuition still followed me—could the ghosts of Eden be responsible for these accidents?

I brought my EVP equipment up and made several recordings, but the results were indeterminate. I still had Beau MacKenzie's diary, and I read it time and again, hoping for some new insight into the events of the Devil's Night Massacre. If only I could find some clue to the mysteries of that night. Then, perhaps, I'd have a new foothold to use when trying to contact the spirits.

-from A DEVIL IN EDEN by Lawrence Wright

DEVIL'S NIGHT - 1894

Marian paced the dining room. According to the grandfather clock in the corner, half an hour had now passed since Tim shot the porter. The pendulum kept up its ceaseless ticking and swinging. She walked to one side of the room, where she could see the back door. Then to the other side, where she could see through the lobby to the front entrance. No one had yet tried to break down the hotel's doors. But she'd checked from the upstairs windows—faces had peered back from nearby buildings, watching and waiting. They wanted to know what was going on in here.

The clock's ticking grated on her. How much time did she have? Every swing of the clock's pendulum, every shift of its great mechanism, she felt her heart winding tighter.

Douglas had found the safe, and that was good. He'd brought back the cook, and she sat crying with the maid in the corner. The injured porter lay insensible beside them. No one would go free until Marian got what she wanted. But Fitzhammer was steadfast in his refusal to give up the code to the safe. There he sat against the wall, still sneering at her despite her triumphs. She would've happily just watched him suffer, whether or not she got his money. But she couldn't keep on living that squalid life, always on the edge of starving. Douglas and Tim couldn't, either.

This man who'd nearly destroyed her. She would bend him to her will, dammit. *She would.*

She took out Bart's Colt revolver. Her boots thumped against the rug as she marched over. The barrel pressed into Fitzhammer's forehead. His eyes squeezed closed, and his throat made a gagging sound that she found rather satisfying.

"Don't," Douglas warned from the doorway. "We need that code. Nobody else knows it."

"You'll never leave this town alive if you kill me," Fitzhammer said, "you know that."

Douglas took a step closer. She moved the gun an inch back. It had left a purple ring on Fitzhammer's fleshy forehead. The maid and the cook hugged each other, eyes closed.

It was a stalemate. She needed some way to break it.

"He doesn't believe I'll really kill him," Marian said. "He needs to be convinced."

She *had* found something during her searches of the upstairs levels: several lengths of rope, abandoned in a trunk in one of the guest rooms. The rope was new, wound intricately out of strong fibers. Who had left it, she wondered? A traveling salesman with a patented rope design? A wealthy rancher who'd stopped in Eden on his journey home? Marian had always enjoyed making up stories about people she didn't know, imagining their simple and prosperous lives. Wives and laughing children eating hearty dinners at home. Such persons seemed as alien as if they'd traveled down from the moon.

She'd left the rope in the lobby. Now Marian went to fetch her prize.

"Marian..." Douglas began when he saw what she carried. She ignored him. If Douglas didn't have the stomach for this, then he could wait in the kitchen.

The coils thudded into a heap at Tim's feet.

"String him up," Marian said.

DEVIL'S NIGHT

It took forever for Bart to pull free of his bindings and drag himself down that hill. His entire body seemed coated in a thick layer of caked blood and dust. Every time he looked at the red-soaked fabric of his trousers, the world spun around him. But his fury kept him going.

He fell and rolled the last few feet, ending up in the road. With a yell, Bart pushed himself up.

If any of them had a brain in their head, they'd have killed me, Bart thought. *Because I'm coming for them.*

That bitch Marian. He should've killed her years ago, back when she pulled that stunt on Fitz. Acting so high and mighty, like she deserved even more than the old man had given her. She was a gutter rat, nothing more, and she'd been lucky that Fitz picked her out of that hellish life and gave her pretty clothes, an education. More than Bart ever had handed to him. He'd had to work for every single thing he ever got in this world.

She was going to pay. By the end of this day, Bart would see her dead.

Bart took a limping step along the road. The pain was terrible. But the bleeding had slowed, at least. He could walk. Far as he could tell, the shot had passed clean through. Still hurt like hellfire, though.

He kept limping onward, one step, then another. His body was tacky with sweat and blood. Lord, how he hated that sticky redness. The rusty, meaty smell. In his younger days, he'd occasionally been humiliated when he fainted at the sight of it. So he tried hard not to look.

It would take him hours to get to Eden at this rate. The old man might be dead by then. Not that it bothered Bart—few people in Eden cared if Fitz lived or died.

But what if they found the key and forced Fitz to tell them how to use it?

Bart couldn't allow that. He'd spent years bowing to that ass of a man, obeying his every whim. Bart hated how Fitz wasted money. Poured it on the undeserving, as if that would buy him love and admiration. Bart had no interest in such frivolities. He'd grown up in a cruel, hard world, and he'd known nothing else. All a man really needed was respect, and to get that, you needed guns and you needed money.

Lots of money.

Bart wasn't a violent man at heart. He'd never considered stealing from Fitz outright, or turning bandit like Marian had done. He believed in earning his keep. But he'd never been satisfied with the pittance that Fitzhammer paid him. He'd watched Fitz toss around gold like it was water, and Bart had started collecting the drops. Just a few coins here, a bill or two there. Nothing that the idiot man would ever notice. Why would Fitz care? He had so much money that he could've bought and sold a man like Bart a hundred times over.

That was the kind of money that Bart wanted. Enough that you could own anybody you chose.

And Bart would never get that rich by picking up after Fitz, or working the mines, or even by becoming an outlaw. The only way was to hold on tight to Fitzhammer, become indispensable. And when Fitz finally kicked the bucket? Bart would know where every penny was hidden, and he'd take it for himself. Now Marian was trying to steal the money out from under him.

He tripped on a stray root, collapsing into the road. Bart screamed curses at the agony in his leg. Wetness seeped again into his boot. Bart sat up, putting pressure on his mangled calf with his hands. He sat there, panting, for a few minutes. Trying not to pass out.

And then the idea came to him.

It wouldn't be so bad if Marian and her two fools took care of Fitz. Would it? Bart could turn this day to his advantage. If he handled things just right. And he could take care of more problems than one.

Then he heard hooves pounding dirt. He turned around just

as a rider came around the bend. The man slowed his horse. It was the barkeep at the Pretty Eyes Saloon. Not the sharpest card in the deck, but they got along well enough.

"Bart! What in tarnation happened to you?"

"Just help me onto your horse, and I'll tell you. There's a reward in it for you, too."

That was all the barkeep needed to hear.

FITZHAMMER'S TOES barely touched the chair. If you didn't look at his terrified face, the man almost seemed to be dancing. Marian was looking at his face, though. She couldn't tear her eyes away.

She hadn't thought herself a cruel person. But his dancing made her feel giddy inside. It was difficult to keep from laughing.

Marian didn't know how to tie a true hangman's noose, but the slip knot had worked well enough. Douglas had fixed it to the chandelier, and then he and Tim had wrestled the man up there.

He was making choking and squealing sounds.

"Pull it tighter," Marian said.

Tim yanked on his end. His thin arms were shaking. Fitzhammer's struggles grew more urgent, his feet just barely touching the chair. His face had turned the bright red of beet juice, and now the skin was edging toward purple. His bound hands pulled helplessly at the rope.

The servingwomen still huddled together in the corner; the maid prayed in German. The injured porter did not look well.

Douglas glanced away. "That's enough."

Tim looked to Marian. She nodded, and Tim added slack to the rope. Fitzhammer's toes touched the chair once more, and he gasped hoarsely. "Please. Please, no more."

"Tell us the code."

"The rope." He could barely speak. "Take it off. Tell you...then."

Douglas moved forward, reaching for the slip knot around Fitzhammer's neck.

"No," Marian said. "The rope stays on."

Douglas gritted his teeth at her. Her gaze didn't waver from his. Did Douglas really want to show mercy to this man, who'd closed down the mine and stolen their pay? Who'd worked them like dogs?

"At least loosen it," Douglas said. "So the man can talk."

Tim let the rope slide down. Fitzhammer's heels now touched the chair. He started coughing.

Marian pushed Tim out of the way and grabbed hold of the rope herself. "The code," she said.

Fitzhammer was still coughing. The livid color was draining from his face, and the cunning was returning to his eyes. She pulled on the rope, just enough to remind him.

"All right! It's fifty-three to the right, seventeen to the left, thirty-four to the right."

Marian nodded at Douglas. "Go and see," she said.

"No!" Fitzhammer's polished leather shoes nearly slipped from the chair. "I gave it to you, now let me go!"

"Why do I think you're lying to me?" Again, Marian took hold of the rope. She wound it over her fist.

"Wait." Douglas's hand was outstretched. "Just wait. I'll check the code." He ran into the other room.

Tim went over to Marian. "What're you planning to do?" he asked.

"She's a demon," Fitzhammer hissed. "A liar." He began coughing again, and spat out a gob of phlegm that hit the chair beneath him. "She'll see you all killed. Make no mistake."

"You're the liar." Marian wrapped the rope around both fists. She started again to pull, cringing when the rope's fibers dug into her wrists and fingers. It reminded her of all the times she'd been bound, trapped, the humanity scraped away. Both in Fitzhammer's house and later in the asylum.

Fitzhammer's heels left the chair. He wriggled beneath the chandelier like a hooked eel.

"Well, now Miss Marian," Tim stammered, "the code, if he was lying—"

She didn't give a damn about that code. All she cared about was seeing the life drain from that man's face. So he could never hurt another girl ever, ever again.

The maid and the cook were crying and wailing. Didn't they know what he was? Why weren't they rejoicing?

Marian pulled and pulled with all her weight until the shiny black shoes kicked in the air. Tim didn't stop her. Her hands had gone numb. Her arms shook. It was taking so long. *I can't hold him*, she thought, but somehow she did. It was important that she bear this weight. That she hold the rope that was choking the life out of him.

Her child had been born with its cord around its neck. She'd held the baby, its skin mottled blue and going cold, before the nurses took it away. They'd tied Marian down and covered her face with an ether-soaked rag to make her stop screaming.

Douglas came into the room. "Oh, hell!"

She spoke through clenched teeth. "Don't."

"It opened, you hear me?" Douglas was edging toward her. "The safe opened."

Tim held out his arm. "She said 'don't.'"

Fitzhammer was trying desperately to reach the chair with his toes.

"But the code worked. Now let him down."

Never. Marian kicked the chair from beneath his dangling feet. She grunted, struggling to hold on to his weight. His face had turned the purple of old blood, his eyes and tongue bulging. Her own hands were turning a similar shade, but she didn't let go. She pictured the face of her child, and she didn't let go.

"Is Penny ready for this?" my wife asked.

I looked up at the stars. "I think she is. We always talked about wanting our kids to decide things for themselves, right? We never wanted to be the kinds of parents who told them who to be."

"But she's five. Maybe we should wait."

I considered this. But I'd seen how much damage a few months of uncertainty could do to her. Before Helen and Jason arrived, Penny had closed off from us. Now, Penny was finally smiling again. What would it do to her if we said no? I said all this to my wife.

But there was more I kept silent, too. In my heart, I wanted this so badly. I wanted to take Penny to Eden so I could finally—I hoped—find some answers....

But if I knew what would soon happen there, I'd never have brought Penny to Eden. I'd have tried to find some other way.

In just a matter of days, I'd be at risk of losing everything I held dear."

-from A Devil in Eden **by Lawrence Wright**

CHAPTER TWENTY-THREE
2019

PENNY WAITED IN THE CHAIR BY MATTHEW'S HOSPITAL BED. When he went for a CT scan, she allowed herself to doze, her spine curving into the plastic in a way that was going to ache later on. The clock outside by the nurse's station said it was five a.m.

She woke when the orderly wheeled him in. "You're getting the royal treatment," Penny said.

"He asked for a piggy-back ride," the burly orderly said, "but that's where I draw the line."

Matthew had a half-amused, half-annoyed look on his face. The orderly helped him out of the wheelchair and onto the bed. Matthew seemed unsteady, listing to one side as he lay back.

"Doctor should be in again shortly with those test results," the orderly said. "Your Highness."

Matthew smiled and saluted. The doctor had already announced that Matthew had a concussion, probably a mild one. But since he had a lump on his head and a headache, they'd decided to run a few more tests, courtesy of the insurance policy that SunBev had purchased for Devil's Fest.

The injury to his right shoulder was worse—a dislocation, which the doctor had reset after a dose of ketamine. Matthew had been pretty goofy after that, but he'd slept awhile, and now the effects seemed to be wearing off.

She pushed her chair closer to the bed. "What can I get you?" she asked. "A butter pecan milkshake with extra whip and Reese's Pieces on top?"

Matthew smiled. "You remembered." His words slurred, but less than before.

"I only witnessed you order that about ten thousand times."

"And you never got the same flavor of ice cream twice."

He winced as he shifted against the pillows.

"Still hurting?" she asked. "Your head or your shoulder?"

"Both. But I'll live."

"If you hadn't been there tonight..." Penny covered her mouth. She'd already said this multiple times, but the shock still hadn't worn off.

When he caught June and they both crashed, his head had bounced off the lobby's wood floor. Paramedics had swarmed from one of the festival's medical tents. June had been knocked cold. The medics hadn't let Penny ride along with Matthew or June, but she and Linden had driven one of Alpenglow's Jeeps. *Accidents happen*, Linden had said. *They're going to be fine. It could've been much worse.* As if Penny didn't know.

Penny had asked to see June, too, but the nurses refused. Linden was trying to find out how she was faring.

Matthew closed his eyes, hissing as he moved his arm to a different position. Bruises dotted his skin, only partly visible past his hospital gown. His right arm was in a sling.

"I just don't understand what June was doing up there," Penny said. "I should've looked for her sooner."

Matthew held his left hand out to her. She slid her fingers into his comforting grip.

"I should've boarded up the stairways entirely," he said.

"Of everyone involved in this, you're the least to blame. If it wasn't for you, if June—" Her voice was breaking, and the tears she'd been holding back for hours sprang into her eyes.

"Enough of that." Matthew squeezed her hand. "If I hadn't been there, you would've done something. I'm really glad that didn't happen, obviously, because I think my head's a lot harder than yours."

"False humility doesn't look good on you, Larsen. You're the big, brave hero. Get used to it."

Watching June plummet from the balcony had been one of the most terrifying split-seconds of Penny's life. That moment had felt endless, and Penny had simply frozen. She hadn't even thought there was anything she *could* do.

But Matthew hadn't hesitated. He'd reached out and caught June—or at least, broken her fall—and risked himself like it was the most natural thing in the world. Because to him, it *was* natural.

He laughed. "I'm not brave. I'm the guy who's too scared to go back to his own house."

"What do you mean?"

Matthew looked at the wall, as if regretting his words.

"Is that why you're living at the inn?" she asked.

He nodded reluctantly.

"Then tell me. You know so many embarrassing things about me, I could use at least one of you."

"It wasn't anything so significant..." Then he stopped and swallowed. "Okay, I guess it was." He closed his eyes, clearing his throat.

"I saw my mother. After she died, I mean. I saw her in our house."

Penny scooted to the edge of her chair, resting her hand on the bed beside him. She felt his warmth through the blanket.

"You saw her ghost?"

"It happened a few days after she died." He spoke slowly, taking time to form the words. "I was sleeping a lot then. I don't know if I was depressed, or if I was just so sleep deprived. I stayed up as much as I could while she was dying. Just caught a nap here and there. She'd spent months holding on, and then those last days she got worse so fast. She was in her bed at home. I could almost feel it in the room—that shift. A few minutes later, Mom was gone."

He sat up, speaking more clearly now. "But anyway, I was sleeping a lot afterward. One day, I woke up around sunset. I'd heard a noise, like a door closing, though I couldn't tell right then if I'd only dreamed it. I wasn't sure of the time until I looked over at the clock and saw it was about five p.m. The house seemed so still. I got up and left my room. Went to the kitchen, thinking I should eat something even though I still wasn't hungry. And then, when I got there..."

He was quiet for almost a full minute.

Finally, Penny asked, "When you got there?"

"All the lights were off in the house, but I could see her outline. She was walking across the kitchen, stopping every few feet and glancing around. Like she was looking for something. And I could hear her. Not out loud. I mean, in here." He tapped at his temple. "It was just like you described it. She was saying, 'I can't, it's not right.' Over and over. I have no idea what that meant. It was so surreal. I guess I thought maybe I was still dreaming. I went toward her, and I said, 'Mom, what's not right?' Without even thinking, I reached out and tried to touch her. It wasn't cold, exactly. But my fingers went numb. I knew then that it wasn't a dream. I grabbed a few things, and I got the hell out of there."

Penny tried to catch his eye, but he wouldn't look at her.

"Your mom didn't ask too many questions when I asked for a room at the inn. She seemed to understand there were things I didn't want to discuss, and I am really grateful for that. I didn't know how to explain it. Even though I grew up around you and your family, and all the stories about ghosts in Ashton, I didn't know how to say what happened. Until, I guess, now. With you."

Penny nodded. She'd heard stories like this before. But even though she was used to seeing spirits, she'd never seen a ghost of a person she'd known well. It would've been intense.

"Have you tried going back?" she asked. "It's possible your mom isn't there anymore." Most of the ghosts she saw were like that. Just passing through.

"I can't experience that again. She was so scared, and I don't even know why. I just feel like I failed her. I tried to make sure she was comfortable and felt loved those last few days, and it wasn't—" His voice faltered. "It wasn't enough."

Penny rested her hand on his leg through the blanket. "That's not true. It might not have been about you at all."

"But it was. I felt it. She was scared because of *me*. I just don't know why."

A nurse came in, and Penny moved her chair back to make room. While the nurse asked Matthew questions about his pain level, Penny thought. Even though she'd lived with this ability for most of her life, she still understood little about ghosts. She'd absorbed some things over the years, but she hadn't gone out of her way to learn more. There were sophisticated research teams studying paranormal activity, but she'd stayed away from them— too many memories of her father's paranormal club. She had no interest in being studied. As for other mediums, she avoided them. Just because Penny knew ghosts were real didn't mean that she bought into every single person who claimed to see them, too.

But of course, she believed whole-heartedly that Matthew was telling the truth.

"Will I be able to leave soon?" Matthew asked the nurse.

"The doctor will be in to discuss it soon. Shouldn't be too much longer."

"I wish you had told me before," Penny said when the nurse had gone. "About your mom."

Matthew looked rueful. "I didn't tell you because you weren't here. And it's not like there's anything you could do. It's my problem, not yours."

His body language had closed off. They hadn't talked yet about what he'd said last night—her moving back to Ashton.

The whole idea was a non-starter. But her heart was doing all sorts of funny things in her chest.

"I pay someone to keep the house up," Matthew continued, "check on it every few weeks. I'm going to sell it eventually, when I feel ready."

"You should be able to go home."

"I thought home was overrated."

Perhaps she deserved that. But his tone was light, not critical. Penny sat gently beside him on the bed. Her fingers grazed his cheek. His blue eyes regarded her.

How had she ever imagined that she'd gotten over this man?

"Knock, knock," Linden said, and tugged at the curtain blocking Matthew's bed from the rest of the room. She peeked in and saw Penny sitting beside him. "Oh, sorry—"

Penny stood. "It's fine, come in. What's up?"

"Checking on our patient, though clearly he's in good hands." Linden's hair was up in a messy bun, and her face was scrubbed clean of makeup. Penny recognized the signs of lack of sleep in her friend—a slight redness to Linden's eyes, a crease between her eyebrows.

Matthew shifted his weight on the bed, sitting up higher against the pillows. "Penny's taking good care of me. But how's June? We haven't heard much."

Linden gave them a quick update on June's condition. She'd broken the tibia and fibula in her left leg, fractured a couple of ribs, and suffered a concussion.

Matthew spoke up. "The way she looked in the ambulance—it was rough. When she woke up on the way, she was terrified. She didn't know where she was."

"Is June's family coming?" Penny asked.

Linden shrugged. "They said something about June's roommate? Tripp's been meeting with the SunBev execs, so I don't know their plan. Or whether June's going to be well enough to stay for the rest of the festival." She was playing nervously with the cuff of one sleeve, a very un-Linden-like tic. There was something else bothering her. Something she hadn't said.

"What else is going on?" Penny asked.

Linden smiled apologetically at Matthew. "I don't want to stress anyone."

"You're starting to freak me out," Penny said. "What is it?"

Linden took a shaky breath. "June wasn't the only one who had an accident at the festival last night."

CHAPTER TWENTY-FOUR

BY THE TIME THE DOCTOR OFFICIALLY ANNOUNCED MATTHEW could leave the hospital, Penny had already gone.

Bryce was waiting in his car by the curb. An orderly wheeled Matthew outside. The day was beautiful—just a few clouds, eye-watering sunshine, seventy-five degrees. The kind of day Matthew and Bryce would've met up for lunch, maybe even played hooky from work for an extra hour or two to play bocce ball on the inn's lawn. But today, Matthew had a sore shoulder and a concussion, he'd only gotten a few hours' sleep, and he still felt spacey from the drugs they'd given him. Plus, he had way too many other things on his mind besides.

Bryce got out of his car and opened the passenger-side door. Matthew got up from the wheelchair.

"You look like you're half dead."

"Exactly. Only half."

The doctor had given him a Tylenol 3 prescription and told him to take it easy for a few days. *Avoid alcohol and screens, if you can*, the doc said. *Try not to think too hard. Give your brain a rest.* Which wouldn't be easy with Penny around.

Once they were both seated and belted, Bryce put the car in

gear. They drove through the parking lot toward the main road. It was about a fifteen-minute trip back to the inn.

"Have you talked to Penny?" Matthew asked.

She'd stopped by his room to say she had to go. Between the two accidents last night, she was once again doing damage control. And that was only the first night of the festival. Had it been doomed from the start?

Or is this my fault? Matthew wondered. *It was my job to make Eden safe, and somehow I screwed up.* But he still couldn't wrap his head around what had gone wrong. Maybe it was the drugs, or the concussion. His brain was fuzzy this morning. Moving too slowly.

Just like his impression that Penny had been about to kiss him earlier. His brain was definitely deficient, because she'd made it clear last night that she had no intention of trying to rekindle their relationship. Hadn't she?

Bryce was always a stickler about the speed limit. Right now, he was driving ten under, like he thought Matthew could break.

"I haven't spoken to Penny, no," Bryce said, "but everybody's talking about last night. You're the big hero. Maybe even saved that girl's life? You always knew how to get attention."

Matthew rolled his eyes, which he stopped when he started feeling dizzy. "But what about Scott? Is he okay? What even happened?"

Bryce sighed, running a hand over his thick, dark hair. "Man, I hardly know. But it's embarrassing. Apparently, he was drunk and high and someplace he didn't belong. He got caught up in some wires, I guess? One of the people who works with Penny found him."

"Was it Anvi?" Matthew wondered aloud.

"Dunno. But he got shuffled off to the hospital behind you."

"Poor kid. Krista's close with him, right?"

"Yeah, they were at the festival together last night. It's an all-hands-on-deck family emergency according to my dad, so it's a good thing you're well enough to come home. We need somebody who's not a Wright to insert a little sanity into our discussions. I tried to remind Dad that people get injured skiing or hiking around Ashton every single year. But he won't listen."

"So you're okay with Penny holding a festival in Eden?"

"Our business around here is tourism. My mom is fine with it, too. It's just Dad, and that's only because of his weird fixation on the paranormal. I mean, some people around town are criticizing Penny's motives, saying she's sweeping in like a carpetbagger, helping big companies make money off of tragedy. Some lady actually confronted Penny at the inn."

"That's completely unfair." Matthew shifted against the leather seat, remembering that he might've said something similar to Penny when she arrived. "Penny's doing the best she can."

Bryce raised an eyebrow in his direction. "Yeah, man, I know. Relax."

But Matthew gripped his door as they drove. Everybody, from the doctor to his best friend, was telling him to relax, and he'd never felt more wound up.

"Just don't start with Penny when you see her," Matthew said. "That's all I'm asking."

"Why would I start with her? I'm not mad at her. Besides, I barely know her anymore."

"Exactly. So give her a chance. You were always way too hard on her growing up."

Bryce laughed. "Some things haven't changed, I see."

"What does that mean?" Matthew almost never fought with Bryce. An easy-going, live-and-let-live attitude defined their friendship. Bryce was the one with a temper, and Matthew always smoothed things over. Their roles were well-defined after almost fifteen years of friendship. So why did Matthew feel like picking a fight now? He couldn't explain it. But the urge was there from the moment Bryce had said Penny's name.

"I just mean, you still have a thing for her."

Matthew's face instantly began to burn.

Bryce laughed again, louder this time. "You thought I didn't know? Matt, you are not a closed book, okay?"

"But you never said anything." Matthew spoke through clenched teeth.

"And you didn't either."

"You're not pissed?"

They pulled into the lot for the inn and parked in the far corner. Bryce switched off the engine, then looked over at him. "I've never worried about her with you. Not for a second. It's you I've always worried about."

"Me? Why?"

Bryce got out of the car, shaking his head. Matthew followed. But he wasn't letting this go.

"Why?" He stopped there in the parking lot.

Bryce put his hands on his hips. "Look, I'm amazed her job at this LA publicity firm has lasted this long. Maybe she's changed in the last few years. But I doubt it. Eventually, Penny always gets bored—that's probably why she's back. Suddenly, our hometown and our history seem new and interesting again. But it won't last. You know?"

Matthew thought Penny had grown up more than her brother knew. But he wanted to hear Bryce say the rest of it.

"Why does that make you worry about me?"

Bryce closed his eyes and sighed. "I care about you, and I'd hate to see you hurt. I don't want you to be the one she leaves next."

DEBBIE WRIGHT USHERED them into the dining room, which was quiet since lunch wasn't being served yet.

"Dora made something special for you," Penny's mother said, setting the plate on a table.

Bryce reached for a square of cornbread, and Debbie smacked his hand. "Not for you," she said. "For Matthew."

"Mom!" Bryce cradled his hand, though he was smiling. "I'll just get one from Dora in the kitchen."

"That's up to her. But you're not stealing Matthew's. We're supposed to be taking care of him, remember?"

Everyone seemed to know already about his supposed "heroics" the night before. He'd just done what anybody would've done. Mostly, he wanted to go to his room and get some sleep.

And Matthew was still stunned by what Bryce had said—not only that he knew about Matthew's feelings for his sister, but that he thought Penny would break his heart. Matthew had wondered as much himself. That was a big part of the reason he'd convinced himself to let her go. A part of him had wanted Bryce to go all protective big brother. Which would've been fair, considering the things Matthew always longed to do with her. But maybe Bryce could see what Matthew couldn't—that he and Penny just weren't meant to be.

Matthew ignored the various aches and pains all over his body—the pounding of his head, the twisting of his heart—and sat down to eat.

"I'm so sorry about what happened," Debbie said. "All those bruises, you poor thing." She clucked her tongue. "Do you want to talk about it, or do you just want to be left alone for a bit?"

I'm alone all the time, Matthew thought. This had been another realization since Penny arrived back in his life. Seeing her again made him realize just how alone he'd been these past few years, though he lived in a hotel with dozens of people constantly surrounding him.

"Alone's good." He didn't like the reason for all the attention. He certainly didn't feel much like a hero.

"All right. But concussions are no joke, and I've got a key to your room, mister. I will be using it. I don't know if you sleep naked, and I don't want to know. So wear some PJs."

Matthew snickered. "Yes, ma'am." Debbie was part of the

reason he liked living at the inn. She'd always been close friends with his mom.

His mom. The thought of her wasn't easing that twisting sensation in his chest. He loved his mom so much, and it had been so hard to lose her. Sometimes people said things like, *I'd give anything to see her again, even for a second.* But Matthew didn't feel that way. He'd thought she died at peace, but her presence in the kitchen had been so tortured. Had she been hiding something? Had she died afraid, unable to tell her son the truth? Or had she simply been trying to spare his feelings?

Matthew had always thought of himself as strong. But if his own mom was afraid to tell him the truth, what did that say about him? And what about his best friend? Bryce had been worried about Matthew's feelings, too. Somehow, their concern felt more like a betrayal.

But the worst thought of all was that his mom was suffering. She was still in that house, unable to rest.

He stuck his spoon into the bowl of green chili and then shoved it into his mouth. He was nauseous, but he knew the food would do him good.

As he ate, he texted his boss. Now that he'd finished the work in Eden, maybe Sully had a new project for him.

Sully texted back, *Absolutely not. You need to be resting. Doctor's orders.*

Really? Matthew lamented. How did everybody know? That had to be an invasion of privacy.

He was halfway through his lunch when Bryce and Ray Castillo came into the dining room. Matthew nodded in greeting. He knew Ray's older sister. Ray was a good kid, young but he had his head on straight. He'd been a deputy at the sheriff's for just a few months.

"There's the big hero," Bryce said. "They fit you for your cape yet?"

Matthew put steel into his returning glare, but he was smiling. At least Bryce wasn't taking this too seriously.

"Hey, how're you feeling?" Ray asked.

Matthew gave him the rote answer: head hurts, shoulder's sore, but otherwise fine. Nothing to see here, folks. Please look elsewhere.

"Is Penny here?" Ray asked.

Matthew set down his spoon. "I haven't seen her since this morning."

Ray slipped into the chair across from him. "Can I?" he asked, pointing at one of the uneaten pieces of cornbread.

"Go for it." Matthew pushed the plate over. Dora had given him way too much, as usual.

"Hey," Bryce sputtered. "What about me?"

"You already ate half the pan that Dora baked," Matthew said. "Admit it."

"But you gave Ray the best piece."

Deputy Ray devoured the cornbread. "Thanks," he said, his mouth full, "I haven't eaten all day."

"Now I sound like a jerk," Bryce said, spinning a chair around and sitting.

"It's just been kinda hectic today, with the accidents up at Eden," Ray said. "Scott's okay, thankfully. He's in pretty big trouble, though. Got fired from Alpenglow—that's what I heard."

Bryce cursed. "He really messed up, huh?"

Ray nodded. "Nearly got himself killed by being drunk and careless."

"Is that why you're looking for Penny?" Matthew asked. "To give her an update?"

"Oh—no, actually. It's about that, um..." Ray glanced around, then leaned in. "That skeleton that Penny found a few days ago in Eden. A report came in from the CBI's anthropologist. I thought Penny would want to hear about it."

Matthew didn't love the eagerness in Ray's voice when he talked about Penny. Did the kid have a crush on her? But then again, he was—what—twenty? Which was...about as far age-wise as Matthew himself was from Penny. So, yeah. Matthew wasn't enjoying that line of thought.

"She'll definitely want to hear about it," Matthew said. "Let's go find her. Together."

CHAPTER TWENTY-FIVE

WHEN PENNY GOT THE NEWS ABOUT SCOTT FROM LINDEN, she called her little sister. She'd remembered that Krista was a friend of his. Krista had seemed startled yet otherwise fine on the phone. But now that they were sitting in Krista's bedroom, Penny wasn't so sure.

Penny tossed a can of local IPA to her sister, then popped the tab on her own.

"Isn't it early to be drinking?" Krista asked.

"After the night we had?"

Penny took a sip, and the tart flavor of resinous hops coated her tongue. She and Krista had the same taste in beer—the hoppier the better. She'd delighted in taking Krista to a couple of beer bars in Los Angeles the year before—bars that conveniently didn't card—in order to prove that Southern California, too, had a decent brew culture. But who was she kidding? It was nothing like home.

"You want to talk about what happened last night?" Penny asked.

Krista took a long swig and fell back against her pillows. "I don't even know. That's the thing. Scott said he was going to meet Anvi someplace. He disappeared when we were dancing, and I didn't think that much of it. But after a while, I just started to not feel right. Ray—Deputy Castillo—and I looked for him, but I couldn't remember where he was going. And that's when all the screaming started."

Penny had been piecing together last night's chain of events. The screaming had started after June's fall. A bunch of the festival-goers saw it all from the Paradise Hotel's windows. Those screams had covered up Scott's cries for help—or so Linden had heard from Anvi. It had been Anvi who found Scott, tangled up in a nest of electrical wires and suffocating. She freed him and called on her radio for the paramedics team, which was already nearby and having a too-busy night. But by then, Penny and Linden had already been in the parking lot, watching medics load Matthew and June for the drive to town.

"When I saw him today," Krista continued, "he just seemed shocked and humiliated. He lost his job. Everyone's acting like he's the dumbest guy in the world, and I guess sometimes he can be. But I swear, Penny, he didn't mean any harm. Scott's an okay guy."

"I'm sure he is. Believe me, I know what a small town Ashton can be." Penny set her beer on the floor.

"Scott told me that your boss—that guy Tripp Sterling—was threatening him with prosecution if he damaged anything last night. Is that really true? Can you talk to your boss? Because it's not right. Scott's the one who got hurt!"

"I'll do whatever I can." She didn't mention that she doubted her ability to convince Tripp.

Penny felt terrible that not one but *two* incidents had happened on the opening night of Devil's Fest. Everyone involved could've been hurt much worse. Scott could even have started a fire by messing with the wiring.

But Linden had told her not to worry. *Do you have any idea how much shit goes down at amusement parks or big festivals every single year?* Linden had insisted. *This is what insurance is for.*

Penny didn't care about insurance. She cared about Matthew

and Krista, and anyone else who'd been hurt. And dammit, she still cared about her town, even though she no longer called Ashton home. She didn't want bad things to happen to people here, and she certainly didn't want to be responsible for them.

She'd considered whether Eden's ghosts could be involved, too. How could she not?

But it did sound like Scott's accident was a case of being drunk in the wrong place at the wrong time. As for June, Penny hesitated to speculate, but without a doubt the fall never would've happened if June had stayed downstairs. Penny and Linden had already discussed adding to their security team.

Krista folded her legs beneath her. "Scott said something else, too. It could be important."

The door to Krista's bedroom opened. Both of their heads turned; their father was standing there.

"You told her?" their dad said. He was looking at Krista. Krista glanced furtively away, sipping her beer.

"Told me what?"

Krista was teaming up with their dad suddenly?

In a low voice, Penny's sister said, "Scott swears that somebody else was there. But nobody will believe him. They see a flask and a vape pen and they just—"

"Someone else was there? Who?"

"He didn't see the person's face. But he says he felt them there."

"*Felt* them?"

"It was a ghost," their dad said. "Isn't it obvious?"

"That's a pretty big leap."

Penny didn't want to be rude, but there was good reason to dismiss Scott's story. Even taking into consideration all she knew about Eden's ghosts, including her own experiences.

"You think I want this to be true?" Krista asked. "I didn't believe it, either. But after what Dad told me today, I'm scared that it's possible."

Krista got up and threw her beer in the trash. "I thought you might listen, but I should've known better." She flopped onto her mattress and buried her head beneath the pillow.

Penny looked to her father for an explanation. "Tell me what you said to her. Right now."

Krista peeked out from under the pillow. "Just go away, Penny. Everything was better before you came back."

"Let's leave her be." Lawrence gestured at the doorway.

PENNY WENT into her dad's study. For a while, he'd insisted on calling it his "man cave" until her mom objected. But the room belonged, in heart and soul, to her father. All his paranormal books were here, texts about famous psychics like Edgar Cayce and Peter Hurkos, reports published by the Duke Parapsychology Lab. His decks of Zener cards, which he'd once used to test Penny for psychic aptitude. Boxes of outdated AV equipment for the ghost hunting expeditions that he took ages ago. A few years after he wrote *A Devil in Eden*, he'd given up his dream of becoming a paranormal researcher. But he couldn't let all this old stuff go.

Her father closed the door behind them.

"What did you say to Krista?"

"It's something I should've told you a long time ago."

"So, out with it."

"At least have a seat."

She dropped into an upholstered armchair. A captive audience.

"You were so young when I wrote the book on Eden."

She remembered the visits to local bookstores, a few small speaking engagements. *I'm an author*, he said when the books arrived in their cardboard box. He held one up next to his face and grinned. *Check me out!*

She'd been so excited for him. She'd been six in 2001 when the book was published. But it wasn't until Penny was thirteen that she actually read *A Devil in Eden* for herself. She'd had a secret admiration for Marian, a woman who could command a gang of men even back when women struggled to get basic rights. Who was this person who could sway people to her side, who still frightened children in stories passed on the playground?

But she hadn't liked the version of her father she saw in those pages. He claimed that he'd taken Penny to Eden to help her understand her ability. Bullshit. He took Penny there because of his obsession with the paranormal. Because he was *selfish*. He'd cared more about Penny's ability than he did about her.

She'd forgiven her dad a long time ago. He wasn't a terrible person; she loved him. But she wasn't going to pretend that his flaws didn't exist.

Lawrence wiped a hand over his face.

"It goes back before I wrote the book. You remember Helen and Jason Boyd?"

"Sure I do."

Penny had thought of Helen as her friend. The woman would ask her to describe the ghosts, writing every word Penny said. She could picture Helen in her mind, even now—curly dyed-red hair, a heart-shaped face with a broad smile. She'd sit cross-legged on Penny's floor and play pretend, dreaming up the most wonderful stories. Brave girls facing down impossible foes.

When Penny's father took her to Eden, the Boyds came along. But they left afterward and Penny never saw them again, which hurt. Lawrence had mentioned that Jason died. She couldn't recall much about him, except for an inkling that children made him uncomfortable.

Penny had wondered if it was really her dad's fault that Helen never contacted them. Maybe—just like Penny—Helen had wanted to escape the legacy of *A Devil in Eden*.

Lawrence settled back into his chair, thinking a moment.

"I didn't really believe that Marian could be capable of the things they said. She was a mother, and she ensured that her child was cared for. And I guess a part of me saw my own grandmother in her. How could an evil woman have birthed my beautiful, kind grandmother? It didn't make sense. After Beau MacKenzie found Marian's child—my grandmother—on those church steps, he made sure that she had a home. He adopted her as his own." He gestured at the room. "Beau made this inn part of her inheritance. And really, the story of Eden was her inheritance, too. It became mine. And then, you came along. The key to understanding it all."

Penny turned away, shaking her head. But her father kept going.

"Helen and Jason agreed to help us. So we went up there for Devil's Night. You know what happened—the things we saw and heard, how your mother got cold feet and took you home, and Helen, Wallace and Carlos gave up too, but Jason and I stayed. Something..."

He looked over at his shelf of books. Penny noticed now that she couldn't spot a single copy of *A Devil in Eden*.

"Something happened to Jason that night," he said. "I wrote about that, too. He wasn't acting like himself."

"I know." She still couldn't see why her father needed to rehash these things. "Dad, please get to the point."

He smacked his hand against his thigh. "I *am*, Penny. In the years after that Devil's Night, Jason started going up to Eden on his own. Helen asked me for help. But I couldn't go back. I *couldn't*."

During Penny's childhood, ghosts were all that her dad talked about. But as he grew older, he could no longer handle the usual stresses and strains of the business of the inn. Her mom simply left him out of it now. He didn't watch the news anymore, either —it made his heart rate get out of control. Instead, he'd become someone that they all coddled. Their mother didn't tell him half of what really went on at the inn or with Penny's siblings. Yet too often, Penny suspected that her dad *enjoyed* being patronized. He'd failed as a parapsychologist, then as an author. This drama was the only way he still knew to command their attention.

Lawrence's eyes were shining. He paused and rested his chin against his closed hand.

Her father was going to cry.

"Dad?"

He took a deep breath, steadying himself. "Jason died up there in Eden. He went up to the third floor of the bank, and he jumped. Broke his neck."

Penny's hand pressed into her stomach. "Why haven't I heard this before?"

"Helen asked me not to tell a soul. It wasn't just the life insurance—she didn't want people to blame Jason for what happened. I didn't see it that way, though. I was sure that Jason didn't jump on his own."

A sick feeling wound through her gut. She could tell where this was going. But she still asked, "Why?"

He looked over at her. "Something terrible happened in that town, Penny. Not just the Devil's Night Massacre—I think it was something worse than we even know. And it's still being replayed, over and over. Maybe the ghosts there are evil. Or maybe they're just trapped. But I blame them for Jason's death. They made him jump."

She thought of June on the balcony. The way she'd leaned against the railing.

"No." Penny dropped her head into her hands. "No. If that were true, you would have told me."

"You think I don't regret my part in this? I didn't really want to know, either. First I took you up to Eden, my little girl, and put you in danger. Then my best friend paid the price."

Penny got up from her chair. "You weren't even there. You don't know what really happened. This is just your speculation, your belief, like everything else."

Exaggerations. Pleas for attention, like always. He'd nearly convinced her this time. But she wasn't that little kid anymore—captivated by her father, blind to his faults.

He slumped in his chair, suddenly older than she'd ever seen him.

"End this madness, Penny. Don't go back there. I couldn't forgive myself if they took you too. But if it's somebody else who dies, you'll have to live with the same guilt as me. I don't want that for you."

She went to the door and paused, gripping the handle, battling within herself over how to respond. How to defend herself. But what could she say to him now, after everything?

If she lived life his way—always asking *what if what if what if*—the fear would paralyze her. The past, and the dead, would forever control her.

She finally just opened the door and quietly left.

CHAPTER TWENTY-SIX

Linden closed the door to her hotel room and leaned back against it. *I will get through this*, she thought.

She went over to her dresser and dabbed lavender essential oil on her pressure points. Her heart was pounding. But she could handle it. She had everything under control.

She'd just gotten off her fifth call of the day. Or was it the seventh? She couldn't even remember. There was the insurance adjuster—SunBev had given him her number, *you can take care of this, can't you?*—the sheriff's office, June's roommate Kelsey. Then a personal call to Ashton's mayor, assuring him that the accidents were unfortunate and random, but no sign that the festival was dangerous. Plus other people who'd blended together into a single, whining voice. Penny might've been able to help, but she'd been busy with her family most of the day.

Linden slipped off her shoes and fell back against her bed, inhaling the scent of lavender.

Then her phone rang. In half a second, the device was out of her pocket and against her ear.

"What's up, Penny?"

"Hey. Do you have a minute?"

Linden sat up, her heart speeding again. She heard the

anxiety in Penny's voice. She loved Penny, but the girl had been a handful lately.

"Of course. Talk to me."

"I wanted to update you. You're not going to like it."

Not a good start. But Linden stayed quiet.

Penny told her what had happened in the last few hours: that her sister Krista was freaking out over something that Scott, the drunken trespasser, had said. He'd seen "somebody else" in the bank. And then this stuff about Penny's father and his friend who died.

"The thing is," Penny said, "Krista didn't like my reaction to their stories. She went on Twitter to tell everyone not to go to the remaining nights of Devil's Fest."

Linden glanced up, meeting her own eyes in the mirror. She was looking paler than usual, a sickly color that meant she hadn't been eating enough. Her appetite vanished whenever she was stressed or sick. Tripp had noticed as well. *Are you getting your period?* he'd asked that morning at breakfast, nose wrinkling.

He pissed her off sometimes. But Linden had never been into guys who gave her the warm fuzzies. She wanted to be challenged. Stimulated. Tripp never bored her.

She got up and went to the bathroom, opening her makeup case.

"What do you think I should do?" Penny asked.

"Leave it alone. We already put out a statement about the accidents. People will probably assume Krista's a plant, and we're just trying to get more publicity." Linden set jars of foundation, concealer and bronzer on the counter.

"But she's my sister."

"This will blow over. We're beefing up festival security, so everything will be fine. Just relax. Take the night off. Spend some time with Matthew." Linden swept a finger over her eyebrows, checking for stray hairs in the mirror. "Give him a blowjob or something, I don't know. He certainly deserves it."

Penny was laughing—an excellent sign.

"I'll leave it to your discretion," Linden said. "Hand job at the very least. Just have a good night. No more worrying about ghosts."

"Seriously? You don't need me at the dinner?"

They'd planned a small dinner at a fancy French place for the SunBev execs. "Tripp and I can handle them."

Penny agreed, and they ended the call. Linden sent off a text to Tripp, confirming their plans for dinner. He texted back a thumb's up emoji.

Linden washed her face and started applying her makeup. As she worked, she listened for the door to the next room, which would signal Tripp's return. Maybe he wanted to meet her in the lobby instead. She checked her messages from him, but there was nothing specific. Then again, Tripp often expected her to anticipate what he was thinking.

They'd met through mutual friends not long after Linden graduated from UCLA. He was a product of the exclusive private schools of Pasadena, and then college at the University of Southern California, his parents' alma mater. But like Linden, he wanted to be so much more than a legacy. When they met, he already had years under his belt as a journalist. His new PR company, capitalizing on his media contacts, was in high demand. But out of all the people in their orbit, Tripp admired *her*. He courted her, not as a girlfriend but a business partner. And that, frankly, was the sexiest thing of all. They were equals. Well, she was still a junior partner at Sterling PR, and he was five years older. But virtual equals. And wouldn't it be a victory if she could domesticate a guy like him? It was like conquering Mount Everest, only with way better sex.

She got up and opened the closet, where she'd neatly hung her clothes after relocating from the travel trailer. The hangers clinked as she shuffled them, debating what to wear. She selected a silky black blouse and slipped into a pair of stonewash skinny jeans. It was the kind of outfit she'd wear to a weekend brunch in LA. Nothing that Tripp hadn't seen before, so she wasn't trying too hard. Her fingers ran through her long hair, working free the tiny tangles that had developed through the day.

Now, she just had to track down her boyfriend. If she could call him that. He'd made no promises of exclusivity. They weren't openly together, but Linden wasn't actively hiding it, either. If Penny ever guessed, then Linden wouldn't deny it. Sometimes, she did wish that Penny would guess. Linden's mother had, though Mrs. Hao hadn't been very positive.

The elevator was taking too long, so Linden took the stairs. Her thick-soled loafers thudded against the carpet as she jogged down to the first floor.

As she crossed the lobby, she spotted Tripp. Linden was about to say something when she realized who was next to him —Anvi. She'd thought that Anvi was up at Eden already. Linden hung back, pausing behind a pillar to watch them. There was something about the way they stood that she didn't like, Tripp going a little too far into Anvi's space. And Anvi, who normally was so serious, smiled and tilted her head. Was that flirting? She'd never seen Anvi and Tripp interact this way before. Linden wished she could hear what they were saying.

It's probably nothing, she told herself. *They're just talking shop, like all of us do.*

Tripp put his hand on Anvi's elbow and squeezed. Then he leaned back, saying something more. Anvi nodded, her smile slipping. She didn't look happy.

Then Tripp headed for the elevator. Anvi went toward the exit, her expression one of shock, tears in her eyes.

Linden waited until Anvi had passed, feeling ridiculous about hiding behind a pillar. It wasn't her style. She'd never had a problem with confrontation. Her family would have pushed her into submission long ago if it were otherwise.

She walked toward the elevator, intending to catch Tripp on his way up. But then she spotted a phone on the rug. Someone had dropped it. Linden scooped up the device, noticing that the screen was open and unlocked.

She didn't mean to be nosy. But the text window was right there with Tripp's name at the top. *I've been thinking a lot about what you said. Can we talk more in person? I'm in the lobby.*

A flick of Linden's finger revealed more of the conversation, going back days. Weeks. *What happened yesterday in the office, it can't happen again.* But then later, *I dreamed about you last night.*

A few more clicks, and it was clear that the phone belonged to Anvi.

Linden jumped when she heard Tripp's voice behind her.

"Ready for dinner? I spoke to Richardson and the others. They're meeting us at the restaurant."

She slipped Anvi's phone into her pocket, turning around. Linden's face felt numb.

"Of course. Let's go."

THE SUNBEV EXECS hadn't arrived yet, so Linden and Tripp ordered drinks at the bar. Linden watched the bubbles pop in her glass of champagne. Tripp was more relaxed than he'd been in days. Unlike her or Penny, the accidents last night had barely ruffled him at all. He sipped his Grey Goose martini and smiled. The cuffs and collar of his blue shirt were stiff with starch. He'd worn the Tom Ford cologne Linden had bought for his last birthday.

"What's going on between you and Anvi?" Linden asked.

He choked on his martini, coughing so much his face turned red. She waited. She asked again, and this time she took Anvi's phone from her pocket and set it on the bar. She couldn't unlock it now that the screen had turned off, but he recognized it.

Tripp downed the rest of his martini, then raised a hand at the bartender to order another.

"It's not what you think."

"That's your opening salvo? A cliche?"

"Linden, listen to me. Anvi is a flirtatious girl. She kissed me

—once. I should've fired her right then, but I thought she could be an asset to Sterling. To *us*. She's a natural for this job. You can't deny that."

He was right. She couldn't deny Anvi's skills. Which were more varied than Linden had imagined. But Tripp was supposed to be the one in charge.

Linden set her glass on the bar, then dug a fifty-dollar bill from her wallet. "Thanks so much," she said to the bartender, and walked out of the restaurant.

Tripp caught up with her before she'd covered half a block. People were streaming in and out of Ashton's restaurants. Linden cut down a quieter side street, and Tripp followed.

"Listen," he said, "I let Anvi go today, just before I met up with you. She's been calling and texting me way too much. I told her that after Devil's Fest, she and Sterling PR will have to part ways. It's time for a change."

"'Time for a change,'" Linden parroted. "You know, I think I agree."

"I would never choose anyone over you. You must know that. With the SunBev account in place and the Dark Energy launch a success, we're in a much better position. We can cut the dead weight. It'll be you and me, like at the beginning."

She stopped, facing him. "Dead weight? Don't say you're talking about Penny."

His shirt had pulled loose from his jeans. Tripp tucked it back. "We don't need to have this conversation now. I understand how you feel about Penny. I really do. But she's just not working out. The Devil's Fest idea was solid, but her performance here hasn't reassured me. One good idea isn't enough."

Linden couldn't believe what she was hearing. After all Penny had done, all the work she'd put in to make Devil's Fest happen, Tripp was just going to cut her loose?

"Let's talk about this later," Tripp said. "After our dinner."

She looked over. They were being watched. Through a restaurant window, a man stared at her and Tripp, his cheeseburger motionless in his hands. She didn't know the guy. But suddenly she had an overwhelming sense of clarity, as if she were inside that restaurant, looking out at herself. *I'm better than this.*

"You can handle the dinner. If they ask, tell the SunBev execs I'm in Eden. Managing their festival."

She started back toward the inn, chin held high. Tripp let her go.

He obviously didn't love her. She wondered if her mother had seen this coming—the way she'd never invited Tripp to family gatherings, smiled patronizingly when Linden mentioned him.

No one can know about this, she thought. Maybe she'd lost Tripp, but damned if she'd lose her pride.

Penny was in trouble, though. Linden was still the junior partner. If Tripp really wanted Penny out, then Linden couldn't do a thing.

CHAPTER TWENTY-SEVEN

After her phone call with Linden, Penny went looking for Matthew. She found him in his hotel room. He said, "Come in!" when she knocked.

Matthew lay in his bed with the covers kicked aside. He had his eyes closed when she opened the door. His eyebrows raised when he saw her.

"Oh, hey. I thought you'd be your mom."

Penny stopped in the doorway. "My mom? That seems a little weird."

He sat up, rubbing his face. "She's been checking on me."

Penny went in, closing the door behind her. "How're you feeling?"

"Fine. But also tired of people asking me that. I was looking for you earlier, but I couldn't find you."

"I've just been dealing with festival stuff."

She decided not to tell Matthew about what Krista or her dad had said. Linden was right—more security guards would patrol the festival tonight, and even if ill-intentioned ghosts waited inside those buildings, nothing could happen if the festival-goers kept to authorized areas. Her sister could air her concerns on Twitter, for whatever that was worth, and then she'd calm down enough to see the holes in Scott's story.

Part of Penny wished she'd been able to do exactly what they wanted, and more—help Scott Mackey get his job back, right all the wrongs done in Eden. She couldn't, and that was a hard truth to accept.

But maybe she could do something for Matthew.

Penny was about to sit down next to him. But then, Matthew's room phone rang.

"Maybe *that's* your mom," he said.

She glanced at the caller ID. The area code was from out of state. "Only one way to solve this mystery."

He closed his eyes again. "You answer it. Tell them I'm asleep. Or in Siberia."

She picked up the handset. "Hello, Matthew's room. He's left the country."

It was someone named Kelsey Richardson. Penny was confused—and just a touch jealous that some woman was calling Matthew—but then Kelsey explained.

She was June's friend from Phoenix. She'd just gotten to town early that morning, already on her way last night when June fell from the balcony at the Paradise.

"I wanted to surprise her." Kelsey sounded like she was on the verge of tears. "And then I heard she was hurt. She told me about what Matthew did—how he tried to catch her. June's going to head back to Arizona as soon as they release her from the hospital. But I just wanted to say thank you. Since June doesn't feel up to it."

"Of course." Penny looked over at Matthew. He was already sitting up, reaching for the phone.

Penny sat on the bed and listened in while he spoke to Kelsey. June didn't want to talk to anyone. No wonder the nurses hadn't let Penny see her. Even Kelsey couldn't get an explanation for what happened last night—why June had been on the second floor of the hotel—but clearly, June was mortified about disrupting the festival. Matthew passed on his cell number in case June changed her mind and wanted to talk.

Penny stopped him before he hung up. "Could I say one more thing?"

She took the phone and said to Kelsey, "Hey, this is Penny Wright again. We're having that closing-night party tomorrow. If June doesn't feel well enough, I get it, but just tell her she's welcome. I hope she'll still come."

Kelsey sighed. "I really don't know. But I'll tell her."

Kelsey ended the call, and Penny replaced the handset. She and Matthew were quiet a moment. Penny thought about June, and how she wished she could understand what happened last night. But if June didn't want to open up, there was little else that Penny could do.

"Are you heading back up to Eden soon?" Matthew asked.

She folded her legs beneath her. "I have the night off. Actually, I had an idea. I want to do something for you, if you'll let me."

"For me?"

It wasn't Linden's suggestion that had convinced her. He'd been so supportive and helped her pull off this event, despite his personal feelings about it. Not to mention saving June, and therefore the rest of Devil's Fest. Though she would *not* show her appreciation through sexual favors, as much as Linden would enjoy getting those details tomorrow. And as much as it might be enjoyable for all parties involved.

Penny struggled to keep a straight face as these thoughts passed through her head.

"I know you don't like being called a hero," she said. "But at least let me try to even things out between us."

His expression told her she'd chosen the wrong words. "You don't owe me anything."

"Okay, then forget I said that. I want to do something for you because..." She glanced at the rug. "I care about you, and I want to spend time with you. But only if you feel up to it."

He seemed to mull this over. But then, a small smile betrayed him. "As long as you're gentle with me."

So his mind had gone there, too. She felt her cheeks color. "I was thinking about what you said earlier. Your mom? Seeing her in the house?"

He groaned, easing back against his pillow.

"I was hoping you might forget I said that. I didn't mean to drag you into it."

"But I'm already dragged, so you might as well let me help."

"Penny..."

"Please. I need this, too."

He looked up, meeting her eyes.

"You told me a few days ago, here in this room, that I could help people with my ability. I could do something good."

There had to be some reason that the universe made her this way. Something more than being a witness to suffering. If Matthew believed it was possible, then maybe she could believe it too.

"Besides," Penny added, "if you can move back into your house, then you'll be free of my mother."

"I really don't mind your mom. I get to eat Dora's cooking."

"Just come with me. Let me look around your house and see what I can see." Once they were there, he'd probably get over his hesitation.

He looked at her for several long seconds. Heat stirred inside of her. She was very aware they were sitting together on his bed. And now, after what Linden had said, she had all sorts of images playing out in her mind.

"I'll drive." She needed to get out of this room before she did something foolish.

He kicked his legs off the bed. "Okay, I'll come with you. But I'm not going in, so don't get your hopes up."

They pulled into Matthew's driveway. The sun was sinking; the second night of Devil's Fest would begin in just a few hours. Penny tried to put it out of her mind.

She put his truck in park and turned off the engine. Matthew made no move to leave.

"We'll have to get out of this car at some point," she said.

"You do. Or we can go back to the inn."

"At least walk me to the door."

She got out. His house was much as she remembered it. Ranch style, single story, built in the mid-century. The grass was neatly mowed, and petunias grew in the flower beds beneath the porch. Matthew's mom had planted them every year when spring came.

The car door slammed, and Matthew approached behind her.

"You have landscapers plant flowers?" she asked. "Even though you don't live here anymore?"

"I plant them. I don't go inside, but that doesn't mean I don't come here. I mow the lawn, keep the sprinklers going in the summer. I do what I can. I wouldn't want her to look out here and see...well, I want it to look the same."

"It does."

Matthew and his mom had lived here since he moved to Ashton in middle school. Penny had always enjoyed the contrast of Matthew's home with her own. The inn was a grand, sprawling place full of rich woods and dark brick. But Matthew's house was light and airy, full of windows. It had a stacked-stone front wall and a slanted roofline.

She took his left hand and together they walked up the steps. He was just standing there, so she unlocked the door. She stepped inside. No lights were on, but the home still had the airiness she'd loved. It didn't smell the way she remembered—Mrs. Larsen's curried chicken, the snickerdoodles that she always seemed to have on hand. This house smelled of cleaning fluid and emptiness.

Penny set about turning on lights. Everything was tidy, free of dust. In the great room, their family photos still decorated the top of the TV cabinet. Mrs. Larsen's basket of yarn and crotchet hooks sat by the couch.

Matthew was still standing on the porch.

"Want to try coming in?" She beckoned him.

But Matthew wiped his mouth and shook his head. He turned around on his heel and practically ran back to the truck. She thought about going after him.

Instead, she kept looking around. Getting a feel for things.

In the kitchen, Penny glanced through the cabinets. Their blue dishes sat on the shelves. She remembered eating cereal from those bowls on weekend afternoons. A few cans of soup and a stray box of crackers remained, but otherwise someone had cleaned out the pantry. The fridge was powered off, its door propped open to circulate air. The place truly felt deserted.

But Matthew had seen his mother's spirit here. Was she still in the house?

Penny walked out of the great room and entered the small hallway. The four doors were closed. She turned the knob on the first one and pushed. The door moved silently on its hinges, revealing a bathroom with the shower curtain pulled closed.

"Mrs. Larsen? Are you here?"

She didn't expect an answer, of course. But it felt good to say something aloud.

She moved to the next door. This one was Matthew's bedroom. She opened it and lingered in the doorway. The bed was neatly made, books stacked on the nightstand, game controllers beneath the TV. As if Matthew hadn't even left. Though she doubted he'd ever kept it this clean in high school. Pleasant memories passed over her: watching Matthew and Bryce play Mario Kart while she awaited her turn to challenge the winner. And the time when the Wii controller flew out of her hands and knocked over a bottle of Mountain Dew. They'd laughed so hard that Mrs. Larsen came into the room, wondering why they were screaming.

She'd sat on the floor, leaning her back against the bed when she was seventeen. That was after Bryce had left for college, and she and Matthew started spending more time alone. She'd wanted to kiss him so much it was physically painful. And now she knew, from what Matthew had said, he'd wanted the same thing.

Penny closed her eyes, leaning against the door frame, and she felt the shift. A movement in the air, as if someone had sighed. Her eyes flew open and she looked around, but still she was alone.

But perhaps less alone than she'd been before.

There was something disquieting about encountering the dead, regardless of how innocuous a spirit might be. But this house was nothing like Eden. Whatever Mrs. Larsen's reasons for lingering here, Penny knew there was no reason to be afraid. Instead, the longer she spent here, the more she relaxed. It felt like standing up straight after being hunched over for days.

She closed Matthew's door and went to the next room. This was Mrs. Larsen's bedroom. It seemed, like the other rooms, not to have been touched since she died.

Penny stepped inside and immediately felt the woman's presence. A sense of loss flooded into her. Yet still, the ghost did not appear.

Finally, Penny returned to the kitchen. The front door was still open, and Matthew paced outside on the grass. She tried to smile reassuringly, but she needed to stay focused. Mrs. Larsen was so close.

She placed her hands on the countertop and closed her eyes.

"I'm here," she said. "I'm listening."

She tried picturing Mrs. Larsen, but nothing much came. Instead, memories of Matthew surfaced in Penny's mind. The sweet way he'd offer her the last cookie in the sleeve, which Bryce never did. The times in high school that his eyes lingered on hers and she wondered if, just maybe, he was thinking the same thing she was. The way he giggled when they watched cartoons after school, even when they were both way too old to still watch cartoons.

She remembered one evening in particular. She had stood at this very counter with Matthew and his mom when they were cooking dinner. Bryce had been playing video games in Matthew's room. A pan of skirt steak and peppers had been sizzling on the stove, and Penny had been warming up the tortillas on the burner. Matthew and his mom had been laughing about something. Just a sweet moment between them. Penny had never met his dad—they moved to Ashton after the divorce, and Matthew's father had clearly been a sore subject. He lived somewhere in Montana and had a new wife, a couple of new kids. The few times he spoke of it, Matthew hadn't tried to hide the tears that gathered at the corners of his eyes.

This time, the shift in the air was more pronounced. She smelled cinnamon and butter, as real as if a batch of cookies were baking in the oven. She could actually feel the warmth.

Penny slowly turned around, and Mrs. Larsen stood there.

CHAPTER TWENTY-EIGHT

Mrs. Larsen was a small woman, her blond hair cut into a short bob. Smile lines creased the skin around her mouth. Despite the warmth of the room and the spices hanging in the air, the woman's sadness permeated straight into Penny's heart.

She was holding a piece of paper and worrying about Matthew. Her beloved son.

Penny kept the woman in her peripheral vision. She let the emotions wash over her, not trying to banish them, although it felt like a stranger's fingertips grazing the back of her neck. Even with someone as open and loving as Mrs. Larsen had always been.

As Penny watched, the woman crumpled up the paper and held it against her stomach.

He can never know.

"Mom?"

Matthew stood just inside the threshold of the house. The door was still open behind him, and the sky was turning the scarlet and orange of sunset.

"Can she...hear me?" Matthew asked.

Penny shook her head.

"Do you know what she's holding?" Penny asked. "That paper?"

"No. It wasn't like this before—the first time I saw her. She's clearer. Like she's..." His chin trembled. "Like she's really here."

He took a step closer, and the ghost began to fade.

"Just wait," Penny said in a soothing voice. "We need to be open. To listen. I'm worried if we let our own feelings intrude, we'll push her out of the room. Okay?"

Swallowing, Matthew nodded. Only their breathing was audible.

Penny had never done anything like this before, and she felt like a fraud. An imposter. But Matthew was counting on her. One look at his face, and it was obvious how much this meant. The bruises on his neck and the way he favored his shoulder made her want to reach out to him. Hold him and tell him everything was fine.

I love him so very much, Penny thought.

Then she realized—her own emotions were mixing up with Mrs. Larsen's. Which, when she thought about it, was pretty awkward. But Penny leaned into the feeling. This was her path to reaching Mrs. Larsen's ghost.

We both love him, Penny thought. *Why are you so worried about him?*

Mrs. Larsen's spirit began, slowly, to react. Not consciously. It was more like a piece of fabric reacting to a change in the wind —twisting, unfolding, revealing more of itself.

Penny held her breath. She kept her entire body still. She didn't want to do anything that might jeopardize this moment.

"Matthew," Penny whispered. "Come here. Please. But slowly."

His expression grew alarmed, but he did as she asked. He edged toward the kitchen. When he was close enough, Penny reached out her hand. He hesitated, and she said, "I'm still me. She doesn't know we're here, not really. Don't be afraid."

His hand slid into hers.

Mrs. Larsen stood beside him holding the letter, crumpling it up, the same motions repeating again and again.

"The letter's from your father," Penny murmured.

"My dad never wrote me. I haven't heard from him in...years. Fifteen years." The anger in Matthew's voice was palpable, and Mrs. Larsen's spirit reacted, her motions increasing in speed.

I don't want him to know.

"He did write you," Penny said. "When you were in high school. He wrote you dozens of times. He..." She let the ghost's memories flow through her. "He emailed, and she deleted the messages. He wrote, and she threw the letters away. She blocked his phone number."

"That's not possible. Why would she do something like that?"

I can't lose him. Not my son. He'll take Matthew and I'll be alone.

"She was afraid."

"She wouldn't have lied to me." Matthew pulled his hand away. He walked to the other side of the kitchen, leaning against a counter, and stared at the ghost of his mother.

"She blamed herself for your dad leaving," Penny said, "and she was guilty enough about that. But when he tried to reconnect, she was so afraid you'd choose him instead."

Matthew roughly wiped at his eyes. "I wouldn't have done that. Ever. When she got sick, I stayed with her and took care of her. I gave up so much..."

The image of Mrs. Larsen had stopped its endless cycle of motion. But the letter remained in her hands.

"Exactly," Penny said, "that's just it. She feels guilty. You had to give up so much because of her—a relationship with your father, going away to school."

"I did it because I *loved* her."

"Then tell her. She can't hear us exactly. But she'll feel it. She'll know."

Matthew took Penny's outstretched hand, then the other. He closed his eyes. Penny closed hers too. She could feel the spirit beside her, still fearful but calming. They were getting through, a bridge forming between the living and the dead.

"I love you, Mom. I never blamed you. Ever. If you kept things from me, I understand. And I forgive you. I forgive you."

The warmth in the room rose. Sweat rolled down Penny's back. She gasped as she felt something moving through her—one last wave of intense emotion, a mother's love for her son.

When she opened her eyes, Mrs. Larsen had vanished. Matthew still had his eyes squeezed shut, and tears streaked down his cheeks.

Penny pulled him into a hug. "She knows. She's gone."

CHAPTER TWENTY-NINE

THE SECOND NIGHT OF DEVIL'S FEST WAS JUST BEGINNING. The music echoed through the canyon, and the spotlights—green and blue and purple—swept across the clouds. Anvi watched from the steps of the trailer. She took another puff of her joint, held the smoke in as long as she could, and then exhaled it toward the sky.

By her feet, the radio chirped. Voices bantered about needing more toilet paper in the port-a-potties. Then about a scuffle that had broken out near the stage; security cleared it. Anvi didn't bother to reply to any of it. Linden was around somewhere; she could handle it. Or not. Anvi didn't give one single shit about what happened at Devil's Fest tonight.

This just isn't working, Tripp had said. *You should start focusing on other opportunities.*

Tripp hadn't even asked how she was doing. She'd been the one to find Scott last night, wrapped up in those cords. His face turning blue. She'd never meant to lead Scott on; she hadn't even seen the text messages till long after he'd wanted to meet. She'd barely paid him attention. All she could think about was Tripp. How he'd really seemed to notice her lately. His hints that they could be more.

There'd been the kiss after a work dinner, which led to rushed sex in the men's room at the office. She'd felt confused. He was her boss. She wasn't stupid; she knew about the uneven power dynamic. Workplace harassment, etc, etc. But when Tripp Sterling paid attention to her, she felt like she mattered. Like he *saw* her.

Tripp pulled away in the days afterward, saying it wasn't a good idea. Which was true. But then he'd start flirting with her again, staring into her eyes like he couldn't stop thinking about her.

She wished she'd hooked up with Scott last night. Then at least he wouldn't have gotten drunk and high and hurt himself. At least she could feel like *somebody* had really wanted her.

Yesterday, she'd been so close to having everything. And now it was just...gone.

She smoked until she singed her fingers. The butt dropped to the ground, then got crushed beneath her shoe. The bad feelings were more distant, floating away on those light-splattered clouds. The beat of the music vibrated inside of her. Boom, boom. Like a giant heart. Someone else's heart, whole and vital.

She wanted to be a part of that.

Anvi got up and walked toward the festival. When she reached the side gate—authorized access only—she flashed her lanyard. She cut between buildings to reach Main Street, where she joined the flood of people. She let them carry her, a boat traveling with the waves.

For a while, she drifted. She took out her phone and captured a video, watching the crowd around her through the screen.

But the music grew louder. So loud she couldn't think. The smells of sweat and onions and something metallic—like ozone —filled her nose. Someone bumped into her; an elbow slammed into her side. She didn't like this anymore. They were hurting her.

Anvi pushed her way through the crowd. Finally, she could breathe again. Move.

She was standing beside the bank building, right near the stage. Security guards stood nearby, watching everyone warily. A guard told her to step back and then left her alone when he saw the lanyard.

Scott had nearly died here.

Last night, she'd gone through the bank's doors behind the stage. She had a set of keys. She'd called for help on the radio when she found him. Now, her hand went to her side, but her radio wasn't there. She must've dropped it somewhere on Main Street. Just like she'd lost her private Android phone earlier that day—not that she needed it to text Tripp anymore.

She hadn't called her grandpa in days. But what did she have to report? Nothing to be proud of.

Linden would be angry that she'd lost the radio. But Linden could kiss her ass. Linden clearly had a thing for Tripp. But he didn't care about anyone, really. Except himself. That bastard.

He used me, she thought.

Used her for information about what was going on in the office, about Penny and the prep work for Devil's Fest. Tripp wouldn't even know about Penny's history or her "ghost seeing" if not for Anvi. And then Tripp used that information—and Anvi's social media contacts—to make Devil's Fest go viral. But did he give her a single ounce of credit?

Should've been Tripp who got hurt, she thought. Not poor June from SunBev. Not Scott.

After he could talk, Scott had said there'd been someone in the bank with him. Someone who'd whispered things. She had figured he'd been wasted. But what if he wasn't? What if there really was something extraordinary in this town, despite the stupid, pointless festival they were hosting?

Maybe she should've read the rest of *A Devil in Eden*. Could be interesting to know how it had ended.

She went around the rear of the bank, where another security guard was patrolling. He glanced at her. She pretended to be official, looking around like she needed to check things out.

"Looks secure," she said. "Go check the concessions? I'll stay here." Had she sounded strange? Did he notice? But the guard just nodded and walked away.

There was a patch of darkness along the wall, sheltered by overgrown weeds. She just wanted to sit someplace that nobody could find her. When the guard was far away, Anvi slipped closer to the bank building. She pulled some grass stalks and lay them on the ground, creating a seat. That was better. She sat in the shadows, her back against the bricks. Soon, she was drifting off.

There was a voice in her dream. A whisper.

It said, *We can make sure he doesn't hurt anyone. Ever again.*

WHEN WE PASSED ONE OF THE OLD SALOONS—ONCE painted blue with the swinging doors you see in old western movies—Penny stopped, a drooping carnation still in her hand. She looked up at a second-floor window. It was an empty frame, no glass.

"What do you see, hun?" I asked her.

"Someone's up there."

My chest tightened. But I saw nothing in the window, not even a shadow. "What do they look like?"

Debbie and Helen edged closer to Penny. I waved a hand, warning them to stay back. I didn't want to break Penny's concentration. Her expression was placid and curious. Unafraid.

"It's a man. He's worried. He's looking for...the bad people."

She knew about "bad guys" and "good guys," a childish understanding that didn't convey the cruelty that real life humans could be capable of. But I hadn't told her about Marian or her gang, nor the specifics of the Devil's Night Massacre.

Penny shrugged, skipping off again. "There's other people watching too."

-from A DEVIL IN EDEN by Lawrence Wright

DEVIL'S NIGHT - 1894

"Take the rope." She could barely speak. Fitzhammer's weight pulled her arms up over her head. In another moment, she'd drop him.

"But Marian, I think he's already dead, why—"

"Just *take him*, Tim, so help me."

Tim came forward. She screamed as the ropes unwound from her hands. The fibers were slicked with her blood. Marian staggered, nearly too weak to keep standing. But she couldn't rest yet.

"Tie him up there," she said.

Again, Tim protested. But she wanted to leave Fitzhammer swinging in indignity, for all to see. That was all he deserved.

Douglas watched with disgust written across his face. He disappointed her. This vengeance wasn't only hers. But if Douglas needed her to take the moral burden to ease his own conscience, so be it.

The crying of the maid and the cook had become a constant background prattle. Marian continued to ignore it. She bore them no ill will; she simply could not think of them just now.

The room was spinning.

"You best sit down," Douglas said. "You look like you'll swoon any second."

Marian braced a hand against the dining room wall. Red fingerprints marked the wallpaper. "Show me the safe."

Douglas rubbed his palm over his face. His skin was ashen. "Very well."

First, he made her wrap her hands. She used strips of cloth torn from her discarded dress. Then he took her to a room lined with bookshelves. In the doorway, he stopped.

"I did not come here to be an executioner," Douglas said. "You told him he'd go free."

Marian's heart was still burning with vengeance, but she was too weak to manage more than a murmur. "I don't pretend to understand your suffering. Don't presume to know mine."

She heard a cry. The noise was so close, yet also a distant phantom that echoed in her soul. Her child had never cried. Never had the chance.

"The cook said this room is haunted," Douglas whispered.

"So you hear it too?"

Such sounds had haunted her before. If Douglas hadn't heard the cry, Marian would have thought that the noise belonged solely to her tortured imagination.

The ghostly voice shrieked again before it ceased.

"This building is cursed, or so the cook told me," Douglas said. "And I'd rather not become another of its specters, if it's all the same to you. We should hurry."

He gestured at the bookshelves. These were Fitzhammer's records, Marian assumed. Several of the books had been removed from a shelf, and a tiny door was cracked open in the wall.

Douglas swung the safe door wide and began rifling through the contents.

Marian was coming back to herself. Fitzhammer had paid for his sins. Now, she had to finish this. Self-murder had never been her intent. She might've entertained such desperate wishes in the past, but Marian had survived this long. She would keep on, if only because survival was all she really knew.

Douglas turned to her. "This cain't be right."

"Don't say 'cain't.'"

"Marian, *listen*. There's no money here." He pulled out handfuls of documents, letting them scatter onto the floor. Marian grabbed for them. They had legal words on them. Contracts, deeds. Papers of value, but not to her. No gold. No fortune.

Fitzhammer had tricked her. Even in death.

From somewhere else in the hotel, there came the sound of gunshots.

IT HADN'T BEEN difficult for Bart to round up a posse.

He and the barkeep rode straight to the Pretty Eyes Saloon, where Bart hoped to find men both sober and restless enough to join in their fight.

The saloon was a sad sight, nearly empty, almost everybody there passed out drunk. They'd heard gunshots over at the Paradise Hotel, and a few had gone to investigate. But they weren't about to risk their necks for Fitzhammer or his fancy friends. So they decided not to get involved in whatever was happening over there. The town wasn't too fond of Fitzhammer, as a rule. He was notorious for stiffing men their wages.

"It's just three of them: a woman, a tall, quiet fellow, and a puny kid," Bart explained. "They caught me unawares, shot me in the damn leg. But they're no match for all of us."

The barkeep pulled out a revolver from behind the counter. He handed it, butt first, to Bart. Bart wasn't happy about using another man's weapon, but that she-devil had taken his.

"I don't believe you," one man said—an Irishman named O'Connor. He slurred all his words. Bart wasn't sure if it was the harelip, or the rye whiskey. "A woman?"

"An evil woman." Bart told them about Marian, how she was

sired by a whore, how she slithered her way into Fitzhammer's household intent on seduction. "I took pity on her myself. Shoulda killed her when I got the chance."

The barkeep frowned at that. "I don't much favor killin' women."

Bart inspected the revolver's chamber and mechanisms. It was no Peacemaker, but it was not a poor weapon. It would do. "Then you'll be the first she sends to hell. She ain't natural, this one. Wicked, through and through."

After a couple more shots of rye—for fortification—the men made their way to the Paradise Hotel.

Bart made a wide loop around the building's perimeter. The curtains were drawn, and the doors were locked. There didn't seem to be anyone watching from the upstairs windows. Bart dashed closer, pressing his back against the brick. When he neared one of the dining-room windows, he heard voices.

Through a crack between the curtains, an awful tableau met Bart's eyes.

Fitzhammer was dead, swinging by the neck from the chandelier.

"God damn." He looked away, though the horrid sight had singed into his memory. So Marian had really done it. But did they find the key? Through squinted eyes, he looked again.

No. He could still see the chain between the folds of Fitz's shirt.

There was one man guarding the remaining prisoners—the scrawny kid with the sparse beard. That one could shoot, though. Bart's leg throbbed a reminder.

Marian was somewhere else in the hotel. Looking for Fitz's money, perhaps? If she found the safe, she'd get a nice surprise.

Bart ran back to where the others were waiting. "We'll go in from the back."

A few swift kicks from O'Connor, and the back door's lock was in pieces. There were shouts from inside.

"Go!" Bart said, pushing the other men ahead. "Before they have time to react."

One of O'Connor's friends went first, screaming and firing his weapon. An amateur. Marian's skinny friend took him down right quick. Caught him in the chest—blood spurted on the kitchen walls. Bart shivered in disgust, watching the man's body fall. O'Connor went next, faring better. He crouched by the dining-room door, avoiding the shot. He returned fire, laying down cover.

"That way," Bart told the barkeep. "Find the woman." He pointed at the hallway off the kitchen, which led to several rooms and a back stairway.

"You too!" Bart said to O'Connor. Keeping his body low, O'Connor followed the barkeep into the hallway.

Bart waited with his back against the stove. Now it was just him and Skinny. His ears were ringing, but he could still hear the womanly cries coming from the dining room. The other prisoners. Bart wished they'd shut up. He had to concentrate.

Gunshots rang out in the hallway where O'Connor and the barkeep had gone. Then more yells. Bart's nerves jumped, but he forced himself still. He kept one eye on the hallway, one on the dining room entrance.

Bart saw a brief flash of movement—Skinny was in the doorway, his gun wheeling in Bart's direction. Bart got off the first shot. Wide. A cabinet erupted in splinters. *Damn.* He ducked as Skinny's gun flashed. The sound of the bullet against metal was deafening—it had hit the stove's chimney. Bellowing, Bart charged at the man. He hit Skinny's middle, throwing him up against the wall.

They struggled for a moment. Then Bart held his revolver to the man's chest. Skinny's hands opened. His gun dropped.

"I surrender," Skinny said.

Bart fired.

Skinny's eyes bulged. His body slid to the floor, leaving a

smear of blood down the wall. Bart cringed away from it. The blood was on his clothes, too. He felt faint.

The others were still firing in the hallway. Bart had to hurry. He limped into the dining room. Sticky wetness ran down his calf again—that blasted wound had started up.

Fitzhammer was listing to and fro from his rope. Bart tried not to look.

"Oh, thank Heaven. Bart!" It was the cook. She and Helga, the maid, were tied up in a corner. They both looked terrified, yet relieved to see Bart here. Though Helga a little less so. She'd had the misfortune of meeting him alone at night a time or two.

The cook held up her bound hands. "Hurry!"

You're right about that, he thought. *I've no time for this tomfoolery.* And he didn't need witnesses, either. He glanced quickly behind him. O'Connor and the barkeep hadn't returned.

Bart shot the cook between the eyes. Helga screamed, holding out her hands and trying to turn away. She took the shot just above the ear, slumping over the cook.

The silvery bit of chain still peeked from beneath Fitzhammer's vest. Bart grabbed the chain and pulled. It snapped easily, and he stuffed the chain—and its charm, the all-important key—into his pocket.

Just before leaving the dining room, he leaned into a corner and vomited.

Then he went back to the kitchen, wiping his mouth, and stood listening at the entrance to the hallway.

PENNY WAS BREATHING HARD. SHE WHISPERED, "I HEAR her, Daddy. She's in there. She's angry."

"Who?" I went closer and knelt beside her. "Penny, who do you hear?"

Suddenly, Penny screamed and pulled her hand away from the bank's doors. In that same instant, one door burst open, throwing Penny backward into the dusty street. I scrambled after her. Debbie and Helen ran from the other direction, all of us converging on Penny.

"What happened?"

"Are you all right?"

"Daddy, she's mad," Penny said again. "She saw us. She knows we're here."

Debbie gasped. "But you said—"

"Honey," I interrupted, "you told us before that the ghosts are confused. They can't see us."

"But she can. Marian can."

-from A DEVIL IN EDEN by Lawrence Wright

CHAPTER THIRTY
2019

As night fell, Penny and Matthew both decided not to go back to the inn. Matthew went room by room, picking up objects and setting them down, trying to reorient himself into his old life. He'd forgotten how good he felt in this house. Penny asked if he'd rather be alone, but he asked her to stay. He *needed* her to stay. To emphasize the point, Matthew took her hand as he continued to walk through the house. But he didn't mention his mother or the extraordinary things they'd just experienced.

Eventually they went back to the kitchen. Matthew ordered pizza, and he found a forgotten bottle of red wine in a cabinet—for Penny, not for himself. But he didn't open it yet. Instead, he put a hand on the counter where his mother's spirit had been standing.

"Do you think she's gone now? For good?"

"I think so," Penny replied. "There was this sense of peace about her right before she disappeared. She understood how you felt. I'm sure of it."

Matthew nodded, looking around the room. "I miss her. But I'm relieved that she can rest."

Penny ran her fingers down his arm—the one that wasn't injured. It nearly undid him when she touched him like that.

"Will you call your father, do you think?" she asked.

He started pulling the foil from the wine bottle. "After all this time, it's hard to know what to say. But now that I know he tried to contact me...I guess I might."

He'd given up so long ago on having any relationship with his father. The rejection had hurt more than anything in his life. Even more than losing Penny. For years, he'd tried not to think of his dad or his half-siblings at all—a boy and a girl. He'd seen pictures of them on the internet, during one of those really dark moments of wallowing. His dad had a new family and had washed his hands of Matthew, as if he'd never existed. It had made him feel worthless and, at the same time, fiercely protective of his mom. He was well aware of all he'd sacrificed to take care of her. But not for one second did he resent his mother for it.

But now? This new information about his mom was difficult to process. She'd lied to him. But Matthew understood why she'd done it. For his dad to suddenly contact him as a teenager, after being absent from his life for years by that point—it wasn't really fair. Maybe his mom worried that Matthew would be so starved for his dad's affection that he'd forgive too easily. As a man, Matthew couldn't imagine doing that. Even setting aside the efforts at contact, his dad didn't really deserve his forgiveness or his unconditional love.

Then it hit him—the truth of what he, Matthew, had done to Penny. He had let her go and hadn't even tried to talk to her for years. *Years.* Just like his father had done to him.

Matthew's hands had frozen on the wine bottle. He'd forgotten what he was doing.

"Let me get that," Penny said, and took the bottle from his hands. She worked the corkscrew into the top and began twisting it free. Matthew watched her. Penny's eyes were down, her eyelashes splayed, her mouth barely open. God, he wanted to kiss her.

She did this for me, he thought. *I'm home again because of her.*

Matthew found two glasses. They were slightly dusty, so he rinsed them in the sink. Penny poured herself some wine, and got Matthew a glass of water. The pizza arrived—mushroom, bell pepper and tomato, Penny's choice—and they ate right there at the kitchen counter. After, they piled their plates in the sink and took their glasses to the living room. They sat on the couch, facing one another, their knees touching. Matthew's stomach was warming, and the house was taking on a pleasant, nighttime glow. Every minute he'd look around, realizing that his mom was really gone and that his old life would never come back. Yet when his gaze returned to Penny, all felt right.

Just the lamp by the couch was on. Penny's wine glittered as it moved in her glass. The rest of the room seemed soft, but Penny was in sharp relief. The freckles that dusted her cheeks. The wisps of hair that curled at her forehead. He needed to touch her. He let his fingers graze her leg.

"I'm sorry I stopped writing back to you," he said. "I acted like my dad and you have no idea..." The words caught in his throat. "No idea how ashamed I am to realize that."

She put a cool hand on his cheek. "Tonight's about good memories only. Okay? We have plenty."

They did have good memories. But that wasn't enough anymore.

He took her hand, threading their fingers together. He remembered the softness of her lips when they'd kissed all those years ago, how she tasted of whiskey. She was beautiful then, and he'd thought he could never want anyone so much. But Penny when she was grown—she made him desperate.

Matthew brought his hand to her face. She leaned her cheek into his palm. She was looking at his mouth.

He'd waited six long years to kiss her again, and the thought of waiting a single moment more was impossible. He drew her closer and caught her lips with his. Her mouth opened to him, and she tilted her head, deepening the connection. They didn't rush. This wasn't a stolen moment in a forbidden place. Yet this kiss was more reckless than their first, because he was old enough to know better. She could break his heart, like Bryce said, but he had to take the risk. His head hurt and the room spun, and he didn't want any of it to stop.

But the last time, he hadn't told her how he really felt. He didn't want to make that mistake again.

When they paused to catch their breaths, he said, "I do want you to move back to Ashton. I know that's a lot to ask. But I don't want you to do it for me. Do it because you belong here. Isn't that what Devil's Fest is really about? You coming home?"

Her eyes widened. But she was listening.

"You can connect with ghosts," he went on. "Do you know how incredible that is? And it's part of who you are. You said to me this morning that you wanted to find the good in your ability. You have. Right?"

"Maybe." She'd whispered the word. Her lips were pink and swollen. He almost kissed her again, but there was more he needed to say.

"You could help other people. The way you helped me."

Penny stood up—he was instantly colder—and she downed the contents of her wineglass. "You don't understand what you're asking. I don't want to leave Sterling. Besides, 'ghost hunter' is not a practical career choice."

"But there must be some way to—"

"I don't want to discuss this," she snapped.

"Okay." He sighed, putting his hand over his eyes. "I overstepped. Can we go back to a few minutes ago?"

This conversation had veered in the wrong direction, and he didn't know how to get it back on track. He'd just been kissing her. He'd been trying to work up to telling her that he loved her. Why hadn't he done that—or better yet, shut up instead?

Because she'd helped him get back here, where he belonged, and he'd wanted to do the same for her.

"I'm really tired," she said, "and I'm sure you are too." She set the empty glass on the table. "Should I go back to the inn? Or—

am I supposed to check on you, make sure your head is still okay?"

"My head's fine. Just fuzzy. But stay anyway. It's late." He got up. "We have the spare room. I'll get sheets from the linen closet. Pretty sure my mom had a box of extra toothbrushes in there, too."

"I've got it. Thank you. I'll see you in the morning." She kissed him on the cheek, averting her eyes, and then she disappeared into the hall.

Matthew sat back down on the couch.

He picked up his wine and took another sip. So he could finally come back home, after all this time. But why? What was the point?

He'd been okay before Penny came back. Living at the inn, hanging with Bryce's family on the weekends. He'd had just enough to tell himself he was satisfied. Now, after a few days with her back in his life, he realized he'd just been pretending.

CHAPTER THIRTY-ONE

"Anvi?"

The trailer door slapped shut as Linden stepped inside. But Anvi wasn't here. Linden had already tried the radio, and though several security guards answered, they hadn't seen Anvi in over an hour.

Linden was still pissed off that Anvi had been sneaking around with Tripp. But she was torn between anger at Tripp—completely justified—and anger at Anvi, which wasn't as fair. Linden's own relationship with Tripp had never been appropriate. Even worse, her feelings for him had blinded her to what was really happening in that office. Tripp never should've put Anvi into that position.

But had Anvi and Tripp talked about Linden behind her back? Laughed that she was so easily fooled? She couldn't stand the thought of it.

Linden kicked the side of her bunk, which only scuffed her boot and made her toes sore. On the little counter beside her, a canvas tote bag tipped over, its contents rolling onto the floor. Bottles of sunblock and bug spray. A couple of booster cans of supplemental oxygen, though she'd been fine with the altitude. There was a little can of bear spray, too, something she'd bought at the inn, thinking it was a mildly funny souvenir. According to Penny, bears weren't likely to be visiting this canyon. But Linden couldn't resist that snarling bear on the side. It had reminded her of Tripp, his beard that he let grow a bit too long. How his whiskers tickled her neck when he kissed her ear.

She didn't bother picking up the bottles. Instead, she went back outside, walking a circle around their travel trailer. They'd parked about half a mile from the central Eden site, among a few ruined cabins that once lay on the outskirts of the town. The festival was over for the night. Two down, one to go.

For so long, she'd assumed her life would only get better. She adored going to work every day in their gorgeous Santa Monica building, just off Main and Ashland, a short stroll to Ocean View Park. There were so many things she loved about LA: the year-round flowers; the breezes off the ocean in the mornings; the perpetual yellow sun that bathed everything, even the ugliness, in light. In LA, she felt like she lived in the center of the universe. Well, New York had its attractions too, but that wan blue light made her feel anemic. Linden had never wanted to live anywhere but Southern California, and she still didn't.

Yet this trip to Colorado had exposed the parts of her life that she hadn't wanted to see.

Tripp had been good to her some of the time. In the past, she'd fought to get what she wanted, and she'd assumed that Tripp wouldn't be any different. But maybe, all this time, he'd been playing her. Getting what he could before he moved on to something else. Someone else.

The shuttles rumbled on their way out of the canyon, taking the last few guests back to their offsite campgrounds and hotels for the night. Through the radio, she listened to the security guards do their last rounds and give the all clear. But still, no one had seen Anvi.

Had she gone back to Ashton on one of the shuttles? Did Tripp call her after Linden bailed on him? Were they together right now? That shouldn't have stung so much, but it did.

Linden went back into the trailer. It was too late to catch a ride back to Ashton—nor did she want to. The only reason she'd booked a room in town was Tripp.

She grabbed her laptop, sat on her bunk, and pulled up her flight info. Tomorrow would be the last day of Devil's Fest, and she was scheduled to stick around for a couple of days after. But maybe she could move the flight earlier. She'd drive to the airport by herself if Penny wasn't ready.

There was a noise outside. A brief snippet of radio chatter. Her radio was on the counter, switched off. Somebody was out there—probably Anvi. Finally. Linden had locked the door, but Anvi had a key.

There was a loud knock. Linden jumped slightly.

"Anvi?" she said.

"Hello?" was the response. But that wasn't Anvi. It was a male voice.

She glanced down at the can of bear spray. After a half second of hesitation, she pocketed the spray and went to the door.

"Who is it?"

"It's me. Deputy Castillo?"

She exhaled, rolling her eyes at herself. Just Deputy Ray. He was moonlighting tonight on their security detail. She flipped the lock and pushed open the door.

"What can I do for you?"

The light from inside the trailer shone onto the ground. Deputy Ray came closer. He wasn't wearing his sheriff's deputy uniform tonight, but rather a windbreaker that said SECURITY in yellow letters at the breast.

"I just wanted to check on you before I took off for the night. Did Anvi turn up?"

"Not yet."

"Huh. I'll spread the word in Ashton. Maybe she forgot to check in with the shuttle driver." That was their procedure, so nobody got left accidentally in Eden.

"That's what I thought." Linden nodded like this made perfect sense, though she was reeling. Were Anvi and Tripp together right now?

"But anyway," Deputy Ray said, "I wanted to make sure you're secure here. Honestly, I don't think it's a great idea being here alone. Some of those people at the festival—they get pretty worked up."

"I appreciate that, but I'm completely fine. I was about to head to bed. Thanks for checking on me."

"No problem. There's something else, too. Unofficial, but the sheriff's office got that forensic report. I tried to catch up with Penny today, but she was busy. I don't blame her, all that stuff with Scott and that other woman last night. Really terrible. Penny's sister was really upset. But anyway, did you want to hear about the report?"

That skeleton. Linden didn't care. "I'm sorry, Deputy, but I'm exhausted. I'm sure Penny will be in touch tomorrow. Good night." Hopefully, Penny was having some fun right now. Maybe she'd finally get Matthew in bed and out of her system. There certainly wasn't much else to look forward to—for Penny or Linden—once they returned to LA.

He seemed disappointed. "Okay. Night." Deputy Castillo started walking away, heading back to the parking lot.

Linden let the door slam shut. She dug around the cabinets until she found a bottle of white wine, one with a screw top. She was about to find a glass, but then muttered, "To hell with it."

She unscrewed the cap, put it to her lips, and drank.

Things went a bit downhill from there. The same self-defeating thoughts kept swirling in her mind, images of Tripp and Anvi together in his hotel room. She landed heavily on her bunk. A sound came out of her—a heaving, heartbroken sob—and it wasn't like anything she'd ever uttered before. Linden did not fall apart this way. She was above such maudlin antics.

Once again, there was a noise outside. Like a boot scraping in the dirt that surrounded the trailer.

"Shit." She wiped at her face, forcing the tears to stop. Had Ray heard her? Had he come running back to check on her again? God, this was mortifying. She started inventing excuses as she went to the trailer door. But when she opened it, Ray wasn't there. She didn't see anybody.

But she could feel someone watching her. Somebody was out there in the dark.

"Who's there?" she asked. "Ray? Anvi?"

There was no answer in words. But she could hear breathing. She grabbed the bear spray from her pocket and held it out. She'd had enough. She wouldn't let anyone treat her this way. In the heightened energy of that moment, she realized exactly how to deal with Tripp—she and Penny would start their own firm. Screw the Sterling partnership agreement. Nobody, not even Tripp Sterling, was going to brush them aside.

"I can hear you," she yelled. "You'd better show yourself or get the hell out of here."

Linden stomped out. She realized she was still holding the white wine bottle. She took a drink as she aimed the bear spray into the dark.

"Whoever's out here, you better run. I mean it. I'm armed."

She walked farther out, her boots crushing the dried-out grass. Then she spun around. Someone was behind her. She'd felt it—a presence, the moving of a shadow.

"Show yourself."

She added a few choice swear words, but there was no answer. She was panting, the wine bottle clenched in her left hand, bear spray in the other.

For endless seconds, nothing happened.

Then she heard footsteps in the brush. Coming at her. Fast.

She forgot the bear spray. Forgot everything. She dropped what she was holding and ran.

CHAPTER THIRTY-TWO

Penny lay awake, staring at the ceiling of the Larsens' spare room. She couldn't stop thinking about her conversation with Matthew. It hadn't been an argument, exactly, but neither of them had been happy.

But that kiss...she touched her lips.

Her stomach was burning, and she doubted it was the red wine.

Matthew wanted her to "help people" with her ability. She now realized that might be possible. Maybe, somehow, she could stay herself and also be the medium her dad described in his book. But what would that even look like? She'd hire herself out as a psychic for money? Go searching for ghosts every day, letting them take up residence in her mind? Sharing in their sorrows and regrets that could never be remedied? She didn't want that to be her life.

She couldn't be the person that Matthew wanted her to be.

Her phone buzzed. She rolled over and picked it up. Matthew had just texted.

Hey Penn, forgot to tell you. Ray was looking for you earlier. Some news about the skeleton you found. Sorry, distracted. Blame it on the concussion. Milking that excuse for all it's worth. Thank you again.

"Oh, Matthew," she whispered at her phone.

She wanted to know Ray's news, at the very least because she was curious. From what she could tell, the festival's second night had gone smoothly. Thank goodness. But at this moment, her biggest concern wasn't Devil's Fest or Eden.

She hated that Matthew had been so isolated from his father and his siblings these past years. Penny had been mostly alone, too, in all the ways that counted. She had Linden, some casual friends, her colleagues at work. There'd been a few Tinder hookups that Penny wasn't proud of. A boyfriend or two. But all that time, the one person who mattered most had been missing from her life.

She could've told him that. Instead, she'd stomped off, acting petulant, as if he'd done something unforgivable by voicing his opinion.

She couldn't stop thinking about that kiss. *Feeling* it. She'd never wanted anyone more than she wanted Matthew—both then, and now.

He was obviously awake, like her. Right across the hall. And for the first time, they were completely alone—together. *This is probably a bad idea*, she told herself, even as she was kicking off the covers.

His door was cracked, and the light was on. Still, she knocked softly.

"Matthew?" she whispered.

"Yeah?"

She pushed open the door. He sat on the edge of his bed wearing an old pair of sweats and a tee, both emblazoned with "Ashton High Eagles, Class of '10." His injured arm was still in the sling.

"Can I come in?"

His eyes traced over her. She wore one of his old t-shirts—it said "Project Prom" in bubble letters—which she'd found in a drawer. Her legs were bare.

"Unless you're tired?" she added.

"I'm not tired."

That wasn't exactly an invitation. But she walked into the room, keenly aware of her body, the distance between them.

"I'm sorry I got upset earlier," she said.

"No, I shouldn't have pushed you about the ghost stuff. I just thought..."

"It's okay." She didn't want to talk about ghosts anymore. Though her own past haunted her. Everywhere she looked, she saw the life that she hadn't known she missed. Penny touched the books on his shelf. Ran her fingers over his old clothes, hanging in the closet.

She turned around, and Matthew was still watching her intently. He scooted back on the bed, leaning against the headboard.

"I think you outgrew those." She pointed at the several inches of ankle that his sweats didn't cover. The shirt was tight across his chest. Her pulse increased.

He looked down, smiling. "I guess it's been a while."

She'd been here earlier without him, and already the room felt more lived-in. The place smelled like him, the way it used to. Never in her life had she been in this room at night. Wearing not much more than his old t-shirt, no less. This was the stuff of her teenage fantasies.

"Your room looks pretty much the same," she said. "Too bad we couldn't read each other's minds back then."

"I used to think about you here. All the time. I imagined us together." His voice was dreamy, his eyes closed.

Her heart rattled her ribcage.

"I thought about you, too. I still think about you."

Those blue eyes opened, fixed on her. Her heart raced, the beats so fast they blurred together.

She sat beside him. Leaned in; she couldn't help herself. Their lips met. He sat up, returned the kiss and intensified it. The stubble on his chin scratched her palm. This was why she'd come in here. Not to talk. *Definitely* not to think.

Then Matthew pulled back, breathing hard. His gaze swept over her. It held the same heat that she remembered from six years ago, and from the living room that evening. But she saw indecision, too.

"What are we doing?" he asked softly.

"I have no idea. You're probably supposed to be resting." She started to get up. He held her wrist.

"I want this to happen, believe me. But I need to know what it means." He ran a fingertip along her arm, setting off waves of tingles across her skin.

"Penn, I've loved you maybe since the day we first met as kids. I never stopped. But if you don't feel the same way I do, just tell me. I can take it."

She put her hand on his chest. His heart thumped in time with hers. He seemed to be holding his breath.

"I've fallen in love with you so many times, I lost count," she said. "I've never loved anyone but you."

He leaned forward to kiss her again, but she stood up and backed away. Heat rose from her skin, her whole body heavy and aching with desire, but she didn't want him to misunderstand.

"I'm not moving to Ashton, though. It's just not going to happen."

"Okay. Then I could...try moving to LA." He sounded hesitant. Like he'd only come up with the idea a second ago.

She laughed without a trace of humor. "You don't want to move to LA. Your friends are here, your job. You just got back into your house."

"You're not even giving the idea a chance?"

"Because I don't think you're serious." And even if he was, he'd already sacrificed so much for his mom. She couldn't let him do that again. There was always the long-distance thing. But that just seemed like drawing out their goodbye.

Matthew got up and crossed the room toward her. Penny's back touched the window, the glass cold through her thin t-shirt.

His eyes were intense on hers. He was taller than he used to be, broader. He could surround her, if she let him.

"I'm serious, Penn. I love you. And you just said you love me. But you're acting like how we feel doesn't matter."

"Of course it does."

He braced his left hand against the window, leaning over her. His scent and his heat were all she could think about.

Back when they were kids, the future was an amorphous, abstract thing. She'd just wanted Matthew to touch her. Undress her. Of course she'd wanted his love, too, but it hadn't mattered that they might not be "forever." Why did that have to matter so much now?

"Can't we just love each other, in this moment," she said, "without worrying about tomorrow? I don't know how to make this all work. I just want you, Matthew. So much."

He slid his arm around her waist. Pulled her to him. His mouth found hers. Holding onto her, he stumbled backward toward the bed. Matthew sat heavily. Penny straddled his lap. She felt how much he wanted her, too, pressing against her inner thigh through his sweats.

Lost in his kiss, she put her hands on his shoulders and squeezed, forgetting all about his injury. He hissed in pain.

"Oh, crap, I'm sorry. Should we stop?"

He took off the sling and tossed it aside. Gritting his teeth, he fisted his shirt with his left hand and then pulled it off in a single, unpleasant-looking movement.

"Worst is over now. Come here."

She stared at the constellation of bruises on his neck and right arm and down his torso.

"What about your concussion? I don't want to hurt you."

He lay back carefully, then reached up and pulled her down against him.

How many times had she imagined them together, in this very bed? Every other man she'd compared to Matthew, how it might've been with him. Part of her was still that eighteen-year-old, wishing he were her first.

They laughed as they undressed each other—the old sweats, the prom t-shirt. When her skin was completely bare, Matthew ran his hand along her collarbone, then down to cup her breast.

"You are so beautiful," he murmured. "It's killing me."

Then his hand moved down farther, and she sighed, tipping her head back and closing her eyes.

Slowly, they made their way together. Sometimes she paused, just looking down at him, wanting to memorize everything about these moments. His spiced scent, the cool roughness of the sheets on her knees. His palms on her hipbones. The way he bit his lower lip when she began to move. She kept holding back, wary of his injuries, but he didn't want to be gentle. Soon there were no coherent thoughts at all, only sensation. Breath. Rhythm. The whole world was only Matthew.

After, she lay her head against his chest. His lips touched her forehead at the hairline.

So this is how it feels with him, she thought.

Maybe it would've been better not to know—because no one else would ever live up to this.

CHAPTER THIRTY-THREE

AFTER HE LEFT LINDEN AT THE TRAILER, RAY STARTED toward the parking lot. But then he looked back at Main Street. Something bothered him, though he couldn't say what. Maybe it was all that caffeine from the can of Dark Energy he drank. He was going to have trouble getting to sleep.

One more check of the perimeter wouldn't hurt. He walked back toward the old buildings.

There'd been plenty of speculation in Ashton about the incidents last night. Apparently, there'd been some accidents in Eden over the years. Add in the legends about Devil's Night and the book by Penny's dad, and you had an endless source of gossip. Almost everybody, it seemed, had a ghost story to tell about the place. *My cousin's high school boyfriend said...*

Ray had his own version, of course, sourced from his father. Dad had seen something weird up here, years ago. Things moving of their own accord. Dad probably wouldn't like that Ray was working up here tonight. But they'd needed extra security, and Ray had enjoyed the festival last night. Until the accidents, anyway. Why not get paid to go for night two? Better yet, maybe he'd run into Penny. Though that hadn't worked out.

He just wished the festival had better music. Ray liked metal, anything from old school Metallica and Megadeath to industrial to hardcore Power Trip. Nothing like a relentless guitar riff fortified by a distortion pedal to clear the clutter from your mind. The boundary between order and chaos was thin, indeed, and metal never failed to remind him of that.

He took the flashlight from his belt and started walking along the fence. The cleaning crew had already been through for the night; the vendors had packed up their booths. The festival grounds were deserted. But still he couldn't shake the feeling that something was out of place. An event like Devil's Fest attracted people from all over the state, maybe even all over the country. Where there were crowds, there inevitably were troublemakers.

Maybe somebody had stuck around, planning a little mischief?

Ray hadn't gone to school in Ashton growing up. He never made the pilgrimage up to Eden on Devil's Night as a teenager. But he'd spent every summer here with his dad since he was four. He knew this place inside and out, but he didn't quite belong. Penny Wright was the first person he'd met who seemed to share that same status. It was a problem that she'd be leaving in a few days. If he wanted to ask her out, he needed to act soon. But first, he had to show how vigilant and dedicated he could be. She was the kind of girl that a guy needed to impress. Older than him, more worldly.

His phone vibrated. He'd just received a text. He'd chosen his cell carrier carefully, the one that had the best reception in the region. As a patrol deputy, he was often out in rural areas, off the usual grid. You never knew what might happen.

The message was from Penny. Instantly, a grin lit up his face.

Sorry to write so late, but Matthew said you had a message for me? Call if this is a good time, otherwise I'll try in the morning.

He called her right away. "You're up late," he said.

She laughed awkwardly. "Can't sleep, I guess. What about you?"

"Working at your festival tonight. Everybody's safe and sound, and it's all packed away for the night."

She exhaled. "You have no idea what a relief that is, thank you."

"No problem at all. I wanted to let you know about the forensic report on those bones—if you want an unofficial summary."

"Yes, please tell me. I'd like to know."

He told her the conclusions of the report. The body was at least a century old, belonging to a young woman who'd given birth at some point. There'd been signs of malnourishment, which wasn't uncommon in those days. She'd died of a broken back, probably after falling from a decent height. The obvious conclusion was the roof, or maybe an upper floor.

"There was a window," Penny said. "Pretty high above the place where I...where the body was found. Could she have fallen from there?"

"Sure is possible. She wasn't buried very deep. Might've fallen there and was never found until now."

A pause. "Will there be a burial?"

"Sure, that'll be arranged once the paperwork is all finished. I just thought, since you seemed in such a rush before..."

"Thank you, Ray. I really do appreciate it."

Are you free for coffee tomorrow? he wanted to ask. But maybe that would seem presumptuous. He wished he'd been able to talk to her in person. "Hey, by the way," he asked, "have you seen Anvi? Did she go to Ashton? Linden was asking, and I wasn't sure if you spoke to her."

"I'm not at the inn, actually. You could try there."

Penny said goodbye and ended the call.

Not at the inn. Well, huh. Where was she, then?

He shook off the disappointment. He was working tomorrow night—he'd see her then. Which meant he should finish up here, get home, and get some sleep so he'd feel his best.

Ray continued along the perimeter of the fence, rubbing the

sleeves of his windbreaker. There was a little more moisture in the air than usual, and that made the cold seep into his bones.

That sense of unease still irked him. He spun around, suddenly sure that there was someone behind him.

He lifted the flashlight. "Hello? Anybody there?"

He felt eyes watching him. Ray's pulse thrummed in his neck. He wasn't like some of the older patrol deputies, always talking about gut instincts and intuition. Even so, he felt those eyes without seeing them.

Could be a mountain lion. Wouldn't be good to run into one of them. He'd look like a colossal idiot tomorrow at the office—even worse, in front of Penny—if he got mauled.

By that same instinct, his hand had already gone to his service weapon, which he'd concealed under his jacket. Though he was off duty, he had a legal right to carry, and Linden hadn't specifically asked him not to be armed. He was glad for the extra protection of a Glock 19 against aggressive a-holes, but he didn't want to shoot some animal.

Just call it a night and go home, he thought, turning to go back toward the parking lot.

Then he spun. He'd heard a thump and a cut-off scream that sounded like, "Help." That was no mountain lion. But it hadn't come from inside the Eden fence. It was somewhere out in the canyon.

Drawing his weapon, he ran toward the noise. His flashlight beam swept over the landscape before him.

A figure appeared, illuminated by the beam. A person standing still, arms at his sides. Wait—it was a woman. She turned, and he recognized her face. Short pixie hair, pouty lips.

It was Anvi.

What was she doing out here? He lowered his weapon slightly so he wasn't aiming at her. "Anvi, you need help? I'm Deputy Ray Castillo, remember?"

She stared at him, her eyes shining in the light. He realized what was so odd about her face—she wasn't blinking. Wasn't reacting. But she was holding a large, elongated object. A thick piece of wood.

Something moved near her feet. He couldn't tell what it was. He took a few careful steps closer.

A person was lying in a heap on the ground. The person moaned. Her head moved, and her hair slid from her face.

Linden was lying there.

"What the—?"

Anvi's arm came up, pointing something at him. He moved his gun up before realizing it was just a can with some kind of nozzle. But by then, Anvi had already pressed the trigger. A cloud of stuff, somehow both water and fire, spewed into his face. Bear spray. She'd hit him with freaking bear spray. He coughed and retched, rubbing his eyes. It wasn't anywhere near lethal, wouldn't even stop a bad guy in his tracks, but it stung like hell.

It had distracted him, though. Enough that, just as he noticed that Anvi was now beside him, he felt a heavy blow to his head.

Ray fell forward onto the ground. The heavy thing smacked into his head again, and he was out.

CHAPTER THIRTY-FOUR

Penny slept until almost noon. She woke to find Matthew facing her from the other pillow, those blue eyes studying her.

"Hi," he said.

She sat up, running her fingers through her tangled hair. "Hey. Hi." The room was different in the midday light. Everything was different. Matthew was lying next to her with his arm propped under his head. His bruises were purple, and his skin was smooth and pale, and there was so much of it. She forced her eyes back up.

He tugged playfully at the sleeve of her t-shirt. "You put this back on? Are we awkward again now?"

She laughed, but she did feel strangely shy. Her eyes kept drifting downwards, and he'd kicked off his blankets.

"I couldn't sleep," she explained, "so I got up to make a call last night. Ray told me about the skeleton I found. It was a woman. Old. Could've been from the Devil's Night Massacre." It wasn't recent—that had been a relief.

Matthew sat up and readjusted the blankets. "Do you think it's important?"

Was it? She would never forget that hidden room. The helpless, overwhelming terror she'd felt there. The report might reveal a few more details about the woman's death, but she doubted she'd ever know what really happened. She didn't want to go back to that place, even in her memories.

"Probably not," she answered. "I guess Anvi could post something about it, since it's Devil's Night tonight." One hundred and twenty-five years exactly since the massacre. "But the festival's over tomorrow, anyway. Ray said there'd be a burial at some point."

They didn't mention that her visit would also be over soon.

Matthew picked up her hand and kissed her palm. His gaze grew more intense.

She wasn't feeling so shy anymore. She tossed aside her shirt and crawled over to him. They were more urgent than the night before, knowing that every minute together now was stolen time.

They showered and ate stale crackers for breakfast—or perhaps it was lunch, given the hour—and Penny finally picked up her phone to check her email and call Linden. She wondered if her best friend would know about Matthew just by hearing her voice.

Linden didn't answer, so Penny left a voicemail.

A silence descended between them as they drove toward the inn. Penny tapped her fingers on the steering wheel. What was there to say now? Nothing that would fill the absence that Matthew would leave once he was gone.

She parked near the back of the lot.

"Should we go in together?" he asked. "Or..."

"I'm going to take a walk." She handed him the keys and got out.

Her family might have already guessed. They had a preternatural sense of such things that were none of their business. But that wasn't the reason she preferred that he go inside without her.

"Can I see you tonight?"

She paused and looked back. He was standing beside the open passenger's side door, hand on the car's roof.

"I'll be busy at the festival. There's a party and a dinner and..." She'd didn't bother listing her other obligations tonight. Neither of them cared.

"Tomorrow?"

"Matthew. I don't think we should."

Spending the next three nights just like the last would be wonderful, but it wouldn't make it any easier for her to get on that plane.

He walked toward her. "I meant everything I said last night."

"So did I. I don't want to move back here, and I *know* that you don't want to leave. Long distance isn't realistic. If none of those options work, what else is there?"

"There's no discussion? Nothing that will change your mind?"

She blinked away tears and walked out of the parking lot.

In the meadow behind the inn, a trail led through an aspen grove and out into the greater valley. On the dirt path, a bicycle zipped past her. A creek ran alongside, filling her ears with quiet music. Inside, she was a wreck.

Matthew thought she had her mind made up. That wasn't true. She wanted to run inside the inn and find him and tell him she'd stay. Every single second, she had to keep choosing the thing she knew was right, no matter how much it hurt. Unless she came up with some new stroke of brilliance, then she couldn't see any alternative.

To distract herself, she scrolled through her feeds. There was a new post from Anvi. A live Instagram video from last night showed the crowd dancing at Devil's Fest. There was no sound at all, no caption. The camera caught Anvi's face only once, and her eyes were glazed. It wasn't Anvi's usual style. Actually, there was something eerie and even ominous about the video, with the writhing bodies of the dancers and the garish lights and the backdrop of ruined buildings, all in silence. Not a single shot of a Dark Energy can or its logo, which might've been for the best.

Penny remembered that Ray had asked about Anvi last night. For a moment, Penny wondered if everything was okay. But then she heard someone running behind her. She stepped to the side of the path to let the runner pass, but the woman stopped, panting.

"Please, Penny. I need to talk to you."

She looked up from her phone. It was that woman from the other day—the one who'd thrown the ice water in her face at breakfast. She wore the cardigan with the missing buttons. The same wild look shone in her eyes.

Penny took a step back. "Leave me alone. I have nothing to say."

"I'm sorry about the other morning. I was upset. But you need to listen."

Penny turned to go, and the woman grabbed her arm. Penny shook her off. "Are you kidding me?" She lifted her phone. "I'm calling the police."

But then the woman said, "I'm Helen Boyd. You really don't remember me? Helen and Jason Boyd?"

Helen.

Penny searched the woman's face. She'd changed so much, at least from the image in Penny's memory. The red hair had turned dishwater gray, and frown lines creased her mouth. Yet there was something familiar about Helen's eyes that tugged at her memory.

"How do I know you're really her?"

The woman dug a tattered wallet from her pocket. She produced a driver's license that said "Helen Boyd," and then a wrinkled photo—Penny's mom and dad with their arms around a man and a red-haired woman. Penny looked from the photo to the person in front of her. Helen had aged, but her features were definitely the same.

"What happened to you?"

Penny had so many questions. She couldn't believe that

Helen Boyd had accosted her at the inn. How could this be the same woman she used to know?

"I'll tell you everything," Helen said. "If you'll listen."

"But—you just yelled at me before. Why do you want to talk now?"

Helen knit her hands together. "I'd driven all night to get to Ashton after I read about your festival online, and it was so overwhelming to be here again..."

Penny closed her eyes. The initial shock of seeing Helen again was wearing off. "I don't understand what you want."

"To tell you the truth. That's it. *Please*, Penny."

"My father already told me. This is about Jason's death, right? I'm sorry for your loss. But it's nothing to do with me."

"Your father doesn't know about this. And it's *everything* to do with you."

Penny started down the path, pulling up the Ashton police department's number on her phone. Another bicycle flew past. If Helen didn't leave her alone, she'd hit call.

Helen kept up with her, still talking. "We tried to understand your power when you were a girl, and we failed you. *I* failed you. But I've learned so much more. I know what you can really do."

Penny's thumb lingered over the call button. After a moment's indecision, she put her phone back in her pocket.

"You really impressed me, that first time I met you," Helen said. "When you were little."

They were sitting on a bench overlooking the creek. Penny had moved as far to one side of the seat as she could, arms crossed over her middle. She was still angry about that ice water. But she'd been wrong about Matthew when she first arrived, too. They'd misunderstood one another. Maybe the same was true of Helen.

Besides, Helen represented one of the few bright spots from

Penny's young childhood. The least she could do was sit and listen.

"We'd spent college imagining that we were paranormal investigators," Helen went on. "Your mom and dad, Jason and me. Reading all those books and playing with equipment. After we graduated, we went our separate ways. I figured those days were gone. Just childish fantasies. But then Lawrence called me up one day and told me about *you*."

Helen looked over at Penny, starting to smile. Somehow it made her eyes even sadder. When Penny said nothing, she went on.

"Things weren't going well for Jason and me at that point in our marriage. I don't want to get into it. But let's say it was a rough patch. *Really* rough. It was my idea to come to Ashton to see your family. And when I met you, you were everything Lawrence had promised and more. You were so open. Innocent. But you already knew so much—about how ghosts interact with our world, how they *feel*. How incredible to think that so much survives after death. I was in my thirties, and I barely comprehended mortality, but here was this little kid who spoke about death like some guru on a mountaintop."

Penny chewed the side of her lip, shaking her head. All that pressure that her dad put on her, the assumptions he'd made. She hadn't wanted to believe that Helen was a part of that.

"I didn't know anything. I was a child."

"You knew plenty."

"But I didn't understand consequences. How a single day could follow me for the rest of my life."

Helen pulled at one of the remaining buttons on her cardigan. "Maybe I didn't either. But believe me, I came to understand."

She shifted on the bench. The creek rushed past them.

"After Jason spent that Devil's Night in Eden with your father, he couldn't get the experience out of his mind. He had nightmares. I took us on a vacation, hoping that we could get past it and reconnect. I'd hoped he would work on things between us, like he'd promised me. But after Eden, he wasn't the same."

Helen gestured with her hands. "I don't mean that his personality changed—if anything, he was more himself. Distilled. His problems had intensified. He'd been aimless in his career, but now he stopped even trying to find a new position. Eden became his escape. His obsession. He read everything he could about Eden's history. He'd disappear, and I'd get a call that he was found asleep at our local library, facedown at a table full of books. He even tried to help some with your father's book—they were supposed to be co-authors, but Jason was too erratic. He didn't finish the parts he was supposed to write.

"This went on for almost two years. By then, I'd had enough. I wanted to ask for a divorce, but I was afraid that he'd stop taking care of himself if I did. All he cared about was getting back to Eden. He said he'd heard some woman speaking in the hotel, and he was sure that he could contact that ghost again. Find out what happened to her. This mystery woman, maybe Marian, who knows—she was more important to him than I'd ever been. That really hurt. But I agreed to go up to Eden with him. Just so he wouldn't be alone."

She wiped tears from her cheeks. "After he died, I was the one who got obsessed. I tracked down everyone who'd had 'accidents' in Eden. Anybody who claimed they'd witnessed something paranormal there. I talked to mediums, too, people like you. I spent all the life insurance money, all my savings. I gave up everything just so I could understand what I'd experienced."

Penny's phone buzzed in her pocket. She resisted the urge to look at it. Probably just Linden responding to her voicemail.

"You said you 'know what I can really do,'" Penny said. "What did you mean?"

Helen went on like she hadn't heard. "The hotel and the bank—those are the places where the hauntings are concentrated. People described hearing a woman's voice in the hotel.

Knocking on walls. Sometimes it came from the first floor; other times they were drawn to the upper levels. Some said they felt despair. Others said it was fear. But the bank was different. The presence there was dark. Angry, like you'd said that Devil's Night when you were there. You'd told us it was Marian."

"Because I'd heard other people talk about her."

"No matter what year the incidents took place, they always escalated near Devil's Night in July. I learned a lot in my research. Hauntings are often more powerful around anniversaries. More people visit a place, more emotions are at play. Ghosts can draw on that energy. But when a really sensitive person arrives—someone like you—paranormal phenomena can skyrocket. A medium amplifies the ghosts. Brings them more into the physical world. Old memories of events will replay over and over. But it's vulnerable people like Jason who suffer for it."

Penny got up from the bench. "You're saying it's *my* fault? What happened to Jason?"

"Of course not. We were the adults. We should've known better than to play with things we couldn't understand. But Jason was permanently affected. You can't deny the truth of that. Of the people who were injured in Eden over the years, almost all were men. I don't think that's a coincidence. That boy just the other night who got hurt at the bank—what about *him*?"

So this was the "truth" that Helen wanted her to know? It was just another version of Penny's father's theories. She stood at the creek's edge, watching the water slosh over the rocks, wondering again if she should just leave. Helen could be out of her mind.

"I'm sure it's easier to think a ghost caused Jason's death," Penny said gently. "But ghosts aren't capable of that."

A small push, maybe. A bruise. A lingering sense of violation. But it wasn't enough. *Couldn't* be.

"There's no proof," Penny said.

"But there is."

"What is it?"

"I...it's hard to explain."

"Then I've had enough."

"I'm the proof," Helen cried. "I was there. I saw him die."

Penny turned back. "What did you see?"

"It's so hard. I was...I never meant..."

Helen closed her eyes and took a stuttering breath.

"We went back on Devil's Night. Two years after that first visit. We started at the hotel—that's what Jason wanted. But he didn't feel any presence. It just seemed like a dead place. I don't know if it's because you weren't there. Or if the ghost simply wasn't active. All I know is, Jason was disappointed. But he didn't want to give up. He decided we should go to the bank."

Tears slid down her cheeks.

"I felt nothing when we went inside the bank. But Jason did. He said he heard a woman's voice. He thought it could be her—the one from the hotel. She wanted him to come up. Come find her. The inside of the bank is all burned up, and the upper floors are mostly collapsed. But at the very back of the building, there are stairs built out of brick. Steep. No railing. Jason insisted on going up, and I...I followed him, trying to convince him we should leave. I was so frustrated with him for his stupid obsession, how it was ruining our lives. I started yelling. The feeling was all-encompassing—I hated him for what he'd done to us. To me. We made it to the third floor. Jason was looking out a window. It didn't have any glass. It faced the canyon. I could see those cliffs with the sun setting over them. It was so bright it made my eyes water. It was a tall window, and he was right there on the edge. Just standing with his back to me. Like I wasn't even there. So many strange thoughts were in my mind."

Abruptly, Helen cut off her narrative. "I need a moment. Please. I'm trying."

She wiped her face with her cardigan sleeve. When she spoke again, she barely reached above a whisper.

"I pushed him."

Penny stared at her. "You...I'm sorry, what?" It had sounded like *I pushed him*. But that couldn't be right.

Tears poured down Helen's face.

"He didn't move after he hit the ground. I drove back to Ashton and notified the police. They said his neck broke instantly. He didn't suffer. I kept waiting for them to figure it out. But so many accidents had happened up there. Your dad assumed the ghost made Jason jump. I let him. He said I should go along with the accident story so we could spare Jason's memory. But I guess I was saving myself."

Penny had no idea what to say. The woman had just admitted to murder.

Helen lunged forward, grabbing Penny by the arms. Her eyes were wide and glazed.

"You have to believe that it wasn't me. *It wasn't me.* It was her—Marian. She made me push him. That's why I *know* Eden is dangerous. It could happen again. And with you there, given that power that you have? You've drawn her out. You're responsible now. Whoever she hurts next, it'll be your fault."

Penny wrenched out of Helen's grasp. "I need to go."

She started backing away. Then she ran. She was afraid that Helen would follow. But when she looked back, the woman was sitting on the bench again, looking at her empty hands.

CHAPTER THIRTY-FIVE

Penny burst into her room, already pulling up Linden's number on her phone. Somehow she'd avoided her family, which was good. She couldn't handle them right now. Only her best friend could talk her through this. Make her come back to reality. Because right now, she was panicking.

Those things that Helen had told her—

You've drawn her out. Whoever she hurts next, it'll be your fault.

Penny's father had made similar claims. But Helen's story had a different level of gravity. So much of what she'd said rang true. The woman's voice in the hotel, the way no one on Matthew's crew had any ghost encounters until Penny had arrived. *A medium amplifies the ghosts.* And Helen had actually confessed to pushing Jason from that ledge.

Linden didn't answer her phone.

Penny had a text waiting—the one she'd received while with Helen—but it wasn't from Linden. It was Tripp. *Please tell Linden to call me.* But why would he ask that? Couldn't he just contact Linden himself?

Maybe Anvi knew where Linden had gone. She called Anvi's number. No answer there. Anvi didn't respond to a text either.

What was going on? If there'd been some emergency related

to the festival, wouldn't they have notified Penny? And why did it have to be *now*, when Penny was barely holding herself together?

She changed into fresh clothes, walked over to Linden's hotel room and knocked. Then banged.

A door opened, but it wasn't Linden's. Tripp stuck his head out from the room next door. "Are you looking for her, too?"

"She hasn't responded to my calls or texts. Neither has Anvi."

Tripp's eyes widened in a way Penny couldn't decipher. "That's odd, but I doubt they're together. Could Linden be up at the trailer, but not getting service?"

Why wouldn't they be together? Penny thought. "Maybe, if suddenly everything stopped working. When's the last time you saw her?"

"Last night at dinner. Not since."

Something didn't sit right. Maybe it was just that unnerving conversation she'd had with Helen Boyd, but Penny was getting worried about her friend.

"I'll call my mom and see if housekeeping has been to her room. What if she's sick?"

A few minutes later, Debbie was striding down the hall holding a master key. She said hello to Tripp and turned to Penny. "Linden's room hasn't been serviced yet. I also spoke to Becky, our night receptionist, and she didn't see Linden come in last night. Let's go ahead and check on her, shall we?"

Penny's mother was upbeat as always, but she must've been worried too. Why else would she be here, about to open up Linden's room?

Debbie knocked brusquely for several seconds. She unlocked the door. "Linden, honey? Are you in here?"

The lights were all off, bathroom door open. The bed didn't look slept in.

"Where else might she be?" Debbie asked.

Penny looked at Tripp. "We should go up to Eden," he said. "Check the trailer."

Debbie seemed like she might say more, but Penny didn't want to wait. She grabbed her phone and purse, and they went to the parking lot.

Tripp had rented a Landrover in Aspen—he'd flown into their airport so he'd have access to luxury vehicles Ashton couldn't provide. The seats were soft black leather, and the engine purred at a low hum. Penny realized she'd never been in a car alone with him before. Actually, they'd almost never spent time alone, except for the occasions when he'd stop by her desk or pass in the hall at work.

"Did Linden say anything to you last night?" Tripp asked. "Maybe she was upset?"

Penny was pulling nervously at the stitching on her seat. "Last night? No."

She hadn't spoken to Linden since before she left for Matthew's house. *And I didn't think of Linden once till this afternoon.* What if Linden needed her, but she hadn't called because Penny was, well, *busy* with Matthew?

"Why would she be upset?" Penny asked.

Tripp grimaced, then laughed. "Because I was getting on her nerves? We had a tense conversation about work. Nothing major. She probably just wants to make me sweat."

But what about me? Penny thought. Linden didn't play games with her like this.

Something could really be wrong.

It was after five o'clock when they reached Eden. The vendors were setting up concessions, and a honey wagon had arrived to pump out the port-a-potties. Penny and Tripp drove past the parking lot and went straight for the Sterling PR trailer, which was out of sight from the main road.

Penny unlocked the door with her key. She went inside, the door banging after she'd shoved it.

"Linden?"

There were bottles all over the floor. Linden's purse lay on her bed. But no Linden. No Anvi, either.

A phone sat on the kitchen counter. Penny grabbed it and hurried outside.

She held up Linden's device. "She wouldn't go anywhere—not to the bathroom, not across a hallway—without her phone."

Tripp cursed. He walked a few feet and leaned down to pick something up from the ground. An empty white wine bottle, caked with grass on its side.

"Unbelievable," Tripp said.

"We have to call the police." Linden could've been assaulted. Or she might've been wandering around lost somewhere in the canyon or nearby hills. Penny stuck Linden's phone in her purse, then pulled out her own device.

"*No.*" Tripp tossed the wine bottle aside, strode over, and plucked the phone right from Penny's hand. "That's exactly what she wants. She's mad, and she's trying to punish me by ruining the last night of Devil's Fest. She knows I can't afford to lose SunBev. I'm not playing along."

"Ruin the—are you kidding? Linden would never do something like that."

"Sorry Penny, but I know her a lot better than you do. She can be a manipulative bitch."

Penny stared at Tripp, mouth open. She held back the insults she wanted to throw back at him, but only because he was her boss.

"Give me my phone back."

For a moment she thought he'd refuse, but then he did.

"Linden is missing right now," Penny said. "She could be hurt. I'm going to find her, and if you won't help me, the security guards will."

Penny headed toward Main Street. She passed a white tent where workers were setting up that night's VIP closing party.

Ray, she thought. *Maybe he's working here again tonight.* He could notify the sheriff's office, talk to the right people to get this taken seriously. She looked up his contact on her phone and called.

"Whoa, whoa, whoa," Tripp said, rushing after her. "Linden is the most resourceful woman I know. She's completely fine."

Penny kept marching through the grass, holding her phone to her ear. But Ray didn't answer. *Really?* she thought. *Does no one answer phones anymore?*

"Okay, how about this," Tripp said. "You and I will look. We know she was up here at Eden because her phone's here. Where could she have gone? Somewhere on Main Street, maybe? She might be over there screwing some security guard right now and just left her phone behind."

Penny glared at him. Then a message came up on her phone—a text from her sister, Krista. Quickly she opened it, wondering if their mother had found some sign of Linden at the inn.

The message read, *Did you see what Anvi posted this morning? Creepy much?*

Krista had sent a link to Twitter. Penny clicked it. At three a.m. this morning Anvi had tweeted, *Devil's Night in Eden is when the guilty are punished.*

Then a follow up text from Krista. *This is your idea of marketing? Really poor taste, considering what happened to Scott two days ago. Not cool.*

Too many things were happening at once. Penny's head was spinning. She sent off a quick, apologetic reply to Krista, then tried again to call Anvi.

"Who are you calling?" Tripp demanded.

"Anvi." Still no answer. Why did she have to disappear now, at the same time as Linden? She was off somewhere posting videos and tweets.

Penny left a voicemail—she was getting sick of those—and she held out her phone for Tripp to see.

"Anvi's been posting weird stuff. She's going *way* off our campaign."

As he read the tweet, all the color drained from Tripp's face.

"I don't know what's going on," Penny said, "but it seems like the entire world has gone insane today."

Unless Linden was abducted and driven somewhere—too far-fetched an idea, even for the day Penny was having—then she had to be here in Eden. According to Tripp, Linden had been upset last night. And now, she'd gone missing.

Anvi was gone, too, after writing that disturbing tweet...All on the anniversary of Devil's Night.

Hauntings are more powerful on anniversaries. Helen had told her so.

Nausea swept through her.

She'd spent so many years dismissing her father's version of the events in Eden. She'd spent the last few days doing the same, even as the evidence kept piling up. The accidents in Eden; Scott's claim that someone else had been inside the bank. Her own experiences inside the hotel. The hands around her neck and the voices intruding in her head. Now Linden and Anvi had gone missing.

She had to tell Tripp what Helen Boyd had said. He wasn't going to believe it. But she had to try.

AFTER SHE FINISHED, Tripp didn't speak for three full minutes. She knew because she kept checking her phone while she waited, hoping that somehow Linden or Anvi or even Ray would respond. All the while, Tripp's jaw muscle twitched. She knew this look. He was in deep strategy mode. At meetings, she'd never known what to expect when he came back to the surface.

Over on Main Street, music played through the massive sound system: ACDC, "Highway to Hell." A few weeks ago in Los Angeles, that might've seemed funny.

"Is this worth your job to you?" Tripp finally asked. "This—" He waved his hand. "Ghost story?"

"You're making me choose between Linden and my job?"

"I'm not the bad guy here. I just need to know how serious you are about this."

Penny had given up so much for her position at Sterling. If she got fired...She couldn't think about that.

"A hundred percent. If I'm risking my job, then so be it." Though she hoped to God she was wrong—even if Tripp fired her, at least Linden would be safe.

But what about everyone else at the festival? She had to push that possibility aside for the moment. Tripp definitely wouldn't want to hear it. Once they found Linden, they could consider what other steps might be necessary.

Tripp studied her another moment. "Let's say you're not crazy, and this is true. There are malevolent ghosts in Eden, and they can have a powerful affect on people. Even kill people. And Linden—or maybe Anvi—could be in some kind of danger. Then...what? Where would they be?"

"The hotel or the bank. Those are the places where all the past incidents have occurred."

The secret room at the hotel, she thought with dawning horror. What if Linden was in there?

Tripp looked toward Main Street, where the cleaning crew was making its final rounds. "It's not even six yet. I'll ask security to go check the bank; we'll take the hotel."

She nodded. Maybe he didn't believe her, but he was actually giving her a chance. It was more than she'd expected. "But if we don't find them? We can't ignore the fact that they're missing."

"If they haven't turned up, then we'll call the sheriff. Okay?"

"Thank you."

They headed toward the hotel. The song had switched from ACDC to Linkin Park's "In the End."

On the way, Penny wrote a text to June, just in case June was still in Ashton.

Hi, I can't find Linden, she wrote. *Getting worried. If you hear from her or Anvi, please let me know?*

The text went through. Next, Penny started on a similar

message to Matthew. She wished he were here. Matthew thought so clearly in an emergency. He steadied her, and she desperately needed that right now. But Matthew was miles away.

"Are you texting someone?" Tripp glanced at her. "It's best if we don't raise any alarms yet. I don't want to jeopardize the festival for nothing."

Is Linden "nothing"? she thought. But she nodded, putting away her phone. She could finish writing to Matthew later.

They reached the hotel. Tripp had a quiet word with a security guard, who handed over a key to the padlock on the hotel's door.

"Did you ask him to check the bank?" she said.

"I will after we're done here. I don't want rumors starting without reason."

He was already changing what they'd agreed. But Penny let this go. If they didn't see any sign of Linden or Anvi at the hotel, they could go with the security guards to the bank.

They went inside. The lobby was dim. There was no hint of the catastrophe that had happened at the opening party, when June dove off that balcony. The similarity to Jason Boyd's death was unsettling, though his fall took place in a different building. She thought again of what Helen had told her: people in the hotel often felt compelled to the higher floors.

She thought she saw something move in the shadows near the dining room—a swirl of fabric—but when she looked again, nothing was there. She hugged her arms at the elbows.

Penny went to the base of the staircase. "Linden? Are you up there?" Her voice echoed in the rafters.

"What about that room you found?" Tripp asked. "The hidden one."

"I thought of that. I don't know why she'd be there, but it's possible." If the ghost was talking to her. Drawing her. Penny suppressed a shiver, thinking of her friend trapped. Terrified. Like Penny had been.

They walked through the bar, then into the dining room. "If

she's there," Tripp said, "wouldn't someone have heard her yelling through the open window? Or if she went in that yard where you found the bones?"

He'd asked the questions so coldly.

Don't let him find me, a voice whispered.

She forced the ghost out of her mind. "I think someone would've heard her before," Penny answered. "But now, with all the noise outside, I'm not so sure."

Penny glanced up at the crack in the dining room ceiling. The room was in shadow, the chairs skeletal, placed legs-up on the rental tables. But the view from the window still showed blue sky. They had hours until night. Plenty of time for an ample search. *Breathe*, she told herself. If something terrible had already happened to Linden, they would know. She had to believe that.

From the kitchen, they veered into the long hallway. Penny pointed to the anteroom with the bookcase, where she'd found the secret entrance. She didn't want to go in. She remembered the last time, and her throat tightened, as if those invisible hands were on her.

"You'll have to show me," Tripp said.

"I don't..." *I can't go in there*, she thought. *Please don't make me go in there.* But Linden could be inside—pushed down. Hurt. Tears burned Penny's eyes.

A faint cry rose in the air. It was coming from the other side of the wall. The ghost.

Or was it Linden?

"Do you hear that?" Penny asked.

"It's something outside. A truck backing up."

Be brave, she told herself. Holding her breath, she marched to the wall and felt around for the gap in the paneling. The room was so dark that she could hardly see Tripp beside her. But she heard his breathing. Felt his exhale, hot against her neck, and smelled the sweat underneath his cologne.

"I can't see anything."

He held up his phone and switched on the light. She found

the gap and pulled the latch. The door swung wide. The hidden room beyond was a little brighter because of the window, though still dim. The tattered curtain shifted with the sudden rush of air.

It didn't look like anyone was inside. She let out her breath, relieved that Linden hadn't been trapped in that terrible place. But then, where was she? They'd have to search upstairs, but it might not be safe. They would need help.

"Aren't you going in?" Tripp asked.

"She's not there."

"But you should check."

"*No.*"

Penny tried to step back, but Tripp grabbed her by the bicep. "I'm sorry, Penny. I can't let you ruin the festival tonight. It's just one night, all right? I'll be back for you in the morning."

He took the leather backpack from her hand, shoved her into that horrible room, and slammed the door.

"We're going home," Debbie said. "Now."

We'd retreated to the cars. Wallace and Carlos were scuffing their shoes in the dirt, unwilling to get involved in our family drama. Helen and Jason had likewise settled a few yards away.

Penny was lying on a blanket on the bed of my pickup truck, eating Goldfish crackers. She'd calmed down rapidly, in that way that children can suddenly smile and laugh after being upset. She'd bounced back like a little rubber ball. But Debbie was freaked.

"Babe," I said to my wife, "just slow down. Let's talk about this."

"There is nothing to talk about."

"Daddy?" Penny sat up in the truck bed. Orange crumbs were scattered over her shirt. "Can we go in that hotel now?"

Debbie whimpered. "Why would you want to go in there?"

Penny looked at me, as if she expected me to understand. I couldn't help thinking of her words from less than an hour before: *She knows we're here.* The chills came back.

"Why honey?" I asked.

"Somebody's lost in there. They need help getting found."

-from A Devil in Eden by Lawrence Wright

DEVIL'S NIGHT - 1894

THE MINUTE THEY HEARD THE SHOTS, MARIAN WENT TO THE door. She drew the revolver from her boot—the gun she'd taken from Bart earlier that day. In her other hand, she held her tiny derringer.

Douglas grabbed her arm. "Wait," he said. He too had his gun in his hand. "You'd better stay here."

"Like hell I will." Such grammar. She was forgetting herself, wasn't she?

Douglas twisted the knob. He opened the door by a few inches, then paused. He put a finger to his lips. Tilted his head to listen.

Marian looked back at the papers littering the floor. There was no money in the safe. Nothing of any value to her. She, Douglas, and Tim would walk away with nothing—except their lives, if they were lucky.

But Fitzhammer was dead. She took solace in that.

Outside the room, a floorboard creaked. Somebody was out in the corridor.

Douglas pointed his gun into the hallway and fired. More gunshots responded. He pulled back.

"Two men," Douglas said. He leaned out again. Fired.

Someone yelped. Douglas pulled back just as bullets slammed into the wood. Marian gripped her weapons, aiming at the open doorway. She still couldn't see the intruders. Her pulse was picking up, thrumming in her ears like the ticking of that grandfather clock.

Douglas leaned out again. There was a shot. He screamed and reared back. He'd been hit. Marian didn't hesitate. She stepped over him, aimed into the hallway, and pulled both triggers. Bart's revolver bucked so hard she barely kept hold of it. She might've laughed at herself, firing both Bart's enormous gun and her own undersized one, if the moment hadn't been so fraught.

There was a man out there, red headed with a harelip. He pointed his weapon at her, but he didn't fire. Instead, he looked down at his stomach, where red was seeping into his brown shirt.

Marian pulled the triggers again. The bullets tore a hole through the red-haired man's chest. He stumbled back a few steps, then fell atop the other body sprawled on the hallway floor.

Panting, Marian kept her guns trained on the end of the hall, where a doorway opened into the kitchen. But no one came.

"Tim?" she hissed.

A constant hum whined in her ears. But she still imagined she could hear the ghostly cries.

She returned to the small room to check on Douglas. He wasn't breathing. Poor man. Blood soaked his shirt. She went to the hall and tore a strip of fabric from the red-headed man's shirt. Douglas gave no sign of life as she tied the fabric around his wounded shoulder.

A noise came from the kitchen.

Back against the wall, she crept her way along the corridor. At the doorway, she stopped. Was that breathing in the kitchen?

No—creaking. The rope. Keeping time with the ticking of that blasted clock. But where was Tim? She took a step forward, crossing the threshold.

A still-warm circle of metal touched her temple.

"Hello, Marian," Bart said. "If you want that pretty head to stay in one piece, you'll drop your weapons."

"Where's Tim?"

Still holding the gun to her head, Bart grabbed her by the back of the neck and jerked her forward. Tim lay sprawled in a pool of blood just inside the dining room.

"Your weapons," Bart said.

She dropped the derringer. But her finger remained on the big revolver's trigger. Could she swing it toward him in time? Not soon enough to stop him from killing her. But he was probably going to kill her, anyway. Her heart pounded so hard that her entire being was shaking. Yet somehow, she'd never felt so alive as in this moment.

She didn't want to die.

The gun clattered to the kitchen floor.

"Where's your tall friend?" Bart asked.

"Right behind me. I'd run if I were you."

"I don't think so. I think he's dead. That's what all that fuss was in the hallway. But now what do I do with you? That's the only thing I haven't figured out."

He backed up a few feet, still training the gun on her. She wondered where he'd gotten the new weapon.

Bart leaned casually against the wall, assessing her. "You've done me a favor, you know. Killing Fitz. I would not stay here much longer, anyway, and you've made my exit a far sight easier. So I thank you."

She spit between her boots. "I did it for myself. Not for you."

Bart scratched his scalp with his free hand. "Only thing I can't figure—why'd you want the old man to suffer like that? After he took you in. Educated you."

Her calm broke. "He cast me aside, destroyed me! I'd kill him again if I could for what he done to me." *Did to me*, she corrected. *Did*. Her chest heaved and her shoulders trembled.

A vicious smile spread across Bart's face. "Well hell, you don't know? You don't *know*?"

"What are you talking about?"

He threw back his head and laughed. She'd have lunged for his gun if she wasn't frozen in place. His laughter chilled her straight to her core.

"And I thought you were sharp, Marian. For a woman, anyhow."

He grabbed hold of her arm and dragged her into the hallway. The gun pressed into her lower back. He brought her to the small records room. Douglas lay against one wall, his skin pale as sand. Bart nudged him with a boot.

"Dead. Just as I thought. Now it's just you and me, once again."

When Bart saw the open safe and the scattered documents, his laughter increased in pitch.

"You even got into the safe! A surprise, wasn't it? You had the wrong end of the stick yet again. Fitz was always careless with his funds, but I convinced him to take more active measures. So many outlaws about, this day and age. And he built the damn bank, so he might as well use it."

Bart dug into his pocket and produced a key dangling from a length of silver chain.

"Fitz had it around his neck the whole time. The key to his fortune—safely stored in a deposit box in the Eden Bank vault. You killed an innocent man and got absolutely nothing for it."

He threw her to the floor. Marian backed into the corner, papers crinkling underneath her.

"Liar," she said. Fitzhammer wasn't innocent.

It was all lies.

She heard crying. Her child. Her poor, lost child. Doomed before she ever had a chance at life. But Marian had known whom to blame. That knowledge kept her alive—that drive for revenge.

She put her hands over her ears, but they couldn't block the child's cries or Bart's cruel laughter.

No, she thought. *No. It can't be true.*

"No!" she screamed.

Bart cringed. "I've heard enough from you to last me the rest of my days." He went to Douglas's body and ripped away part of the man's shirt. Bart used it to tie Marian's hands. He ripped another reddened strip of fabric and used it to gag her mouth.

"That's much better. Now you can be quiet and listen. That obedient little girl is still in there somewhere."

He knocked his fist against her forehead. She turned away, trying to burrow into the corner.

"Now, Fitz was an old letch," Bart said. "But he couldn't seal the deal, if you catch my meaning. So he always liked to have pretty young things around for the view. But I thought to myself, why should all that loveliness go to waste? You weren't the first, nor were you the last."

Her gorge rose. Bile filled her mouth behind the gag. She had to swallow it down to keep from choking.

She remembered the darkness. The hands holding her down. The smell of Fitzhammer's cologne. She'd known it was him. She'd been *sure*.

"The crux is," Bart said, "that I need to make it seem this is all *your* doing." He thought a moment.

Marian barely listened. She was lost in the world of her memories, suffocating in the dark. But she hadn't seen him in the light, had she? The smell of him was clear. His outline in the doorway. But back then, Bart and Fitzhammer cut a similar figure, didn't they?

No. No, no, no.

"Let's see, now," Bart mused. "You're holding Fitzhammer as your prisoner. Threatening his life, unless I deliver his fortune into your hands. Right? And your men killed O'Connor and the others, so what am I to do?" Bart clapped a hand to his thigh. "Go to the bank and retrieve the money, of course, at all costs.

Which I then deliver to you. And I'm left here to mourn my dear master, Ernest Fitzhammer, who you so viciously dispatch even though I do everything you ask. Doesn't that sound like a grand little drama? Half of it's true, thanks to you."

He squatted in front of her. "Only, *you'll* need to disappear to make it convincing."

She made a desperate grab at his gun, which he easily pulled out of reach.

"I'm a man of many secrets. This room is one of them. I fitted out the design myself during the construction— Fitzhammer may have paid, but he wasn't ever one for details, was he? He didn't see what he didn't want to see. If there were cries in the night, he believed the ghost stories."

She screamed her rage into the gag. The child's cries picked up again.

"So you see," Bart said, "you aren't my only problem here in Eden. But I do believe I'll work out my solution." Keeping the gun trained on her, Bart reached around one of the bookcases. He pulled some sort of latch, and it swung open. The child's cries grew louder, filling the room and Marian's head.

He picked her up by the back of her shirt. Shoved her inside a dim room. It smelled like an unemptied chamber pot. Her knees hit the ground. Immediately she turned, trying to get back through the doorway.

He kicked her backward. The hidden door swung closed.

She threw herself against the wood, choking on her muffled screams.

MARIAN'S EYES watered from the smell. The child's cries still filled her head.

Slowly, very slowly, she turned around to face the room.

She examined the tiny, dark space. It took a moment for the shapes to take on meaning in her mind.

Bottles, jars, boxes and tins covered a set of shelves. Emptied containers were piled into one corner. A cot was pushed up against a wall. Blankets sat in a bundle on top.

But it wasn't just blankets. There was a *person* inside.

A woman. She had her eyes squeezed shut and her small, grime-streaked face turned to the wall, as if she were trying to hide. The child's mewling cry was coming from the cot. Somewhere in those blankets, the woman held a baby.

"Shhh," the woman said in a faint whisper, "shhh."

My God, Marian thought, though she'd never in her life been a church-goer. Bart had said he had secrets. *If there were cries in the night, he believed they were ghosts.*

But these were no ghosts.

Marian got up. She tried to pull the gag from her mouth, but it was too tight. Using her bound hands, she pushed back the curtain over the window. Wan light filled the room. The woman on the cot flinched.

No, she wasn't a woman. She was a girl. Gaunt enough that her cheekbones made sharp lines, but she had not a single wrinkle or sign of age. She was just a few years younger than Marian. Perhaps sixteen.

This could've been me, she thought.

Marian made a grunting sound through her gag. The girl wouldn't look at her. How long had Bart been keeping the girl here? Since the pregnancy, maybe before, Marian guessed. It was horrifying to contemplate the girl's life here.

"Please, leave me alone," the girl whispered.

Marian got onto her knees by the cot and held out her bound hands. She made a small whimpering sound through the gag, hoping the girl would respond. Because if she didn't—if they didn't help one another—they were both going to die. Bart had a purpose for them yet, but Marian was sure he wouldn't let them live long.

The baby was quieting. The blankets moved, and Marian thought that the girl was giving the baby the breast. Finally, after several agonizing minutes, the girl looked over.

Marian made another grunting sound. The girl's eyes widened, scanning Marian's bonds, her clothes. The blood stains.

The girl turned away again, burrowing even further beneath her blankets.

Marian started grunting in protest, but then the girl emerged holding a pointed stick. It looked like a piece of wood sharpened to a spike at one end.

So the girl had a weapon. What did she mean to do with it? Marian forced herself not to move.

The girl wrapped a blanket around herself, with the baby tucked securely inside. Then she beckoned Marian closer. "So you can breathe better," she murmured. She gingerly held the gag and began sawing at the fabric. She was so weak, though. Each movement of her arm seemed to take tremendous effort.

Marian held out her bound hands and nodded at the spike. *Give it to me.* The girl hesitated. Then she set the spike between Marian's palms. After a few tries, Marian sliced through the gag. The fabric fell away. She panted, licking at the scrape the spike had left on her lip.

"Who are you?" It came out too harsh. Marian tried to soften her voice. "I'm Marian. What is your name?"

"Shhh," the girl whispered furiously. "We can't. He'll punish us."

Marian focused on her wrist bindings instead. These were trickier. It was hard to get enough leverage with both hands still bound. The girl had to help her hold the spike at the right angle, while Marian applied the pressure. Finally, her wrists were free.

Marian sat back. All was quiet for a few more minutes.

"Anabel," the girl eventually said. "And this little one's Bea." Her voice was thin and high. She was a mother, but she looked and sounded like a scared child. She tucked the spike back into its hiding place.

"Why haven't you used that spike against him, Anabel?" Marian asked.

She rocked the baby back and forth.

"You don't ken."

"Oh, but I do. You're not the only girl who's been used in such a way."

The girl's eyes met hers. Pale brown, intelligent if weary. "When I was little, my father come out here. He'd claimed some land after they made the Utes leave. My mama and the rest of us came to the ranch later. But my father done raised his hand one too many times to me. I hated him, and I thought anythin' would be better than living under his roof."

She glanced around the room. There was no hatred in her eyes, not even sadness. Just a profound exhaustion that didn't match her years. "There was a boy I rather liked, and I think he cared for me well enough. Rex. We run off together, and he found work in one of the mines near Eden that Mr. Fitzhammer owns. We told people we'd married. Didn't live in much more than a hovel we shared with another family, and near starved. Then Rex died last year. Crushed by some falling rocks. Mr. Fitzhammer gave me a little money, and that's when I met *him*."

The baby whimpered in its sleep. Anabel put a hand on the little one.

"He came for me a few days later. Told me that Mr. Fitzhammer had took a liking to me and wanted to help me. I wasn't blind to his intentions, but what else was I to do? So I went. Bart brought me here. I didn't ever see Mr. Fitzhammer, nor anybody else. He said he'd kill me if I made too much noise and I was found out. Sometimes I couldn't help myself, though."

She described how Bart would bring her food and water every couple of days at first. She was supposed to empty her chamber pot through the window. But it opened onto a tiny, closed-in space between the buildings. No means of escape without trying to climb the walls. And before too long, her condition prevented any such attempt.

"But what was the use of even tryin' to get away? If I got out, or if he just put me in the street, how'd I be any better off? I had a roof, and I had food. There wasn't nothing else for me. Not anywhere. Don't you see?"

Anabel's speech had gotten slower and slower, and here she stopped. She stared into the empty space of the room. Marian thought of her own darkest days and nights. That feeling of hopelessness, that the future held nothing but coercion and pain.

It was hard to see all of that in the mirror of this girl. Part of Marian hated Anabel for it. She eyed the window—there had to be some method to get out that way. The girl hadn't tried hard enough.

But I didn't escape either, did I? Not until the asylum, when Bart and Fitzhammer both had already cast her aside. If they hadn't, she would've stayed in Fitzhammer's house. She'd truly believed she had no other choice. It was terrible, the things that subjugation did to one's mind.

Forgiveness was not easy for Marian, least of all for herself.

"And the baby?" Marian asked.

"Bea came a couple of months ago. Bart—he was angry when he saw I was in such a state so soon. I like to think she's Rex's. She has pale hair like him."

She touched the silky strands on her child's head.

"But it's hard to keep her quiet. I'm afraid of what he'll do. That's why I sharpened the wood, just in case he tried to take her away...I think she's the only thing that's kept me alive. In my heart, I mean."

"Then we have to get her out of here. Before he returns."

"We can't. There's no way out."

Marian went to the narrow window. She opened it and stuck her head out. There were four sheer walls surrounding a tiny patch of dirt. Night was coming soon. There was only a bit of graying sky visible from this pit. As if she was inside a well and looking up. The air smelled stale and rotten, but still fresher than Anabel's prison.

Ignoring the pain in her scraped hands and wrists, Marian went outside and started rapping on the various walls. There were more of the slot-shaped windows on the second and third floors. If they could climb up there, though...

"What're you doin'?" Anabel hissed through the open window. "Get back inside."

"I will not die here."

"*Please*, you're just makin' things worse."

Marian squeezed back through the window into the horrible room.

"Bart is set on seeing me dead—I've a long history with him, just as ugly as yours. I fear he intends you for the same fate. But even if you live, do you want to raise Bea like this? Trapped in this hell?"

"But where would we go?"

"Someplace they cain't hurt us!"

Despite everything, Marian still believed that such a place might exist. Tears had filled her eyes. "Even if we die of starvation in the wilderness, at least we'll be free. Your daughter will be free."

Anabel looked at the sleeping child. "D'you really think that's possible?"

"I'll help you," Marian said. "I've survived as much as you, and more."

Anabel bit her lower lip. She shook her head. But the girl was merely warring against her own thoughts, rather than expressing a conviction. Marian waited.

"I'll try, if you wish," the girl finally said. She spoke without hope, as if resigned to a new but equally bleak fate. *How can she make it with so little will left?* Marian wondered. But she couldn't leave the girl and the baby here. That would be like leaving her own soul behind, tattered though it was.

Marian instructed the girl on how to prepare. The climb would be difficult. And escape from Eden would be ever more tenuous. But staying in this room meant certain death. If not for their bodies, then without a doubt for their hearts and minds.

Marian went back outside, and Anabel tossed items to her

through the window. The blankets, spare linen, food. Anabel handed out the baby and finally emerged herself.

The two of them took almost all the space in the yard. Anabel wrapped some blankets into a bundle. She tucked her few belongings inside, including the wooden spike. Then she held it out to Marian, who slid this bundle around her body to carry it.

Next, they constructed a sturdier sling, in which the baby could travel against Anabel's body.

Marian held the little thing as Anabel wound the sling around herself. The baby felt awkward in her hands. Squirming and warm, pink lips and cheeks. Tiny veins ran along her eyelids. How could such a fragile creature survive? This beautiful child could be crushed as easily as a flower, and this world seemed utterly indifferent to her fate.

Anabel was probably right. There was nowhere for them to go. No place that would be safe for this child. But this knowledge made Marian want to scream in defiance.

We're alive! We live and breathe and feel.

"Would you be able to carry her, too?" Anabel said.

"What? No." She tried to hand the child back, but Anabel was removing the sling. She draped it around Marian instead, crossed oppositely from the bundle that Marian already wore.

"Please. You're stronger. If I drop her while I'm climbing, if I fall..." Anabel's expression was so plaintive.

"All right." Marian adjusted the sling and tucked the baby inside. The warm weight of her rested against Marian's right torso. It felt lovely and natural and monstrous all at once.

It was getting dark when they began to climb. Anabel started first, so that Marian could help push her up. "The brick is far more uneven than it looks," Marian said. "Feel with your fingers."

"But it's madness! I can't!"

"Then use your legs to push against the opposite wall."

It took several more minutes of cajoling before Anabel tried in earnest. Marian followed, moving at a quicker pace. Her hands were still raw and bleeding from holding the rope earlier in the day. The baby wiggled against her side. Right away her hand slipped, and she tore skin from her finger pads. Blood once again made her hands slick. Every inch up the building was both triumph and agony. But the pain meant nothing. This was the only way. This, or death.

"I can't," Anabel kept moaning, "I can't." But she crept upwards like a spider mounting a narrow shaft.

Marian braced herself against the other walls, forcing her way up. The space between the buildings was only a few feet across, and for that, they were lucky.

Quickly, Marian overtook Anabel. She reached the second level. Here, the metal roof of the wooden building sloped up into a peak. But it was steep. Escape would be far too dangerous that way. Balancing her weight, Marian tried the hotel window. It wouldn't budge. Painted shut from the looks.

"We'll have to reach the next window up." If it too didn't open—but she wouldn't think on it.

Anabel moaned. Marian kept climbing.

After a while, Anabel began to quietly sob. She'd stopped trying to speak.

Marian was first to reach the third-floor window ledge. Her muscles were trembling. She rested her left side against the stone lip, still hanging precariously. A glance down reminded her of the audacity of what they were doing—two skinny, exhausted women climbing sheer brick walls.

Marian forced up the narrow window. It wanted to stick, as if it had rarely been opened. She was looking into the corner of a guest room of the hotel. It was a grand room, full of large windows on another wall overlooking the moonlit canyon. She lowered the baby inside first, then levered herself over the sill. The baby whimpered.

"Don't fuss now," Marian murmured. "You must wait a bit longer yet for your dinner."

Leaning sideways out of the window, Marian reached for Anabel's hand. "You're almost here. A little farther, come on."

Anabel moved up her hand by another inch. But she was still too far below for Marian to grab hold of her. Anabel's fingers were turning white from holding so tightly to the brick.

"I can't."

"You *must*."

Anabel's limbs shook. She screamed as her hand slipped. Marian leaned her whole torso out of the window. The sill cut into her stomach. She grabbed for Anabel's arm and caught it by the wrist. They slipped against one another, but Marian held tight. *Come on, damn you*, she thought.

Anabel's foot slipped. Her legs swung, colliding with the brick beneath the window. She was dangling in mid-air.

Marian could hardly breathe, the window was pushing so hard against her. Behind her, the baby began to cry.

Marian hauled Anabel upward. The girl was frail and far too thin for a healthy young mother. But she was still heavy enough for Marian, exhausted and bloodied, to struggle. She could barely hold on to the girl. Marian's jaw ached as she bit down on a scream. They were so near safety, yet still so close to the edge.

Anabel's wrist was slipping from her grasp.

"Give me your other hand," Marian said through gritted teeth.

Anabel's body was limp. "I can't."

"You must try. I can't do it myself!"

The girl didn't answer. She was still slipping.

"God damn you, try! Your baby needs you."

The girl's brown eyes lifted. "She has you now. Take care of her. Please. I'm so tired."

"Give me your hand. *Now*. You *must*." Marian screamed and cursed at the girl. She didn't care who might hear her and discover them. She couldn't let Anabel go.

But Marian couldn't hold her there. The weight was too much.

It had taken them endless minutes to reach the third floor. But now, the girl plunged through the same distance in less than a second. Her body hit against one wall, then another. She crashed to the ground, which was now hidden in shadow.

THE MINUTES TICKED BY AT A SNAIL'S PACE. I HAD TO STOP myself from chewing my nails. The only sounds were our footsteps, our breathing, the occasional click from Jason's video camera or the electromagnetic detector.

Penny started whispering.

"What honey?" I asked. "What're you saying?"

"I'm not talking to you. I'm talking to her." Penny looked toward the hotel.

Helen inhaled sharply. Debbie was shaking her head, the tears starting up again.

"Do you mean Marian?" Helen asked. "Is it her again?"

"I don't know. She's really upset, though. And scared."

Just as she had in front of the bank, Penny stopped at the hotel's threshold. We all gathered behind her. The street was quiet.

Then Jason, suddenly animated, pushed his way to the front. "There's someone inside. Do you hear that?"

I couldn't hear anything. I looked from Debbie to Helen, and they both shook their heads. But Penny said, "Yes, that's the lady. She's crying."

-from A DEVIL IN EDEN by Lawrence Wright

CHAPTER THIRTY-SIX
2019

Penny banged on the door and screamed. "Let me out! Someone, help!"

He couldn't keep her in here all night. Tripp couldn't be serious about this. She clawed at the paneling, but the wood was just as solid as it had been a week ago.

He didn't care about Linden or Anvi or anyone else. He'd never believed Penny at all. And she'd fallen for it completely, let him lead her straight here like it was really her idea all along. How had she been so stupid?

She could go to the police. But that consolation wouldn't get her out of here any faster. Besides, would they believe her word over Tripp's? She'd gotten herself trapped here before.

She turned around and faced the room. Her mental walls were up. She didn't want the ghosts to come back. Yet she knew they were already coming, already here. She'd heard the baby's cries and the woman's whispers.

"I'm Penny," she said aloud, over and over. She paced the tiny room. "You're gone. Stay out of my head."

But she couldn't keep the emotions from seeping in through the cracks. The anguish, despair. Those confused, contradictory thoughts.

Please let me go. I hate him. What if he doesn't come back? What will become of me?

"Go away!"

She went over to the window, peering out. The dirt was turned over, the bones dug up and gone. Only a few plastic markers hinted at the investigation. But the ghost remained. Had it been her body, this woman who'd been trapped here? Who was she?

Penny felt a presence beside her. The baby shrieked, and then its cry was muffled. She looked over.

A woman sat on a narrow bed. She was gaunt, her dark hair long and stringy. She bent over a tiny child wrapped in blankets, begging it to stay quiet. *Hush*, she said, *hush, little one. I'll catch a beating if you don't.*

Anabel. The name appeared in Penny's head. Her name was Anabel.

The woman looked up suddenly. Penny thought at first that the ghost was staring at her, but then she realized that Anabel was looking at the door. Anabel started wrapping her baby around and around with the blanket, as if she were muffling the despairing cries of her own heart.

He's here. He's come.

Anabel's fear flooded into her. Yet it was also relief—a hateful, detestable relief—because without the food and water that he brought, she would die.

Anabel hated herself for that sense of relief.

"This isn't happening," Penny said. But she couldn't keep Anabel out.

Cold blew in from the window, pushing Penny to the center of the room. Hands slammed into her back. "Let me go! Stop!" But the hands pulled her up, only to force her roughly down once again. She contracted her body into a ball, tears blurring her vision.

Her body lifted from the ground, then fell. Penny's breath left her lungs.

The hands gripped her throat. They squeezed.

We have nowhere to go, Anabel said.

She couldn't fight the images any longer. Penny felt her own self fading away as Anabel's memories invaded her mind.

CHAPTER THIRTY-SEVEN

LINDEN SWAM IN AND OUT OF CONSCIOUSNESS. HER HEAD hurt when she turned it a certain way. She was sure that she was dreaming. This awful, burned-out place couldn't be real. Sometimes, she thought she saw things moving in the depths of the shadows.

Anvi's face appeared, kneeling over her. "Drink." Anvi held the spout of a water bottle to Linden's mouth. Linden tasted the water, then drank.

"Where are we?" Linden heard music playing.

She was starting to remember things. Being chased in the night. The blow to her head. Walking—no, being led—through a gate, then down a darkened street. The clank of a padlock opening, an enormous door swinging wide like a mouth. And being swallowed up into something's charred insides.

I'm in the bank at Eden, Linden realized. Anvi had brought her here. But she had no idea why.

"This is where the guilty are punished," Anvi said.

That didn't sound good.

Anvi set down the water bottle next to Linden. "You've been asleep all day. You need to get up now."

Linden tried sitting up. Her head ached, and she felt nauseous. Her hands were bound in front of her.

"Anvi, whatever you think I did—"

"I know it wasn't you. It was *him*."

Did she mean Tripp? Linden was about to agree, but she wasn't sure that was a good idea, either.

"I really need to pee," Linden said. Anvi nodded.

"We can go over here."

Anvi helped her up. Blue and green light flashed in through the building's upper windows.

She and Anvi stepped over a conduit which organized the cords along the floor. Before now, Linden had only peeked inside the bank. Most of the electrical for the music show passed through this building and out to the scaffolding around the stage. This was also the place where Scott had gotten tangled up in the cords along the wall. Almost strangled. It was an awful thought. Linden couldn't imagine a worse place to die, surrounded by these charred walls.

Could she scream? Would anyone hear her? Not over the music. She heard the DJ's voice shouting at the crowd. Their answering cries. It was the third night of the festival.

Devil's Night.

Linden looked down at her hands. She was wearing handcuffs. Where did Anvi get handcuffs?

"We really should go." Linden kept her tone even. "They'll need us at the festival. It's starting."

"Not yet. We have to wait."

"Wait for what?"

"It's him who's guilty." Anvi paused and glanced to the side. "Only the guilty are punished."

That again. "Do you mean...Tripp?"

She hesitated. "Yes. I think so."

They reached the far corner of the bank. It smelled bad over here. So this was the bathroom, apparently. Linden breathed from her mouth, accepted Anvi's help with her pants, and did her business. This was not the moment to panic.

Alright, think, Linden told herself. She didn't know what was wrong with Anvi's mind right now, and really, she didn't want to know. She just wanted out of here. In one piece, preferably.

When they'd crossed the room again, Linden said, "I'm pretty angry at Tripp too. Maybe he deserves to be punished for what he did. But I've got other plans tonight, so..."

"He won't give me the code," Anvi murmured. "He could end this if he wanted."

"What code?" Linden asked.

Anvi looked at her sharply. "You don't understand."

"Hey, I get it. He hurt me, too." *Tell her the truth*. Maybe that would get through. Linden laughed, though her eyes stung. "I was convinced he was going to marry me. Can you believe that? But he doesn't love anyone but himself."

"I gave him so much." Anvi knelt by Linden's side, her eyes suddenly more focused. "And then he took more, and he threw me away when he was done. Everything I worked for is gone." Anvi brushed away tears. "It means nothing to him."

"I'm so sorry, sweetie. Truly. But is he really worth..." Linden nodded at the surrounding space. "Whatever this is?"

Anvi rubbed her face. Her eyes were going distant again. She got up and walked a few feet away. Her body stilled, her head tilted. Like she was listening to something. The music?

"There are other options," Linden said. "We can end him online. With our contacts—"

"*He has to pay for what he's done*," Anvi screamed.

She dug into her pocket and produced a gun.

"Oh, shit." Linden held up her cuffed hands, like that would help protect her. "No, no, no. I'm on your side, okay?"

Anvi wasn't pointing the gun at her. But Linden was glad she'd already peed, because if not, she'd be a mess right now.

"We're in this together," Linden said. "You and me. Just tell me what to do, and I'll do it."

Anvi nodded. "When he gets here."

Still holding the gun in one hand, Anvi took out her phone with the other. Her face glowed in the screen's light. She started typing with her thumb.

Linden heard a sliding sound. In the shadows of the room, something was moving.

CHAPTER THIRTY-EIGHT

I'm Penny Wright.

I was born...April 18, 1994. My father is Lawrence Wright. My mom is...my mom...

Penny struggled to remember. "Debbie," she whispered. "My mom is Debbie."

She opened her eyes. She was lying with her back on the hard floor. Everything was dark. Slowly she sat up, her body aching. Her throat was sore. She coughed, but the pain only worsened. Music thumped from some distant place.

She'd been trapped inside Anabel's memories. Penny had spent days, weeks, months inside this stinking room. She'd felt the utter desperation of knowing she'd never leave. Even if that door suddenly opened, she could never leave. Because if she did, who would take her side? Who would give her a roof? Food for her baby? No one cared if she lived or starved.

Except him. The man she hated most.

And he'd given her the single comfort that she had in the world. A baby daughter.

But it hadn't been *him* who held Penny down. There was no ghost here but Anabel; Penny understood that now. Anabel was reliving the most terrible moments of her existence in this room.

She had died, but she'd never been able to go beyond the hallways of the hotel. Always, again and again, Anabel returned to this room and endured her torture anew.

But Anabel had retreated. Why? Had Penny been able to push her away? Perhaps even freed her, like she had Matthew's mother?

Right away, Penny knew that was impossible. Anabel's spirit was infinitely more disturbed than Matthew's mother had been, and Penny had no way to form a bridge with her. She'd been so helpless there on the ground, those images playing out in horrifying detail in her mind.

Then she remembered the very last of them—the terror of falling through the air. Her frail body shattering on the ground. That was what made Anabel leave; in Anabel's lingering mind, she hadn't perished after that fall. She'd merely returned to her torment. She couldn't accept that she was dead.

Marian had tried, but she couldn't save Anabel. She had taken the child—the child that had never been hers.

Penny pushed onto her hands and knees, then stood. She swayed, catching herself against the wall. The wood vibrated just slightly with each beat of the music. She had to get out while she still could. But she could hardly see. She looked to the window and realized—night had fallen. She might've been lying there for hours, for all she knew.

It was Devil's Night. But what had happened to Linden? Or Anvi?

At the window sill, Penny lifted herself up, arms shaking. She got one leg over, then the other. Jumped down. The softened earth caught her fall. Dirt slipped inside her shoes. She looked up at the small square of dark sky between the buildings. Dizziness made the square spin. She braced her hands against her knees.

I can't.

No. That wasn't Penny's thought, but Anabel's. Marian had climbed out of here with a baby and supplies strapped to her.

She'd reached that narrow third-floor window. Penny was healthier and had no such burdens. She could do it.

But it was dark. She could hardly see.

I can't, that voice insisted.

"You must," Penny said. Linden was out there somewhere, maybe still in trouble. And Penny couldn't endure any more time in the secret room with Anabel.

She began to climb.

At first, she visualized the rock-climbing wall at her gym in LA. This one was more challenging. She had to search out the hand and footholds almost entirely by feel. She used the opposite walls for leverage. Just like at the gym, she found a rhythm.

Then she felt the presence again at her side.

I can't do this. I'll never be free of him.

A weight sunk onto Penny's shoulders. Yet she kept propelling herself upwards. She had to make it out. She passed the boarded-up second-floor window and kept going.

After countless minutes, her fingertips touched the next stone windowsill. The glass and frame were entirely gone, leaving the rectangular opening. She didn't look down, but she sensed the open chasm beneath her. That terrifying drop.

No, Anabel cried inside of her. *I can't go.*

Freezing air blew through the window into Penny's face, forcing her back. Her fingers slipped from the stone. She brought a hand up again, groping for better purchase.

I'm so tired, Anabel said.

But the ghost's power was growing. Penny's muscles shook. She wasn't strong enough to keep holding on. She would never see anyone she loved again—Linden, her parents, Krista, Bryce. And Matthew most of all.

The spirit of the dead girl was pushing her back down. She was going to fall.

"Anabel, please. We have to go."

The ghost couldn't hear her. Had no consciousness of her as a separate being. But Penny reached out to her, just as she had to

Matthew's mother the night before. The terrible images—the shame and aching despair—once again engulfed her. But she let them come. She'd helped Mrs. Larsen. So she could do this, too. She had to.

"We can be free. If we go. If we leave this place."

I can't be free.

Anabel's voice was hesitant. The deluge of memories slowed.

Penny's fingers were nearly giving out. She made one last desperate grab. Her hand closed over the inside curve of the windowsill. She pulled herself up and through the window's opening and rolled onto the floor. The floorboards creaked beneath her. Her chest heaved, lungs sucking in air.

Anabel was still there. But she was tentative. Confused.

"Your baby is safe," Penny whispered. "But you fell."

The ghostly presence started to retreat, returning to her prison, but Penny held to her. Penny played back the memory of Anabel plunging through the air. The shock of the impact.

Tears spilled down Penny's face.

"You died. You're free now. It's time to go."

The ghost lingered there another few seconds. And then suddenly, Anabel's presence was gone.

Penny's mental defenses were gone, too.

She was aware of the scores of people outside on Main Street, the energy of hundreds of souls. Most living, some dead.

Further down the street, an immense darkness hovered, far deeper and colder than the night that surrounded them all.

But here, in the Paradise Hotel, Penny was alone.

CHAPTER THIRTY-NINE

Ray kicked the metal sides of the cargo trailer. He was lying on his back, staring into the pitch-black space.

"Can anybody hear me?"

Of course, no one responded. Nor had they for all the hours he'd been here. He was losing his voice. His only sense of time was the crack in the cargo trailer's door, which he'd discovered while trying to find a way out. For a while, he saw daylight through the crack. The stem of a lock and dirt on the ground. He could hear the generator trucks humming somewhere nearby, that distinctive rumbling noise they made. The metal trailer had gotten unbearably hot.

But now, the daylight had faded, and night was coming back. At least it would cool off again.

Ray had tried thinking about it from every angle, but he just didn't understand why Anvi would do this to him. She'd left him his wallet, but she'd taken his gun and car keys and everything else—including his pride. She'd attacked Linden, too. Why?

He went to the door and pushed, sucking in the fresh air from the gap.

His throat was painfully dry. His clothes were stiff with evaporating sweat, and his mouth tasted like bile. His eyes were still sore from the bear spray, weepy and ringed with crust no matter how much he rubbed them. And his head hurt so bad. There was a bump on the back of it that almost made him pass out when he touched it.

Ray had only moved to Ashton to spend more time with his dad. Sometimes one of them didn't sleep at home, and that was fine. They'd go to work the next day and not see each other till dinner, without a single comment on where they'd been. Ray and his father had a convenient understanding—no questions, no need to give answers. But that meant his dad might not even be looking for him yet.

Then again, was he that eager for his sergeant to find out about this? Failing to maintain control of his weapon? Getting overpowered by a girl who couldn't be taller than five three? That was going to look outstanding on his termination report.

Ray slammed his fist against the trailer door. Then again. He hollered and pounded until he'd spent his energy again. His body slumped against the cool metal.

Then he heard a noise. "Hello? Is somebody in there?"

It had come from outside. Ray sat up, his veins flooding with adrenaline. He banged against the door. "Help! Get me out of here!"

He heard the clank of the lock, and then the door rolled open. "Holy—Ray, is that you?"

Ray tried to step out, but his knee buckled. He landed face-down in the dirt.

CHAPTER FORTY

June thumped her way into the white tent, where the servers were setting out platters of appetizers on a long table. Linden and Penny weren't here yet; hardly anyone had arrived. June's crutches dug into her armpits, and the cast on her leg was already starting to itch.

Kelsey put a hand on the small of June's back. June was exquisitely aware of that touch. But she doubted it would happen again once the other guests arrived. God forbid Kelsey's father—SunBev VP Jeff Richardson—saw them as anything more than friends. But Kelsey had come to the festival, at least. It was more than June had expected.

"Do I need a name tag or something?" Kelsey asked.

June's girlfriend had her hair up in a twist. She'd worn a pair of dark jeans with a sparkly tunic, and let June borrow the dress she'd brought—June couldn't fit into pants because of the cast.

"No name tags," June said. "We wanted the party to be more...low key." She glanced around. They'd brought in potted plants to make it feel organic, less like a temporary space. LED candles twinkled on the bar-height tables. She'd gone over the final plans with Linden and the Sterling team just last week, but it felt more like last year.

After leaving the hospital yesterday, she'd wanted to just slink away and hide. But Penny had asked her to stick around, and Kelsey had promised not to leave her side. Even so, June wished to be anywhere but here. What would she say to her co-workers? Sorry about ruining the other party two nights ago. Clumsy me.

Because she certainly couldn't tell them the truth.

Despite endless questions from the doctors and her bosses and from Kelsey, June had struggled to explain why she'd been up on the second floor of the Paradise Hotel. Her memory was hazy. Partly, it was the concussion, which poor Matthew Larsen had apparently also suffered by having to save her. But her recollections from that night also didn't make much sense. She'd felt sick, upset. She'd imagined that she heard a voice. Maybe it was a ghost, or maybe June had just made it all up in her mind.

Yet all day today, and especially during the shuttle ride up to Eden, she'd been thinking about what happened in the hotel. When she and Kelsey walked through the festival gate tonight, the Paradise had loomed ahead of her. The memories had only gotten stronger. She remembered that voice, calling out to her. She couldn't hear it anymore, but she could feel it. The pull to go closer, as if that despairing voice had called to the ever-present sadness that June kept hidden inside.

Last night, she'd wanted to explain it to Kelsey. That voice in the hotel. How it had drawn her to the second floor. But the words wouldn't come.

Whatever happened, it wasn't your fault that you fell, Kelsey had said. Maybe she was right.

June *had* heard someone in the hotel. Penny would've believed it. But even if nobody else did, the truth was still the truth. And it wanted to come out.

"What's wrong?" Kelsey asked. "Do you need to sit?"

June was shaking. A few people were trickling into the party, and she retreated farther from the bar, hoping they wouldn't notice her yet.

This wasn't the right time. She was supposed to be smiling,

chatting with the SunBev sales team, talking about their imminent product launch. But she didn't think she could keep this inside anymore. Being here in Eden again, with Kelsey this time—it had made something crack and spill over inside her.

"I need to tell you," June said. "Now. It can't wait anymore."

"Okay." Kelsey found a chair, took June's crutches, and made her sit. Kelsey sat beside her, leaning in. "What is it?"

But when June opened her mouth, she didn't talk about the ghostly voice. A different truth came out.

"It's about your father."

In whispers, she told Kelsey about what happened several months ago. How he'd touched her. Humiliated her, and then acted like it was nothing.

Kelsey's face turned red, and then tears filled her eyes. "Why didn't you tell me before?"

Then, Jeff Richardson's voice boomed across the space. "Kelsey, honey! Isn't this a surprise. What're you doing here?"

June's stomach dropped. She knew that Kelsey wasn't close to her father. He'd barely been present while she was growing up. But nobody wanted to hear this kind of thing about her parent.

Please don't leave me, June thought.

Kelsey wiped her eyes, standing. "We'll talk more about this later, okay? I'm so sorry it happened. But right now, tell me what you want me to do. If you want a scene, I'll make one. If I should stay quiet, I can do that too."

Suddenly, everything was lighter. Easier. June reached for Kelsey's hand. "Just stay with me."

Now wasn't the time for confrontations. But she felt braver than she had in a long, long time. When Mr. Richardson approached, June gave him a vicious smile. *Kelsey knows the truth now*, June thought. *And she believes me.*

He blanched, taking a step back. June had never seen that look on his face before: uncertainty.

"Nice to see you, hun," he said to his daughter. A glare was Kelsey's only reply.

"We can catch up later," he added, glancing at Kelsey's hand clasped with June's. He didn't ask. Didn't dare. Instead, June's boss walked away, quickly finding another colleague to fawn over. Rings of sweat had darkened the underarms of his dress shirt.

"Well. That was awful." Kelsey squeezed her hand. "But I love you. Always."

June had no idea how all this would turn out. Maybe her job was in jeopardy. But that moment of victory, small as it was, had felt damned good.

She was lucky to be standing here with Kelsey. Probably lucky to be alive, or at least not in the hospital right now. She had Matthew to thank for that. Kelsey had already said thanks to him, but June hadn't done so personally yet.

While Kelsey went to the bar to grab a couple of beers, June took out her phone to send Matthew an email.

There was a text from Penny, sent a few hours ago. June hadn't seen it before.

Hi, I can't find Linden. Getting worried. If you hear from her or Anvi, please let me know?

June looked up. Neither Linden nor Penny had arrived. Anvi hadn't shown, either. That was strange. She quickly tried calling their numbers. Each one went straight to voicemail.

Maybe it was nothing. But June felt uneasy. Why would Penny send a text like that, saying she was worried, and then not follow up? June knew that Penny and Linden had been looking for *her* the other night, before she fell. What if something bad had happened again, but to *them* this time? She thought of that ghostly voice in the hotel. How she'd felt confused. Compelled.

On instinct, June decided to call Matthew. He and Penny were close. Once again the call went to voicemail, but she left a message.

Kelsey came over and handed her a foamy glass of stout. "Who were you talking to?"

"Just voicemail."

June considered the situation—was she being too paranoid?

—and decided to forge ahead. She set the beer aside. "You spoke to Penny yesterday on the phone, right? From the PR agency I'm working with?"

Kelsey nodded.

"Help me find her? I'm worried that something's wrong."

CHAPTER FORTY-ONE

AFTER THE SUN HAD SET, MATTHEW DRAGGED HIMSELF OUT OF bed. He'd slept the whole afternoon in his room at the inn. His joints still ached, especially his right shoulder. But his head felt slightly clearer. Clear enough that his immediate first thought was Penny.

He didn't regret their night together. But he'd thought that it would make some difference to her. He'd woken up beside her, watched her sleep with her cheek on his pillow. It had felt so right. When they made love again, it hadn't seemed like it would be the last time. Not to him. She certainly hadn't seemed dissatisfied, despite the injuries that—only slightly, mind you—handicapped his performance.

Saying goodbye to her would be so much worse this time around. Because he knew exactly what they were giving up. But Penny did, too. It just hadn't been enough to change her mind.

"All right, Larsen. Stop feeling sorry for yourself."

He rubbed a hand over the stubble on his jaw. He was going to get cleaned up, get some actual food in his stomach. Then he was going to get some beers with Bryce. He wasn't supposed to drink. But he figured that his best friend wouldn't have to ask why he was getting drunk.

He lumbered over to the desk, where he'd left his phone. The battery was dead. He plugged it in to reset. He went for a shower and then came back to check his messages.

Nothing from Penny. But June Litvak had left him a voicemail.

"I wanted to thank you for helping me the other night. I hope you're well...And I'm calling about Penny, too. Have you seen her? She couldn't find Linden earlier, but...maybe they're busy. Just have her call me if you see her? Or let me know she's okay? Thanks."

His pulse jumped straight into overdrive. He texted Penny first. Called. Then tried calling June, but she didn't answer. Next he called Linden. And then Anvi, because she should be with them at the festival. Nobody was answering. Maybe cell coverage in Eden was acting up. Maybe they were busy, like June thought. But then, why hadn't June seen them up there? Why had June been worried enough to call him? It didn't feel right.

He threw on clothes, grabbed his keys, and left his room.

He found Krista behind the front desk.

"Do you know where Penny is?"

Lawrence and Debbie came out from the office while Matthew explained his concerns. He played June's voicemail.

"I haven't been able to get in touch with any of them," Matthew said. "Something could be wrong." He thought of how she'd gotten hurt in the Paradise Hotel last week. Those bruises. She'd been genuinely frightened.

Lawrence's face seemed carved from stone. "It's Devil's Night."

"So what?" Krista put both hands on the counter. "Penny doesn't want our help or our input. She's made it clear she's fine on her own."

"She's in trouble," Lawrence said. "I know it. We need to get up there."

Debbie held up her phone. "Just wait a minute, both of you.

Before you go charging up to Eden, let's call Harry. He's at the festival tonight, isn't he? If anything's wrong, he'll know."

CHAPTER FORTY-TWO

Tripp Sterling walked toward the white tent, smoothing the front of his shirt. Beneath strings of lights, guests were already sipping on the free booze and nibbling toast with Iranian beluga caviar. A little gift Tripp had personally provided. It was probably over the top for SunBev—they were from Phoenix, for God's sake—but Tripp had wanted the closing party to leave them wanting more.

He scanned the faces for Linden, but she wasn't here. He couldn't believe she was really angry enough to miss tonight.

"Evening, Mr. Sterling," said the beefy head of security, who was monitoring the entrance to the party just outside the tent.

"Evening. Have you seen Linden yet, by any chance?"

"No, sir. Not yet. Should I ask around on the radio?"

"No, that's fine. She's probably running late." He stepped away, then doubled back. "What about Anvi?" If she tried to screw up the last night of Devil's Fest, he would end her. She'd never find a job in PR again.

The guard thought. Then his face lit up. "I saw her earlier. Near the stage. Want me to find her?"

"I'm sure she's busy. But if she shows up tonight, come get me before letting her in, all right?"

The man nodded, and Tripp continued on.

He'd gone back to Ashton to get cleaned up after that unpleasantness with Penny. Maybe he'd been too harsh with her. Especially now, when his entire team was falling apart. He checked Twitter again; at least Anvi had posted nothing else. If she tried to tarnish his name, he'd have his lawyers on her by tomorrow morning. He'd hoped she would handle his rejection with a little more dignity.

Hadn't he done enough for the women in his office? The above-market pay, generous bonuses, theater tickets. The lattes and lunches that he always paid for. He never screamed at his staff, unlike his sister, whom the employees at her art gallery called "The Great and Terrible." He expected a lot, but he'd made no secret of that. He'd made a mistake with Anvi, but plenty of people did far worse.

But all that still couldn't keep Penny or Anvi loyal. His generosity had made them overestimate their importance. Even Linden. He liked her, and he knew her to be capable. She came from a well-known LA family, and she gave phenomenal head. Before, he'd had every intention of continuing their partnership long term. But she was far from irreplaceable.

A dozen heads turned when Tripp entered the party. He shook hands, smiled, laughed and traded flattery. He loved this part of his job. Anybody could put together events and keep track of spreadsheets and talk on the phone. But he was the essence of the Sterling PR brand. There was a reason that the firm bore his name.

If the client believes in me, he reminded himself, *then nothing else matters.*

He got a martini from the bar, and then June Litvak assailed him. She was swinging herself around on a pair of crutches.

"Tripp?" June asked. "Have you seen Linden or Penny?"

"Not yet." His hand was growing slick against the martini glass. "They're running late. Should be here soon."

June frowned, as if his answer didn't satisfy her. He was

surprised she'd even shown her face tonight, given the trouble she'd caused at the opening-night party.

Tripp excused himself and moved on. He stopped to chat with Jeff Richardson from SunBev and Harry Wright, their grease-man in Ashton.

"Where are your beautiful colleagues tonight?" Richardson asked. "We don't have nearly so nice of a view."

Tripp's jaw tightened. Why was everyone so interested in his female employees? "I wish it were otherwise. I hate to disappoint."

"Other responsibilities, I'm guessing?" The ice in Richardson's drink rattled. "I'm sure they have *many* roles in your firm."

Tripp grinned. He hated Richardson, actually. The guy's casual sleaziness, as if he and Tripp were on the same level. But it was good that Richardson felt comfortable.

"They do," Tripp said. "Help's not essential, but it comes in handy."

"Are you saying Penny's not essential?" Harry Wright asked. The man was still smiling, but somehow those teeth looked a little sharper.

Damn. Tripp had forgotten for a moment that Harry was Penny's uncle. So he wasn't such a good old boy after all, at least about his niece. Tripp laughed and clapped Harry's shoulder.

"Of course Penny's essential. In fact, I'm considering giving her a raise."

The idea had just occurred to him. When he let Penny out of that room in the Paradise Hotel, he could offer to keep her on at the firm if she zipped her mouth.

Harry's phone rang. He looked at it. "Excuse me, I need to take this. Debbie?" He walked away from them.

"I just saw June," Tripp said to Richardson. "She seems to be recovering from her accident."

"Good thing. I'm not sure we'll keep her on, though." Richardson looked into his glass, which he'd nearly drained. "She's not as reliable as I'd hoped."

I know how you feel there, Tripp thought.

Harry came back over, still holding his phone. "Gentleman, sorry to interrupt, but have you seen Penny at all this evening?"

Who was Harry talking to? "Why do you ask?"

"My sister-in-law is on the phone. Penny's mother. She says nobody's heard from Penny, and they can't reach her. Apparently she was looking for Linden earlier?"

"Right," Tripp jumped in. Sweat was suddenly soaking his undershirt. "Penny and I tracked down Linden on Main Street this afternoon. The two of them took off afterward to prep something for tonight. I think maybe a presentation for after dessert."

That had sounded asinine, but it was what came into his head. So Penny had told someone about Linden. He'd instructed her not to, but she hadn't listened. He cursed at himself for not making sure. At least he'd taken the battery out of Penny's phone and stored it in his hotel room, just in case her family had some way to track it. He'd done the same with Linden's, which would hamper her ability to cause him trouble tonight.

"Penny's off doing her job," Harry said into the phone. "She's fine."

Tripp thought that was the end of it. He went back to greeting his guests, being sure to prompt Richardson about SunBev's goals for the next quarter. Just in case he could help.

But then, after about twenty minutes, June tapped his back again. He'd always thought she was cute with all those blond curls, her slight frame. But that frown brought out the ugliness in her.

"I still can't find Penny or Linden," June said. "I've asked the security guards and most of the people here. Nobody has any clue where they are."

Then Harry Wright walked over. He'd been listening. "You know, I agree. I'd feel better if I could check in with Penny myself. Just so I could tell her parents I saw her. Can't you find out where exactly she is?"

Tripp smiled. "How about you both enjoy the party, and I'll track Penny down? I'll have her call home, so her mom doesn't have to worry."

June nodded, the frown barely shifting.

"Thank you," Harry said. "That would be very kind."

"Not a problem."

There was only one thing to do—he had to go have that conversation with Penny about the raise right now. Better yet, he'd offer to make her a partner. Then she'd do anything he asked, at least for the near future. And it would teach Linden a lesson too, for thinking she could leave him in the lurch.

This would be easier if I'd made Penny the damn offer in the first place, he thought. But she'd been acting so irrationally. Hopefully, these hours locked away had put some sense into her. He'd use the back door of the hotel—the same way he left earlier. He had the set of keys he'd gotten from the security guard. This would all work out fine.

Tripp left his martini on a table and went straight for the exit. It was just in time, too. His hands were shaking.

His phone chirped. He stopped to look. A text from Anvi.

If you don't want the entire world to see all of our texts and emails, then come to the bank. Alone. Plus, Linden says she has a video?

He muttered a string of curse words.

"Everything okay, Mr. Sterling?" It was the beefy security guard, staring at him.

He waved, slipping his phone into his pocket. "All good. Carry on."

Of course Linden was behind this. That conniving, selfish...

He'd deal with Anvi and Linden first. Penny wasn't going anywhere, thankfully. He wished he could lock up all these troublesome women until he was ready for them. It would've made his job a helluva lot easier.

CHAPTER FORTY-THREE

Debbie set down her phone. "Harry thinks that Penny's fine. She's just working."

"But she should be at that party," Matthew said. "She told me earlier that it's important. It makes no sense that she's not there." A terrible feeling was gnawing at his stomach, eating at his mind. Penny wasn't safe. He had to do something or he'd lose any semblance of calm.

"I don't like this," Lawrence said.

"Me neither," Debbie agreed.

Matthew dug his keys from his pocket. "I'm going to Eden. Now."

"You shouldn't be driving," Debbie said.

Lawrence came out from behind the desk. "I'm coming with you."

"Dad—" Krista protested.

Debbie caught her husband by the wrist. "Lawrence, are you sure? You haven't set foot in that place in almost twenty years. The last time..."

"You think I've forgotten the last time? But it's Penny who could be in danger now. I have to."

Lawrence drove, pushing the limits of the truck's engine and tires on the rough road. Every bump meant a lightning-sharp jolt of pain in Matthew's head, but he gritted his teeth and ignored it. Before they could reach the parking lot, an attendee ran out, waving his arms. Matthew buzzed the window down.

"You can't come in here," the guy said.

"It's an emergency."

"I'll call Harry," Lawrence said. "He'll make them let us in."

Five minutes later, Harry met them in the parking lot. "You shouldn't have come, Lawrence," Harry said as they got out of the car. "Tripp just went to look for her. Everything's fine."

Matthew didn't care what Tripp was doing. They'd never officially met—Linden and Penny had handled that side of things. Matthew thought Tripp seemed like a douche bag. But he also wondered if he was stereotyping the guy unfairly just because Tripp had a smarmy, self-satisfied grin and wore shirts with cuff links even on the weekend.

But if Tripp Sterling had done anything to jeopardize Penny's safety, Matthew would permanently remove that grin from his face.

He started toward Main Street. Lawrence followed, and Harry cleared the way at the festival gates, speaking into his radio. A voice squawked back.

"Wait, hold on," Harry said, "the security guards found somebody."

They veered toward a tent, which had been set up as a headquarters for the security team.

But it wasn't Penny. It was Ray Castillo.

Ray was inside chugging a bottle of water. The man looked awful; his clothes were stained. He had dark circles beneath his eyes and a day's worth of beard on his chin. He finished the water, droplets still trickling from his mouth. He started telling a wild story that Matthew couldn't follow. Something about bear spray.

Then Matthew felt a tug on his sleeve. It was June—she was balancing on crutches, wearing a ruffled black dress. A young woman Matthew had never seen hovered by June's elbow. *Maybe that's Kelsey*, he thought, remembering his phone call with June's friend yesterday.

Without preamble, June said, "You're here for Penny?"

"Yeah. Did you hear from her?"

"Not yet. She and Linden and Anvi are all missing. Somebody needs to check the hotel. I'm worried."

Matthew knew exactly what June meant. Too many bad things had been going down in that old brick building.

"I'll go right now." Matthew grabbed Lawrence. "We need to get to the Paradise Hotel."

They left the security tent. As they neared the festival proper, the music and crowd noise grew more intense and the bright lights waned. Beams of green and blue swept across the crowd in time with the beat. Glowing bracelets and necklaces twirled as people danced.

Lawrence stopped, staring at the scene. "So this is what Penny's created. Devil's Fest."

Matthew pulled Lawrence along. They wove between festival-goers, then had to push as the crowd got denser.

Near the hotel, Matthew leapt over the wooden barrier. His head spun, and he stumbled as he ran up to the entrance. He tried the door. Locked. As he expected. He was furious at himself for not keeping a key, but Sully had it now. How could he have known?

"Hey, what're you doing!" Behind them, a security guard was waving his arms. "You can't go back there."

"I'll distract him," Lawrence said. "You keep looking for Penny."

Matthew nodded. He didn't recognize the guard, and he didn't want to stop and explain or wait for permission. He'd have to go around the side. There were some boarded-up windows near the back, and he knew which ones were a little loose. His crew had tried their best, but the brick was a bit soft in places. He just needed a tool. Some leverage.

He started toward the far side of the building. But as he passed the front windows, Matthew heard banging. He turned, scanning for the source of the sound.

Penny was looking out from the dark lobby, her palms pressed against the window glass.

"Lawrence, take a look at this."

Jason was standing before the open doorway to the bank building. I climbed the steps. Inside, the building was little more than a shell. The wooden rafters and beams were exposed, everything blackened by fire.

But there was a bit of rope hanging from one of the floor joists. The end of the rope swung steadily back and forth, back and forth. The creaking sound matched the rope's rhythm, as if there was a heavy weight at the end. Yet there was nothing tied there. No source for that creaking. No natural source, I should say.

"Jesus," I murmured. I thought of Beau MacKenzie's diary, what he'd seen and heard in the Paradise Hotel. But we were far from the hotel.

What the hell was happening?

-from A Devil in Eden **by Lawrence Wright**

DEVIL'S NIGHT - 1894

DOUGLAS WAS DREAMING. HE KNEW IT WAS A DREAM BECAUSE his mother was there. He was a little boy, and it was Sunday.

"You'd better wake up now, Deedee," she said. "Time for church. Jesus might wait for us, but the preacher ain't."

Then he heard people singing.

Not singing. Screaming.

He gasped, sitting up. He was in a dark room. His body hurt. Oh Heaven, did it hurt. He couldn't go to church like this.

But that had been the dream. With his mother, who'd passed. Had she really come to him? If she did, then she'd come for a reason.

You'd better wake up.

Pain or no, he had to get moving. That man had shot him in the hallway of the Paradise Hotel. That was why he hurt so damned bad. His shoulder was on fire. But somehow, he was alive. He felt for the wound, nearly blacking out when his hand touched the crater where the bullet had gone in. But the blood was tacky. It seemed to have clotted. Someone had tied fabric around the wound.

Marian. Where was she? And what about Tim?

Had he really heard screams, or just dreamed them?

Douglas staggered through the dark. It was night, and he had no idea how much time had passed. The hotel was quiet. He nearly tripped over something—a body. The men in the hallway. Flies buzzed. His hands met congealing wetness. The stench of feces gagged him.

There was light ahead. Douglas came into the kitchen, where moonlight was coming in around the curtains. A worse smell hit his nose, metallic and rancid and noxious. He could make out shapes in the dark, but nothing was clear.

"Tim? Marian?"

All he heard was incessant, unearthly creaking.

He reached the window and pulled back the drape. Light flooded the kitchen. A terrible scene came into view. Blood had pooled on the floor, black as tar in the low light. Tim was sprawled in the middle of it, partway into the dining room. The man was very dead. Flies hummed around him.

Douglas breathed in and out. The smell was making him even more light-headed. He had to get outside to fresher air.

He found the back door. The air was sweet and cold in his nostrils, filling his lungs. He bent over and retched.

You'd better wake up now, Deedee.

"I'm awake, Mama," he said. "I'm awake."

After a few minutes, Douglas started to walk. Every step was an effort. His limbs and joints were stiff. The town seemed deserted, as if everyone had vanished. Or were they dead? *Is this some hell?* he wondered. *Punishment for my sins?*

But he wouldn't see his mother in hell. That gave him hope.

He stumbled onward along the backside of Main Street's buildings, past outhouses and stinking trash piles. The stables were somewhere this way. East—that's what the porter had said to Tim that morning.

The porter was dead. Tim was dead. Maybe Marian was dead, too.

He couldn't bring his thoughts together. All Douglas knew was that he needed a horse. Right now, that was enough.

After some minutes, a more wholesome smell met his nose. Hay and animal manure. He heard something large moving, and then a loud sneeze. He'd never spent a lot of time around horses—not like his cousin Ronald, who'd found work driving cattle—but he knew that sound well enough.

The stable door was not bolted. Someone had left it ajar. Douglas went inside. His mind kept blinking in and out of awareness, but his hands seemed to know enough on their own. The horses were braying, stomping in their stalls. Douglas found a calm one and led it out into the open space.

Next he needed to tack up. His foot bumped into a curved shape on the ground, and he nearly fell—it was a saddle. There was more tacking scattered on the ground, as if someone had been here in haste and knocked everything about. But they weren't here now, so Douglas didn't worry over it. He began to prepare the horse. Marian had saddled their rides to get to Eden. His wife was good with horses, too. But even before that, Douglas remembered watching his cousin Ronald on rare visits. Ronald's horse, Sunflower, had hated Douglas. Bared its huge teeth at him. Never let him ride.

But this horse was placid. It could tell something was wrong, and it scuffed nervously at the dirt. But it let Douglas lay the blanket down, tighten the buckles on the saddle, and position the halter and bridle. He was sure he'd attached something wrong. But he'd done his best.

Finally, he led the horse out into the street. He kept expecting someone to come out and stop him. But no irate stable hands appeared.

His only doubt was about Marian. Where was she? Dead in the hotel? Had she escaped, somehow?

But what if she was still here someplace, alive?

I don't owe that woman a damned thing, he thought. She'd been nothing but a curse to him. He never should've listened to her mad ideas. He'd been such a fool. Seeing that empty safe was one of the worst feelings he'd ever had. All the things he'd done—thieving, holding Fitzhammer prisoner, refusing to let the cook go—it had all been for nothing. Nothing except evil. The Paradise Hotel was indeed an accursed place, just as the cook had said. For all Douglas knew, this entire town was cursed.

He thought these things as he led the horse through the shadows. Then he saw the canyon walls narrowing and realized he'd been going the wrong way. Heading not toward the road, but away from it. He spun around, and that's when he saw her.

Marian, lit up by moonlight.

She was walking haltingly down Main Street, looking like a vengeful spirit. Like she'd risen from the depths. Hair in a wild corona around her head. Eyes so wide and shining, he could see the fury in them from his hiding place. She had a thick bundle wrapped across her torso, carrying something.

Douglas pulled the horse behind a building. But she hadn't seen them. He wished for his weapon. The horse tossed its head, and Douglas petted its neck.

"Calm now," he whispered. "You're all right."

He wasn't sure if it was really Marian, or some monster that had taken her form. In the dark and in his addled state, both possibilities seemed equally likely. He remembered how she'd killed Fitzhammer in the hotel dining room, pulling on that rope until the life squeezed out of the man. She'd never intended to let Fitzhammer live. Douglas understood that now.

Perhaps Fitzhammer had deserved this fate, for whatever evil he'd done to Marian in the past. But that wasn't justice. It was simply more evil.

Evil that I helped to do.

Whatever Marian really was—woman or devil or vengeful force of nature—Douglas bore some responsibility for what she'd done here today.

He tied the horse to a railing. "I'll be back." He followed Marian's form down the street.

When she neared the bank, she stopped. Douglas stopped as

well, watching. There was another horse—this one tied up in front of the bank, with saddlebags attached.

Marian took off her bundle. She looked inside it. Seemed to be *talking* to it. An odd sound carried across the street to Douglas—a sort of choked cry. Marian tucked the bundle into one of the horse's saddlebags. She walked up to the bank's entrance. She tried opening it, but it was locked.

Then she starting banging with both fists on the double doors.

BART HAD NEVER SEEN SO much money.

He was inside the bank's vault, and he'd lost track of time. There was more wealth here than he'd even imagined. Fitz had kept some things to himself, the old rogue. Bart kept piling the cash into bags. Gold bars and purses of glittering dust, too. A few times, he caught himself counting. How was he even going to carry it all?

That didn't matter. He'd be able to carry enough. But he couldn't keep wasting time. It was already dark outside.

His only regret was killing the bank teller. All that filthy blood. Bart's stomach did a turn, thinking of it. He'd have to walk through the mess again when he ventured upstairs. But the teller hadn't listened when Bart explained the situation. *Fitzhammer's being held for ransom. I need to get into the deposit box.* Hell, he'd had the key! Everybody in town had heard the gunshots at the hotel, all dozen or so souls who were left. Those who hadn't fled. Bart had seen the dust rising along the road.

The stable boy, Pete, was one of them. Bart had gotten rid of him easy enough. *They're killing everyone,* Bart had said. Scared him real good. Bart had the bloodstains on his clothes to prove it. Pete saddled up his little donkey and got right on out of town, hadn't he? This town was full of cowards. Especially with O'Connor and the Pretty Eyes Saloon's barkeep dead.

He just wished he didn't have to deal with the women at the hotel. And the baby. Damn little pest probably wasn't even his. If he'd been a violent man, he'd have killed Marian already. But he wasn't some mindless monster. He didn't go around killing for no reason. He was clever. He looked for solutions to his problems.

Marian was going to be his solution.

He'd laid even more of his clues at the Paradise before coming here. Scrawled the name "Marian" on the dining room wall with that skinny man's blood. It had a whiff of melodrama about it. Like some tale of gasping women in a gothic castle. But in such situations, subtlety didn't pay. When the law men finally came riding into town, Bart wanted no doubt about the true culprit. He'd make sure that neither Marian nor Fitzhammer's money were ever found to contradict him.

As for Bart himself? By morning, he'd be on Main Street with the few remaining townspeople, ready to tell his tale. He'd have to leave out the part about visiting the bank, now that the teller had been so stubborn. But he could blame that death on Marian as well.

Anabel made him sorry, though. She was still pretty in a certain light. He'd have to get rid of her, too, and he hated to think on it. Perhaps he could find a cliff, and she'd have a fall. As long as he didn't have to touch her when she died.

He'd nearly finished packing up his satchels when he heard a noise above him. The ground floor.

Bart left the bags and crept over to the stairs. It had sounded like banging. Could the bank teller still be alive? No. That was impossible. Had somebody else worked up their courage and come sniffing around? If he was seen, that could be a problem.

Carrying his lantern, he slowly went up the stairs, weapons at the ready. He'd retrieved his own revolver from Marian's possession, and he still had the one from the barkeep, too. The rhythmic banging started up again. It was coming from the bank's entrance, which Bart had been careful to lock.

Someone was banging on the double doors.

Bart unholstered his revolver.

MARIAN STOPPED KNOCKING and crouched to one side of the bank's entrance. Darkness shrouded her. She felt the shadows permeating her soul as well, turning her into a wraith. A creature made of night.

That had to be Bart's horse tied up outside the bank. He hadn't ventured out in response to her knocking. But eventually, he would come. She'd be waiting.

Nothing seemed to be left in the world except for *him*. Not even the baby changed that fact. Once, however briefly, Marian had been a mother. Somehow, she might have learned to love that child. But now? It wasn't possible. She had taken the life of an innocent man. Sullied the little bit of purity left in her soul.

When Anabel had fallen, the last human part of Marian had died too.

She still heard the thud on the hard-packed dirt, the scattering of pebbles against the walls. Faced with that horror, Marian's mind had gone strangely quiet. As if sleepwalking, she'd stumbled through the hotel. The baby had burbled and cooed in her sling against Marian's side. In the kitchen, she'd ignored the grisly remnants of the earlier battle. There was a bottle of milk inside in the icebox. Marian had tasted it—goat's milk, not yet turned. She'd dribbled the white liquid into the baby's mouth.

She would find some safe place to leave the child. She owed that much to Anabel. But Marian no longer cared what happened to her own miserable self.

So long as Bart Adams was dead.

From the bank's entrance, there came a faint click—the inner bolt sliding free. The door opened. The hinges were well-oiled, silent. Light spilled from the opening. A man stepped out, pausing to look around. His gun glinted silver.

Him.

Her breath quickened. Her skin flushed. *Not yet*, she told herself. *Wait.*

Bart walked down the wooden steps. He carried a heavy sack. The planks creaked ever so slightly. His head swiveled left and right. Watching for the person who'd banged on the bank's doors. He glanced behind as well, straight at Marian. But she was still hidden among the shadows.

As soon as he turned and started toward his horse, she rose. Anabel's sharpened spike dug into her palm.

When he reached the horse, Bart tucked the gun into his belt. He lowered the sack beside the horse. A sound came from one saddlebag. The baby, grizzling in her sleep.

Bart stepped back. "What in the—"

Marian closed the distance between them, her boots moving in silence over the dirt. Now, she couldn't hesitate. If she gave him a single moment's warning, he might overpower her.

She grabbed for his weapon, wrenching it sideways from the holster. At the same moment, her left hand rose in the air. The spike slashed downward. The point of the wood sunk into Bart's lower back. He screamed and thrashed, knocking her aside. The spike snapped. She dropped the blunted end.

But she'd taken his gun. Marian braced both hands together and pulled the trigger of Bart's revolver. The shot sent bits of brick flying from the bank building. He was running for the still-open entrance doors. Then Bart spun around. His arm lifted. He was holding another gun—Marian hadn't realized he had a second.

Heat sliced across her side. But she kept after him, firing the revolver once more. This time Bart screamed. He tripped and fell forward, halfway across the bank's threshold. He crawled the rest of the way inside.

She reached the doorway just as he tried to kick it closed. The door landed against her bruised and bleeding torso. More shots rang out as Bart fired again and again. They echoed against the bank's thick walls and tin ceiling. She felt a punch to her thigh. Her knee buckled.

Then came the clicking of an empty chamber.

Marian had fallen back slightly, crouching partway behind the door. The pain was like a massive weight. Her eyes went dark. She blinked, and her vision cleared a bit. Only half a second had passed. In that brief pause, Bart had retreated farther inside the bank. Blood poured down Marian's leg.

She realized that she still held his revolver in her hands.

She lurched forward, dragging her wounded leg behind her. A cry came out of her with every step. A sound of pure rage.

The room was lit by a kerosene lantern, which sat on the wooden counter. Bart crawled along the floor. He'd gotten past the bank teller's desk and was now heading for a set of stairs. They led down to a cellar. Marian realized what must lie below—the bank's vault. He thought he could shut himself inside. Hide from her, like he'd hidden behind darkness and lies for so many years. Perhaps he'd die in that small room, wasting away like Anabel.

But that wasn't enough for Marian. She wanted to see it happen.

He'd reached the railing. He pulled himself up, trying to stand.

Marian's arm shook. She could barely lift the revolver. She fired—a miss. Bart slipped on the top stair. He clung to the railing. His body twisted and he looked up, his eyes meeting hers. She saw terror there. She felt nothing—not pity, not mercy, nor pleasure. Simply emptiness where her heart had been.

Marian steadied her hand and fired again.

The bullet hit him in the chest. Bart let go of the railing and careened down the stairs. Marian dropped the gun and fell to her knees. She lay on the floor at the top of the staircase. She couldn't see Bart down there at the bottom. But she could hear Bart's labored breathing.

Finally, the breathing stopped.

She thought of the baby, still tucked inside the horse's saddlebag. Most likely someone would find her. And if not, the child would avoid all the suffering that was a woman's inheritance in this world.

Marian made no move to get up. She doubted that she could.

She wished she could reach that lantern and dash it against the wooden furniture. But no matter. Her body was already on fire. She was in hell—she and Bart, together. Right where they belonged. And together they would burn.

"This is the one I took at the bank," Jason said.

He rewound the tape and handed me the camera. I put my eye to the viewfinder, my stomach a swirl of anticipation. I watched Penny mount the steps in front of the bank's double doors. I gasped when the door blew open and Penny was thrown to the ground, even though I knew it was coming....

Then my daughter vanished from my mind. The shot had now moved forward. Jason had pointed the camera into the open doorway of the bank.

I continued to watch the soundless video. And then, in the background of the shot—far in the shadows of the bank—an outline emerged.

I swore aloud.

"What?" Jason asked. "What'd you see?"

The outline had vanished almost immediately. But it had looked like a woman. Narrow shoulders, thin waist, hair loose around her head.

I held out the camera. "Put the video back about thirty seconds. Then look in the shadows. The background."

Jason did as I asked. He exhaled with a small moan. "No way. That's...Hell, Lawrence. I see her."

Marian. Just as Penny had said. Marian was there.

-from A Devil in Eden by Lawrence Wright

CHAPTER FORTY-FOUR
2019

Linden watched the front doors of the bank. Outside, the DJ dropped the beat and the crowd roared. The ground vibrated with the noise.

"Did he say if he's coming?" Linden asked.

"He will. I know he will."

But it had been ten minutes. Was Tripp making them wait? Or maybe Anvi's text hadn't riled him as much as Linden thought it would. She'd even had Anvi mention the video—a moment of drunken foolishness a year ago that Linden had promptly deleted from her phone. But Tripp didn't know that.

This is stupid, she thought. *It'll never work.*

She looked down at her hands. The handcuffs weren't especially tight, but the metal chafed her wrists. The skin was getting raw. Linden just wanted this to be over. But as long as Anvi held the gun and the handcuff keys, then she held the control.

"When he gets here," Anvi said, "we'll make him admit what he did."

And then what? How far was Anvi going to take this? Linden acknowledged she'd been a fool about Tripp, but she didn't want him hurt.

"Couldn't you take off the cuffs now? So I can help?"

Anvi spun around. "Did you hear something?"

Linden didn't know how anybody could hear much over the music. The stage was right outside. But Anvi kept hearing "things." Stopping to listen into the dark. Unlike Penny, Linden had never seen a ghost in her life. Maybe ghosts were real to some people, but to Linden, the supernatural had little bearing upon her experience.

But Anvi's strange behavior and this blackened, gutted building were making her wonder.

"It's him," Anvi said.

Linden didn't understand. The front doors hadn't moved. But then Anvi rushed away into the dark.

"Anvi!"

Linden heard a shout. Then a scuffle, and something heavy falling. A scream.

She backed up until she touched the wall. She stepped on electrical cords and nearly fell over. Her wrists pulled painfully against the cuffs.

The lights from the stage pulsed against the black walls. Green. Blue. Green.

Someone was coming.

Anvi came out of the shadows. She held her hands out at her sides. She wasn't holding the gun. Blood dripped along the side of her shocked face. Green. Blue. Green.

Then Tripp emerged behind Anvi. He held the gun.

"Linden? Where the hell are you!"

Linden cowered against the base of the wall. The electrical cords pressed into her back.

"So you think you're going to ruin me?" he shouted into the dark.

She had been planning to help Tripp when he arrived. Anvi would be distracted, and Linden had figured she could get the gun away somehow. To end this. But would Tripp ever believe that?

He wasn't going to shoot either of them, though. It wasn't possible. Tripp wasn't violent that way.

"You think you can intimidate me? Scare me? Blackmail me?" He raised the gun, pointing it at the ceiling. "Or were you actually going to use this? You're that much of a basic vengeful bitch?"

She stood and stepped out. Tripp's head whipped around, the gun now aiming at her.

"This has gotten completely out of hand," Linden said. "I never meant—"

A series of loud pops made her jump. For a fraction of a second, she thought Tripp had pulled the trigger. But then, black, rope-like shapes shot out from behind her. They wrapped around Tripp's wrists. He screamed and dropped the gun. More of the black things circled his waist. His neck.

Linden's eyes strained in the low light. But this was happening. It was real. The electrical cords had broken away from the wall and attacked him. Anvi looked on impassively.

The cords lifted Tripp into the air. His mouth opened, emitting a strangled, desperate scream.

CHAPTER FORTY-FIVE

THROUGH THE WINDOW, PENNY WATCHED MATTHEW DASH around the side of the hotel. Some of the festival crowd had broken off to stare. Her dad came and put his palm against hers on the other side of the glass.

"We're getting you out." Her dad's voice was muffled.

She nodded, struggling not to cry again. She'd never expected to see her father here in Eden, but right now, she was past feeling shock. Her eyes were bleary and tired already from crying.

There was a crashing sound. She spun to look. It had come from the back of the building somewhere.

"Penny!"

She ran through the dining room and straight into Matthew's arms.

"What happened?" he asked. "Are you hurt?"

"I'll be okay." She put her face against his chest, just breathing him in. The warm, solid weight of him. She looked up at him, though she could barely see him in the dark.

"I really missed you," she said.

"You saw me this morning."

This morning? Penny thought. In her mind, she'd been trapped here for so much longer.

He kissed her forehead. "Why are you in here? June was the one who called and said nobody had seen you. I don't understand what's going on."

"It was Tripp."

"*What?*"

She waved the question away. Penny would deal with that asshole later. More important things were happening.

"Where's Linden?" Penny asked. "Has anyone found her?"

"June said she's missing, too. Tripp supposedly went to look for you—maybe both of you—but I have no clue where he is. What did he do? Did he hurt you? I swear, if—"

"We just need to go," she said. "This isn't over yet."

Penny's Uncle Harry had arrived, and he forced the security guard to unlock the hotel's front door. Penny's dad hugged her the moment she got outside.

She asked again about Linden.

"I haven't seen her all night," Uncle Harry said.

"You're looking for Linden?"

Deputy Ray limped up the steps beside Harry. He looked ragged, like he'd been through his own drama while Penny was trapped in hers.

"I saw her last night," Ray said. "Anvi too, unfortunately. That's what I've been trying to tell everyone." Quickly, he told her how Anvi attacked them both, how she'd taken his gun.

"A gun?" her father said. "Somebody's got a *gun* up here?"

Penny tugged Matthew's hand, pulling him close to her side. "Listen, please, Dad. Uncle Harry, Ray, you too." They stood in a semi-circle in front of Penny, huddled together to hear over the music.

"Something terrible is happening at the bank. I think Linden and Anvi are both in trouble. But everybody in Eden could be in danger, too."

She saw the fear in her father's eyes.

"It's her, Dad. It's Marian."

Her dad knew, maybe better than anyone else, what that meant. *I was wrong*, Penny thought, *from the moment I came back here*. But she'd told the truth when she was a little kid. Marian *was* different. She was like no other ghost Penny had ever encountered, even Anabel.

Marian was awake.

"Then we're leaving," her dad said. "Right now."

"I can't. All these people are in danger because of me." Penny had seen the black fog hanging over the bank. Anvi had already been pulled into that rage and confusion, Penny was sure. But Marian's anger was growing still.

"You're not going to that bank. Matthew, you agree with me, don't you? She has to come home."

Matthew had said nothing yet.

"I trust Penny. We need to do what she tells us."

"Wait." Ray touched her shoulder. "Anvi has my gun. I called this in. Backup's on its way, and we're not doing anything until they get here."

"I'm not waiting. It's really Marian who's causing this, and nobody else can stop Marian but me."

"Then we'll send every security guard with you." Her father's voice was pleading. "To protect you."

"You know that won't work. They'll just get hurt. Please. I can do this." She hugged her father again and spoke directly into his ear. "Convince Harry and anybody else you have to, but get all these people out of Eden. I'm begging you, Dad. Tell me I can count on you."

Tears streaked her dad's face. "You better come home. And Matthew—you take care of her."

RAY INSISTED ON COMING. He, Penny and Matthew approached the bank from the rear, passing the concessions and picnic tables. They carried flashlights, borrowed from the security team. Penny looked at all the people who still had no idea anything was wrong. She wanted to yell at them to go, run. But she'd have to trust her father and Harry and the security team to handle that.

Penny's knees weakened, and she stopped. Some kind of surge had passed through her. The hair on her arms stood on end. It had felt like a flash of lightning at the head of a storm.

"You okay?" Matthew asked.

Marian. Penny felt the ghost drawing on the energy of the crowd. Drawing from Penny herself. She never had imagined any of this could be possible. But this was Bloody Marian, and tonight was Devil's Night.

What have I done?

"We have to hurry." Penny ran.

They rounded the side of the bank, coming up behind the stage. The DJ still played, the crowd oblivious. A sound engineer sat before a console, and he barely glanced at them as they passed.

Then a few of the overhead stage lights flicked off. The music dropped in volume—a speaker had stopped working.

It's her, Penny thought.

The sound engineer stood. "What's going on? Is somebody messing with our electrical?"

"I'd get out of here if I were you," Ray said to the man.

"But—"

Penny dashed toward the bank's doors, which were in the shadow of the stage. The padlock hung loose.

"I should go in first," Ray said. "My weapon—"

"It has to be me." Penny mounted the steps. The right-hand door swung wide before her.

Marian knew she was here.

Matthew rested his hand on Penny's waist. "I'm right behind you," he said in her ear.

Someone was shouting, but the music was still loud enough

that it muddled the sounds. The beat pulsed like a racing heart. *Boom. Boom.*

Penny stepped over the threshold. The interior was dark. She swept her flashlight over the space. Her light found someone, but it wasn't Linden.

Tripp hung in mid-air, black cords circling his neck and chest.

"Let him go." Penny walked forward.

The force of Marian's rage hit her, pushing her back. Matthew caught her before she fell.

He won't hurt anyone else, she heard in her head. *Ever again.*

"Penny, do something!" Linden was to her left. Anvi was here, too, standing a few feet away.

Tripp's legs kicked. His face was turning red. He was going to die, just like Fitzhammer did so many years ago.

Penny pushed herself upright. "Marian. Let him go." Whatever he'd done, Tripp didn't deserve this.

She flinched as Marian's voice again entered her mind, sharp and cold as a knife.

The guilty will be punished. I won't suffer them to live.

"This man is not Bart Adams. He's innocent of those crimes."

The flashlight flew from Penny's hand and broke into pieces against a wall.

They're all guilty.

"But Fitzhammer wasn't guilty. Was he?"

Marian screamed. Penny fell to her knees, holding her hands to her ears. But the awful sound was inside her head.

Abruptly, the scream ceased.

Tripp collapsed onto the ground, the cords retreating. Then one of them darted at Penny. Wrapped around her wrist. Pulled her forward, toward the dark recesses of the bank.

"No!" Matthew grabbed hold of her other arm.

"Just let me go, I'm okay," Penny said over her shoulder. "Get everyone out of here."

Matthew held on. The cord kept pulling. Penny's joints popped as she was jerked in one direction, then the other.

"Please!" Penny cried.

Ray dashed forward, took hold of Tripp beneath his shoulders, and dragged the man toward the door. Anvi ran out after them. Linden remained, crying and shouting Penny's name.

"Take Linden and go," Penny screamed. She looked back at him. "Matthew, *please*."

With a look of anguish on his face, Matthew let go of her arm. Penny flew forward, landing on her knees.

She heard them running. Then the bank's doors slammed closed. Matthew and Linden were gone.

The cord unwound from Penny's wrist and slithered away.

She stood, panting, staring into the dark.

"Marian. I know you're still here."

Outside, the beat of the music suddenly died. Shouting came from the sound system.

Something moved in a corner, and Penny spun to face it. Then the noise echoed from a different corner. She heard the electrical cords sliding along the floor, just out of sight.

What do you know about Fitzhammer? Marian whispered. *About anything?*

This wasn't like experiencing Anabel's memories. Penny didn't see Marian's past in images. But she knew. She felt the truth inside of her, like the memories already belonged to her. A terrible knowledge that she could not escape, much less deny.

"I know you killed him. You didn't understand it was Bart Adams who was to blame. But Bart's dead, too. You saw to that long ago. You're the one who's trapped here, Marian. Just like Anabel was."

Penny felt something brush her neck, and she whirled again. Her chest moved up and down as she breathed. The room was cold. Things rustled and whispered indistinctly in the dark.

"But you could be free," Penny went on. "I could...I could help you."

You know nothing.

The cords still slid across the floor. One touched her shoe.

Penny tried to force herself not to move, but her entire body trembled, waiting for them to strike at her again. To grab hold.

You're afraid.

A cold fingertip—she swore it was a fingertip—traced down her back. She tried to stay still. But finally she turned, desperate to bat the thing away.

But she wasn't in the bank anymore. At least, not that gutted ruin.

A plush carpet lay beneath her feet, a tin ceiling over her head. Polished wood lined the walls. A high desk sat before her with huge, leather-bound books stacked on its top. A stairway led to a lower level, its balusters intricately carved. Soft, flickering light came from a lamp which hung from a hook on the wall.

A woman strode toward Penny from the back room of the bank. She passed the desk, leaning an elbow against it. Her dark hair was braided but loose around her face. Her features were attractive and youthful, if solemn. She wore slim pants made from rough material; tall, scuffed leather boots; a stiff shirt and vest. A gun belt peeked from inside the woman's coat.

"Bart is not dead. He's here in Eden still. But we can stop him. Together."

Marian held out her hand.

CHAPTER FORTY-SIX

LAWRENCE DIDN'T KNOW HOW TO MAKE THEM LISTEN. His brother Harry was arguing with a thick-necked man in a dark blazer—apparently, the Devil's Fest head of security. Some puffed-up, pseudo-military type. Lawrence wanted to give him a swift kick in the ass.

"No way," the security man said, "I'm not shutting anything down until I hear from Mr. Sterling."

A few minutes ago, Penny, Matthew, and Ray had crossed Main Street and disappeared. Yet Lawrence and Harry were still in front of the hotel.

"Sterling is missing, can't you get that through your head?" Harry shouted back.

It was a massive load of bull crap. Penny was risking her life right now. They couldn't just stand here.

My daughter gave me a job to do, Lawrence thought, *and by God, I'm going to do it.*

Lawrence turned and jogged down Main Street.

Ever since Penny left home after high school, he'd regretted writing *A Devil in Eden*. But never so much as the past week. Once, he'd believed he was doing a public service by telling the world about his experiences here. But that was just another steaming pile. Penny knew it, and Lawrence knew it. He'd written the book for his own ego—he was proud of his family ties to Marian, and even prouder of his daughter's talent. He'd wanted to claim some small part of that luster for himself. But he'd driven his daughter away from home. He'd given her something to prove.

Devil's Fest was the result.

He plowed headlong through the middle of the crowd, ignoring cries of protest.

"Move!" he said. "Coming through!"

At the foot of the stage, a pimply security guard tried to stop him.

"Let me pass," Lawrence bellowed. "I have hemorrhoids that're older than you."

He scrambled up onto the stage. A DJ was dancing in front of some fancy music setup that Lawrence couldn't make heads or tails of. The DJ was a skinny, tall kid wearing mirrored sunglasses, as if that made any sense at night.

The kid glanced at him, then did a double take. Lawrence pulled the headphones right off the DJ's ears.

"Hey, you can't—"

"Turn off the music. *Now*. Or I start pushing buttons myself."

For a moment, the DJ stared. "Okay Gramps, okay. Calm down." He pressed a few buttons, and the music stopped. The crowd booed and yelled.

The DJ picked up his microphone, but Lawrence leaned over and yanked it from the kid's hand.

"Listen up, you idiots." Feedback squealed from the speaker.

Something popped overhead. Lawrence glanced up at the metal scaffold over the stage. Electrical wires were pulling free, snapping like rubber bands into the air. Sparks flew from the lights.

Marian, he thought. *She's really here.*

"Devil's Fest is over," Lawrence said into the microphone. "Time to go home. No, this isn't a joke—stop filming me! Yeah, you! Turn around, take your little glow sticks and Halloween masks, and proceed toward the exits in an orderly fashion."

Lawrence jumped as a spotlight crashed down onto the stage. The DJ screamed. Flames shot out of the ruined light, then dissipated. Another light fell, this one closer. Lawrence turned away as glass peppered his clothes.

Then suddenly, the entire stage went dark.

CHAPTER FORTY-SEVEN

MATTHEW HAD GOTTEN LINDEN OUT OF THE BANK. RAY WAS helping Tripp, and Anvi was sitting and crying on the ground.

But something bizarre was happening up on the stage.

Matthew could only see it from behind—Lawrence was yelling at the crowd. He watched Penny's father dodge a falling light. Then another light careened down and exploded in sparks. Another. People in the audience screamed. The electricity on the stage cut out.

And that's when Matthew saw the flames. One of the superheated falling lights had ignited the fabric concealing the understructure of the stage.

The flames spread faster than it seemed possible. In an instant, the fire was licking at the plywood sheets covering the bank's windows.

Penny.

Matthew turned to Linden. Her hands were still cuffed, and tears had left trails on her cheeks.

"Take Anvi and get out of here. Go with Ray. Take the side gate, not the front. Just get as far from Eden as you can."

"But what about Penny?"

"I'm going back in the bank to get her."

He ran for the bank's front doors. He was afraid Marian had locked them to keep him out, but the door opened when he pulled.

Matthew went inside, and the cacophony of Main Street receded. He couldn't see the flames in here yet. But he smelled the smoke.

The door clanged shut behind him.

He spotted her. Penny stood near the center of the room, her back to him.

"Penny, we have to go!"

Matthew went over and took her by the arm. She didn't react. Didn't respond. She was staring at nothing.

"Penn? It's me."

Too late, he heard the cords sliding along the floor. They grabbed hold of his ankles. He sprawled face-first, catching himself with his hands. Pain seared through his head and his injured shoulder. The cords dragged him away from Penny. He rolled over, trying to kick them off, but more cords wrapped around his middle.

The flames licked at the inside of the plywood, glowing in flickers of red and yellow and blue.

He looked over to see Penny walking toward him.

"Penn, you need to wake up and *help me*. This place is going to burn."

But her eyes were still glazed. Something clattered across the floor and then flew in a blur at Penny—her hand reached out to pluck it from the air.

A gun.

She pointed it at Matthew.

CHAPTER FORTY-EIGHT

"You see?" Marian said. "I told you he was here."

Bart Adams lay on the ground of the bank, blood oozing from his leg onto the lush carpet. His sneer was cruel.

"You weren't the first," Bart said, his eyes fixed on Penny's. "Nor were you the last."

She remembered the hands on her back. The smell of cologne, taken from his employer to disguise the truth.

"He thinks he can hide in the darkness," Marian said. "But we can stop him. He won't ever hurt anyone else."

Penny shook her head, trying to clear the images. Yet they remained.

"But he's dead already. You're dead."

Marian tilted her head thoughtfully. "That may be true. Sometimes Bart hangs. Or he falls from the heights, or dies with a bullet in his chest. Sometimes he wears the face of Ernest Fitzhammer or countless other men. But I know him. I will *never* forget, and he will never, ever stop. He's shown us no mercy. Why should we give it to him?"

"No mercy..." Penny repeated.

"That's right. Do what must be done."

Penny looked down. She was holding a gun. The metal was warm and comforting in her hand.

She pointed it at Bart. He bared his teeth at her. She knew in her soul, in her indelible memory, the terrible things that he had done. He intended to do them again. This man deserved to die.

Her finger tightened on the trigger.

But then Bart's eyes softened. "Penny," he said. "Penny, listen to me."

She blinked, and the bank returned to ruins. Matthew lay at her feet, held down by electrical cords.

"Penn, I know you're in there. Plea—"

A cord wrapped around his neck, halting his words.

Another blink, and Bart returned.

"Kill him," Marian whispered.

The gun shook in Penny's hand. This wasn't real. Bart Adams was dead, and his spirit was gone.

She smelled smoke. Heat pressed against her side.

"I'm Penny Wright," she said, the words catching in her throat. She coughed. "I was born in...1994. My father is Lawrence. My mother is Debbie."

She blinked and again the face before her changed.

Matthew. Not Bart.

I don't want to hurt you, she thought.

Penny threw the gun across the room. "You've had your vengeance. You have to end this, Marian."

Marian's face changed before her, the flesh melting, eyes bulging. Her mouth opened, and her shrill cry was more animal than human.

The illusion vanished piece by piece. First the carpet dissolved, then the polished wood blackened. The desk and the lantern vanished.

Matthew was struggling with the cord around his neck. Penny bent over him and pulled it free. She yanked the others away from his legs and torso.

"I'm sorry, I'm so sorry."

"Tell me later. We gotta go." He pushed himself up.

The room was growing hazy with smoke. Penny looked at the front wall—flames now engulfed several of the plywood sheets. There couldn't be that much in this building left to burn, but already it was hard to breathe. She coughed into her elbow.

Matthew put an arm around her shoulders. They hunched over and ran for the doors. He pushed them open. Fresh, cool air rushed inside. But before they could step out, the doors slammed back into place.

Matthew pushed the door again. She tried the other. He kicked at the knob. But the doors wouldn't budge.

They were trapped.

Don't you see? Marian said. *There is nowhere to go.*

Penny turned.

From the smoke and the shadows, Marian emerged, her outline glowing with silver. Blood darkened the front of her shirt and the leg of her pants. Her hands were wrapped in strips of stained cloth. Her mouth hung open in an obscene grin.

The guilty will be punished.

Matthew continued to pound on the bank's doors. Penny put her hand on his arm to still him.

"Open the door, Marian," Penny said. "We can leave—all of us. We can go free."

I can never be free of this.

"You want to stay here in this hell?"

Marian screamed inside Penny's head. A wind rushed through the bank, whipping Penny's hair. Cinders burned her skin and stung her face. Matthew grabbed her and pulled her down to the ground. They crouched against the doors.

If this is hell, then it's his making, Marian cried. *He took everything good and pure out of me. He killed me again and again and again, and he has to suffer for it.*

The wind continued to whip around the space—a vortex with Marian's ghost at the center. Electrical cords writhed and snapped in the air.

"The roof." Matthew pointed. Flames were dancing across the rafters.

He held Penny against his chest. She squeezed her eyes shut. Both of them coughed. Every breath hurt. Penny didn't know how to stop this, how to get through. Marian was too far gone. She believed she had no other choice but this awful place. Just like Anabel.

Penny opened her eyes. *Anabel.*

She crawled forward. Matthew tried to pull her back down.

"You said you trusted me," she said. His eyes searched hers.

Matthew let her go.

Penny faced the vortex that was Marian.

"Do you remember what you told Anabel? You told her you'd help her escape."

There was no answer but the rushing of the wind, the crackling of the flames. But Penny was sure that Marian was listening.

"We'll go someplace they can't hurt us."

The wind dropped immediately. But the heat was everywhere. Penny covered her mouth with her sleeve, coughing, trying to breathe through the fabric. The flames had spread over most of the roof. The plywood over the windows was turning black.

When Marian spoke again, her voice was weak.

But I can't.

Penny could barely speak for her coughing. Her eyes watered. But she kept whispering into her sleeve. Marian heard her well enough. "You must. Anabel is free now. So is her child."

It's my fault she died. I tried, but I couldn't...

"It wasn't your fault. It was Bart's. But now it's over."

Still, Marian fought.

Penny felt her anguish. Her fear.

Please, Marian, Penny thought. *You can set us all free.*

A small voice replied, *I don't know how.*

"Give me your hand," Penny said.

A coolness brushed her face. For a moment, a stillness fell. The flames vanished, and silver streaked across her vision.

Her ears rang, as if at a sudden silence.

Then the world around her resumed. The flames leapt back. The bank's doors swung open. Matthew took her arm, and they ran.

They emerged into a different sort of chaos—emergency lights, shouts. Somebody else grabbed hold of her. Her dad. He shoved a plastic thing over her face. Glorious oxygen flooded into her lungs. He made her keep moving.

They ran all the way to the chain-link perimeter fence, a few dozen yards from the bank building. Lawrence was holding her, keeping her upright.

Ray was beside them, helping Matthew.

There was a tremendous crash. Penny cowered, her hands going to her head. The roof of the bank had just caved inward.

Over his bright green oxygen canister, Matthew's gaze met hers.

We're really out, she thought. *It's over.*

AT FIRST, HELEN DROVE PAST US. WE WERE MILES AWAY from Eden, sitting on a slope overlooking the dirt road. I stood up when I heard the car coming, waving my arms. But she didn't expect to see us here.

Then she did a double take and slammed on her brakes.

"Come on," I said, pulling Jason by his shirt.

He'd barely said anything since we left the ghost town. He seemed exhausted. My body had the opposite reaction—as we'd walked away from Eden, following the dirt road out of the canyon, I'd felt more and more awake.

"What're you doing out here?" Helen asked, shocked at the sight of us. "I thought you wanted me to pick you up by Main Street. What happened last night?"

Jason lay in the back seat. All I could do was shake my head. "I don't know, Helen. I can't think about it right now. We just need to get home."

When I got back to the Ashton Valley Inn, the first thing I did was hug my wife. Then Penny and Bryce and Krista. I kept apologizing until Krista, my youngest, finally piped up.

"Daddy, you do somefing bad?"

I started sobbing, all the events of the last twenty-four hours finally too much to bear.

The next day, Wallace and Carlos drove up to Eden to retrieve our equipment. They said the memory cards were wiped, all the tapes blank. My research was gone.

-from A DEVIL IN EDEN by Lawrence Wright

DEVIL'S NIGHT - 1894

When Douglas found her, he thought she'd passed. But then she spoke to him.

"Leave me." Marian's words slurred. "I'm already gone."

"You ain't dead yet," he said, lifting her into his arms. Blood had already ruined his clothes, so he paid little attention to the mess.

"Don't say…ain't."

He smiled ruefully. Marian wasn't gone yet, but she was close. She probably wouldn't survive. But she'd saved his life at the Paradise Hotel—of that, he was sure. If Marian hadn't shot that man in the hallway and wrapped his shoulder, Douglas would've met his maker by now. The least he could do was make sure she didn't die here in Eden. This accursed town.

As he'd been watching the bank, Douglas had seen Bart—Mr. Fitzhammer's servant—come out of the bank carrying a heavy load. And then Marian had attacked. The two had fought viciously. Douglas had thought of intervening, but he had no weapon, unlike Marian and Bart. Too many bullets were flying for him to poke his head up.

He'd guessed that Bart had lost the battle. Douglas might've asked Marian for an explanation. But she was in no condition to be telling stories. She'd probably carry her many secrets to her grave.

Douglas carried her out of the bank. Now that the gun battle was over, the street had returned to its eerie quiet. The moon was climbing higher in the sky.

"The horse," Marian was saying, "Bart's horse."

"I know. It's yours now. Let me calm her."

The horse was badly spooked from the gunfire. He whispered to her and rubbed her side, surprised to find himself managing quite well with the animals. His cousin Ronald would be proud.

He picked up Marian and lay her across the saddle. He assumed she'd been planning to take this horse to escape from town—he'd seen her place her bundle into the saddlebag.

But there was also the large satchel that Bart had carried out of the bank. Now Douglas went to inspect it. The flap fell open.

"Holy Mother of..."

Gold. Bart's pack was full of gold bars and bank notes. Douglas regretted what he'd done today, yet this temptation was more than he could bear. He lifted the heavy pack into his arms.

"Fitzhammer's," Marian explained. "Bart meant to steal it."

Douglas reached for one of the saddlebags.

"No," Marian said, lifting her head. "The other side."

Shrugging, Douglas skirted around to the other side of the horse. He stowed about half of the small fortune in the saddlebag. The horse was a little lopsided, but it would be all right. Douglas would carry the rest of the load with him.

"I've got my mount, too," he said. "Wait a moment." As if she could do anything else.

Douglas retrieved his horse and led it over to the bank. Then he grabbed the reins of Marian's horse, mounted his own, and they set off into the night.

THEY WERE in the hills above Eden when Douglas heard crying.

He stopped his horse. "Marian, is that you?"

It hadn't sounded like her. She'd been quiet except for her halting efforts at breathing. But this cry was loud. It was coming from one of the saddlebags on Marian's horse. The one she'd said not to touch.

It sounded a bit like the cries Douglas had heard inside the Paradise Hotel.

Douglas had been through many things this day. But when he unbuckled the bag and found a red-faced, screaming baby inside, he nearly fainted from the shock.

"Marian, where in hell'd you get this child? Who does it belong to?"

They'd left the road some miles back and had been making their way into the foothills. Douglas had wanted to avoid attention. There was sure to be activity in Eden once morning came. Perhaps even law men coming in via the road into the canyon.

He couldn't go back to Eden now. Not unless he wanted a noose around his neck. But he couldn't take this child, either. He'd been a party to far too much evil already.

Marian was murmuring something. Douglas went closer so he could hear over the baby's wails.

"Child...my child is dead. She was born in blood."

Dark secrets lived in this woman's heart. Douglas hoped she'd find the peace in the afterlife that she lacked in this one. But he had more urgent problems at the moment.

"I have to give this baby back to its mother."

Marian struggled to breathe. "Her mother...dead. Anabel. Bart was...the baby..."

"Mr. Fitzhammer's servant? He was this child's father?"

She hesitated. Then nodded. "Born from evil. But innocent."

Douglas shook his head. *What do I do? What on earth do I do?*

Then his mother's voice came to him. *Time for church.*

There was only one thing he could do.

Douglas held the baby for a little while, trying to soothe her. She had soaked through her wrappings, so he found fresh cloth.

Marian was doing poorly, so he carefully lifted the injured woman from the saddle. She lay on the ground and stared up at the stars. She couldn't ride anymore, not in such condition.

"You have a chance to get right with God, Marian." He rocked the baby in his lap. "I suggest you take it." *Just like I intend to*, he thought. Now that he had a second chance.

She didn't answer. Her breaths were getting slower, further between.

"My mother used to love looking at the Milky Way," Douglas said, swinging the baby in the crook of one arm. "All the stars out there. The realm of the angels. If you ever think the night is dark, you just look up, and it's there to light your way."

He couldn't tell if Marian heard. Eventually, he drifted off.

When the sun rose, Douglas woke. The baby was sleeping against his chest.

He looked over at Marian. She lay in the same position as before. Her chest was still, her eyes gazing up at the sky.

HE SPENT the morning burying Marian on the hillside. Then he moved on. The baby wouldn't stop screaming. He knew why—she was hungry. Yet he had nothing for her.

He found a red currant bush and mashed up a handful of berries. The baby sucked the sweet, red juices from his fingertips. Her eyes were light brown, and she stared straight into his soul. She didn't seem to find anything there unworthy. Finally, she quieted.

Perhaps he and Sara would have a child someday, as they'd so often imagined. This day was the first in a long while that he'd even allowed himself to hope. It was not because of the gold or the bank notes in his saddlebags. The money was merely an illusion of security. In the past, he'd feared that he shouldn't bring a child into such a harsh world. But now, he suspected that sharing in a child's innocence was the only remedy for the horrors he'd seen.

As the sun set, he spied the town of Ashton on the horizon. He waited until the sky had turned fully dark. He tied his horse to a tree, loaded up Bart's pack, and then set out on foot toward the town.

The baby didn't cry when he lay her on the church steps.

"I'm sorry, little one," he said. "I have to leave you now. This part's up to God. Hopefully He's paying attention."

But he couldn't bring himself to go completely. Douglas crossed the street, found a hiding spot on the edge of a nearby wood, and waited.

About half an hour later, he heard the beat of horse hooves. A man was riding up the street. Just then, the baby began its healthy, piercing cry. Douglas slipped into the woods just as more townsfolk emerged from nearby buildings, searching for the source of the noise.

They'd soon find the bag he'd tucked into the baby's blankets: a large portion of the riches from Bart's pack. Douglas couldn't be sure what the people of Ashton would do with the money—whether they'd use it to care for the child as he hoped. Some matters simply required faith. As for the rest of the money, he intended to distribute it into church collection boxes as he made his way across Colorado. Perhaps then the stains of evil on that money could be washed clean.

He reached his horse and rode onward, thinking of his Sara's beautiful face.

EPILOGUE

2019

Penny walked across the meadow behind the Ashton Valley Inn. She'd already said goodbye to her mom and dad and Bryce. But Krista had been conspicuously absent. Penny sat on the bench by the creek and waited.

Before too long, Krista ran down the path in her trail shoes, dark braid bobbing. She stopped when she saw Penny.

"Oh hey, is it three already? You're taking off?"

Penny stood. "Tomorrow morning, yeah." She'd wanted to spend her last night in Ashton with Matthew.

Krista shifted from foot to foot. "Well, I'm sure I'll see you soon."

Penny was less sure. But things were still a bit tense between her sister and herself, though almost a month had passed since Devil's Night.

She'd been spending half her time at Matthew's, half at the inn with her family. She'd had some long, sometimes difficult, conversations with her dad. But they were in a better place now. Lawrence had offered to re-release *A Devil in Eden*—complete with a revision of their family history and a foreword written by Penny, to tell her side of the story—but she'd declined. She'd had enough media attention already.

Helen Boyd had also made a few more appearances at the inn, this time with the express invitation of Lawrence and Debbie. They'd spent some late nights in the dining room, reminiscing about Jason and their college days. Penny hoped that Helen might find some solace.

"Mom said you heard from Scott Mackey?" Penny prompted. Scott had gotten caught in the electrical cords on the first night of Devil's Fest. "I was really sorry about how things turned out."

Though Penny tried to defend him to Alpenglow Guides, they'd refused to give him his job back. Scott's ex-boss hadn't been too impressed by Penny's explanation. Apparently some people in Ashton still didn't believe in ghosts, despite all the evidence.

Krista looked down the trail, as if longing to return to her run. "Scott's in Oregon visiting his brother for a while. He sounded good on the phone, though. Happy. I'm sure he'll be back in Ashton once ski season starts."

As for the ghost town itself, the fire hadn't caused too much damage. The bank was in worse shape than before, and a nearby wooden structure had burned to the ground along with the stage. But the Paradise Hotel was getting some further renovations, after which it would open as a museum. Penny's Uncle Harry was spearheading the effort for a share of the profits. Penny had asked for the real story of Marian and Anabel to be told, albeit in a family-friendly way. It would inevitably get watered down into nothing but hints and innuendo, but it was better than nothing.

Penny was still trying to make sense of Devil's Night. But the rest of Ashton was quickly moving on. Everyone from Sterling PR—except Penny—had returned to LA. Ray hadn't been fired from the sheriff's department, despite an investigation, and was even getting accolades for his role in evacuating the festival-goers. There'd been a few injuries in the crush to escape Main Street, but thankfully no one had been killed that night.

"When are you coming back?" Krista asked.

"I don't know. Probably not for a while."

Penny had just told her parents the news. But Krista hadn't yet heard.

"Linden is starting her own PR firm, and she wants me to be her partner."

"That sounds big."

"Yeah. It really is."

Linden had been meeting with her contacts since the moment she returned to Southern California. She'd spoken to June at SunBev, and June was in favor of moving with Linden and dropping Sterling. Penny didn't know all the details, but apparently June had reported the VP Jeff Richardson to their HR for harassment. And it wasn't his first complaint. Richardson had taken a leave of absence, and that left June as the head of their marketing department.

I need you, Linden had said on FaceTime a few days ago. *I wouldn't even have the nerve to do this if not for our trip to Colorado—and that was all you.*

Penny didn't have the money to buy into a partnership, but Linden had promised they'd get a business agreement in place and work out all those details. *There's the whole partnership divorce and the no-contact clause*, Linden had explained. *But my lawyers are better than Tripp's.*

Penny had no doubt Linden would come out ahead. They had Tripp's behavior at Devil's Fest to use as a bargaining chip. If he agreed to back off, then Penny might "forget" about the way he'd locked her in the hotel.

She and Linden would be in charge of their own firm. Just the idea made her giddy.

Linden had even talked about bringing Anvi into their company. At the moment, Anvi was dealing with several criminal charges in Ashton County, including first degree assault, obstruction of a law enforcement officer, and a bunch of other scary-sounding things. But Linden was helping to fund her legal defense. *I want to believe in second chances*, Linden had said, *espe-*

cially where murderous ghosts are really to blame. The last Penny heard, Anvi would probably plead guilty to kidnapping and third degree assault and get probation.

Krista stepped aside to let another runner pass on the trail. "But...what about you and Matthew?"

That was a good question. Penny'd had a month already to figure out the answer, and she still wasn't sure.

About a week ago, they'd stopped at a roadside stand for peaches, and Matthew had insisted on buying a set of handmade ceramic wind chimes. "Our house needs one of these," he'd said. Just slipping that in casually—*our house*. Like a test.

"Your mom would've loved it."

Matthew's mouth had tensed, trying to hide the frown. But he still bought the chimes.

Krista was shaking her head.

"I cannot believe you. Bryce said you'd do this, and I told him he was full of it."

"Full of what?"

"But here you are," Penny's sister continued, "a month into a honeymoon, practically, for all the sex that *everybody* knows you and Matthew are having—"

"Krista, *jeez*."

"C'mon. Even Dad's not that clueless. And you're just going to ditch him? *Thanks Matthew, it was fun playing house. Gotta go.*"

Playing house. That was exactly how it had felt. A fantasy, but a really lovely, comfortable fantasy that was so damned tempting to make real.

"Seriously Penny, how is this so hard? He's kind, he adores you, your family loves him. Most straight women would give anything for a man like Matthew to look at them the way he looks at you."

Penny quirked an eyebrow at her sister.

"Not me. Ew." Krista wrinkled her nose. "I just mean, you have no idea how good you have it. Nothing's ever enough for you. 'Perfect Penny.'"

"So I'm supposed to give up my life and move back here to be with him? Like some twentieth-century housewife?"

"Not what I said. You're smarter than this, Penny. Think of a freaking solution."

Krista started to leave, then turned back around. "And I'm not saying this for myself, okay? Because things were easier without you around. I got a tiny bit of attention sometimes. But I don't want to see you throw away such a great guy, and I *really* don't want to see Matthew hurt. *Figure yourself out.*"

WHEN THEY LEFT Eden after Devil's Night, Matthew had stayed at the inn. He and Penny had been treated for smoke inhalation at the hospital—Matthew had never seen so much of that place in his life—and then released. Penny's family had swarmed around them, offering advice and comfort. As they usually did.

He'd lay in his bed, coughing, chest aching—head still in a fog—and unable to sleep. But then the knock came. Penny stood at his door, her eyes red and skin blotchy. It was their first moment alone since what had happened at the bank. Matthew hardly even understood the events himself, and he'd been there.

But neither of them said a word. Penny shut the door behind her. They got under the covers, held each other, and slept over twelve hours.

They'd stayed together every night since, either at the inn or his house. He'd gotten used to sleeping beside her. He'd tried to take one day at a time, not expecting too much. First, she asked to stay with him a few days. Then an extra week. Linden had gone and the many interviews with police and insurance had slowed down, but still Penny wanted to stay in Ashton a little longer. Matthew had let himself imagine she wouldn't go. But he'd already decided he wouldn't try to convince her.

He'd taken some time off work, and now he didn't want to go back at all. Getting his contractor license, running his own business—these now seemed like genuine possibilities. He could use the house as collateral on a loan. It was scary, the thought of doing something so adult, but hearing Penny's conversations with Linden had inspired him. He wanted a lot more than the life he'd been living before Penny came back. Even if she might not be in it.

On her last full day in Ashton, Matthew stayed home making dinner while Penny said goodbye to her family. He kept one eye on the picture window in the great room, expecting to see her car drive up any minute. She'd rented a sedan to ferry herself around town. He'd offered his truck, but of course, she wanted to be self-sufficient.

His house was messier now, more lived in. Everywhere Matthew looked, he saw signs of Penny. Her laptop lay on the couch. Her clothes hung next to his in the closet—still his childhood bedroom, not the master. He hadn't packed up his mom's old things. But he could see himself doing it, and that was something.

But Penny was leaving tomorrow. Matthew would drive her all the way to Denver—the concussion-induced fog was finally gone from his brain, so he'd insisted—to catch her flight to LAX. He didn't like it, but he'd accepted it. He wasn't going to ruin their time together by rehashing the same conversations.

Matthew glanced at the window again and saw her coming up the sidewalk. He opened his front door just as Penny was reaching for it.

"There you are. Where's your car?"

"I walked."

"Five miles?"

"I needed to think." She went inside, slipping off her shoes by the door. "I'm going to change."

"Wait." He brushed aside her hair, kissed the back of her

neck. "I missed you," he murmured, which was true. But he also meant, *I'm going to miss you.*

She turned around and kissed him back.

They'd fallen into certain habits in the last weeks. Never getting out of bed till after eleven; always leaving the dishes until the morning. And talking only of the past, never the future.

She'd told him everything that happened inside the Paradise Hotel and the Eden bank. He knew that those memories—Anabel's, Marian's, her own—still haunted her. Especially the thought of what she'd nearly done. Those minutes inside the bank had been some of the most harrowing of Matthew's life. He'd never had a gun pointed at him, and definitely never expected Penny to be the one to do it. When he'd looked into her eyes, he hadn't seen his Penny at all. She'd been something *other*. Of course, he didn't admit that to her. *I knew you wouldn't hurt me*, he'd told her. He wanted to believe that. He *did* believe it.

"You got three more calls while you were gone," he said.

Penny groaned. "I don't even want to know." She went to their bedroom and closed the door.

When she came to the dinner table, Penny was quieter than usual. She picked up her fork to spear a tube of pasta, then set it down again.

"So Krista gave me a lecture today."

"Did she?"

"About you."

"Oh."

"She said I'm selfish, that I act like nothing's good enough for me."

Matthew started to disagree, but Penny waved her hand. "Let me finish. She was maybe a little bit right. I disagree that it's wrong for a woman to be selfish sometimes. But she's right that you and I..." Here, Penny's eyes flicked up to meet his. "I'd like to see where this goes. If you still do."

His heart jumped straight into the red zone. *Do I give her the stupid grin that my face wants to make?* he wondered. *Or do I play this cool?*

"Of course I do," he said.

"I'm still going back to LA. But you could visit in a few weeks. I mean, I'm *asking* if you'll visit. And I'll come visit Ashton a few weeks after that. It's expensive, but I was looking at these credit card airline reward things, and—"

"Yes." He caught her hand and twined his fingers through hers. He decided not to tell her about the plane tickets he'd already bought to LA for Labor Day weekend. There was never any possibility he'd let this girl go without a fight. But he'd let her think it was her idea.

"My roommates are awful," she warned. "And my room is tiny, and the walls are thin, and—"

"So I'll try to be quiet. I don't care. Tell me when, and I'll be there." The stupid grin was sneaking out, so he stopped stifling it.

THEY ATE THEIR DINNER, making so many plans for the next few months that Penny couldn't keep them straight. She was just relieved that Matthew had agreed. A long-distance relationship wasn't ideal, but maybe it could work until they figured out something else. If the right "something else" even existed. But she wouldn't think about that. They were happy and dreaming about all the good things that would come next.

So Penny was surprised when Matthew let go of her hand and brought up the subject she hated most. A subject she thought she'd already dismissed today.

"You know," he said, "those calls are going to keep coming."

She sat back, staring hard at the table.

She'd stopped answering any unfamiliar numbers on her cell, so the randos had taken to calling the landline at Matthew's place. How they'd found out she was here, she didn't know.

Penny picked up their plates and took them to the sink. "I'm sorry. I'll pay for you to change your number. Or do you really need a landline anymore?"

"That isn't what I meant."

He followed her to the kitchen. She grabbed a paper towel and started wiping the counter, wishing they could go back to their pleasant conversation. Anything but this.

"Penn, if you heard these messages, these people..."

"I've heard them."

At first it was more interview requests, which she'd summarily denied. Then accusations that she'd faked the ghost activity in Eden and caused the fire, either on purpose or through negligence. Threats of lawsuits.

But then the calls had turned more heartrending.

I didn't get a chance to tell my dad I loved him. Please, can you help? Or, *I think there's a spirit in my house, a murdered woman, can't you free her?* And worst of all, *My daughter is missing, can you see if she's on the other side?*

Every one of those messages kept her awake at night. She wished she could help. But even if she could manage the feats they were asking—which was far from certain—she didn't think she could stand it. Taking on the painful memories and the suffering of all those people, again and again...it was too much.

And she couldn't stop thinking about that gun in her hand. How she'd almost killed Matthew, *Matthew*, because a ghost told her to do it.

Her father had told her she was special. *You have a gift.* But it wasn't a blessing or a talent. She had a weakness. Without even knowing, she'd made the haunting in Eden so much worse by her very presence. Before this trip, Penny had believed that she understood how hauntings worked. Now, she realized that she knew almost nothing at all. She was afraid of what might happen if she faced a ghost like Marian again.

"I'll keep telling them what I've been telling them," Matthew said. "That you're not available. But you're going to keep seeing these things, right? The next time—"

"I don't want there to be a next time."

Penny didn't want to be ghost girl. She didn't want to be ghost *anything*. But those words kept repeating in her mind, like a promise.

Next time.

"But if there is—*when* there is—don't think you have to do it alone."

He put his arms around her. She leaned into him, closing her eyes.

Penny Wright returns in Angel Eyes, *available now!*

Everyone in Ashton, Colorado, knows that January House is haunted. It's been the site of grisly murders and unsolved disappearances. When a reclusive painter dies there, medium Penny Wright reluctantly agrees to investigate. But the walls of January House conceal a terrifying secret. And this time, it might be the living who pose the greatest threat.

Read the free prequel to *Devil's Night*— Sign up for the author's newsletter at http://bit.ly/anwillis to download the exclusive prequel FREE.

ABOUT THE AUTHOR

A.N. Willis writes supernatural suspense, gothic mysteries, and science fiction for teens and adults. She loves the creepy, the thrilling, and the otherworldly. To learn more about her writing and hear about her new releases, sign up for her newsletter at: http://bit.ly/anwillis

ALSO BY A.N. WILLIS

THE BYRNE HOUSE DUOLOGY

Evelyn Ashwood is the last to see her classmate the day he disappears—just a pale face in the tower window of the mansion across the street. She must uncover Byrne House's secret history...or become its next victim.

Under Glass and Stone (Book 1)

Doors of Gold and Rust (Book 2)

HOW MUCH IT MAY STORM

1943: When Dinah sees a young soldier out in the snow—a soldier who supposedly died in the last Great War—she follows him into the woods. But what she discovers will force Dinah to confront the dangerous darkness hiding inside those she least suspects.

Made in the USA
Columbia, SC
05 November 2021